RELIC

DEL REY | NEW YORK

RELIC

Alan Dean Foster

Relic is a work of fiction. Names, places, characters, and incidents either are the products of the author's imagination or are used fictitiously. Any resemblance to actual events, locales, or persons, living or dead, is entirely coincidental.

Copyright © 2018 by Alan Dean Foster

Published in the United States by Del Rey, an imprint of Random House, a division of Penguin Random House LLC, New York.

DEL REY and the HOUSE colophon are registered trademarks of Penguin Random House LLC.

LIBRARY OF CONGRESS CATALOGING-IN-PUBLICATION DATA
Names: Foster, Alan Dean.
Title: Relic / Alan Dean Foster.
Description: First edition. | New York : Del Rey, [2018]
Identifiers: LCCN 2018009535 |
ISBN 9781101967638 (hardcover : alk. paper) |
ISBN 9781101967645 (ebook)
Subjects: | BISAC: FICTION / Science Fiction / Adventure. |
GSAFD: Science fiction.
Classification: LCC PS3556.O756 R38 2018 | DDC 813/.54—dc23
LC record available at lccn.loc.gov/2018009535

Printed in the United States of America on acid-free paper

randomhousebooks.com

2 4 6 8 9 7 5 3 1

FIRST EDITION

Title page image: © iStockphoto.com

Book design by Dana Leigh Blanchette

FOR BETSY MITCHELL,

with whom I went through a darned lot of words together. With thanks, friendship, and appreciation.

RELIC

1

He was the last one.

The others, the rest, the balance, the remainder: they were all gone now, in their mass and multitudes. Memories and ghosts of memories. No one knew how many of them there had been before they were no more, least of all him. There had been a time when countings were done, but such behaviors belonged not to his time but to others. There had been several such times, he knew. Eras as well as countings.

First came the Expansion. That was followed by the Consolidation. Then there was the Union, which birthed the Empire, which gave way to the Collapse. After a long, slow climb there came the Reunion. It dissolved into the Second Empire, which was followed by the Interregnum. The Interregnum was long and prosperous and offered, among other things, something new to humankind: time for reflection. It was an age when inherent and inherited stupidity finally surrendered to understanding and common sense, and saw among humans the first firm grasping of those things that really matter. As a result, the Conclave that followed lasted even longer than the Interregnum. It showed what could be done. Humanity spread out and flourished. Did some grand things. Noble things, even.

But in the end, or perhaps it should be said in The End, it was revealed that the species' baser instincts had not, after all, been laid to rest but had merely been slumbering. They reasserted themselves with a vengeance. Human fought human over things that, in the end, mattered little. There was shouting and screaming and cursing. There was slaughter and destruction and aggrandizement.

Finally, in every sense of the word, there was the Aura Malignance.

That was when everything began to come apart. As the Conclave disintegrated, the bold and the hopeful and the vainglorious made an attempt at a Third Empire, but the inexorable spread of the plague known as the Aura Malignance had weakened the species to the point where that sort of racial energy could no longer be summoned in quantities sufficient to sustain any kind of functioning organization across the spaces between the stars. Gradually the means to conjoin, and eventually even to communicate, began to fade away.

He didn't know if this was due to a forgetting of knowledge or the loss of the rare elements that underlay the necessary technology. Worlds lost contact with worlds. The society of man splintered, then fractured, and before long commenced a long, slow slide toward total collapse. Only this time it was different. This time there was no recovery, no reconsolidation, not even a last desperate reach for Empire.

On Seraboth, where he was from, society had been slowly crumbling for several hundred years. Everyone thought they were safe from the last of the self-seeking spores, that final folly of human ingenuity that always seems to burn brightest in the service of war. But they weren't. Shards of the self-dispersing, all-pervasive biological weapon arrived, and began to kill. Missing no one, the infection ruptured neural connections in the brain. People who thought they had no more than a bad headache flinched, winced, and collapsed, never to rise again.

Serabothian scientists, and there were many who were as dedicated as they were competent, worked together across political boundaries. Like all who had tried and perished before them, they could do nothing. The Aura Malignance was too virulent, too mutable, and, most critically, too swiftly spreading. The kind of inter-world science that had bolstered the various federations and alliances and empires had degenerated. Not only did the facilities to share and communicate no longer exist; neither did the individuals or intelligent machines that might have had the capacity to find a cure.

So on Seraboth, as on every other inhabited world, the people began to die. In an earlier time they might have gone down fighting, raging at the futility of their situation, shaking defiant fists at the stars, battling to the last in search of a solution to the problem. Instead, once it was felt that nothing could be done, the only response was a vast cultural sigh and a grim acceptance of the inevitable. People perished in silence and, to a certain extent, in peace. They did not know theirs was among the last of the settled worlds to succumb. He certainly did not know he would be the last of the last, the only one to survive the otherwise all-destroying, fast-moving contagion.

All of this he knew only because of the aliens. The Myssari were very good to him. They found him wandering, tired and hungry and approaching old age, and immediately set to work to fortify what was left of his bodily processes. When they told him what they knew, that human civilization had long since fallen, that all the many and innumerable of his kin on the dozens of settled worlds were gone—cities empty, countrysides returned to the unhindered fecundity of nature, vast space stations drifting in emptiness that were staffed now only by the drifting dead—he decided he might as well die, too. But even when all else slips away, the tiny flame that is the urge to survive still flickers in the sole surviving representative of a species.

So he didn't fight it. He let them fix him up, as much as they could. Their xenologists were accomplished, their surgeons expert, their machines advanced. They could not restore him to youth, of course. The Myssari could repair, rebuild, refresh, but they could not reverse time. Taking into account their limitations and his, by the time they finished their work he felt better than he had in decades. Though to what end he could not imagine. He did not particularly look forward to a twilight career as an artifact, but though confused by what had happened to him he understood that the aliens had done what they had done out of genuine interest. It had taken some time and effort on their part to preserve and extend his life. Could he do less in return than live?

Thus he became, quietly and with resignation, a living exhibit. Ruslan: the last *Homo sapiens*.

There was a time when he had possessed more than one name, but now found he could not remember it. Somewhere in the course of his aimless wanderings on Seraboth, it, like so many other things, had become lost. He could not even recall if "Ruslan" was a first name, a last, or something else. Not that it mattered. There were no other Ruslans with whom to be confused. There were no others at all.

One thing in particular about the situation in which he found himself was wonderfully ironic. Humans had spent thousands of years believing they were the only intelligent species—or at least the only space-traversing intelligent species—in the galaxy. Ultimately they became convinced of it and no longer even bothered to ponder the possibility that there might be others. Human civilization rose and fell, rose and fell, finally falling for the last time, and when only one last solitary wandering soul remained, the aliens arrived. Delicious. And not just the Myssari. According to Anu'lex, one of his restorers, there were dozens of intelligent species out there. All thriving and exploring and arguing and advancing and pushing their own particular species-centric agendas. All the while that humankind was rising and falling, it was unknowingly doing so on the empty side of the galaxy, the existence of its prolific and multifarious neighbors masked by distance, their communications obscured by intervening radiation.

Striving to be a good and grateful artifact, he told the inquisitive Myssari what he could. He helped their linguists decipher the floating photonic files that were present in every city center and information repository on Seraboth. This allowed the aliens to access corollary records on dozens of other now-empty human worlds. While such records differed in matters local, the general sweep of the past many hundreds of years remained the same. The story of the tailless bipeds was a heroic tale with a sad ending. Human history had ever been thus.

It was too fine a day, he thought, to dwell on what might have been. But he could not help himself.

Composed of a solidified cocktail of carefully engineered binding molecules, the pedestrian promenade was wide and white, easy on the feet yet impervious to heat, cold, and the weather. There were no vehicles about. In Pe'leoek both mass and individual transit ran belowground, pollution-free, out of sight, and, except for an occasional slight humming as a line of capsules passed underfoot, out of hearing. Citizens of all three sexes strolled beneath the intense light of Myssar's sun, the youngest still attached to their birth mothers by the strong, flexible, cartilaginous tube that would keep them under control while supplying them with supplementary nutrition until they reached the age of separation. Ruslan smiled as he watched one mother snap an unresponsive offspring back to her side by contracting her muscular leash.

Several varieties of short, broad-leafed growths provided shade from the powerful UV rays beating down on the walkway. Shading in hue from pale lavender to deep purple, their upturned leaf-like pads were round, flat, and held perfectly parallel to the ground.

In bloom now, they put forth flowers of intense crimson that at-
tracted waiflike multi-winged pollinators. The botanical rationale
behind their enchanting colors had been explained to him. Like
much other information supplied by his hosts, it had already been
forgotten. Having to cope with and survive among an entirely
alien civilization left little room in his aged and overstuffed mind
for such choice bits of information, however enchanting or en-
lightening they might be.

A child came up to him. Tube-weened, it was attached to nothing but its own curiosity. If not for the restraint imposed upon
their offspring by Myssari parents, Ruslan would have found himself unable to move, so dense would have been the crush of curious youth around him. This one looked to be about halfway along
the path to adulthood. The narrow, ribbed skull with its small,
bright blue eyes with horizontal pupils gaped up at the peculiar
two-legged creature. As a sophisticated city and the capital of its
homeworld, Pe'leoek saw its share of visiting aliens. This routine
influx did nothing to mitigate Ruslan's uniqueness.

"I am a human." Ruslan had long since grown used to pre-
empting inevitable questions.

The half-adult had no trouble understanding his excellent Myssarian. An adept if not especially enthusiastic student of the language of his saviors, Ruslan had been well coached by tutors both
live and inorganic. His fluency had progressed to the point where
his speech was colloquial. Ingenuously expecting nothing else, the
youngster was eager to converse.

"What's a human?"

Ruslan sighed. "I am the last representative of my species. Its
sole survivor. A relic."

"You speak well for a relic." The adolescent regarded the
strange biped appraisingly. "So if I was to kill you, there would be
no more of you?"

There were times when characteristic Myssari directness could
diverge from the refreshing to the appalling. Looking on from

nearby, Ruslan's friend and minder Kel'les appeared as if s'he was about to intervene, but Ruslan raised a hand to forestall him. A gesture, he reflected, that was shared among many intelligent species.

"I cannot swear to that. My kind settled a great many worlds. But I am the last that I know of. So, yes, if you were to kill me, then there would be no more of me. Beyond me I cannot say."

On the other side of the promenade, the half-adult's mother, father, and intermet looked as if they wished they were somewhere else. They were too polite to say anything and too conflicted to intervene physically. In Myssari society curiosity among youth was a trait highly prized. This parental triad did not want to inhibit their offspring. At the same time, they worried that his inquisitiveness might spill over into prying.

They need not have worried. The youth pondered the peculiar biped's response, then gestured with a three-fingered hand that was one of a trio. "I won't kill you, then."

The last human smiled. "That's very considerate of you. It seems that I'm very hard to kill anyway." Opening his eyes wide, he leaned toward the youth. This action was sufficiently startling to cause the youngster to step back. In addition to having evolved small eyes due to the intense light of their sun, the Myssari could not "open" them in the manner of humans. Their enclosing bony orbits were fixed and inflexible. Turning, the bemused and now slightly frightened youngster loped off on his three legs to rejoin his parents.

Ruslan straightened. The special slip-on lenses the Myssari had made for him allowed him to move about in Pe'leoek in broad daylight without damaging his own large, sensitive eyes, just as the third lung they had grown for him from bits of his own lung tissue enabled him to breathe comfortably in air that was thinner than Seraboth's. The organ lay deflated behind his two normal, larger lungs, expanding and contracting with them in perfect unison only when his body demanded additional air. In the event he found himself once more on a human-settled world, it would not inhibit his normal breathing. Myssari surgeons were very adept.

Other than the third lung and the artificial lenses that protected his retinas, his body was much as the Myssari had found it. Manufactured to his own suggested design by a local crafts-professional, the broad-brimmed hat he wore protected his head from the strong sunshine better than did his close-clipped gray hair. Finding clothing of any type or style was no problem, nor was anything else he might desire. He could pick and choose from among the miscellany of a hundred worlds. Artifacts to fit the artifact.

More than once he had grudgingly admitted to himself that his was not a terrible way to finish out one's life. Other than the absence of company of his own kind, he wanted for nothing. The considerate Myssari did not even have to synthesize food for him. Secure in its varied packaging, enough remained on the now-silent human worlds to sustain him until the end of entropy.

He would be dead, he knew, rather sooner than that.

Meanwhile he lived on and did his best to enjoy the delights natural as well as artificial that the Myssari homeworld and others presented. He had even made a few friends: locals who came to regard him as an individual worth knowing and not just a specimen. Chief among them was his soft-voiced, tripodal official minder and companion of the morning.

Kel'les was an intermet. A neuter, s'he was unmated. The use of the conjoined identifier was a deliberate choice by Ruslan. He needed a way to refer to Kel'les without employing a name, and it would not do to think of or refer to Kel'les as an "it."

Visiting metropolitan locales like the seaside promenade enabled the Myssari functionary to participate in activities beyond his assigned task of seeing to the needs of the human. That s'he chose to spend some of it in nonofficial consorting and communication with the human was a tribute to Kel'les's character as well as curiosity.

Ruslan paused to bend and smell of a deep blue, trumpet-shaped flower. He did not hesitate. Here on one of the city's main pedestrian walkways, there would be no dangerous flora. He struggled to identify the scent. Vanilla, he decided. Or possibly the wonderful *balume* that in the days of interstellar commerce had been imported to Seraboth from Porustra. Once, such things had been common on his homeworld—until the Aura Malignance had halted imports and every world had retreated into its own increasingly desperate self-imposed quarantine. Such thinking brought yet again to the forefront of his thoughts a notion he had never been able to shake.

"I've always wondered, Kel'les: if your people had made contact with mine a couple of hundred years earlier than they did, would your scientists have been able to find a cure for the Malignance? You would have been immune. The lightning-fast mutable vectors were designed to attack only human neuralities."

Raising right hand to mouth, Kel'les fanned the three fingers so that two flanked the lipless gap while the third bisected the opening: a sign of uncertainty.

"It is impossible to know, or even to speculate." The alien's voice was soft and breathy, a loud whisper. Even now Ruslan had to be careful to keep his voice down when speaking with the people who had found him. To their decibel-sensitive organs, normal human speech came across as excessively loud. Though he had never attempted to do so, Ruslan suspected that a good, hearty shout could do real physical damage to his hosts' organs of hearing.

He persisted. "Speculate anyway." A spangled *lorpan* soared low over the treetops, looking for food it could steal with a quick thrust of its coiled, sticky proboscis.

Though s'he might have been wanting on the necessary specific knowledge, Kel'les was not lacking in imagination. S'he was also too polite to continue refusing. "I am a supervisorial consort, not a scientist. I understand how to keep things functioning and individuals content, but not always how they function or why they are content. Having been assigned to . . ." The Myssari hesitated.

With a slight nod Ruslan indicated his understanding. "To my case?"

"To you. To your individuality. In the course of being assigned to you, I have naturally been obligated to learn as much as possible about your kind so that I may provide the best support to you of which I am capable. Among many other things, this required me to learn as much as I could about the great tragedy that overcame your people." Once more the alien paused. "You do not mind my talking about it?"

"If I did, I wouldn't have asked you to hypothesize about it." Ruslan looked away. "It's not like there's anyone else to offend."

Kel'les's head tilted slightly to one side—a Myssari gesture of compassion. "Then since you ask, it is my opinion that nothing would have changed had my people, or the Hahk'na, or any of the other advanced races, contacted your kind once the plague had begun its spread. To this day the method and means of its propagation remain a mystery. From the histories we have scanned, it appears that your biologists first tried to contain it by quarantining the afflicted individuals, then the affected cities, then entire worlds. Nothing worked." Kel'les's voice was softer now even than was usual for a Myssari.

"Whoever designed the pathogen was very specific. As you point out, only humans were affected. It did not afflict even your nearest genetic relatives. It burrowed into your cerebroneural system and nothing else. Perhaps that is why your other—I believe the correct term is 'primates'—were not harmed. As a weapon of biowarfare, it was as precise as it was unstoppable." Small violet eyes focused on the human. "Whoever schematicized it knew exactly what they were doing."

"Not quite." He made no attempt to keep the bitterness out of his voice. "I doubt their intention was to kill every last human being in the galaxy—with one exception." He did not smile. Smiling he reserved for those isolated occasions when it was justified. Not knowing when one might be his last—humanity's last—smile, he rationed them.

"No one has proposed a cure," Kel'les continued, "especially since the agent has now died out. With no hosts in which to dwell, it has officially vanished from the canon of galactic illnesses as mysteriously as it first appeared."

Ruslan found himself growing tired. One of the glistening, metallic, free-form strandstands that had been provided to give promenaders a place to rest cast a hopeful loop in his direction. Though it was too narrow even for his aged and shrunken human backside, he settled himself against the semifluid surface as best he could. It rippled uncertainly beneath him, trying to accommodate buttocks it had never been intended to support. At least it allowed him to take the weight off his feet, if only for a little while.

Settling in far more comfortably beside him, Kel'les eyed the biped who had become his friend. "Despite uncertainty and reluctance, I have answered a question of yours. Now you must answer one of mine. Why do you object so strongly to allowing yourself to be cloned?"

Ruslan's face twisted. Familiar with them as s'he had become, Kel'les still had difficulty interpreting the human's many expressions. Myssari facial construction was relatively inflexible.

"It doesn't matter what I think. Your scientists are going to attempt it anyway."

Once again Kel'les's head bobbed sideways: this time in the other direction. "You know that we believe that the preservation of any species, especially of an intelligent one, far outweighs the personal preferences of any one individual. I would just, as a matter of personal curiosity, like to know why you continue to object." The tone of the alien's voice, to which, with time and instruction, Ruslan had by now become sensitive, had changed to one of deference.

They're so damn courteous, he thought. It made it hard to refuse the Myssari anything. Had they been other humans, or aliens
whose attitude more nearly resembled that of his own confrontational species, he would not have bothered to respond.

Instead of replying directly, he continued to evade. "You may
succeed anyway, without my cooperation."

"That is so," Kel'les admitted. "We have more than enough
genetic material from you. Only a few cells are necessary, and
while we were restoring you we acquired many thousands. It is a
pity you are not female. It would make things much easier if we
had access to eggs."

"Sorry." Ruslan's tone clearly indicated he was not.

Innocent of the sarcasm, Kel'les continued. "Helpfully, your
species is bi- instead of trisexual, so there is no need for the inclu-
sion in the reproductive process of an intermet like myself. Still,
without eggs, I am told it will be difficult. First we must successfully produce human eggs via genetic manipulation. Then these
must be impregnated in the hope of bringing forth viable embryos.
Once this has been achieved and adults brought to maturity, the
ongoing process will become easier. Additionally, genetic material
has been salvaged from bodies on your world that had not yet
reached advanced stages of decomposition. This will permit chro-
mosomal variation to be introduced into your . . . offspring.
Whether it agrees with your personal preferences or not, your species will live."

"After a fashion." Ruslan squinted into the distance. Pe'leoek
had been built on a peninsula, and from the rise on which the
promenade had been constructed he could see the glint of alien
sun on alien sea. The latter exploded with life in waters that were
saltier than those of Seraboth. Under the watchful eyes of minders
like Kel'les, he had been allowed to go swimming many times. In
his youth he had been quite an athlete. In his youth he had been . . .
in his youth he had been . . .

His youth was gone, along with everything else he had known. He was not caged. It only felt that way.

"I just don't like the whole idea." He turned to face the Myssari's hairless, largely frozen face. Shepherded by the customary trio of adults, a covey of youngsters ambled by. They made no attempt to conceal their curiosity. He was locally famous, in his way, but he could still never quite get used to being the object of so much attention.

"Is it the idea of you, personally, giving rebirth to your species that offends you?" Kel'les's questioning was as earnest as ever. Ruslan wondered if s'he was trying to satisfy a matter of personal curiosity, as s'he claimed, or just subtly working for the benefit of the Myssari scientific community. He found that he was too tired to parse.

"I don't think the result, if your biologists do succeed, will justify my history. True, if successful it will mean that humans will continue to exist. But how human will they be? No matter how much 'variation' your scientists manage to induce by utilizing genetic material from deceased others, every individual that lives will still essentially be a variant of me. And believe me, I'm not the one I would have chosen to serve as the foundation for such a resurrection."

Amusement crept into Kel'les's reply. Even their humor was strenuously polite, Ruslan had found.

"We can only work with those poor materials that are available to us."

Ruslan looked away, staring off in the direction of the pale blue sea. "Like I said, you're going to do it anyway. You don't need my cooperation. What do you want me to do—bless the results?"

"We want you to be happy. We want you to be—"

"Stop it," he snarled abruptly. "Just stop it. Stop being so damn *nice*!"

Kel'les recoiled and, as much as it was possible to do so, an abashed Ruslan could see the mixture of fear and revulsion in the alien's visage. A trio strolling nearby was visibly shocked at the un-Myssari outburst and accelerated their pace.

"What was that?" His minder was visibly unsettled.

"That was . . . being human. I hope it provided some insight. It should have. Look, I'm sorry. I just wish it wasn't going to proceed like this. It's not that I object per se to what your biologists are wanting to do." He looked down at his hands: leather-brown, the veins prominent as a geological upheaval. "I just wish you had . . . better materials to work with."

Poise recovered, Kel'les inhaled deeply. Beneath the bright red sweep of his overshirt, the conical upper torso where the tripartite lungs were situated barely heaved.

"I think you underestimate your cellular composition. With luck and time, you will become a multitude. And that is another reason why we wish, why we *need*, your cooperation. We are fairly certain that we can bring your species back to life. We can remake, according to your peoples' classification system, *Homo sapiens*. What we cannot do is make a him, or a her, fully *human*. There are great quantities of historical material showing what human society was like, but that is not the same thing." Ruslan saw that Kel'les was trying to be very specific without saying anything that might offend. S'he need not have worried. Ruslan was long past being offended by much of anything.

"What I am saying is that while we can reproduce human beings," the Myssari went on, "what we cannot do is imbue them with humanness. In a society such traits are acquired from watching others of one's kind, from one's parents, from one's peers and equals, and from education systems. We can re-create a little of that. But for the scientific venture to be a real success, we need you to instruct those we bring forth in how to be human."

It was an eventuality Ruslan had already considered. "Once again, I think you're working with the wrong material."

Kel'les was not dissuaded. "Once again, I think you underestimate yourself. My superiors concur. In any event, you are all we have to work with. We will bring forth humankind again whether you cooperate or not. How human they will be is a decision that rests largely upon you."

I'm not the person to be making such decisions, he thought irritably. *There were better, far better, people than I.* Unfortunately, Kel'les was right. The choice was up to him. Where humanity was involved, all choices were now up to him. He was torn. He was confused. He vacillated.

Kel'les had learned enough to recognize uncertainty. Straightening all three legs, s'he rose and stepped away from the flexing, tubular bench. Two of three hands gestured toward a nearby transport booth. "Come with me to Tespo. My superiors have been empowered to present something that may interest you."

Ruslan looked longingly toward the horizon. "I would rather spend the afternoon at the beach."

Kel'les's head slowly spun a full 360 degrees, the eyes coming once more to meet Ruslan's. It was a physical contortion that a human skull, set atop a fixed vertebra instead of a bony gimbal, could not hope to duplicate. Among the Myssari a full rotation was heavy with understated eloquence.

"You spend so much time in the water that I have to remind myself your species was not amphibious. Is there a reason other than simple pleasure that you so enjoy immersing yourself in another environment?"

Ruslan nodded as he rose. "It helps me to forget."

Side by side, biped and triped started toward the booth. Noticing the human, a pair of unmated females gave them a wide berth.

"To forget." Kel'les pondered. "Anything in particular?"

"Yes. How ignorant we were. Thousands of years of development, achievement, and supposed maturation, and in the end we were just as stupid as we were when we first came down out of the trees. We deserved to go extinct." He looked sharply over at his friend. "As I've told you, I think we still deserve it."

"Then, much as my kind strives always for consensus, I am afraid I and my colleagues must disagree with you. Provided we can manage the bioengineering, your species will continue to exist in spite of your distrust of the arrangement."

Ruslan grunted as they approached the booth. The Myssari were going to do what they wanted to do no matter what he said. Politely, of course, the same as they did everything else. That much had already been made clear. Even if he killed himself, he could not stop them from preserving a humankind he was convinced was better off dead and gone. That was his one consolation. Soon enough *he* would be dead and gone. Despite their best efforts, he would not live long enough to see the results, or more accurately the consequences, of their strenuous efforts on behalf of his all-but-vanished species.

At least he had something to look forward to.

2

Ruslan knew that his kind had developed short-range teleportation, though the service had never been widely distributed on Seraboth. The energy requirements were enormous and an outlying world like his own had never been able to justify the expense to construct anything more extensive than an essential-services network. It had long since ceased to function and had entered into a state of serious decay by the time the Myssari arrived.

In contrast, analogous technology was readily available on many Myssari, Hahk'na, and other civilized worlds. It was omnipresent in Pe'leoek. But just as had been the case on human-settled worlds, the system functioned only over short distances. The energy required to sustain a transfer to another world or even a satellite increased exponentially with distance. To send someone to an orbiting ship or station, far less a moon, required an enormous amount of power. That did not keep Kel'les's scientific superiors and others from striving to solve the problem. With any intelligent species it is failure, not success, that drives science.

Additionally, successful teleportation required direct line-of-sight between sending and receiving stations. While this offered hope for future transit across spatial distances, it ironically reduced its usefulness on planetary surfaces. A teleported individual or object could not be relayed. One had to enter a departure booth, step out of another, and enter a second booth to cover anything like a significant distance. The tall, needlelike towers that dotted the landscape were teleportation senders and receivers. By employing the technology, one could circle an entire world, but doing so required a significant number of stops, of repeated entries and exits.

Tespo being a suburb of Pe'leoek, this was not a problem for the two travelers, especially since they were journeying from the high peninsula of the capital to a community lying at sea level. Using Kel'les's priority identification, they were able to jump the queue. None of the individuals or families waiting to use the transport system begrudged them this advantage. Leastwise, not visibly. To do so, especially in public, would have been unforgivably impolite.

"I wish I could have examined a human teleport system in action." Kel'les entered their destination and stepped backward onto the platform. Ruslan had preceded him and stood waiting. "So much potentially useful technology lost." His epiglottal membrane vibrated to indicate his regret.

"Your people have found some valuable remnants," Ruslan reminded him. "The Aura Malignance destroyed people, not physicalities."

"That is so." A rising electronic prattle that sounded like millions of tiny seeds being poured onto a flat glass surface began to fill the chamber. "But it is astounding to see how swiftly Nature reclaims that which has been abandoned. Too many of your centers of knowledge and systems for retaining records were over-

whelmed by the elements or destroyed by anarchic elements of
your society before we could reach them. We are continuously
searching for more, of course. As are the Hahk'na and others who
now know of your demise."

*So the Myssari were not too polite to engage in a little salvage
competition,* Ruslan thought. "I'm sorry I'm not a scientist. If I
were, I would be able to help you more."

Kel'les looked surprised. "You would do that?"

The human shrugged, a gesture the handler had come to recognize. "Why not? The survival of knowledge is more important
than the survival of a race. Knowledge transcends species."

Kel'les was about to comment when s'he disappeared.

Their actual physical selves were not moved. They were destroyed. As they were obliterated, duplicates of themselves that
were exact down to the simplest molecule of the last cell appeared
in a reception booth within the scientific complex at Tespo. Billions of such transits had taken place without a single accident,
though the urban legends of the Myssari whispered of the occasional traveler who arrived sans a limb, or with two reversed, or
absent more sensitive portions of their anatomy.

Ruslan never gave the process a thought. The worst that could
happen was that he would die. Darkness would steal upon him
soon enough anyway. Despite his situation he did not long for it,
but neither did he waste time lamenting its increasing proximity.
The air around Pe'leoek was too fresh, the sun too warm, the
strange sounds that passed for laughter among Myssari youth too
effervescent. When the time came, he would depart readily, with
no regrets.

Tespo was comprised of twelve identical large structures. Half
were given over to the cause of science, the other half to its support. Each edifice was shaped like a giant teardrop that had flowed
uphill; the smaller end terminated at a narrow beach, the much
larger bulbous end ballooning up into the rolling hills. They were
substantial buildings rising to twenty or thirty stories in height at

the thickest point of the structures and descending several stories or more into the ground. Slathered in exteriors of a muted golden brown, they absorbed more of the intense sunshine than they reflected, rising up the hillsides like gargantuan droplets of molten bronze.

Emerging from the arrival booth deep inside one of the buildings, Ruslan saw none of this. If anything, he was more of an object of great, if respectful, curiosity here than he was in the city proper. To those Myssari of a scientific bent, he could not be otherwise. He was fluent enough now to understand even their whispers.

"The last of its kind . . . Two legs and no tail, how does it stay upright? . . . Such large eyes, what do they see? . . . Why is an Ordinary escorting it? . . ."

An Ordinary. Such was Kel'les's general professional classification. To Ruslan the Myssari intermet was anything but an Ordinary. S'he was a friend.

The three members of the Humankind Research Sectionary would have liked to be accounted his friends, too, but Ruslan found that he was unable to release his emotions to them. With Kel'les he had gradually gained the feeling that the Myssari was more interested in him than in whatever knowledge of a lost species Ruslan might be able to supply. Whenever he found himself in the presence of the trio of scientists, he felt the reverse. They tried hard enough to be convivial. Probably too hard. Though he realized this, it did nothing to sway his opinion. He had no interest in furthering emotional accommodation.

Nevertheless he was as cordial as any of his hosts as they greeted one another. The chamber he and Kel'les had entered was nearly devoid of furniture. There was no need for it to occupy floor space when whatever was necessary could be summoned with a command. Bac'cul did just that, bringing forth from the floor places to sit, liquids to drink, and a transparency of the far wall that boasted a fine view of green-blue hillside on which could be seen grazing, with infinite slowness, small groups of what looked like dog-sized orange slugs. Beyond the field lay yet another massive, teardrop-shaped structure, and beyond it, another.

Dogs. Ruslan found himself remembering dogs. On Seraboth as well as elsewhere, they had rapidly gone from being man's best friend to scavengers and predators. In a way, he envied them their simple and straightforward regression. It would ensure them the survival that had eluded their masters.

In addition to Bac'cul he recognized Cor'rin and Yah'thom. Two males and one female. As it did frequently these days, he found his mind wandering. Did they look at an intermet like Kel'les with lust, or purely as a colleague? As it required three Myssari to procreate naturally, were emotional relationships correspondingly far more complicated? Despite all the time he had spent in Pe'leoek, he had never been able to successfully appreciate or analyze Myssari feelings. It was not that they were reluctant to discuss such matters; they were too polite to do so.

In keeping with contemporary Myssari design, there were no sharp angles or corners in the room. This extended from the architecture to the limited amount of scientific equipment on view to personal items. Every surface was opaque. A diurnal folk with sensitive eyes were not fond of reflective surfaces. The view out the back wall would automatically dim as the sun rose.

The cylindrical container from which he sipped a mixture of sweet and bitter liquid posed no difficulty for his simian hand. The dark green metal surface was lightly pebbled to provide a better grip. Though his fingers were shorter than those of a Myssari, he had five on each hand to their three. What they could not understand was why human manipulatory digits varied in length. The evolutionary engineering behind the thumb they could comprehend, but not Nature's rationale for making each of the remaining four digits a different length, nor why this should vary even among individuals.

"I couldn't tell you," he had replied when they had asked him about it. "All I know about anatomy is what I see in a mirror. If it helps, I don't understand the evolutionary reasoning behind a lot of what I see, either."

As she regarded him, Cor'rin's narrow mouth twisted and she blinked. Since the bony orbits in which her oculars reposed were entirely inflexible, she could not narrow her eyes in the human manner. The mouth twist was the Myssari version of a welcoming smile. Though she was female, nothing about her voice was particularly feminine. Save for those who had for entertainment or other purposes deliberately chosen to have surgical manipulation performed on their vocal apparatus, male, female, and intermet Myssari all sounded the same. It forced Ruslan to focus harder on physical discrepancies in order to be able to identify and recognize individuals.

"How are you, Ruslan?"

"I'm still alive."

"And as taciturn as ever." Yah'thom was by far the senior member of the group. So old that, on occasion, his inherent politeness sometimes gave way to sarcasm. Ruslan liked him a lot.

A whistling sound emerged from Cor'rin's throat as she cleared the breathing passage. It was a far more mellow sound than a human cough. Beside her, Bac'cul turned his head 180 degrees to study something outside before returning his gaze once more to the non-Myssari visitor.

"Has Kel'les explained why we have asked you here today?"

The human glanced at his minder. "S'he said you had something to present to me." He wanted to be equivalently polite, but he also wanted the meeting to be over. Beyond the arching bronzed walls of Tespo, the beach beckoned. Its aspect was maternal and not at all alien.

"An offer. We have an offer to make you." Though Bac'cul would defer to the elder Yah'thom when it pleased him, among those present it was the younger male who held the senior administrative rank. "It has been determined that the project to clone your cells and attempt to reestablish your species is to move forward with or without your consent."

How refreshingly impolite, Ruslan thought mordantly. "Your position is well known to me. From a scientific standpoint I suppose it makes sense." He grinned deliberately, knowing it would unsettle the panel. Having no teeth of their own, the Myssari were always shocked when a civilized being chose to flash them. "Aren't you afraid of what a resurrected humankind might do? We were highly advanced in many ways and thoroughly uncivilized in others. Look what we did to ourselves."

"If you refer to the biological weapon that resulted in the demise of your kind, we are not afraid of dead science. From the studies of records found on your world, it is plain there is, or was, much good in you. Your people were aesthetically inventive. There is a spontaneity to your art that we, the Hahk'na, and others feel should not be forgotten. Then there is the important philosophical point that no intelligence should be lost. We firmly believe that every species, no matter their individual or collective failings . . ."

Yah'thom let out an unequivocally loud whistle. Bac'cul chose to ignore him.

". . . has by their inherent uniqueness something important to contribute to the ongoing advance of civilizations. This therefore includes humankind."

"I can't give you my consent." Raising the beautiful metal utensil to his lips, Ruslan took another long draft. Alien flavors lacquered his tongue. "The best I can do is promise you my indifference."

Cor'rin gestured with two of her three hands. "That is why we requested that Kel'les bring you here today. We would prefer to proceed with more than that. And we are prepared to bargain to acquire it."

The human's gray brows drew together, another gesture designed to unsettle the inflexibly visaged Myssari, though this time it was unintentional. His gaze traveled warily across the semicircle of scientists.

"What's this really all about?"

The Myssari scientist did not hesitate. "Ethics."

He repressed a smirk. "Yours or mine?"

"Ah." Yah'thom's whistle was more subdued this time but no less unmistakable. "Always you jest. No matter the seriousness of the subject or lack thereof. A general characteristic of your people?"

Ruslan shrugged. "I couldn't really say. I always had a tendency to veer to the caustic."

"The answer is: more our ethics than yours," the elder Myssari told him. "If you will accede not only to our intention to try to restore your species, which you admit you cannot in any event prevent, but to actively participate in the effort, then we have been given permission to grant you anything you wish."

The lone human in the room—the lone human anywhere—frowned. "Except permission to live out the remainder of my life in peace and quiet while taking with me the last memories of my kind."

"We would not prevent that in any case." Heretofore unmoved, Yah'thom was now staring at him intently. The senior scientist's small eyes were a startling shade of yellow-gold that made them clearly visible to Ruslan even from where he sat.

The human considered. "Anything?"

"Within reason." It was Bac'cul who added the hasty caveat. "Our resources are limited. Though we regard the attempted resurrection of your kind as an enterprise as important as it is noble, we are not the only scientific project the Myssari Combine finds worthwhile. We must submit our requests for support like any other group."

"So you may not be able to deliver on your promise." This time

Ruslan did not grin, even though among the assembled only Kel'les might have interpreted the facial gesture appropriately.

The three scientists were clearly uneasy. "No promise is a fact until it has been requited," Cor'rin said finally.

"Then I accept, since if you fail to deliver on your end I will be just as happy to withdraw my cooperation as to provide it."

It took a moment for the triumvirate to ensure they understood his meaning. When they finally decided that he had indeed accepted the offer, their relief passed into gratitude.

"This means much to us." Cor'rin's earnestness was palpable.

Yah'thom's gratitude, on the other hand, rapidly gave way to circumspection. "What is it you would most like, Ruslan? What is your ultimate wish?"

The precision with which the scientist pronounced the human's name showed how seriously he was anticipating Ruslan's reply. Carefully the old man set the drinking utensil aside. His big-eyed human gaze passed over each of them individually.

For the second time that day, his thoughts turned to dogs. Wherever mankind had gone, wherever he had eventually settled, dogs and cats had gone with him. It would have been nice to have a dog. It would have been nice to talk in something besides Myssarian again. And there were plenty of wild dogs on Seraboth. But he decided against it. Even though gengineering had made it possible to extend the lives of dogs and cats and other animals much as it had those of humans, those of most quadrupeds still remained brief by comparison. As much as a dog taken from one of the blighted human worlds might bring him comfort, he knew it was entirely possible he could die before it. He would not leave a dog to the Myssari. Kind as they were, advanced as they were, their culture did not include any provision for keeping other creatures as pets. A cat, now, would handle the situation just fine. But he had never been able to talk to cats.

"I want to go home."

Bac'cul exchanged an unblinking glance with Cor'rin. Yah'thom did not take his eyes off their guest.

"That is all? You want to go back to Seraboth?"

Ruslan shook his head irritably. "No. I want to go *home*."

Leaning leftward, Kel'les gently rested the three equally long fingers of one hand on his friend's arm. "They do not understand, Ruslan. Nor do I. Is not the world your people called Seraboth your home?"

"It's where you found me." Ruslan's voice was taut, though whether with anger or frustration not even he could have said. "It's where I was born and where I lived. But it's not 'home.' Not *the* home." He returned his gaze to the expectant, bemused scientists. "I want to go to the home of my species. The homeworld. Humankind's equivalent of Myssar. Earth."

"That is its name?" Bac'cul was plainly amused. "How quaint."

In contrast to that of his colleague, Yah'thom's tone was entirely serious. "I have myself studied the great majority of general knowledge that has so far been gleaned by our researchers from the information storage facilities on your world. While we are still a long way from having all of it properly catalogued, far less studied in detail, I do recall mention of this homeworld, this 'Earth.' But not its location."

Ruslan nodded somberly. "I didn't say it was going to be easy. According to the legends on Seraboth, all records as to its spatial location were obliterated or maladjusted or spasmed more than ten thousand years ago."

Cor'rin's mouth was too small to gape, but she came close. "Why would that be done? Why would any species deliberately eliminate all traces of its homeworld's galactic coordinates?"

"I said according to *legends*. There are many. Some say people were angry that the center of civilization didn't or couldn't do anything to stop the Aura Malignance. Some insist that the plague originated on Earth itself and was spread from there. As a mid-level administrator, I had access to a lot of records. Other stories insist that the Malignance did not originate on Earth and that its inhabitants themselves destroyed all references to its location in an attempt to preserve at least the homeworld from the devastation that was afflicting all the others."

"Ah." Bac'cul felt he understood. "Erasing their steps backward. If this Earth could not be found, then it could not be infected." He waved a hand to indicate his excitement as he regarded his colleagues. "Consider what such a scenario might mean. If we can find Ruslan's homeworld, it might be intact and healthy! Not only would our xenologists then have access to all of human culture and civilization, Earth's people could help us to interpret and catalog and classify all the knowledge that we have acquired from studying their colonized worlds."

"Be reasonable." All three of Cor'rin's hands were in motion. "If his homeworld escaped the cataclysm wrought by the Aura Malignance, would its people not, when it was subsequently determined to be safe to visit other worlds again, long since have done so?"

Bac'cul was taken aback by her observation. Not so Yah'thom. With his every response, Ruslan's respect for the elder rose another notch. As he spoke, the senior scientist was gazing at the gleaming, curving ceiling. Or perhaps beyond it.

"Possibly there does still exist a surviving human civilization on Ruslan's Earth, but one that has not yet determined it is safe to visit other worlds. They may be restraining their explorations out of caution, or uncertainty. Or fear. I should imagine that racial suicide of the kind induced by this species-specific contagion would be enough to keep every means of transport on any unaffected world severely, if not permanently, locked down."

"Then it is up to us," Cor'rin declared, "to locate this place and, if such is the case, free them from their concerns."

I'd just like to see the place before I die, Ruslan thought. As Yah'thom declared, enough generalized information about humankind's homeworld existed in the records on Seraboth to pique his curiosity, if not reveal its location. Everyone (before they died) knew of and was taught about Earth. It was just that for a very long time no one knew any longer where it was.

Bac'cul was speaking again. "I would think that if anyone on Seraboth had access to your homeworld's coordinates, it would be an administrator such as yourself."

"Not necessarily," Ruslan countered. "I didn't rise into the higher echelons of my classification. I would think the global astronomy organizations of Seraboth would have had far more such knowledge."

Yah'thom emitted a soft, sibilant Myssari sigh. "The records of your world's astronomical societies were among the first to be accessed and translated when the Combine began studying Seraboth. Unfortunately, there was little to be learned from them about the immediate galactic neighborhood that we did not already know, and certainly nothing about a human homeworld that had been safeguarded through deliberate isolation. Our scientists were frankly surprised. One would think that, included among the description of your species' homeworld, there would at least have been hints as to its location."

"There was much that was forgotten." Ruslan was instinctively defensive. The population of Seraboth had not been composed of the mentally deficient. It was just that knowledge had shrunk in proportion to the population. Now only he remained. Perhaps he was not the brightest or the most educated individual his world had ever produced, but he was no fool. Dying of old age he might be, but he would uphold the honor of Seraboth to the last.

As for upholding the honor of humankind, that did not concern him. As far as he was concerned, that was no longer an issue, the species having forfeited it with the development and dispersal of the Aura Malignance.

There was a long pause on the panel until Cor'rin said, "Then what are we to do? How can we proceed?"

Ruslan had no suggestions, but Yah'thom certainly did.

"If there are no clues as to the location of Earth on Seraboth, then we must look elsewhere. A request for such information will be distributed among the other civilized species: the Hahk'na, the Lelopran, the Kastorii, and any others who might have access to or an interest in such knowledge. Many times one seemingly unrelated fragment of information will lead to another, and another, until greatly to everyone's surprise all the many broken pieces of knowledge combine to form a useful theorem or fact."

Present as an escort and handler rather than a participant, Kel'les had kept silent. Now s'he spoke up. "Sending forth such an appeal is certainly a fine idea, but it will take time to be dispersed. The Hahk'na and the Lelopran will not devote to it the resources we would like. This is understandable. They have their own priorities." S'he glanced sideways at the human. "I doubt that the prospect of fulfilling such a request, even if it is made at the behest of the last surviving representative of a species, will bestir their researchers to much action."

"True," Yah'thom readily agreed. "While we have plenty of time, Ruslan does not." It was a cold assessment of the situation, but not a brutal one. He turned his attention from handler to guest. "Are you familiar with a world settled by your people called Treth?"

Ruslan's thick gray brows drew together. "I've heard of it. Can't say I'm familiar with it." Where he expressed doubt, Cor'rin and Bac'cul showed no such uncertainty.

"It is the world we encountered after finding Seraboth," Cor'rin explained. "The most recently human-settled planet yet found."

Yah'thom gestured affirmatively, then returned his attention to their guest. "Human civilization appears to have persisted on Treth longer than on Seraboth or on any of the other several dozen worlds settled by your kind that we have thus far found and explored. Therefore it is reasonable to assume that knowledge that has been lost elsewhere might still exist in the records of such a place."

Within Ruslan's mind the tiniest flicker of interest began to froth. "As an administrator, I have to agree with you. That doesn't mean there's anything more to be learned about Earth's location in the planetary records of Treth than there was on Seraboth, or anywhere else your people have visited."

"No," admitted the elder scientist, "but it strikes me as a good first place to look. We will begin our search there." He did not need to seek confirmation from his colleagues. The proposal was too rational to debate. "Do you wish to accompany the expedition?"

Ruslan was visibly startled. Coming to the meeting, he had not expected to be presented with a blank tender. Now that it had been made and accepted and a plan of action decided upon, he realized that for him to participate would mean giving up the bland but comfortable life that had been made for him on Myssar. Mightn't it be, he considered, that he was too old to go exploring? It was not as if his presence on such an expedition would be necessary. If by some miracle the Myssari actually located Earth somewhere in the vast firmament, he could then accompany the initial expedition designated to explore the ancient homeworld. That was what he sought: the result, not the work.

But he felt he could not refuse. While he saw his physical presence as contributing little more than deadweight, it might add a sense of urgency to those doing the actual research. He had never been to Treth, of course. Being a human-occupied world, it might hold some things of interest, some things worth seeing, even if its surviving records did not contain the location of old Earth.

"Of course I'll come along." His apparent enthusiasm belied an unspoken uncertainty. "Does Treth have oceans? Water oceans?"

Yah'thom ventured the Myssari equivalent of a smile. "Yes, as I recall, it most certainly does."

That was enough to reassure Ruslan concerning his decision, if not fill him with conviction. "I'll be ready to go whenever you can mount the visit. Assuming I'm still alive."

Bac'cul did not smile. "That is all you have to do, Ruslan. That is all you have to work at. Not dying." A three-fingered hand gestured at the figure seated beside the human. "Kel'les will endeavor to assist you in achieving that end. Or rather, non-end."

Noting the suggestion of apprehension on his handler's sharp-edged, triangular face, Ruslan struggled not to smile. "So we will go to Treth and try to find a hint as to the location of Earth, and meanwhile Kel'les here will attempt to keep me breathing long enough to complete the journey." He covered his mouth with his right hand and coughed into it.

Then he added, "I think s'he has the more difficult job."

3

___

The snapweft pilot was already deep in dream down in the center of the twilldizzy. From the beginning of his acclimatization to Myssari culture, Ruslan had always had the most trouble learning scientific terms. His general ignorance of physics of any kind only rendered comprehension that much more difficult. Trying to understand a nonhuman version only tied his thoughts in knots. So he asked for explanations, freely accepted the results, and translated them into terms that made a vague sort of sense. To him, anyway. Since there were no human physicists around to correct or contradict him, his improvisation served his needs quite well.

It was all magic anyway, this business of traveling between the stars. Certainly his own species had been quite efficient at it, though the last starship to visit Seraboth had come and gone two or three hundred years before he was born. Whether humans had utilized a system similar to that employed by the Myssari he had no way of knowing. When queried, Kel'les could only convolute his nine fingers and surmise that it must have been the same or very much so, because all known space-traversing species used a variant of it.

Once aboard the orbiting starship, Ruslan had a few moments before it would be time for him and the other passengers to enter stasis. He used them to query Cor'rin. Bac'cul was nearby, chatting with another traveler. Among the trio assigned to monitor and study his life, only Yah'thom remained behind. Smitten with assorted infirmities of old age, the crusty senior scientist felt that his presence would slow the group's progress. They had not yet departed Myssar orbit and already Ruslan missed the elder's insightful personality. He even missed the scientist's sarcasm, perhaps because so little of it was ever directed his way.

"I have two questions," he said to Cor'rin. "One involves the means and nature by which interstellar travel is accomplished. The other is about sex."

The scientist replied without hesitation. Now, as on previous occasions, he was struck by the bright metallic violet of her eyes. The insouciance of her response emphasized how at ease she was with his queries.

"An odd coupling, one might say, though both involve thrust. I am expert in neither."

"Your best take, then." Around them, other passengers besides Bac'cul and Kel'les were seeing to final preparations. Since his minder was taking care of necessary details Ruslan did not understand anyway, he had time for casual conversation. "Firstly, as near as I can tell, you, Bac'cul, and Kel'les are of similar age and maturity. Together you could constitute a reproductive trio, a potential procreational triumvirate. Aren't you concerned that working together away from the supervisorial strictures of Myssarian society could result in a romantic entanglement that might interfere with your work?"

"You really have learned a great deal about our society." The dimmer illumination in the access chamber had caused her eyes to darken from violet to purple. "Bac'cul is already mated elsewhere. I am not, nor is Kel'les, but I can assure you our scientific interests easily outweigh and would dominate any thoughts that might incline to the physical."

Ruslan nodded his understanding. "I was just curious. From what little I know and what lots I read, my kind were different. Second then, can you give me a better idea how this ship and its ilk actually work?" He gestured at their tubular surroundings. The curved floor underfoot posed no problems for its tripodal designers and builders, but he had to be more careful where he stepped.

"It is hardly a specialty of mine." Though she was plainly keen to enter her own travel pod, she was too courteous to arbitrarily dismiss his question. Listening closely, he did his best to assign meaning to her response.

"As I understand it, the cosmos is not uniform. There are lapses, holes, walls, currents. Different kinds of matter. Some things stable, others less so. Some are fixed, while others move about. By navigating these exceptions, these oddities in space-time, it is possible to shortcut ordinary space and arrive at a destination made suddenly congruent to the point of one's departure. To do so requires the skills of a snapweft: a highly trained pilot who is half organic and half machine. He or she or s'he is physically attached to the great contorting complex called the twilldizzy, which delicately tracks the disruptions in non-normal space-time. The body of the ship remains steady within while it spins around it, its course directed by the snapweft.

"Manipulation must be constant, unyielding, and faultless. Once control of a twilldizzy is lost, a ship can emerge anywhere in space. If that happens, sometimes a snapweft can reposition it within an anomaly and resume course. Sometimes that cannot be done. Then a ship is lost, never to be heard from again." She gestured confidence. "But such occurrences are rare. Twilldizzy travel is safe."

He was unable to forbear from pointing out, "Except for those unfortunate enough to have been designated the exception."

Her reply was even, her tone enigmatic. "It is good to see that you are feeling like your usual self. I need to ready myself for departure now. You should do the same."

Having silently joined them mid-conversation, Kel'les now put a hand on Ruslan's shoulder. "It is possible you will perceive the overflow from the snapweft. A pilot's projections are very powerful. There is no need to be alarmed. Such reception is perfectly normal."

Uncertainty further corroded Ruslan's already rugged features. "Why would I sense mental emanations from a representative of another species? I didn't when I was brought to Myssar from Seraboth."

"You made that transfer while under heavy medication. It would have dulled your awareness. As to being a member of a non-Myssari species, snapweft projections are sensed across multiple intelligences." A hand gestured meaningfully. "It is something that transcends species. Sensitivity depends entirely on the architecture of one's sentience. You may feel nothing at all."

They had entered the passenger torus. All around them, other travelers were slipping into waiting pods as calmly and efficiently as he would have slid into bed. Quite unexpectedly he felt a rush of uncertainty. Confronted with the possibility of death, rare as such occurrences might be, it developed that perhaps he was not quite as ready to die as he supposed.

They halted before a pair of open pods. Bac'cul and Cor'rin had already entered theirs. The transparent covers were closed, the occupants awake and relaxed. He noticed that Cor'rin was wearing a customized sensory eyeband. One of her three hands was conducting a diversion silent and unseen. Interstellar travel was plainly not for the claustrophobic. He eyed his own waiting deuomd nervously.

"What do I do if I get inside and find that I can't stand it, or that I'm having trouble?"

Kel'les eyed him tentatively. "What kind of trouble?"

The human's mouth twisted slightly. "If I knew, I'd tell you now."

His handler's voice was soothing. "I have seen how you deal with the unfamiliar, Ruslan. You will have no trouble. But if you do, simply announce the nature of the difficulty. The information will be relayed to the appropriate personnel and your problem will be dealt with promptly."

Kel'les's patient, confident tone was reassuring. Climbing into the deuomd, Ruslan lay back against the cushioned interior. Engineered to accommodate travelers with far more outrageous physiognomies than his, it had no trouble molding itself against him. He felt better already. His weight activated the deuomd's functions. There was a soft hiss as the cover began to slide from his feet toward his head. He spoke quickly but calmly before the lid could shut out the rest of the universe.

"If I do have trouble and declare it, what will be the likely response?"

"Your unit will analyze your observations and react accordingly." The cover was nearly closed now. "Most likely you will be appropriately sedated and sleep through the remainder of the voyage."

After that he could no longer hear Kel'les. It did not matter. The intermet had nothing else to tell him and he could think of nothing else to ask.

It was utterly silent within the deuomd. There was a surprising amount of space in which he could move around, doubtless because the wider triangle-shaped pelvis of the Myssari demanded it. He did not feel cramped. Whether he would feel the same way in another hour or so was a different matter. With all that had been going on, he had forgotten to ask how long the trip was going to take. Since no one had said anything to him about emerging for meals, or exercise, or voiding wastes, he assumed it would not take very long. No more than half a day, surely. Although it was all relative. The time that transpired inside the deuomd, inside the ship, might not be the same time that passed outside. So much depended on the skill of the cyborg pilot.

What would snapweft overflow feel like? He looked forward to possibly finding out with a mixture of awe and trepidation. Surely it was not potentially fatal or Kel'les would have so informed him. Unless his handler and the two scientists thought it better to keep certain information from their prize specimen.

There was a lurch. The ship starting out and away from Myssar orbit? he wondered. Or entering a distortion, an anomaly? Feeling nothing, he was suddenly disappointed.

An hour passed. In response to his verbal query, the flexible deuomd supplied diversions. Music, visuals, olfactory refractions: anything he could think of that he had learned from the Myssari. It was all very unextraordinary. The deuomd in which he lay was designed to promote sleep without the aid of drugs.

Somnolence was a state he was on the verge of entering when something stuck the dull blade of demand into his mind and he was cast outside himself. He remembered Kel'les's words.

Overflow.

The snapweft was struggling with a current. Along with the other passengers who had remained awake, Ruslan found himself swimming hard to keep his consciousness from descending into madness.

The longer it lasted, the more he came to realize that he was overdramatizing. Focusing on regulating his breathing calmed him. No system of interstellar transport that regularly risked the sanity of those who utilized it would remain long in favor. That didn't mean he was not unsettled.

He was receiving, or perceiving, a fraction of what the mech-asymbiote pilot was sensing as he fought to utilize the outré physics that permitted travel between star systems. The more Ruslan

tensed and twitched and grimaced and whined within the security
of his deuomd, the more his respect for the unseen snapweft grew.
Outside the spherical ship was a universe that was beautiful only
in images. In person and up close its aberrations and contortions
manifested themselves in shapes and sensations that ran the gamut
from off-putting to nightmare.

What was the thing that brushed against the hurtling orb and
left bits of its incomprehensible mentality clinging to those
stretched out within? Shards of id, like strips of seaweed damp
and chill, stuck to his mind until the snapweft lurched the ship
leftward and a force to which Ruslan could not put a name brushed
off the subconscious silt. Tendrils of another eldritch shape bigger
than a star, but stretched so thin that the atoms of its being seemed
stitched together only by lines of cooperating positrons, swallowed the ship. To Ruslan and the other travelers, it was less than
a breath; to the snapweft, a mind-wrenching throb. Shrugging it
off, the pilot pressed on, dodging and dancing, a juggler of lives
and machinery and instrumentation. It was the ship and the ship
was it.

Outside and beyond, stars and nebulae and blobs of unidentifi-
able matter and antimatter and far smaller things maintained their
stately dance through the firmament, coldly indifferent to a minus-
cule sphere bearing tiny knots of sentience. So easy to vanish in
that vastness, such a simple matter for beings that were less than
nothing to disappear. Not out of maliciousness but from Nature's
deadly apathy did those who braved the gulf between star systems
occasionally perish.

Finally Ruslan slept. Slept and dreamed and remembered.
Even while trapped on a world of the dead and dying, his had
been a childhood full of questioning hope. He had passed through
adolescence and on into young adulthood while those around
him, everyone he knew, had expired from the Aura Malignance.
It was the speed that was so daunting, the absoluteness that was
so appalling. There was no remedy, no vaccine, no escape. Walk,

think, then shudder. Sometimes panic when realization set in. No time for much more as the cerebroneural connections failed. Eyes fluttering, people staggered, stopped, and toppled over. Usually individually, sometimes in groups, occasionally in rows. He remembered entire streets full of people collapsing like dominoes. No wonder a cure had never been found. Despite walls of redundant prophylactics cast up in attempts to protect them, the scientists and physicians who had tried desperately to find a cure for the apocalypse had perished before they could even understand what it was they were struggling to fight.

Gradually the streets had grown empty. Eventually even automated public transport stopped. As it had on every other human-occupied world, a stillness and silence descended on Seraboth that was quieter than the inside of his mind when he was sound asleep.

There had been an old man. Ruslan had encountered him decades ago while wandering the streets of his home city. Searching for others—hopefully at first, then reluctantly, and at last with only the most bitter resolve—found him with only corpses for company. Until the old man.

The slender elder, his clothing worn, his visage weathered, had not simply dropped dead like hundreds of thousands of others. Something in him, genetics or resolve, had kept him upright a while longer than was typical. When young Ruslan had come upon him, he was leaning against a wall, coughing and starting to slump. With a cry Ruslan had rushed to him, thrilled to find someone else, another human, alive. As he drew near, the man turned toward him. Shaking his head slowly, he bestowed a sad smile on the young man.

"Don't worry about it, son. It doesn't hurt."

Then he closed his eyes, slid the rest of the way down the wall, and expired. Upon which Ruslan, beyond frustrated, beyond angry, clenched his fists and cursed the sky before howling at the newly dead body before him.

"You can't die! You can't!" His youthful self looked around

wildly. At the lingering corpses. At the dead city. "Don't leave me alone! Don't, don't!"

He pounded on the thin, motionless chest until his hands hurt. It didn't do any good. The brain didn't function, the heart didn't start. It wasn't fair! To meet someone else, to encounter another living person, only to have them greet you with a dying farewell.

Afterward came the guilt. Why should he be spared? Why out of the thousands, the millions, did he continue to live? His health stayed good, his mind sound. Several times, overcome by despair, he had contemplated killing himself. Why live on alone only to die among the greater loneliness that surrounded him? Why had he been singled out to become the last old man?

Then the Myssari exploration team had found him. Their astonishment at encountering a surviving human far outpaced his own at the sight of their trisymmetrical bodies. After centuries and ages of his kind searching the cosmos, he was the first human to encounter an intelligent alien species, and the last. He let them take him (not that, courteous though they were, they gave him any choice). He let them keep him alive. To remember, and to dream.

He woke up to the soothing sounds of a cloisteram stream: not quite strings, not quite woodwinds, all reminiscent of spring and running water—aural honey. He did not remember when reminiscence had replaced apprehension, but he was glad of the change. Better to lie abed in the grasp of old bad memories than incomprehensible nightmare realities. Humming softly, the lid of his deuomd retracted toward his feet and out of sight.

When he sat up, the first thing he did was silently salute someone he would never meet.

All praise to the snapweft.

He tried to push out the thought as forcefully as he could. Whether even a twinge of it was received, or perceived, or otherwise picked up by the half-Myssari, half-machine pilot he did not know. A slight shiver passed through him. Just cooler air outside the capsule, he told himself.

Less activity eddied around him than he had anticipated. Only a few other pods had opened to permit their denizens egress. As soon as he could stand he vented his curiosity on Kel'les.

"There is no reason for them to come out of stasis. Most will not do so until the ship arrives at their intended destination."

"Then what's the story behind these?" He indicated the clutch of awakened who were presently shuffling off in the direction of a nearby corridor. Bac'cul and Cor'rin were among them, chatting energetically. "Are they all assigned to work down on the planetary surface?"

Two of his minder's hands gestured elaborately, though it was not quite an explanation. "Some are, certainly. But there are those for whom a stop at a previously unvisited world is worth being roused from stasis, if only to garner a glimpse of it from orbit." S'he extended a third hand. "Come, Ruslan. We must go one way and our supplies another."

The human trailed slightly behind. "Will we be in the first group to go down?"

Kel'les looked back at him, almost facing him. "There is no teleport system here. No string of linked platforms like we used to reach the ship from Myssar's surface. The Myssari presence is modest and wholly scientific in nature. The demands required to construct and sustain even the most basic, conjoined teleport system would cost more than maintaining the entire scientific outpost. We will descend to the surface via the ship's cargo transporter."

That seemed fitting. He'd thought of himself as little other than cargo ever since the Myssari had recovered him.

Treth was beautiful from orbit. Ruslan had never traveled off-world until the Myssari had found him, but he'd had access to millions of stored images of other worlds. He did not specifically remember looking at or reading information about Treth, but with dozens of human-settled worlds to choose from and thousands of uninhabited others, it was hardly surprising that he should fail to recall a specific one.

Nor was there anything especially distinctive about the blue-green-brown orb turning slowly beneath the great interstellar craft and its much smaller orbit-to-surface transporter. The oceans Yah'thom had promised were smaller than those on Seraboth, the mountain ranges less imposing, the deserts widely scattered. It could have been Earth and he would not have known it. That it was called Treth was proof of nothing. With the passage of time, names change as readily as does history.

Though he was in excellent health, additional precautions were taken to ensure his safe arrival. Dropping from orbit via a cargo transporter could sometimes be rough. *Wouldn't do to damage their prize specimen.* There were straps and pads and sensors, so much so that he felt far more confined than he had within the deuomd.

The descent to the surface was cheerily anachronistic: all bumps and bangs, sideways slews and howling, as flowmetal and composite squabbled with atmosphere. The discomfort went away as soon as the transporter touched down. Kel'les was at his side almost instantly, unpacking him. There was a dose of medicine, a shaky but increasingly steady trek down several corridors, further descent via a mechanical lift, and then he was standing on the surface of a new world. His third.

Visually it was anticlimactic. Low hills off to the right dusted with vegetation that was reassuring shades of green. Ordinary dirt underfoot. A sky that shaded to yellow but was blue enough to be comforting. Ahead and to the left, the ruins of a once extensive metropolis. Even at a distance he could clearly make out crumbling towers and collapsed domes among the rest of the decomposing, verdure-encrusted infrastructure. Wherever intelligence fled, Nature took over. In that, conditions on Treth were no different from those on Seraboth. He felt almost at home.

A driftec was waiting for them, hovering a handsbreadth above the ground. Glancing upward, he saw no sign of the orbiting starship. When the next might arrive here he did not know and it did not matter. He had no control over such things and had not for some time now. It had been many years since he had been the captain of his ship.

Not a good attitude with which to begin, he chided himself. *A little optimism, if you please.* They were here to find something that might lead them to old Earth. If nothing else, it should be an invigorating change from daily life on super-civilized Myssar.

The driftec was composed of completely transparent ripples. Looking toward the stern, one could see its drive and other components encased in something like clear jelly. As soon as everyone and the first load of supplies were aboard, the driver activated the craft's systems. From a handsbreadth it rose to the height of Ruslan's waist, turned, and accelerated silently toward the ruined city.

On the way, they passed several lines of enormous trees that rose higher than anything he knew from Seraboth. At intervals the massive growths extruded branches that themselves were greater in diameter than most of the plants with which he was familiar. Each bole was topped by a crown of dark pink tendrils that waved in the wind. The straight lines in which the trees grew were a strong indication they had been planted here, perhaps to impressively flank some long-disintegrated boulevard leading to the city. Wrestling for sun-space among the massive trunks and exposed roots was a riot of lesser, opportunistic vegetation.

Of native fauna he saw nothing, though Bac'cul assured him it was present. "Some of it is hostile. Keep that in mind if while we are here you are tempted to wander off on your own."

"Where would I go?" he protested.

Seated in front of him, Cor'rin swiveled her head completely around. "We know you, Ruslan. You like to explore. Another characteristic of your people that you personally possess."

"Maybe I did once, but not anymore." He leaned back against soft transparency. "Now I leave the exploring to others. I'll do mine via readouts and let the Myssari do the heavy work."

Her responding gesture indicated that she understood the

humor underlying his remark. He quite liked Cor'rin. Bac'cul was all right, too, but more somber—as befitted the one in charge of their little hunting expedition. Ruslan did not hold the male alien's attitude against him. With age comes tolerance.

The headquarters of the Myssari scientific expedition on Treth was situated deep within the city, in the center of what once must have been a park. Or so Ruslan deduced from the density of the vegetation that had taken over the vast open space between high, now vine-covered buildings. Predominant among the flora was an interesting growth with dark purple bark that grew parallel to the ground before extruding numerous vertical trunks that in turn linked together to form yet another horizontal branch. Plant or not, it looked more engineered than evolved. A number of smaller growths aped the fascinating configuration, while innumerable vines ran parallel to one another instead of fighting for space. When tended to, he reflected as he climbed carefully out of the driftec, the luxuriant open space between the buildings must have been some long-dead horticulturalist's pride.

Despite their innate cultural sensitivity, in establishing their base camp the Myssari had opted for practicality over preservation: the plant growth occupying the center of the park had been vaporized to clear an open space.

To Ruslan's eyes the outpost was substantial. In typically orderly Myssari fashion there were well-defined locations for vehicle storage, maintenance, living quarters, research, and much more. As his companions disembarked, other Myssari were busy with smaller driftec, unloading supplies from secondary vehicles. An unusually squat Myssari ambled over to greet them, his stout physique lending him an unflatteringly insectoid appearance. Introductions were made. Project supervisor or not, San'dwil could not keep at least one of three eyes from constantly straying toward the only non-Myssari present.

"It's all right." Even when it was expected, Ruslan's fluent Myssarian never failed to surprise new acquaintances. "I'm used to it."

San'dwil's reply was marked by a slight respiratory stumble. "Used to what?"

"Being stared at. Especially by children." The indirect reprimand ensured that in the future the supervisor would strive to treat the sole human as simply another member of the visiting scientific team.

"Chilly here." It was the tone of her voice that told Ruslan that Cor'rin was already uncomfortable. He could not tell just by looking at her: the Myssari did not shiver. Along with his companions he had already noted the heavier garb worn by the outpost workforce. "Could you not have found a more climatologically amenable part of the planet on which to base operations?"

"We are here because the human science of Treth is to be found here." Turning, their host started toward a two-story structure of dull whitish construction foam. It had been poured as a solid; holes for windows and doors had long since been cut out and filled. "Not because we like the weather."

"I find it quite pleasant." Ruslan inhaled deeply of the fresh air. "Reminds me of Seraboth."

Cor'rin bobbed her head, a gesture intended to show what she thought of his opinion. Though there were exceptions, Myssari-settled worlds tended to run hotter and dryer than those that had been favored by humans.

The doubled entranceway admitted them to a heated interior. As opposed to the frenetic commotion he had half-expected to encounter, Ruslan was surprised by the lack of activity. It made sense, though, if one thought about it. Those engaged in research had little time to spare for casual chatter. Good science demanded plenty of silence.

Though he had seen similar displays on Myssar, he was still suitably impressed when San'dwil led them through one door and into an unexpectedly large room. It held little other than a massive dimensional visual of Treth that extended from floor to ceiling. Embedded indicators showed the location of outlying study camps, some of which were situated halfway around the globe. Markers could be enlarged to show where the ruins of human cities and towns had been discovered, as well as which had been investigated and which awaited initial exploration. With a wave of one hand, San'dwil brightened the network of orbiting recorders that were working tirelessly to map the planetary surface in ever increasing detail.

"I did not realize your work here had progressed this far." Bac'cul did not try to hide his admiration. "You have accomplished a great deal."

"With such extensive facilities, you must have learned much," Cor'rin added.

Focusing his attention on her, San'dwil dismissed the praise with a wave of two arms. "You asked why despite the less than convivial climate we chose to place our main base here, and I replied that this was where human science was to be found." He raised his center leg, then brought the booted foot down emphatically. "Deep beneath our feet, beneath this ruined and overgrown public space from which we had to carefully clear many bones, lies what we believe to be the core processing center for Treth global information. In a modern society all information is readily available to the population, but ultimately there has to be a central storage facility, an origination point. On this world it lies, we think, directly below us.

"Our linguistics specialists have been translating data as fast as the technicians can extract it. Some things wonderful, some depressing, much that is ordinary and of no especial importance." He paused, glanced at Ruslan, and resumed. "As one would expect, there is in the last days much discussion of the Aura Malignance. The results correlate with what is known from other human worlds, including Seraboth. No explanation, no reasoning, and certainly no solution. Eventually information input ceases, to be followed not long thereafter by the cessation of inquiry."

An uncomfortable silence ensued that Ruslan felt bound to

break. "I don't suppose that in the general course of doing their work any of your translators happened upon any reference to co-ordinates for a human-populated world called Earth?"

San'dwil's mouth twisted as much as was possible for a Mys-sari. "It peers no toplift to me, but as I am responsible for keeping the entire scientific program on Treth functioning, not to mention keeping the scientists functioning, I might easily have heard or seen multiple references. To me such fragments of new knowing are like seeds in the wind: important no doubt, but dispersed be-fore I can have a look at them." He proffered a formal gesture of welcome.

"You have traveled a long way. Come and have something to eat. Later, if it is important to you, I will pass you along to a data-base specialist and a search can be run for evidence of what you seek."

"It *is* important." Cor'rin walked alongside their hosts. "Find-ing that particular human world is the reason we have come here."

San'dwil gestured back that he understood. Meanwhile his eyes questioned the human.

4

———

Neither the food nor the accommodations were as pleasant as what he had grown used to on Seraboth. The Myssari base on Treth was a scientific outpost. As was the case with scientific outposts since the beginning of time, food and shelter were suborned to work.

That is not to say that he was uncomfortable. Though he insisted on being treated the same as any other worker in the camp, be they members of the support team or leading researchers, he was all too aware that everyone considered him an irreplaceable commodity, to be respected as such. Beyond the tiny room that had been assigned to him, it was virtually impossible to find any privacy. Someone was always following, leading, flanking, or otherwise looking out for him. He hated it. But it would have been loutish to argue that he was being treated too well.

So he tolerated the presence of escorts where none were wanted and listened to guides who were not sought. Despite this, time passed on Treth devoid of boredom. It was, after all, a world that had once been populated by humans. There was much to see and much to learn. In that, he was in complete accord with the emplaced science team.

He helped where he could. With the identification of found objects, by demonstrating how everything from furniture to still-functioning gadgetry was to be used, even to explaining the taste and smell and rationale behind certain foods. Meanwhile San'dwil's knowledge-extraction team and linguists did their best, when they had time, to try to search out the small bit of information that had brought the human and his minders all the way from Myssar.

"I am sorry we have not been able to supply the details you seek."

San'dwil reposed within his indentation on the other side of the irregularly shaped table. Though food and drink were present and amenable, they could not compensate Ruslan for the outpost commander's news.

"It has to be somewhere." Ruslan was muttering aloud, discouraged and unafraid to show it. "The location of the original homeworld of an entire species doesn't just vanish from every last one of that species' records, no matter how carefully and thoroughly they're wiped."

"If it is here, in these local records, my team will eventually find it." San'dwil did his best to sound encouraging.

"I fear that the keyword for my friend is 'eventually.'"

A surprised Ruslan looked over at Kel'les. He could not have voiced his feelings any better than the Myssari. True friendship, he thought, is knowing what the other person is going to say without having to inquire.

San'dwil took a long sip from a coiled drinking utensil. "I have excellent people working here. What I do not have is all the equipment I would like. We cannot translate knowledge faster than we can extract it. Although the buried central records facility is in excellent condition, the material it contains is frequently in differing or multiple formats."

Seated nearby, Cor'rin reached out to put a three-fingered hand on the back of Ruslan's forearm and another against the back of his neck and another around his waist.

"During their period of expansion your people settled on a great many worlds. The Combine has extensive resources, but not all can be devoted to science—far less to one particular discipline."

Bac'cul's words supplemented as well as supported her own. "There are currently four teams such as this one working on four ex-human worlds."

Ruslan nodded tiredly. Out of his original wishful thinking had come hope, which had soon given way to reality. Dozens of worlds. Four research teams. Trillions of bits of information generated in languages and by technologies not their own. The Myssari were doing the best they could. It was consolation writ small.

And yet—and yet—it was still a wonderment to him that so basic a piece of knowledge should have been utterly obliterated from the general records of any world, much less all of them. Such had been the fear engendered by the Aura Malignance. Had it really originated on and been propagated from Earth, as some legends had it? Without finding that fabled world, he would never know.

Among them all it was Kel'les alone who could clearly see his pain. "There is a very great deal to catalog, my friend, and far more catalog than there are cataloguers."

"I know, I know." At a touch, his Myssari chair, functional but uncomfortable as ever, slid him away from the table. "I just have to endure."

"The most critical quality in good science." San'dwil pushed back and stood as well. "More important even than insight or intellect."

Ruslan dredged up a wan smile. "Then I'd make a good scientist, because I sure have more of the former than the latter two."

Not for the first time swallowing his immense frustration, he informed Bac'cul and Cor'rin that he was going to watch some of the external retractors that were working on the deeply buried knowledge center. Halfway there he told Kel'les that his stomach was giving him the slightest of arguments and that instead he'd better retire to his room. Though it was only late afternoon, he explained that he was going to take some of the medicine that he had brought with him and retire early. Halfway to his room he turned sharply down a different corridor.

The horizontal service shafts brought and distributed power from the energy cube and water from the treatment plant. On a walk-by the previous day, he had noticed that the latter was undergoing repair. Ensuring that for the moment no one was watching him, he bent, lifted the currently unlocked access door, and eased himself outside. Though he was more massive than many Myssari, their wide tripodal lower torso demanded broad portals. He had no difficulty slipping through the gap.

Both of the buildings that housed the outpost's living quarters backed onto the northern end of the old park. Walking quickly but trying not to draw attention to himself, he avoided the last tubing and conduits only to find himself confronted by a security fence too tall to jump and too highly energized to touch without risk of electrocution. But by climbing up a vertical tank on the base side of the barrier and down a convenient native tree on the other, he managed to surmount the problem.

His knees complaining mightily, he landed on the other side. Save for breathing a little faster, he was intact. For the first time since he had landed on Treth, he found himself truly alone. A glance back the way he had come revealed no minder patiently waiting for him to resume his little expedition. There was not even an automaton. Turning, he struck out through the last remnants of the park.

The density of the vegetation made for slow and difficult going. It would have been easier with a cutting tool, or a dissolver, but requesting the use of either one would have aroused suspicion among his well-meaning handlers. No matter. He pressed on without, enjoying the feel of verdure against his body even when the occasional black thorn nicked his flesh and brought forth blood.

He would not have dared the solitary excursion had the wildly overgrown park been substantial in extent. With much of it having been cleared to permit the expansion of the Myssari base, however, he soon found himself through the thickest flora and able to contemplate the city proper.

What struck him immediately was how familiar it was. The architecture was sufficiently similar to the prevalent urban style on Seraboth to send a momentary jolt of dislocation through him. Years had passed since he had been "invited" away from the world on which he had been born, but he had lived there long enough for memories of even small details to stick. The way professional and commercial buildings were spaced, how defiantly residential towers thrust toward the clouds, the spiderweb of interstructural links designed to convey everything from power to people, the covered pedestrian walkways . . . all might have been lifted straight from the cities he remembered from his wanderings. There was even a wall formed of material against which an old man might once have slumped.

One thing that was different and reminded him he was not on the world of his birth was the nature of the enveloping vegetation that was rapidly reclaiming the buildings. On Seraboth it had been primarily green. Here on Treth it tended to shades of purple and lavender. Green remained a highlight but was not dominant, though as the local sun set it was growing increasingly difficult to distinguish colors. The intensifying evening sounds were different, too. Buzzes and hums rather than the squeaks and whistles of Seraboth.

One more human world, he thought. One more vast cemetery. He started forward . . . and almost immediately stumbled over something. Glancing down, he instantly identified the cause of his near fall.

It was a doll. A large one, simple and devoid of technological enhancements. Or detractions. It all depended on how one regarded the purpose of such objects. Until they reached a certain age, children had a remarkable lack of need for electricity. The doll was outfitted in rural attire. Its flat, nondimensional face had features that had been heat-pressed on. The ears did not flex, the nose did not expand and contract, the mouth was incapable of speaking, burping, or coughing up internal fluids. The blue eyes, however, laughed.

He put it down. In the course of the post-plague years he had spent roving a silent Seraboth, he had encountered many such forlorn relics of vanished individuals. All the crying they engendered, and there had been all too much of that, had finally faded away to nothing after the first few months of realizing that he was alone. He had wept tears the way a tree sheds bark, until, like a tree, nothing but bare heartwood remained.

The girl who had owned the doll was dead. Her parents and any siblings she'd had were dead. Just as on Seraboth, every human on Treth was dead.

No, that wasn't quite right, he corrected himself. Now he was here. Humanity lived again on this world—and would at least until he departed.

The skeletons he encountered in the first building he entered were largely if not wholly disarticulated. Complete breakup would come with the further passage of time. The calcium and phosphorous and other elements would be gratefully taken up by the soil and thence by the plants that now blocked the long-gone windows and fallen doors. Deeper into the first room, which struck him as possibly the foyer of a once great hotel, plant life thinned out. It was a place where only those growths that could thrive without direct sunlight could survive.

In the center of the room, which boasted an atrium that soared all the way to the apex of the structure, was a fountain. It was dry as dust, its once decorative motile structures now home to bioluminescent growths and small scurrying things. Due to the failing light he could not make out the shapes of the latter, but they were at best unsightly. Every fully evolved ecology has its vermin, he mused.

It was time to leave. He had been gone longer than he intended. Although he had not strayed far from the base and it was impossible to miss (he simply had to avoid the tall human structures), he did not relish plowing his way homeward through the small but dense wooded area that was all that remained of the city park. Leaving behind the tall tomb that was the unidentified structure, he retraced his steps until he was once again standing on the pedestrian way outside. Two of Treth's three moons were now rising in the sky. While they did not provide enough light for him to see clearly, they did supply sufficient illumination to allow him to find his way back.

He had not taken three steps when the cough stopped him.

Neither a buzz nor a hum, it was deep and ominous and unlike anything he had heard since arriving on this world. Above him unfamiliar stars had begun to background the two moons, one spherical, the other jagged. The silhouettes of ruined buildings seemed to bend forward, admonishing him. He fancied he could hear the reproachful moans of the dead millions.

"Shouldn't be out by yourself at night."

"We are gone and this world has reverted to those who dominated before us."

"Alien world equals alien dangers. Stupid human!"

He picked up his pace, looking around uneasily as he headed for the thicket from which he had emerged earlier. The intensifying moonlight bathed everything—buildings, pavement, oddly geometric plant life—in a silvery softness that was as false as it was beguiling.

The cough came again. Louder this time. Nearer.

He could hear himself breathing as he tried to move faster still. Though still in decent shape he was not the athlete he had been in his youth. That might not matter, he knew, depending on what was responsible for the now repetitive cough that was somewhere behind him and closing fast. He considered calling out, but most of the Myssari would already be inside their living quarters, while the night team would be preoccupied with their work.

Abruptly, the coughing stopped. A look back showed nothing behind him, nothing to block out eternal stars and human architecture. Ahead loomed the wall of park vegetation that marked the boundary between Myssari life and human demise. He started into it.

Something stood up in front of him.

He sucked in his breath as he stumbled backward. Whatever it was that rose before him in the night was far more massive than any Myssari. It had come not from the camp but from the depths of the crumbling city where it and its kind had assumed the mantle of dominance once worn by the planet's human colonists. In lieu of the intellectual capacity of a human, this new master of Treth boasted a more basic but no less efficacious round mouth full of backward-angled teeth, enormous scute-covered front paws, and a counterbalancing tail of inflexible gray bone. Even in the dim light, Ruslan could see that its two eyes were located one above the other instead of side by side. They differed in size, color, and shape, perhaps to allow the creature to see different portions of the spectrum—or as well by night as during the day. He took only hasty notice of such additional characteristics. What mattered was the mouthful of teeth. Unmistakably, the cougher was a carnivore.

It struck him that the creature might well have been stalking him ever since he had left the safety of the scientific compound.

He could run: the beast had long, powerful hind legs that would doubtless catch up to him within a few strides. He could attempt to find a vulnerable area and fight back: if there was a sensitive place located within the mass of long yellow-and-black fur, he couldn't see it in the dark, and probably not even in daylight. He could dodge to left or right: one of those massive paws would probably crush his skull before he could get beyond reach. His only hope was to make it into the dense park brush and try to wriggle into a place the predator could not reach. All these thoughts ran through his mind in a matter of a few seconds, subsequent to which he made up his mind and ran.

Straight at the creature.

A deep-throated cough crackled around him as bony forepaws descended toward his head. He could feel the air they pushed ahead of them as he dove between the upright carnivore's legs. By the time it whirled, he had rolled and was up and running for his life. He did not know if his bold charge had surprised it, nor did he care.

He was taken aback when the branches and twigs he encountered did not snap under pressure from his flailing arms or body weight. Whatever their internal integuments were composed of was tougher than the vegetation he remembered from Seraboth. The inability to force a path through the wood left him at the mercy of his pursuer. From the cracking and coughing he heard coming closer behind him, he realized that the animal was encountering no such impediments. Looking back, he had a moonlit vision of a face as big as his entire upper torso, a nightmare cross between a parasite and a panther. He was too old to fight and too tired to scream.

The Myssari will be greatly disappointed, he found himself thinking as rows of teeth began to shift back and forth within the round gape. Where the proposed cloning project was concerned, his hosts would now have to make do with salvaged DNA in the absence of his future cooperation. Assuming they could find his body. Or enough of it.

As wide as his hips, a branch running perfectly parallel to the ground momentarily slowed the carnivore's charge. It gave him time enough to duck beneath it. Under no further illusions as to his chances for survival, ancient instinct nevertheless compelled him to press on.

A shadow appeared in front of him. Though it was much smaller than the monstrosity on the verge of chewing into the flesh and bone of his back, its appearance did nothing to raise his hopes. It was not Myssari. The smaller offspring of his pursuer, perhaps, hovering expectantly as it awaited its share of the kill. Or perhaps an unknown species of scavenger appraising an incipient meal.

The shadow raised a limb. At the end of the limb was something small and shiny. There was a sharp, metallic, almost musical intonation. Light flared from the shining and passed close enough to scorch the floundering human's left ear. He yelped more in surprise than pain.

Such was not the case with the predator that was almost upon him. It let out the loudest cough so far, one that broke and descended into an intermittent gargle. Turning, Ruslan saw flames rising from the creature's right shoulder. He could hear clearly the sputter of burning hair and smell carbonized flesh. A second shot flared from behind him to strike where the monster's neck would have been had its head not emerged directly from between its shoulders. The result was more flames and a burst of insane gargle-coughing. Whirling, the monster dropped to all fours and fled back along the path it had made through the brush. The smashing of additional flora as it took flight faded into the distance along with the flickering light cast by its flaming flesh and fur.

Sucking air as if he had spent the previous several minutes being smothered beneath a heavy blanket, Ruslan rose and turned to thank his savior. As soon as the individual took a step toward him, Ruslan saw that there were going to be difficulties in extending his gratitude.

His initial impression had been quite correct. The weapon wielder was not Myssari. In the shadowy wood he could just make out a vertical shape. Taller than the average Myssari, it was also slimmer. From the bottom of a pair of linked fleshy ovoids, two limbs extended downward. He thought they were pseudopods until his eyes adjusted enough for him to see that they were bony legs similar to his own. The difference lay in the number of joints. Where a human leg had three, this being boasted a dozen or more. It was the same with the two thin but highly flexible arms. The head was a hairless horizontal bar that sat atop a short but wide neck. At the right and left termini of the skull, bright eyes swiveled sideways and forward. There was a long slit of a mouth and no immediately obvious nose. Atop the long skull fluttered a row of small brown appendages like the petals of a flower. Whether these were sexual attractants, merely decorative, or organs of unknown function he could not say.

The creature was garbed in tight-fitting material that changed color and pattern as it moved. Camouflage gear, Ruslan decided. As his breathing slowed he essayed a few words of thanks in sub-dued Myssarian.

The muzzle of the weapon rose until it was aimed directly at his forehead.

Spreading his arms wide, he spoke again, this time more quickly. "Did you save me just to kill me? I don't know your kind, but based on what I've seen and see now, you don't strike me as inher-ently counterproductive."

"I did not fire, *ssish,* to save you. The *barunkad* would have killed you first and then come for me. Eaten one first before carry-ing off the other."

Having initially been slowed by the predator's disappearance, Ruslan's heart was now pounding anew. "Practical rather than altruistic. I can accept that. But why kill me now?"

The muzzle of the weapon did not shift away from the human's head. "You have seen me. It will be better if you do not tell your . . ." As the battle with the local carnivore receded from its thoughts, the alien's thinking shifted gears. "You are not Myssari. What are you?"

Looking past the alien, Ruslan gestured at the eroding metropolis beyond. "I am a human. A member of the species that settled this world and raised this city."

The strange bean-shaped head dipped to the left. "You define yourself as a member of a species of liars. There are no more humans. None have been seen for . . ." He named a figure in his own language that did not translate into Myssarian.

"Until now." Ruslan spoke as calmly as he could. Liars grew nervous as lies unfolded. If he was going to survive this encounter, it was vital for him to appear as self-assured as possible. "If you know of humans, then perhaps you have seen visual representations. Or within this city, statues. If I am not human, then what am I? Why would I claim to be a representative of an extinct race when I could as easily claim to be a member of an existing one?"

While the alien hesitated, the multiplicity of joints in its remarkable legs twisted and popped as it shifted on its feet. The latter extended backward from the ankle as far as they did forward.

"You claim to be a surviving human yet you speak perfect Myssarian. Far better than I. How do you explain that?"

"They found me on another empty human world and have cared for me since."

"Then you are a pet." The alien's exceptionally wide mouth gaped to reveal dozens of small peg-like teeth.

If it was trying to provoke Ruslan, it failed. He had long ago come to terms with his status. The alien's comment was interesting in and of itself. The Myssari did not keep pets. It suggested that this being's species did.

"I am alive. If I were a pet, would I be out and about, exploring this place at night? Unless our respective kinds differ extensively on the definition of a pet, you know that if that was my status I would not be permitted to go out on my own." For obvious reasons, he did not add that had they known about it the Myssari would surely have prevented his late afternoon excursion.

The alien appeared (or at least to Ruslan's mind appeared) confused. He pressed his advantage.

"Why is it awkward for me to have seen you?"

"Because I should not be here," the alien murmured.

Ruslan shrugged. "According to you, I should not be here, either. So we have something in common."

Again the alien paused before the wide mouth parted once more. "I am thinking, *ssish,* that you are attempting irony. If so, that would be two things we have in common. They are not enough to keep me from killing you. But your existence, if you are truly a human, is. Most valuable information to take back with me that will become worthless if I kill you."

Though the alien's Myssarian was far from perfect, Ruslan felt sure enough of its meaning to comment. "Now who's being ironic?"

The sounds of breaking branches interrupted the alien's intended reply. With another long, appraising stare, the strange biped took the measure of the self-proclaimed human standing helplessly before it. The muzzle of the hand weapon held steady. So did Ruslan's return gaze and respiration. Then the alien pivoted on its remarkably flexible legs to vanish in a thrashing of underbrush and camouflage. Ruslan exhaled heavily.

San'dwil was first at his side. The anxious base commander was followed seconds later by Kel'les and a clutch of concerned Myssari. All except Ruslan's friend and minder were armed. While the others spread out to search the surrounding vegetation for threats, San'dwil and Kel'les confronted the human.

"What happened?" Kel'les's small round mouth was flexing so fast it appeared that it was actually vibrating. "You were missed. When you could not be found, there was confusion, then some panic. Destructive energy was detected in this sector and confusion was multiplied."

"I wanted to go for a walk." A relieved Ruslan was by now far calmer than the still-apprehensive Myssari. "Without supervision. Without handlers." At the look on Kel'les's face, he added quickly, "Nothing personal. My kind needs occasional privacy, and I've had very little of it since we left Myssar."

Kel'les was only partially mollified. "Bac'cul and Cor'rin are beside themselves, as was I. This might once have been a civilized world but it is a dangerous place now. You could have been killed."

"Twice," Ruslan agreed without hesitation. Both Myssari eyed him uncertainly.

"Would you care to explain the specific numerality of your response?" his friend inquired.

Turning, Ruslan pointed at the tunnel of broken vegetation that now extended back through the wood. "I was on my way back to base when something big and knobby and full of teeth tried to make a meal of me. I can't be certain, but I think it must have been following me for some time. I probably had less than a minute to live when this funny-shaped specter arrived and shot it twice. Didn't kill it, I don't think, but drove it off. The shooter admitted he shot only to protect himself, not to save me. He was about to shoot me, too."

Kel'les indicated his incomprehension. "Why did he not?"

"I'm not sure." Ruslan thought back to the confrontation. Though it felt as if the entire episode had taken place hours ago, only minutes had passed. In his mind's eye he could still see the alien standing before him, weapon upraised, pondering how to proceed. "You arrived before he could come to a considered decision, I think." A thin, humorless smile creased his face. "Maybe he's a conservationist, like you. Maybe he thought that if he shot me, you'd pursue him. Maybe he simply enjoyed our brief conversation."

San'dwil's outrage was barely constrained. "We will find out who is responsible. Someone out operating on their own, without official permission. Whoever it is should be commended for saving your life, but at the same time . . ."

Realizing the confusion, Ruslan hastened to clarify. "It wasn't a Myssari."

Kel'les's tone was sufficient to convey his puzzlement. "Not Myssari? How can you be certain?"

Ruslan turned to his friend. "I suppose it could have been Myssari. As long as it was an underweight, out-of-shape, multiple-amputee Myssari with a serious cephalic condition and terrible grammar."

San'dwil was not amused. "Describe it. Leave out no detail."

The human nodded tersely. "My recollection won't be perfect. I remember the weapon he kept pointed at me better than anything else."

"Describe that as well."

San'dwil and Kel'les listened silently while Ruslan recounted the encounter. When he had finished, it was his minder who spoke first.

"A Vrizan!" The intermet's shock was unconfined.

San'dwil's tone was grim. "A scout. Sent to spy on our work here."

"It will be better if you do not tell your . . ." Ruslan remembered the alien's words. *"I should not be here."* On reflection and mindful of San'dwil's observation, he was more surprised than ever that the intruder had not shot him on the spot.

"Why would anyone want to spy on a base engaged in xeno-archeology?"

Turning back toward the camp, the commander allowed himself to fully exhale. "Come away from this dark and dangerous place and I will explain things to you." He glanced at Kel'les. "Are you also ignorant of the relevant facts?"

The minder glanced sharply at Ruslan, then back at the commander. "My companions and I were given a realistic overview, but it is reasonable to assume certain details were missed."

"Then it will be useful for you to listen as well."

Around them the armed Myssari continued to spread out. Searching for the intruding Vrizan, Ruslan told himself as he stepped over a root rising a thumb's length above the ground and running perfectly parallel to it. He hoped that if they found anything it would be only the alien scout and not the enraged, wounded carnivore.

"In the absence of any other nearby intelligences," San'dwil was saying, "this section of the galactic arm was once dominated entirely by your kind. That you warred among yourselves is a concept so alien to our culture that our xenosociologists are still trying to unravel its reality. Eventually this constant interspecies fighting led to the development of the Aura Malignance and the consequent extermination of your species." He paused, staring at Ruslan. "Near extermination," he corrected himself.

They were through the worst of the brush now and back among the clean, disinfected confines of the camp. Espying the returnees, several Myssari gestured in their direction. Ruslan knew they were not pointing at his companions. He had both upset and inconvenienced his hosts and was feeling increasingly bad about it.

"I know all that."

"Now that human civilization has gone," San'dwil continued, "this quadrant of the galaxy offers many uninhabited worlds that are hospitable to other species. I naturally include the Myssari among them."

"Naturally." Ruslan's careful monotone carried no accusations.

"The Vrizan are particularly competitive and highly expansionist. There are other species interested in the old worlds of humankind as well. The Combine has laid its claim to Treth. So have the Vrizan. There will be debate, discussion, and most probably diatribe. Eventually the matter will be settled. The Combine may acquire rights to Treth while conceding those of another world to the Vrizan. Meanwhile each side seeks in whatever way possible to cement its respective claims."

Ruslan had a sudden thought. "Who has the rights to Seraboth?"

"The Combine." Kel'les did not wait for the commander to reply. Ruslan felt oddly comforted to hear that the Myssari would maintain control of the world of his birth, though for all he knew of the Vrizan they might have proven themselves better caretakers than his hosts. Though not, he told himself, more polite.

"You said that competing claims would be settled 'in whatever way possible.' Although I have only one personal experience to go on, I assume this includes armed conflict as a means of resolving disputes?"

San'dwil looked away, clearly uncomfortable. He answered but did not dispute. "Negotiation is better." Two arms spread out to encompass the totality of the base. "My group here is focused on science, not territorial acquisition. I would prefer it remain so." His attention returned to his guest. "It is quite possible the Vrizan are unaware of your existence. Returning to his superiors with such news would be the second most important thing the Vrizan scout—spy—could do."

Ruslan frowned. "What would be the most important thing?"

"Returning with you." San'dwil emphasized each word.

"So maybe that's why he didn't shoot me. I'm potentially valuable to them as well."

"An unparalleled scientific asset." Kel'les was first through the door to the building that contained their living quarters. "Now that the Vrizan know you exist and are here on Treth, they may try by other means to make contact with you. If they cannot take you by force, they may try to induce you to cooperate with them."

Ruslan smiled as he was enveloped by the warmer air of the building's interior. "You've already given me anything I could want, including your efforts to try and find old Earth. There's nothing the Vrizan could offer that would surpass that."

Unless by some chance the Vrizan know its location, he thought.

"We are here to carry out scientific research and studies on the history and culture of humankind." San'dwil was drifting away. He had a report to compose. "I personally do not wish to be drawn into even the slightest of violent conflicts. We will leave all discussions concerning informal encounters to the appropriate components of the system."

Another thought, this one considerably wilder than its predecessors, entered Ruslan's mind. "What if I, as the last human, claim Treth? Then it will go neither to the Vrizan nor the Myssari."

Ambling on three legs, San'dwil was about to turn a corner and head up another corridor. "In a contest between ethicality and numbers, numbers invariably win. I am very much afraid that to prevail with such a claim, there would need to be considerably more than one of you . . . however enthusiastic you may prove to be."

5

From the first day he had arrived on Myssar, Ruslan had been asked to explain something, or elaborate on something, or identify a missing element of human history or culture, be it physical, philosophical, or verbal. While his hosts had managed to decipher the necessary codes and now had available to them the entire bulk of knowledge that had been stored on Seraboth, there were still times and places where Ruslan, with the simple everyday knowledge of an ordinary human, was able to save time and resources by merely pointing at something and saying, "This is what this does," or "It's intended for that purpose." He knew perfectly well and had long since accepted that he was as much an explicatory shortcut as he was a specimen.

This inherent facility, this basic uncomplicated essence of extant humanness, made his presence even more valuable on Treth, whose Myssari researchers did not have instant access to all the information that had been garnered from Seraboth's storage facilities. While specialists processed his wish and did their best to find any reference to the actual spatial location of Earth, there was a steady stream of experts in other fields confronting him with impatient requests.

"What is this?"

"A device for preparing food," he would explain.

"How did it work? By burning combustibles in this chamber?"

He smiled. "It cooked by means of propagating radiation."

"What was the source of the radiation?"

His hands rose. "I don't know. I'm not a scientist or an engineer. One would voice a request of the machine and wait for the food preparation to be completed. I remember how to use one; I never knew how to build one."

And so it went—with machines, tools, clothing, decorative items, construction materials—until repetition led to boredom and the feeling that while he might be helping his hosts, he was doing nothing to help himself.

Though any further unescorted strolls were now out of the question (he was watched—surreptitiously but continually), he did at least have the prospect of attendant local travel to look forward to. The desire to have him explain or expound upon new archeological finds required that he be transported to various digs around two of the nine continental land masses. After a while even those trips began to bore, one skeletal city looking much like another. The weather changed, and the topography, but not the ruins. They looked little different from those among which he had spent lonely years wandering on Seraboth.

Occasionally he would be struck by the appearance of an edifice whose design lifted it beyond the ordinary. The bridge spanning the strait that divided the two continents, a graceful, once golden and now tarnished thread of spun fibers. A still-standing tower three kilometers high that had been all but hollowed out from within and in a high wind bent like a reed. Lush fields of crimson and sapphire flowers sprouting from horizontal stems that overran an ancient airport as beautifully as if their planting had been the architects' original intention.

It rained modestly on Treth, but enough to counterpoint melancholy and remind him of the grayness that was slowly overtaking the last of his life. Even the best efforts of Kel'les, occasionally abetted by Bac'cul and Cor'rin, failed to cheer him.

It was on such a morning that San'dwil entered the relaxation room where Ruslan and his minder were gazing out the wide, sweeping window. The visibly energized outpost commander delivered an announcement whose import to the slumping human eventually drowned out even the echoing thunder of the fast-moving storm outside.

"We have found an intact human cemetery!"

Ruslan and Kel'les regarded him calmly and without astonishment. "Many human cemeteries have been found on Seraboth," commented the intermet.

"Too many," added Ruslan.

San'dwil's mouth flexed with his excitement. "Not like this. It is a cryocemetery. And when I say it is intact, I mean that the power source is still functioning."

Ruslan sat up immediately. "Then those who were interred . . . ?"

"Are still frozen, yes!"

Ennui fled as the human rose to his feet. "Am I . . . When can I see it?"

The commander was enjoying himself. "A transport awaits even as we speak. I came to get you." He gestured in the direction of the building's private living quarters. "Do you need to gather anything before we depart?"

"Only my expectations." Ruslan was moving past San'dwil and heading for the portal. "Let's go."

Even with three legs Kel'les had to hurry to catch up to his charge. "What about Bac'cul and Cor'rin?"

"Cor'rin is already there." San'dwil hastened to keep pace with the human. "Researcher Bac'cul is occupied elsewhere but can join us if needed." A three-fingered hand reached out to gently squeeze Ruslan's left shoulder. "I have not seen you this animated since you arrived on Treth, not even after your unauthorized excursion."

Ruslan ignored the observation. His thoughts were focused on one thing and one thing only. "You said the facility is still drawing power and those interred are still frozen. Can your people activate the resurrection instrumentation?" He wanted to say *restore them to life* but he was still having trouble wrapping his mind around the possibilities posed by the commander's announcement.

"Such is not my area of expertise. I am hoping that by the time we arrive at the site . . ." He left unspoken the answer to dreams Ruslan had long since ceased to contemplate.

They were outside now and moving fast toward the open, cleared corner of the base that was reserved for transportation. Several vehicles hove into view. Most were designed to provide only ground transport, but Ruslan saw two driftecs among them. San'dwil steered him and his handler toward the nearest. In moments they were on board. As the commander had promised, the craft had only been waiting on their arrival. By the time Ruslan had settled into his liquid seat, the driftec was lifting off. Peering out the transparent wall, he could see the base recede rapidly beneath them.

Leveling out at cruising altitude, the nearly noiseless driftec headed toward the ragged line of lavender-clad mountains that formed the western horizon, accelerating hopes Ruslan had long since forgone.

Only the presence of a roughly cleared landing pad surrounded by temporary self-erecting structures marked the location of the find.

There was no visible evidence to suggest a human presence. Where bare rock did not predominate, alien forest covered the hillside. As the driftec touched down, Ruslan gave voice to his curiosity.

"How did your people find this place?" The thickly vegetated slope into which the landing pad had been cut was unremarkable, in appearance no different from a hundred they had just flown over.

San'dwil pointed to one section of hillside that was slightly darker than the rest. "The entrance was overgrown. A routine automated survey picked up emanations that suggested the presence of functioning electronics. As we have no ongoing operations in this area, a follow-up was ordered. Located, as it is, well below the surface, the efflux was too weak to be detected by our two orbiting sensors, which is why it was not discovered before now." His mouth flexed to indicate humor. "The follow-up proceeded with caution, as one possibility held that the emissions might emanate from a clandestine Vrizan installation."

They were met at the cleared entrance by the xenologist in charge of the excavation. An exceedingly slender representative of her kind, the scientist resembled a triangular box mounted on three angled sticks to Ruslan. For a Myssari she had eyes that were almost soulful.

Her manner was a model of efficiency, however. Despite this being her initial contact with Ruslan and despite her unconcealed interest in the human survivor, she did not let her gaze linger nor did she waste words.

"Follow me, please. Your name/personal identifier is 'Rus'lann,' I believe?"

"Just 'Ruslan.' No epiglottal break in the middle."

"I am Wol'daeen. If you have any questions, do not hesitate to ask. I will answer as best as I am able based on the available evidence we have managed to uncover and interpret thus far. In turn I hope that you will answer any questions I may pose."

Not discourteous, he reflected, but for a Myssari decidedly

cool. It didn't matter. The friends he desperately hoped to make here did not include the members of the on-site scientific team.

A small mobile transport was brought over, into which piled Ruslan, Kel'les, San'dwil, Cor'rin, and the xenologist. As was usual when he was compelled to adapt his bulkier bipedal shape to the Myssari norm, he had trouble finding a comfortable place to fit. Giving up, he opted to sit on the floor.

The reason for the transport soon became clear. Lit by lines of luminescence hastily slapped onto the walls by Myssari technicians, the corridor ran deep into the mountain. It eventually terminated in a series of linked chambers whose contents the Myssari researchers were busy recording and cataloguing.

Guided by Wol'daeen, the visitors made their way to the last room. At its far end was a single elevator. That it still functioned was a tribute to its builders and to the self-sustaining power system they had buried inside the mountain. It had been many, many years since Ruslan had seen a piece of functioning human technology. Simple as was its design and function, when it started downward he found himself near tears. He struggled with his emotions.

If this is how you react to a working lift, he told himself, *how are you going to handle seeing intact bodies?*

Since the elevator shaft penetrated solid rock and there were no floors by which to judge distance, he had no idea how far they had descended when at last the lift came to a stop. Led by Wol'daeen, they exited into a sizable hall. Like the access tunnel, it was lit by luminescence that had been added by the first Myssari investigators. The floor underfoot was slightly ribbed to provide better footing in the presence of condensation, of which there was more than Ruslan had expected. He was estimating the water's depth when they rounded a corner.

There they were. Other humans. Naked, intact, entirely whole, unravaged by starvation or the aftereffects of the plague. A long row of them, each sealed in an individual transparent tube. Their eyes were closed, their lips pressed together and sealed by an organic binder. Each floated, suspended in a slightly bluish liquid, as if asleep in a vertical bath. Their number apparently equally divided between men and women, young and old, their appearances were heart-wrenchingly normal. Though her words completely shattered the mood of the moment if not his hopes, he was glad they came from Cor'rin and not San'dwil or Wol'daeen.

"Hopefully, one of the females will contain fertile eggs."

His mouth tightened but he said nothing. There was no reason to expect even a well-mannered Myssari xenologist to react to the discovery in anything other than an entirely scientific manner. If they could remove fertile eggs, perhaps they could also extract viable sperm. If one or both proved unusable, there remained the option of drawing intact cells from multiple sources. The full import of her detachment rolled over him.

They didn't need him anymore.

No, that was not entirely true. They might no longer need him to clone and preserve his species, but when it came to answering questions and supplying explanations, he was still invaluable. He berated himself for wasting time on such thoughts. None of that mattered here and now. What mattered was the possibility of revivification of others like himself.

Wol'daeen did not object as Ruslan walked over to the nearest tube. Whether it was the first or the last in line he could not say. Hovering in the liquid within was a woman who looked to be only a few decades younger than himself—no more than eighty, possibly younger. Her flesh appeared firm, her skin smooth and unbroken. Periodic electrical stimulation of some kind had kept her muscles toned. Still discernible as blond through the blue, her hair was cut short and restrained by a restricting net. Tubes connected to her body circulated fluid that kept cells alive while she drifted in a state of suspended activity.

Stepping back, he let his gaze travel the length of the corridor. The neat line of tubes held no less than a hundred preserved humans.

"I don't know for certain why this was done to these individuals, or by them, but I can hazard a guess." He regarded his nonhuman companions. "Unable to find a cure for the Aura Malignance or a way to slow its advance, they had themselves put in suspension in the hope that one day a treatment would be found and they could be revived." He shook his head slowly. "I doubt any one of them imagined the plague would die out by itself."

Kel'les placed all three hands on various portions of his friend's torso. "This must be very difficult for you to see."

He nodded. "Difficult and exciting all at once. I'm trying very hard not to get my hopes up." His attention shifted to the site supervisor. "You *are* going to try and revive some of them before you consider dissection, aren't you?"

Wol'daeen tensed visibly. "Linguists are already deeply engaged in translating the relevant surviving operational materials. As soon as they and our engineers feel they have a reasonable grasp of the necessary science, we will certainly attempt resuscitation."

"So we wait."

Cor'rin joined Kel'les in embracing the lone human in their midst. As a demonstration of characteristic Myssari empathy, it was typical, but with six hands on him he felt unreasonably restrained. Cor'rin blew his edgy concerns away with a new thought.

"If resuscitation proves successful, what will you say to the revived? Seeing you will reassure them. Seeing us may have a countereffect."

He blinked. "I hadn't thought that far ahead. I suppose I'd better think of something."

"I am sure anything you can say would prove comforting." Having introduced the human and those accompanying him to the great and wondrous discovery, Wol'daeen stepped past them as she headed back toward the lift. "If you wish, you may remain to carry out further observations. I ask only that you touch nothing lest you possibly damage some of the artifacts."

Artifacts, Ruslan told himself. *Like me.* What was amusing was that, having come to terms with such descriptions of himself during his time on Myssar, he was not half as offended by the appellation as were San'dwil or Cor'rin. In voicing the admonition, the xenologist in charge of the find had mildly called into question their competency as field researchers. He observed his companions' reactions with amusement. The caution was hardly necessary where he was concerned.

If the next moment of life was to be his last, the last thing he would do was risk damaging the revivification of another human being.

Far more time passed back at the main base than he would have liked, far less than he surmised. Though he strove to busy himself with whatever distractions he could find or invent, his thoughts were never more than a moment or two away from the damp crypt. When the call came to return to that underground mausoleum, he had to fight to contain his excitement.

Bac'cul was with him this time as well as Cor'rin, San'dwil, and Kel'les. Little was said on the flight to the site. They had not been prepped on the reason their presence had been requested. Only that a matter of some importance was to be discussed. Ruslan found that his hands were trembling. When a surprised Kel'les remarked on the phenomenon, his charge explained it away as a normal reaction to impending excitement. While the intermet seemed reluctant to accept this explanation, s'he didn't challenge it, no doubt out of politeness.

For the majority of the return journey to the site, it was silent inside the driftec. Touching down on the mountainside, they were met not by Wol'daeen but by one of her subordinates. Without volunteering any information, he led them inside. Ruslan could barely contain himself as the compact transport vehicle carried them down the access tunnel and into the depths of the mountain.

Though she had not come out to greet them, Wol'daeen was waiting for them in the most sterile work chamber Ruslan had seen since he had originally been embraced and examined by the Myssari. Prior to entering, the four visitors were required to don filmy, transparent overgarb. Membranes integrated into the attire allowed them to breathe without additional equipment, filtering the air they took in as well as their potentially contaminating exhalations. Ruslan was not surprised to find that suitable garb had been prepared for him. Myssari efficiency in all things had long since ceased to surprise.

Despite believing he had prepared himself mentally for anything he might see, a soft gasp of amazement escaped his lips as Wol'daeen led him and his friends to a long, silvery platform. Lying on it on their backs, head to feet, were a man and a woman. They looked to be middle-aged, perhaps just shy of eighty. They were as naked as they had been in their respective suspension cylinders. Every detail of their bodies down to the pores in their skin was on display in the carefully climate-controlled room. Structural integrity appeared not to have been violated, though he knew that Myssari scientists and technicians had the ability to enter a body and withdraw without leaving behind any visible evidence of their incursion.

Anticipation inexorably gave way to concern and then to dismay the nearer he drew to the bodies. Neither betrayed any sign of consciousness. Chests gently rose and fell but eyelids did not flutter. Closer inspection showed slight movement of air and skin in the vicinity of the nostrils. Tubes and conduits supplied nourishment. Links to pale blue liquid drawn from their respective capsules kept the bodies from collapsing in upon themselves.

For several minutes no one said anything. Though their interest in the display was purely scientific and they had no emotional stake in the outcome, his companions were every bit as intrigued by the sight as was Ruslan. Finally the site's lead scientist spoke. A female of few words, her commentary was even more brusque than usual, though no less explanatory for its brevity. Her words hung cold in the underground chamber.

"We tried."

Death, which had retreated to a tolerable distance ever since the Myssari had removed Ruslan from Seraboth, jumped unbidden into the room beside him. He could sense it, cool and proximate, against his back. Despite the sudden constriction in his throat, he managed to make himself heard.

"You'll—you'll try again."

"Of course." For a moment Ruslan thought the awkward situation had mellowed the gruff scientist. Then she added, "We have plenty of specimens with which to work."

His lips tightened but otherwise he kept his fury and frustration close. Wol'daeen was a scientist and a Myssari whose specialty was xenoarcheology. But she knew nothing of human emotions, and he had no reason to expect her to be sensitive to them. Kel'les, who knew a great deal more about such things, had turned sharply to the human as soon as the words had been spoken. The intermet was relieved to see that Ruslan was coping as well as could be expected with the researcher's chilly indifference.

Cor'rin pushed her center leg forward. "What went wrong?"

"With the attempt at revivification?" Wol'daeen sounded resigned. Which, Ruslan reflected, was better than sounding defeated. "It was more a matter of not enough going right. We prepared thoroughly. The translations of the relevant human manuals, procedures, technologies were checked several times before we began. In addition we have access to our own Myssari attempts at long-term preservation." She looked back toward the platform.

"The primary difficulty with such a process is the same as it has always been. While the technology for long-term preservation of a physical corpus has clearly been familiar to humans as well as to our own people, no known means exists for reviving thought." A hand indicated the woman. She was still beautiful, Ruslan thought. He preferred to think of her as sleeping rather than brain-dead.

"Stored separately in cylinders behind each preservation tube were quantities of blood specific to each individual. Using this, we carefully filled veins and arteries. Next we succeeded in restarting the natural heart pumps. Restoring respiratory function was more difficult but in the end proved satisfactory." She gestured. "That is as much as we were able to accomplish."

"Electrical cortical stimulation?" Cor'rin wondered.

Wol'daeen signaled understanding. "When the specified drugs that were also stored behind each cylinder failed to produce the hoped-for response, such stimulation was indeed attempted: light at first, then increasing in graduated increments. Muscle stimulation was achieved, but nothing else. It is possible to manually expose the eyes to daylight. This too was tried in the hope that it might initiate a recognizable response where all other attempts had failed." For the first time there was a hint of genuine sadness in the scientist's voice. "Not one of our various efforts produced anything that could be called a cognizant response. The neural readings for both brains are completely flat."

It was left to San'dwil to sum up the totality of the attempt. "So you can make the bodies live but cannot bring back consciousness."

Wol'daeen gestured affirmatively. "It is most exasperating. The resurrected forms have all the appearance of life but none of the necessary cognitive functions. The conclusion to be drawn is that while humankind mastered the means necessary to preserve physical form over the long term, they failed at finding a way to preserve memories in the organic mind. They went as far as they could with what they knew. Perhaps they hoped that whoever eventually resurrected them would have learned of a way to release or revive memories stored within the cerebral cortex. Sadly, we also recognize that such knowledge is nothing more than a flurry of electrical connections and pertinent stimuli. If it is shut down for any reasonable period of time, it vanishes." Her attention fixed on the silent Ruslan.

"Nonetheless, we will try again, and keep trying, in the hope that there may be some critical factor we have overlooked or otherwise neglected to implement. The potential rewards of success are too great to be dismissed by a first failed attempt."

Having heard it before, this time a devastated Ruslan was not shocked by the question Cor'rin posed next. "What about the female's eggs?"

"As our initial interest has been focused wholly on the prospects for revivification," Wol'daeen replied, "we have not proceeded with vivisection. Having failed to revive these two specimens, we will certainly not waste that which can be learned from—"

"Out." Ruslan made repeated gestures in the direction of his mouth. "I need to get out."

An anxious Kel'les confronted him. "Out of your suit?"

"No." The human was looking around wildly. "Out of here. Out of this mountain. Away from this place."

San'dwil looked concerned. "You are feeling uncomfortable at the prospect of work continuing here?"

It was only one of many things he could not run away from: the Myssari proclivity for understatement. He did not even bother to respond directly to San'dwil's question.

"Out, *now*."

Wincing at the volume the human was projecting, Kel'les helped him toward the portal through which they had entered the operating theater. Ruslan looked back and searched the assembled Myssari until his gaze once more settled on the site's senior scientist. "If you don't think you can bring any of them back, I'd prefer you didn't do anything else with them."

Wol'daeen glanced at San'dwil, who neither said nor gestured a response, then turned back toward the human. "I of course do not have the final say in such matters, but I believe that given the expense and difficulty involved in the carrying out of scientific work on this world, such a request will be denied by those who are in charge of the Combine's scientific fieldwork."

"I know," Ruslan muttered disconsolately. He and Kel'les were nearly to the exit where the first of three hermetically sealed barriers was preparing to open and let them pass through. "But I felt it had to be said. If you can't bring back the dead, respect them."

Wol'daeen called after him. "I would think that being able to contribute to the advancement of science would be as virtuous a sign of respect as any intelligent being could wish for. I know for certain that I would feel that way."

The portal was open and Kel'les was trying to help him through. There was time for Ruslan to offer only a few final parting words.

"So would I. But you and I are in a position to make such a choice." He nodded in the direction of the two mindless bodies lying on the gleaming platform, who continued to breathe uselessly. "Not so either of them."

The first barrier closed tightly behind them. Air was exhausted, to be treated elsewhere and swiftly replaced. The second doorway parted, the process of cleansing was repeated, and then they were out in the brightly lit prep room. A trio of technicians who were preparing to enter the restoration chamber eyed the live human curiously in passing.

Slumping onto an awkward and uncomfortable Myssari seat, Ruslan let Kel'les begin the process of extricating him from his visitor's sterile suit. He paid little attention, not caring and not helping. Having returned to the excavation site in hopes of encountering revived fellow humans, he had instead been confronted with living but empty bodies. He had no doubt that the dedicated if diffident Wol'daeen and her colleagues would try their utmost to successfully revive some of the other cold-stored humans. It would be a scientific triumph for them if they could do so. But having seen what he had seen and heard what he had heard, he was not sanguine.

As for Cor'rin's comment, he couldn't halt the Myssari in their efforts any more than his parting words would prevent the senior scientist and her counterparts from digging into more and more bodies in hopes of finding the means necessary to revive conscious human beings. Failing that, they would seek to extract the means necessary to create new ones. Artificial insemination into an artificial womb would be simple enough. All the Myssari needed was the necessary raw material.

He could at least refuse to help with that. He had agreed to cooperate in a process of cloning; nothing else. The thought of what might be asked of him if Wol'daeen and her team succeeded in extracting viable human eggs from one or more of the frozen non-revivable bodies left him feeling queasier than when he had asked to leave the chamber. He wouldn't do it. They could force him to cooperate, but he doubted it would come to that. Desirous as they might be of attempting such a procedure, he did not think they would compel his participation. Given his age, any such effort might well fail anyway.

Cloning. Impersonal and distant. Let them stick with that if they insisted on restoring humankind. If they did try to force him to assist with any other procedure, he'd . . . he'd kill himself.

No, you won't, he thought tiredly. The drive to survive was more powerful than any abstract sense of ethical outrage. He might resist, but in the end he would probably comply.

He knew himself well enough to know that he was too much of a coward to do otherwise.

6

One did not need to possess Kel'les's level of expertise and experience in dealing with a live human to see how depressed Ruslan was on the return journey to base. At Cor'rin's suggestion the driftec detoured to pay a visit to a newly discovered geological phenomenon. The presence of scattered human ruins near the base of the thousand-meter-high waterfall was proof that the spectacular sight had long been appreciated by Treth's inhabitants. Now the vertiginous panorama was the sole province of a small group of Myssari scientists. Even its undeniable magnificence, however, failed to rouse the disconsolate Ruslan from his bereavement.

The pool of depression in which he felt himself foundering was his own fault, he knew. It had been wrong of him to raise such expectations. To imagine that the Myssari were any more adept than humankind in reviving the long preserved. Such techniques had been little more than theory in his own time. But desperation leads people to take desperate measures. It was difficult to imagine anything more desperate than having oneself voluntarily committed to cryostorage, knowing that the technology for revivification did not exist at the time the process was carried out, and might never.

The exhibition of failure he had just witnessed was proof that never was still now and might well be forever. Better to try to store human personality and memories in a fluxbox than in the fragile, fleshy form in which they originated. Possibly somewhere, on some unknown human-settled world, desperate citizens had tried to do just that. Given his age, he was unlikely to learn whether anyone had ever been successful in such an attempt. Even if they had been, any such effort could only be considered a partial success. The resultant revived individuals might be capable of speech, and remembrance, and conversation. But they would not necessarily be truly human. The warmth that was likely to be missing would be more than physical.

While he appreciated the effort on the part of his Myssari friends to distract and revitalize him, he was glad when they reached the base and he could isolate himself in the small cubby he had been allotted. Alone with his thoughts, he was more attuned to his kind than when in the presence of multiple Myssari, however considerate they might be. Kel'les, for one, could not understand how Ruslan could handle so much solitude. In such a situation a lone Myssari would become mentally unbalanced far more rapidly than any human.

"I talk to myself," he had once explained to his minder. "I have conversations with myself. I debate with myself." He remembered smiling. "Sometimes I even win the arguments."

They did not understand.

The door chimed softly for his attention. Responding to his query, it went transparent on the inside so that he could identify his visitor. A sigh of resignation escaped his lips. It was Kel'les again. That much he expected. Seeing to the human's health and happiness was the intermet's responsibility. Despite that, Ruslan would have sent the minder away except that s'he was accompanied by another. Cor'rin was with him. The xenologist had been particularly struck by the human's despondency. Further flinging his depression in her face would be impolite. Not that he much cared. Not at this point. If he died leaving the Myssari thinking his frequent cynicism and disdain were typical of all humans, so be it. But he liked the young scientist. So he directed the door to admit them.

They had not come to offer additional sympathies. There was no need. Empathy had been proffered all the way from the archeological site back to the base. The xenologist got right to the point.

"We have just received word that Wol'daeen is going to try another double resurrection tomorrow, and we need to know if you wish to attend. An alternative procedure will be employed. We are informed that she has a list of several varying techniques, ranked in order of descending theoretical success."

He did not stir from the special improvised bed on which he lay. "When she runs one that has real instead of theoretical results, let me know. Otherwise I'd rather not go back there." Memories of wandering the silent, death-filled streets of Seraboth's cities rushed through his mind, an unavoidable tsunami of sorrow. The early decades of his life had been spent stepping over or around the dead and decaying. He had no wish to relive those moments now, not even if surrounded by the cool white comfort of advanced Myssari technology.

"What's the purpose of it all, anyway?" Rising from the edge of the bed, he walked over to a food dispenser. The liquid he called forth took a moment to brew. He credited the Myssari with accepting without question his insistence that he required the periodic ingestion of alcohol to function properly. Taking a too-long draft from the modified fluid container, he regarded his visitors.

"I've said it before and this seems a suitable time to say it again, no matter what the Science Sectionary feels. Why put so much effort into bringing back a species that's responsible for its own extinction?"

"You know why." Kel'les held his stance as well as his stare. "You have been told repeatedly. The knowledge of and about your kind is important."

"Why, why? Remind me again." He took another heady swallow of the drink that had been concocted to his specifications.

"Because all knowledge is important," Kel'les told him.

"Yeah, right. Lot of good it did my kind."

"Motivation, right or wrong, exists separate from knowledge." Cor'rin was unexpectedly forceful. "It is the knowledge that matters, not what motivates the acquiring of it."

Ruslan grunted, swaying slightly. "Knowledge for knowledge's sake."

"If you will," she shot back. "On one thing, I believe we can agree."

"What's that?"

"You are not the most qualified individual to decide on the validity of that conclusion."

A broad smile creased his face. "Why, Cor'rin, I do believe there are those of your kind who would consider that frank assessment to be borderline uncivil!"

Kel'les stepped forward. "I am more aware than anyone, including probably yourself, of the effect the too-rapid ingestion of alcohol has on the human system. Already you are having difficulty cogitating clearly." The intermet turned to the other Mysarri present and, with as much firmness as Ruslan had ever heard from his minder, said, "Please leave now, Cor'rin, in order to deprive our plainly troubled human charge of any opportunity to further embarrass himself."

She hesitated, then as she turned to leave executed a gesture that managed to convey both compliance and understanding. In a moment she was gone, leaving Kel'les to cope alone with behavior that only further underscored Ruslan's frequent lamentations regarding human fallibility.

He was unsure what woke him first: the distant mechanical hum that suggested the presence of large machinery operating in an area of the base where it ought not to be present, or the subtle but insistent chiming of the door. Verbally activating the one-way view showed Kel'les standing outside. That the intermet looked more agitated than the human had ever seen motivated Ruslan to swiftly rise from his sleeping platform. Without taking the time to dress, he admitted his handler.

Having viewed it on numerous occasions both in person and via detailed biological schematics, Kel'les paid no attention to the biped's nakedness. Nor did s'he comment on what to a Myssari would be the difficulty of dressing oneself with only two hands instead of three. S'he had scarcely allowed the door, which automatically opaqued once more, to close before s'he began speaking.

"I hope you are fully recovered both mentally and physically from your physiological diversion of the previous day, as this morning brings with it a potential awkwardness."

Ruslan frowned as he wrestled a lightweight shirt down over his chest. "What kind of awkwardness? Don't tell me Wol'daeen insists that I watch another potentially botched revivification?"

Further emphasizing that something out of the ordinary was in prospect, his minder's responding gesture involved simultaneous movement of all three hands.

"This has nothing to do with Wol'daeen or the human cryostorage facility. The Vrizan are here."

The vestiges of sleep that were pawing at Ruslan's thoughts vanished like mist caught in sunlight. "The scout who encountered me is here?"

"Not the scout. Many Vrizan." Kel'les glanced back in the direction of the doorway. "There was talk by San'dwil and the other base supervisors of spiriting you away, but there was not sufficient time. The Vrizan arrived without notice. Their craft came in using military-grade concealment and revealed itself only when ready to touch down."

Now fully awake, Ruslan's mind was awhirl with possibilities, most of them disagreeable. "I don't understand. Are we under attack?"

"Not overtly, no. At least, so I have been led to believe. No hostile gestures have been made and no weapons have been brandished. Oppositely, those bent on friendly concourse tend not to arrive under cover of military-rated camouflage." S'he whistled significantly as s'he inhaled. "These are Vrizan, not Myssari. It is difficult to comprehend their reasoning in coming here in such a fashion."

"Maybe they're shy." Sitting on the edge of the sleeping platform, Ruslan eased his feet into the special sandals that had been fashioned for him.

"Whatever else they may be, the Vrizan are not shy." Kel'les's tone was reproving.

"You think they're here after me?"

"Doubtless we will learn their purpose shortly. San'dwil and the others have been theorizing. As you are the most valuable asset at this location, and quite unique, the intent was to move you to a place where your presence could not become an issue. That now cannot be done. Any driftec departing the base would immediately come under scrutiny by the Vrizan."

"I suppose it's flattering to know that I'm still considered that important." He rose from the platform. "I don't want to be the cause of any fighting."

Kel'les's expression, such as was permitted by his less flexible face, did not change. "That decision is not up to you."

Ruslan's lips pressed tightly together before he replied. "I see that something else hasn't changed, either." He nodded toward the door. "Since I am not the master of my destiny, what happens now?"

"We wait."

He could only fume quietly while wondering if he would be allowed to hear whatever decisions were being made concerning his welfare or if they would simply be forwarded to Kel'les to convey to him. He might be nominally independent, but he was also property. Of one thing he was certain: the Myssari would not surrender him easily.

Now he was the one hypothesizing. Notwithstanding the Vrizan's stealth arrival, his alien minders and mentors might be overreacting. The unexpected Vrizan visit might have nothing to do with him.

Via a tiny communicator, Kel'les was listening to words that were not being sent the human's way. The minder eyed him evenly. "We are to make our way to the central meeting chamber. The Vrizan know you are here. They insist, rather forcefully, on seeing you."

Ruslan frowned. "Seeing me? That's all?"

"That is all they have requested. San'dwil has consulted with his aides. It has been decided that under the circumstances, refusing would risk more potential harm than good. Neither the Myssari nor the Vrizan have succeeded in codifying a final claim to Treth. Until ownership has been granted to one or the other, our respective scientific teams must share this world. It is better that this be done on a cordial basis. Also . . ."

"It would be impolite to refuse, given their insistence that they know I'm here," Ruslan finished for the intermet.

Kel'les gestured affirmatively. "With the exception of your regrettably inadequate physique, you have acquired all the makings of a good Myssari."

S'he was trying to be encouraging, Ruslan knew. In return he offered up a smile of his own that was as reassuring as it was fake. As the door opened and they started out, he tried to prepare himself for whatever might come. Somewhat to his surprise he found that it didn't matter. On the heels of Wol'daeen's failed efforts to resurrect any of the preserved humans, it seemed that nothing mattered much anymore. Not to him, anyway.

To the Myssari his continued existence among them still mattered very much indeed.

In contrast to the single individual he had encountered under dark and difficult circumstances, the half dozen Vrizan who awaited him in the meeting room were patently of a different standard indeed. In place of the lone scout's camouflaged field attire, the majority of the visiting aliens were resplendent in silklike garb of some electric-blue material. A few were differentiated from their comrades by garments fashioned from an intense turquoise-hued fabric that shimmered whenever their wearers took a step. The latter also featured a vertical line of rotating gold orbs embedded in the upper left shoulder of their clothing. The optical effect was striking. Despite San'dwil's change of attire into something more suited to a formal meeting, the duty dress and uniforms of the assembled group of Myssari were dull by comparison.

Daylight defined the external anatomy of the Vrizan sharply. Bipedal, they were basically two conjoined ovoids topped by a severely flattened sphere. Bright eyes glistened at either end of the wide skull. The exceptional multiplicity of joints in their legs was matched by a similar number in their arms. These limbs were not quite human, not quite tentacles. Studying them as they moved, an intrigued Ruslan reflected that a Vrizan snapping its joints would generate a veritable symphony of pops and crackles.

The few gasps that came from them as he entered the room were unsettlingly humanlike.

A Myssari technician was about to pass out translators when one of the taller Vrizan clad in the brilliant turquoise garb stepped forward.

"Conversational instrumentation will not be necessary. I and several of my colleagues speak Myssarian."

"Quite well, too." Grateful of the opportunity to respond with a cost-free compliment, San'dwil advanced to meet his counterpart. The wariness with which he approached was well considered.

"I don't suppose any of you speak Vrizan?" the visitor added before his host could continue with an official greeting.

San'dwil maintained his poise. "Several of us are fluent in your language. However, the human is not. I am assuming that in addition to seeing him and verifying his existence for yourselves, it would please you to speak to him. Absent translation equipment, this can only be done in Myssarian."

Startling Ruslan, the Vrizan's long, narrow mouth parted at opposite ends while the center section remained tightly closed. Even though the lone human in the room could not properly interpret its meaning, from an anatomical standpoint the alien expression was fascinating. Was it the equivalent of a smile? A grimace? Or something unknown?

"When working in the field, all scientists must adapt to the circumstances of the moment," the Vrizan murmured. This time only one corner of the extended mouth opened. "We will speak in your language." The widely separated eyes shifted to focus on Ruslan. He met them evenly—or as evenly as he could given their remarkable degree of physical divergence. "How conversant is the . . . creature?"

Bac'cul spoke up. "Fully fluent. He has resided among us for some time now." If the Vrizan recognized the scarcely muted pride in the Myssari scientist's voice, the visitor gave no sign.

"We desire physical contact." One of the other turquoise-clad visitors was unable to restrain herself. "If only to know for certain that the creature is not a cleverly constructed artifice designed to mock us."

"I'd think that the scout I encountered who reported my presence would be able to give you confirmation enough of that," Ruslan told the anxious researcher.

His confident response, wholly as articulate as Bac'cul had promised, sparked an animated babble among the Vrizan. Calling for quiet, their leader turned back to the assembled Myssari.

"For myself I would be content to leave with the evidence of my eyes, but there are scientists among us teetering on the verge of giddiness who have threatened me with all manner of incivilities if their request is denied. So I must ask again: may several of us be permitted to approach the survivor?"

"Survivor." Not "specimen." For all that one of their number had threatened to shoot him on that frantic night when Ruslan had taken his unauthorized stroll, he found himself softening toward the Vrizan, only the second intelligent species with whom he had exchanged more than a passing glance.

As San'dwil's head swiveled to regard the human, Kel'les leaned close and whispered, "I do not think this is a good idea."

Ruslan rejected his minder's appraisal. "Why not? All they want to do is touch me. Where's the harm, if it inspires them to leave quietly and satisfied?"

Kel'les's small eyes were scanning the waiting, impatient visitors. "What if they have something else in mind? Something more?"

"What, like trying to carry me off?" The image this speculation conjured was so absurd that he had to struggle not to laugh. "I'd fight back. San'dwil would not permit it—it would mean the ruination of his career." He nodded toward the Vrizan. "There aren't many of them, some are self-proclaimed scientists, and they're *inside* a Myssari base. They don't strike me as fools."

"They are not." Kel'les's worry remained. "That is why I am concerned."

"Let's put an end to that." Walking toward the visitors, he lowered his arms and spread them wide. "Approach and satisfy yourselves, if this is what you want."

While it was evident that San'dwil was unhappy with his prize guest's willingness to accommodate, there was little he could do about it. Alien and sole survivor of a vanished species, Ruslan was too valuable to risk injuring. It never seriously occurred to San'dwil to try to prevent the encounter by calling for the use of sudden physical force. So he stood where he was and looked on apprehensively.

While it was plain that the Vrizan were sexually dimorphic, Ruslan was unsure which was which. Fearing it might be undiplomatic to inquire, he resolved to ask Kel'les to settle the question later. Meanwhile Vrizan of both sexes took their time inspecting his frame, from running small, narrow, and many-jointed fingers through his brown hair, to marveling at the flexibility of his ears, to trying to understand how his arms and legs could efficiently carry out their apparent functions utilizing only three joints and such heavy bones. As they grew more comfortable in his proximity they began asking questions.

"This stiff but bendable flesh behind your aural openings . . . what is its purpose?"

"You have two kinds of teeth—pointed and flat. Why?"

"There is no proper separation between the upper and lower halves of your torso. How do you keep waste material in the lower half from corrupting and poisoning the organs in the upper half?"

It went on like that for five minutes, then ten, then twenty. Eventually Kel'les relaxed. The Vrizan gave no indication of wanting to hit Ruslan with anything more damaging than a flurry of questions. San'dwil, on the other hand, did not relax, nor did those around him. While occasional glances flashed the way of the visiting researchers, far more of the Myssari supervisors' attention was focused on the Vrizan military personnel who had accompanied them.

As Ruslan stood surrounded, the questions kept coming.

"Your head is impossibly round but you have two eyes. Do you have binocular vision?"

"What is the purpose of the small divided organ in the center of your face? Doesn't it interfere with your consumption of food?"

"How do your limbs function in the absence of a proper number of joints?"

He was growing tired, both of the endless queries and from having to stand in one place for so long. When he expressed his unhappiness, one Vrizan researcher rushed to bring him a Myssari seating bench while the others held their questions until he was again ready to reply. It was not at all what he had anticipated; certainly not from his previous single encounter with the Vrizan scout. Admittedly the circumstances were decidedly different this time. What he had not expected, especially based on the concern expressed by Kel'les and San'dwil, was the respect being shown to him by the visitors. It bordered on awe. In contrast, with the exception of Kel'les, the Myssari treated him as something valuable to be preserved rather than as an individual to be regarded as an equal. Granted, it was possible he was misreading their attitude. More time spent on Myssar did not necessarily breed familiarity.

After he informed them, as he took his seat, that they could continue to ask questions—but please, not too many more, for he really was growing weary—the Vrizan scientists resumed their excited interrogation. This time they did not talk over one another and they gave him more time to respond thoughtfully to each query.

What came next he did not expect at all.

As he was replying to a question relating to an obscure aspect of human culture, one of the heretofore less active interviewers moved very close, leaned over with a multitudinous popping of joints, and whispered.

"Why do you remain in the company of these insipid tripods? You and I, we are both bipeds. We Vrizan are normal bisexuals, like humans. Like you, each of us has more than three digits on our hands. Although they are positioned differently on our heads, our eyes are like yours, large and equipped for marginal night vision as well as excellent sight during the day. Though you have far fewer joints, our means and method of vertical locomotion are similar. We are more straightforward and honest in our dealings. We are bold, as was humankind before its fall. We do not simper and neither did your people. Human and Vrizan have far more in common than human and Myssari."

As Ruslan digested this extraordinary disquisition the speaker straightened. The eyes at the ends of his flattened, elongated skull swiveled inward to face the human.

"Come with us. The Myssari have learned much from you. Why should we not have the same opportunity? They cannot possibly treat you as well as we will. There are more similarities between humankind and Vrizan than I can enumerate in a short time. You will see for yourself if you come with us."

Ruslan was aware that all questioning had ceased. Insofar as he could tell, none of the Vrizan researchers looked surprised by the offer that had just been extended. Their plan of action—respectful questioning followed by unexpected offer—had doubtless been rehearsed and agreed upon long before the science team had left its base. They were all staring at him now, a progression of widely separated alien eyes. Waiting for his reply.

A nervous Kel'les rejoined him. "Is everything all right, Ruslan?" The intermet eyed the now expectant visitors worriedly. "It has gone quiet. Are they finished with you?"

"Everything's fine, Kel'les. Just one more question to answer and then we'll be done here." Given the extraordinary separation of the Vrizan's oculars, Ruslan tried to meet the gaze of the alien who had voiced the offer as best he could.

"You are absolutely right. On the face of it, my people and yours have much more in common than they do with the Myssari. In many ways the Vrizan do appear to be far more humanlike." A startled Kel'les started to say something but Ruslan forestalled his friend. "That is why I will *not* go with you."

While unhappy murmuring rose from among the visiting researchers, it was left to their spokesman to respond. His bemusement appeared genuine. "I—we—do not understand. If we are more like you, then would you not find yourself more comfortable among us?"

"Quite the contrary. As I have inferred, by your words and your actions, you do share many features with my kind. The last thing I want is to be reminded of them. You remind me of failure, of hubris, of arrogance. Of the death of millions upon millions of innocents." He lowered his eyes. "I already have far too many memories of such things." He gestured toward Kel'les, and beyond, to the other intently staring Myssari. "All my disturbing reminiscences will trouble me less if I remain with them, I think. Because they do not remind me of my kind at all." He raised his gaze anew. "I hope you can respect that."

The senior alien researcher paused for a long moment. Then he made a gesture. It was a forceful gesture, delivered in the manner of the Vrizan—or a human.

"Yes, we can respect that." He started backward, the numerous joints in his legs crackling harmonically. "We cannot understand it, but we can respect it. However, we need not agree to it."

His retreat accelerated. Not with as much agility as a Myssari, a tight-lipped Ruslan thought. More like a human struggling not to trip and fall. Weapons appeared in the hands of the researchers' turquoise-garbed military escort. The human sighed resignedly. So the instinctive defensive, antagonistic reaction of the nocturnal scout he had surprised had not been an aberration after all. What a pity. But not a surprise. Faced with a similar situation, representatives of his own kind might well have reacted similarly. He might have done so himself.

What he was seeing now only confirmed that he wanted to live out the remainder of his life among the Myssari. Provided the Vrizan would let him. Their hand weapons were impressively advanced, their determination almost . . . human. The only one in the room who didn't care a great deal what happened next was the subject of the confrontation.

Die today, die tomorrow—what's the difference? On reflection he realized that he had actually enjoyed, as opposed to merely tolerated, all the years he had spent on Myssar. Aliens Kel'les and the other Myssari might be, utterly nonhuman in appearance, reproductive matters, and much of their culture. But they possessed one element that overrode all the others.

They were nice.

That intrinsic niceness did not prevent them from drawing weapons of their own, however. That this was done in defense of property more than of an individual did not trouble Ruslan. He was used to it. He was not only valuable: from a scientific standpoint he was irreplaceable. How far the Myssari were prepared to go to retain him and how far the Vrizan were prepared to reach to try to take him would be known within a minute.

As he sat speculating, Kel'les stepped in front of him. Bac'cul and Cor'rin crowded close at his sides. At the moment, the Myssari in the room were outnumbered and outgunned. That would not last long. A quick sideways glance out a nearby transparent panel showed movement in the base's central plaza. Someone in the room had managed to sound an alarm or relay word of what was happening. Very soon all exits would be blocked and the Vrizans' options would be drastically reduced. They would have to decide what to do in the next few seconds.

In a single smooth swooping motion made possible only by an arm composed of dozens of individual joints, one of the escorts raised his sidearm. Ruslan stiffened.

So this is how the last human in the galaxy dies, he thought calmly. *Being fought over by representatives of two alien species. The central prize in a scientific tug-of-war.* Thinking of the ancient children's game made him smile. It would be good to go out focused on such an antiquated image. Just like his entire species. He did feel sorry for Kel'les and the others. His death would not do their career prospects any good, although the Myssari viewed such things differently than a human. He closed his eyes. The leader of the Vrizan research team was speaking. Kel'les translated for him.

"Do not fire! You might hit the human."

Blinking, Ruslan saw the speaker push down on the arm of the military escort who had started to take aim. A bit, though far from all, of the tension seeped out of the room. Beyond the transparent section of wall, Ruslan could see that the small open area outside that had been carefully landscaped with native Trethian plants was filling up with armed, restless Myssari. It seemed possible that he might live. He was happier for his Myssari companions than for himself.

"No knowledge is to be gained by those who seek it from fighting among themselves." The Vrizan leader stood tall on his slender legs. "I ask your forgiveness for this awkward attempt. My orders to make the attempt came from a higher authority. From off-world, to be exact. I explained that it was unlikely to meet with success but I was overruled. Having complied with our pointless instructions, I assure you that we will now depart quietly." For a last time his gaze fell on Ruslan. "If you should change your mind, human, I hope you will not hesitate to contact us. Since I doubt that your hosts will allow me to provide you with a means of doing so, I trust that should you ever wish to do so you will find a way of managing that communication. Studies show that your species was wonderfully resourceful. I can only hope its last representative is equal to any task to which he may set himself."

Ruslan followed the Vrizan as they were escorted out. There was certainly much to admire about them. He had admired the native predator that had tried to eat him, too, but that did not mean he wanted to live with it or its kind. His relief obvious, Bac'cul turned to him.

"Are you all right, Ruslan?"

"I'm fine. I just want to rest."

The researcher indicated his understanding. "I believe we all need a break after that confrontation. It could have turned calamitous."

Nodding agreement, Ruslan rose and started in the direction

that would lead him back to his assigned living quarters. The three Myssari who knew him best watched him go. Cor'rin was first to comment.

"What do you think?"

"The human has always been as good as his word," a thoughtful Bac'cul observed. "Though it is oftentimes difficult to tell what he is thinking, his speech is invariably straightforward. I do not think he will try to contact the Vrizan. If he was so inclined, I believe he would have stepped across the room to join them here and now."

"I agree," added Kel'les. "I have spent more time in closer contact with him than anyone, and I have never known him to prevaricate. Nevertheless, I believe that as long as we remain on Treth he should be watched, especially when I am unable to accompany him. I will explain our conclusion to San'dwil."

Cor'rin indicated that she was in agreement. Then, bearing in mind Bac'cul's earlier observation regarding the need for everyone to rest, they departed the room as a group.

7

Work at the outpost continued as usual, with the only change being the instigation of greatly enhanced security. San'dwil and his assistants had been leery of the contending Vrizan presence on Treth prior to their attempt to abduct, and then to persuade, the human. Subsequent to those efforts, they initiated security procedures that bordered on the paranoid. No one was allowed off-base without being armed. Duplicate hardened emergency beacons were installed on all driftecs. Researchers who had never encountered, much less handled, a weapon in their lives were put through a course of hasty instruction. It was all very distracting to the scientists, who wished nothing but to concentrate on their work, but San'dwil was insistent.

Having now met multiple Vrizan, Ruslan would have chanced taking them at their word that they would not try anything untoward again, but it was not his career that was at stake. He would have chanced it partly because he was honestly curious to learn more about the Myssari's rivals and partly because his hosts considered him far more valuable than he did himself. Respectfully but firmly deprived of the opportunity for interspecies contact, he had to content himself with learning what he could about the alien bipeds by searching through the research materials available on the base.

These told him that the Vrizan were a bold, space-traversing species who competed with other races as well as with the Myssari for new knowledge and new worlds. Like the Myssari, they had entered the virtually unpopulated galactic arm that contained Treth and Seraboth from well-developed star systems located many thousands of light-years distant. While more aggressive in their expansion than the Myssari or the O'lu, the Chaanoss or the Hahk'na, the Vrizan were not flagrantly warlike. Among civilized species, fighting was a last resort, one extremely difficult and costly to wage between star systems. Far better to find other ways and means to settle disagreements. The extreme behavior exhibited in their effort to acquire Ruslan in support of their research demonstrated how much they coveted the sole surviving representative of humankind as well as how highly they valued that vanished civilization itself. Ruslan did not feel flattered. He felt objectified.

Nevertheless, the enticing words of the Vrizan representative remained in his mind, and refused to fade away.

They were still nagging at him the next day as he stood outside in the sun in the central plaza that formed the physical nexus of the base. Giving Kel'les a break from the task of continuously monitoring the human, Cor'rin had temporarily taken the intermet's place. She was leaning back on one of the tubelike inclined benches that provided a resting place for the tripodal Myssari frame. Ruslan had chosen to sit on the ground nearby, his back against one of the curiously horizontal native growths, his forearms resting on his pulled-up legs, his chin propped on his interlaced fingers.

She found the human's persistent silence personally as well as professionally troubling. "It has been observed that your behavior of late has trended to joylessness."

Glancing up at her without shifting his position, he commented sourly, "Truly nothing can be hidden from the penetrating eye of Myssari science."

She flinched. "I only meant that—"

"Forget it." He waved a hand at her and, by implication, the cosmos in general. "I'm tired and discouraged, and I shouldn't inflict that on you." A hint of a smile crossed his features. "That was very impolite of me."

Uncertain whether he was retracting his sarcasm or emphasizing it, she decided to approach the subject from a different angle. "Your current degraded mental state is making it difficult for Bac'cul, myself, and others to work with you. While the questions that are asked may seem trivial to you, I assure you they are very important to us, both as individual researchers and in enlarging our knowledge of human civilization as a whole."

"A black hole," he responded absently.

"What?" She hesitated, then gestured with two arms. "Is there something about me personally that requires you to triple the degree of sarcasm in your replies?"

Not for the first time since he had been brought to live among the Myssari, he was ashamed of himself. He looked up at her. "I told the explorers who originally found me wandering on Seraboth that I was a poor representative of my kind. When I fail to confirm it, one of you usually manages to do so."

Something small and bright blue landed on her sloping left shoulder. It fluttered to the middle, then to the right one. Looking up from where he was seated, Ruslan could see it clearly. Each of its four wings was mottled with yellow and brown streaks that flashed according to how they were struck by sunlight. *Alien butterfly camouflage,* he told himself, though the creature had single-lensed eyes, a normal mouth, and perfect, tiny nostrils. He had never seen a butterfly anyway. It was a creature that survived only within the extensive depths of recorded human knowledge. Something that had lived on old Earth, the accompanying material insisted. He wondered.

If the Myssari succeeded in locating Earth, would it still have butterflies? He hoped so.

Thoughts of both served to mute his disdain. "I'm sorry. No matter how I feel, I have no right to take it out on you or Bac'cul or Kel'les or anyone else."

Her voice, already Myssari-soft, fell to a near murmur. "Do not apologize. You have no one else to 'take it out on.'"

Dark and wrenching, sorrow welled up in him. It had not paid him a visit in more than a year. He thought he was done with it, that he had banished it to the same cold, remote place where he had put away most of his feelings. Frustratingly, it surged up and out now, manifesting itself in tears that streaked his face like flow channels on a dry world. He wiped at them angrily.

Cor'rin stared, fascinated by a phenomenon she had read about but never seen in person. There were a great many questions she wanted to ask about the biological process. Instead, she said nothing. That much, at least, she had learned about humans. Or at least about this human.

Two hands came down to rest on his shoulders while the fingers of the third draped themselves over his right knee.

"I wish I could find a means of improving your life outlook. There is much that is Myssari for an alien to enjoy. Not just the physical beauty of the worlds we have settled, but in our culture as well."

He sniffed forcefully and rubbed his nose with the back of his left sleeve. "I know that. In my time among your kind, I've seen much of it and certainly enjoyed some. It's just that every once in a while the loneliness takes me by surprise and—it's overwhelming." He looked up at her as she removed her hands. "There's nothing anyone can do to help. It's like a recurring disease. You work through it until it goes away of its own accord. Then you wait for it to come back when you least expect it."

"There is something that would help, but unfortunately it's not possible."

His curiosity was piqued. "Something none of your analysts or xenologists has already proposed? I would've thought they'd tried everything by now."

"They have. Everything psychological. Everything chemical. There are certain biological remedies that are unfortunately not viable."

He frowned. "I don't understand."

"There are—engineering problems. The therapy to which I refer would be akin to trying to build a starship utilizing both Myssari and human components."

"What?" Realization dawned. "Oh. *Oh*." The last of the tears spilled. As they dried he found himself smiling slightly. "I have to ask, Cor'rin: do your thoughts regarding this matter arise out of considerations that are professional or personal?"

"Both." She continued to stare at him. Having brought up the subject herself, she was plainly not in the least reluctant to discuss it further.

"Well. We agree on one thing. None of your colleagues has so much as broached the possibility. 'Engineering problems,' yes, to be sure. But I am flattered that such an outré thought would even occur to you."

"Why should you be so surprised? Your continued well-being is of great interest to all of us. If you are not well and alert mentally, it diminishes the accuracy and therefore the reliability of your re-sponses to our queries."

"Certainly, certainly." He paused a moment. "Tell me, Cor'rin: even though it's self-evident that this concept cannot advance be-yond a hypothetical line of thinking, it must have prompted a mental image or two."

"That is only natural," she replied. "For you as well."

"It surely did." He shook his head. "But I can't, even working at the extremes of my imagination, envision how an intermet would come into play."

"Surely in the course of studying our culture you have had occasion to encounter descriptions of the process?"

"Descriptions into which I can't conceive of inserting myself . . . so to speak."

She rose from where she was sitting. "I have succeeded in getting you to engage the expression called a 'smile.' Therefore I count our conversation a success." Pleased with herself, she started toward the nearest building. "If you ever wish to repeat such a conversation, I am on call to respond to your query no matter what other work I may be doing. We all are. That is how important your satisfaction and well-being are to every member of the science contingent."

"I know." His smiled widened. "Don't worry, Cor'rin. If I want to talk, I'll let you know. I'm not shy."

"Less so than a Myssari," she called back to him. Her head having swiveled 180 degrees, she kept walking toward the building while continuing to stare back at him. She held the gaze for as long as practically possible before her head snapped back around so that she could see where she was going.

With a deep, resigned sigh he once more leaned back against the horizontal tree branches. She *had* succeeded in snapping him out of his funk. Sorrow had been banished, however temporarily, and he could once more see the sky as blue instead of black. He felt better.

Though whether this was the result of the pseudo-butterfly's visit or the image of a complex physical impossibility she had left with him he could not say.

"Gather your personal belongings."

Seated in the midst of frolicking *chelabar,* Ruslan heard the

words only faintly. He was reluctant to comply. Undulating beneath the waves, the school of four-meter-long eel-like *chelabar*
were nearly transparent, a trait that rendered them invisible to
most predators. But when they leaped clear of the surface in their
exuberant mating displays, cells in their skin that were sensitive to
contact with the gaseous nitrogen in the atmosphere reacted to the
exposure by strobing several colors of the spectrum. Males leaned
heavily toward purple and females to pale orange, while the *chelabar* intermets flashed all the way over into the ultraviolet.

Even though he could not perceive the latter hue, the totality
combined to create an exciting, almost transcendent display. Drifting on the surface of the sea in a thin body masque that both
warmed and concealed him, he watched as the gracile, gliding
creatures danced in the air above the foam. No land was in sight,
no support craft. He was adrift in the center of the south Myssari
ocean, alone with the inborn radiance of that world's remarkable
sea life. The only sounds were the lapping of the waves, the splashing of *chelabar* as they returned to the water from their brief aerial
excursions, and the coarse cry of broad-winged *simmets* and
bubble-like *aiau*.

"Please," came the irritating, intruding words again. "A shuttle
arrives this evening. The ship comes only for us. It is a notable
honor. And an expensive one."

No matter how much he wished for it to go away, the voice of
veracity persisted. It belonged to Kel'les. With great reluctance
Ruslan waved a finger in the direction of the controls. Romping
rainbow *chelabar*, wide-winged wind-riding *simmets*, and amusing chirping *aiau* vanished. So did cerulean sky and blue-green
ocean. The displacement bubble and the comforting images that
surrounded him evaporated, as did the relaxed mood in which he
had been immersed. Resigned to reality, he swiveled in his spe-
cially modified chair to confront his determined minder.

"What's all this about a shuttle and a special ship?"

"We are departing Treth tonight."

Ruslan still did not grasp the situation. Or maybe he didn't want to.

"What do you mean, leaving?"

"All of us."

Striding through the human's quarters, Kel'les had begun collecting personal items and placing them in neat piles. There was not much to gather. In hopes of keeping him content and cooperative, the Myssari Combine had offered him nearly anything he wished. Needing very little, he had accepted very little. It was not as if he were going to boast of his possessions to his neighbors.

"We are leaving Treth." The minder spoke as s'he worked, handling even the simplest of the human's belongings with care.

As Ruslan slumped back in the chair visual echoes of the sea scene in which he had just been immersed flickered teasingly across his retinas. "I guess I lost track of time. I thought we were supposed to be here for another thirty-three-day period." A wry smile cracked his expression. "From what you're saying, I suppose it means even Wol'daeen has given up on the idea that I might have something to contribute here. I'm not surprised. Depression is a poor interpreter, and that's all I've had to offer lately. I won't be sorry to get back to Pe'leoek."

Pausing in the work, Kel'les looked over at him. "We are not going back to Myssar. A discovery has been made and a ship diverted to take us to its location. We are to be sent to Daribb."

It took Ruslan a moment to connect with the name. That he recognized it was not surprising. Learning the names of all the human-settled systems had been a part of every child's basic education on Seraboth, as it likely was on every similar world. In the course of working with Myssari researchers, there had been numerous occasions on which he had been obliged to recall such names. Still, he needed to confirm it.

"Daribb. That is a human-colonized system, isn't it?" The busy Kel'les gestured affirmatively. "What do they want with me there?" He raised a hand. "No, let me guess. The Myssari have a

scientific research station there not unlike this one and the staff
desires my inimitable input."

"There is that," Kel'les admitted. "But it is not the main reason. I am told that your presence is requested in the event certain
sightings turn out to be confirmed."

He was only mildly intrigued. "What kind of sightings? Active
automatons? Still-functioning weaponry? Mysterious cultural artifacts that your people cannot comprehend?"

Kel'les put down the pair of pants s'he was in the process of
folding into three layers. "A pair of free-ranging aerial automatics
scouting new territory reported the possible sighting of a live
human or humans."

Delivered in the intermet's usual matter-of-fact tone, the words
went through Ruslan like an electric charge. His mind momentarily blanked and for an instant he stopped breathing. Then he
made Kel'les repeat what s'he had said. Confirmation that he had
heard correctly birthed a thousand questions, to which it quickly
became clear Kel'les had less than a thousand answers.

"Enhancement of the recorded images and careful perusal of
the report have apparently convinced senior researchers on Myssar that whatever the automatics saw, it was not a machine.
Whether it was truly a living human, simply a native creature of
similar shape and stature, or the product of convergent evolution
they cannot say." The intermet paused to ensure s'he was using
the right words. "But should it turn out to be another surviving
human, or more than one, it is considered imperative that you be
present. Not only to confirm the discovery but to aid in acquiring
the new specimen."

Despite Kel'les's customary care in speaking, the use of the
terms "acquiring" and "specimen" were ill-considered. Another
time, Ruslan might have taken offense or responded with a riposte
rich with his trademark sarcasm. Not now. Not this time.

"How did it look?" The questions poured out of him rapidly
and in uncharacteristically bad Myssari. "Old, young, male, fe-

male, in good health or bad, what? By all that is sacred and sapi-ent, *tell me something!*"

Kel'les's tone was mournful. "I have told you all that I was told, Ruslan. There is no more to tell."

Rising from his chair, the diversionary oceanic delights of the displacement sphere now completely forgotten, Ruslan moved purposefully toward the small storage unit that contained the rest of his meager personal belongings.

"Go prepare your own self for travel. I will be ready in nine smalltime."

"There is no need for haste. The shuttle will not arrive until—"

"Nine smalltime. Go on, go!"

Thus dismissed, a complaisant Kel'les departed, leaving behind the sole human on Treth. Awhirl, Ruslan's thoughts clashed so hard that his head began to pound.

Dare he hope? Dare he wish? The Myssari thought enough of the report to send a ship just to transfer him and his small group of attached researchers from one world to another. They might not have convincing proof of the discovery, but they clearly had expectations. Could he, after all these years convinced he was the last human alive, dare to hope otherwise?

What if the report turned out to be wholly inaccurate? What if, as Kel'les had suggested, the scouts had merely taken note of the existence of some native primate-like lifeform? He struggled, he fought, to restrain his excitement. If that proved to be the case, disappointment would not kill him: human beings did not die from disappointment. Besides, why should he expect the report to be accurate? It would not be the first time. There had been previ-ous reports of humans living on other worlds. All had turned out to be false; misperceptions of self-maintaining machines or local wildlife.

But never before had the Science Sectionary gone to the trouble and expense of sending a ship solely to take him to help verify or refute such a report in person.

He had lied to Kel'les about the time he would need to prepare himself. He was ready in a threepart.

The name Daribb was familiar to him, but not the place. On the scale of suitability for human life, it ranked somewhere in the bottom third of habitable worlds. Such a designation indicated that rather than being unsuitable for settlement, it was more awkward and uncomfortable than dangerous. That it was quite literally a messy place had put off the fussy and starry-eyed. Those who had been willing to put down roots and work hard had done well. In the end it did not matter. The inhabitants of Daribb succumbed to the Aura Malignance as readily and rapidly as those who dwelled on more welcoming worlds.

Most notably, Daribb was a flat place. Very flat. Any mountain ranges had long since been ground down. The few geological contusions high enough to be called a hill were few and far between. To these isolated continental bumps humankind had consigned their scattered settlements and cities. When they began running short of elevated places, they expanded out onto the surrounding flats—and onto the mud.

It was everywhere. Slick and sticky and of varying viscosity, it averaged half a dozen centimeters deep no matter where one went. Below the scattered hills the cities, even the farms, were forced to build on raised platforms. It was not terribly difficult, this physical elevation of an entire society. Far less involved than putting down pylons on a water world, for example. Step off a platform onto the planetary surface, however, and a resident would find himself on a world of sodden soil and lugubrious organic goo. Agronomists did well out of the rich muck, miners less so. There was a living to be made, but Daribb required a particular sort of settler. Or rather, one who was not particular. Unsurprisingly, even at its peak the population had never been more than a fifth of that of Seraboth or Treth.

Metropolitan areas were few and far between, with the bulk of the population living in scattered small towns and the agricultural areas that radiated outward from them. Located on an abandoned outcropping, the Myssari research base was smaller and less developed than the ones on Treth and Ruslan's homeworld. Operating with less support and fewer personnel, the scientific complement nonetheless had compiled an impressive list of discoveries. Were the most recent one to prove accurate, it would certainly overshadow nearly every piece of research into vanished humankind since a team on Seraboth had recovered the survivor known as Ruslan.

It was drizzling when he exited the shuttle. Sheltered within the flexed, extendable tubeway, he and his companions were shielded from the moisture. The Myssari reacted to rain much as they did to everything else, with aplomb and a disposition that was invariably sunnier than the weather itself. They evinced none of the gloom that would have afflicted a corresponding trio of humans. To them rain invariably meant growth, renewal, a refreshing of the world. Depending on individual mood, to a human it could mean that, or a moodiness that might linger.

Despite the strain of the journey, Ruslan was too keyed up to be anything other than energized. The director of the outpost and their host, a mid-aged female named Twi'win, tried hard to distribute her attention among the four visitors. Used to putting awed Myssari at ease, Ruslan made it a point to reassure her.

"Go ahead and stare. After years on the receiving end, it has long since ceased to bother me." He smiled, wondering if the director had been better prepped on human expressions than on human appearance. "You should know that I don't consider it a display of ill manners."

Indicating that she understood, Twi'win pivoted and led them along the covered walkway. Outside the transparent protective sleeve the drizzle vacillated between mist and sprinkle without ever turning to real rain.

"Is it like this here much of the time?" Staring out through the curving wall on her right, Cor'rin hinted that she would not be averse to seeing some sunlight.

"It is like this here *all* the time." As they entered the outpost's headquarters the director turned to their left. Busy scientists and techs paused to regard the newcomers and, despite themselves, gape at the human. That they knew Ruslan was coming did not in any way mute their curiosity. Just as he had advised Twi'win, he took the gawking in stride.

Seats were taken and refreshments were brought. Disdaining the Myssari furniture, which in any case was of the temporary and barely adequate kind one would expect to find in such a remote extension of the Combine's research arm, Ruslan leaned back against an insulated wall and crossed his arms. Though she addressed them all, the director's gaze kept sneaking toward Ruslan. Whenever he met her stare, she would look hurriedly away despite his insistence that such attention did not trouble him. As she grew increasingly used to his presence, he knew, such involuntary gaping would gradually disappear.

She did not waste words on small talk but went to the heart of the reason they were present.

"The sighting did not take place here but at an urban location we have not yet explored in person. No staff were available to engage in an immediate follow-up to the automatics' report. We have since sent people to the site. They found nothing. There are no indications a living human being was present anywhere in the vicinity of the report. Or, for that matter, anywhere else on Daribb." Using all three hands, she gestured at the damp landscape outside. "As you may surmise, there are no such things as lingering footprints on this world. Nor handprints either, as the constant mist and showers immediately wash such evidence away. It rarely rains heavily here. The sun occasionally banishes the clouds, but never for very long. The climate is a major contributor to the perpetually slick and sodden ground."

The exhilaration Ruslan had felt on Treth and during the outward journey was fast draining away. "If your people haven't been able to produce anything more convincing than a single inconclusive report filed by automatics operating in bad weather, why request that I and my companions be transported all the way here?" He regarded the director evenly.

A profound gesture executed with all three hands indicated that she appreciated his candor. "I did not make such an appeal. As you correctly observe yourself, based on the available evidence, someone in my position and with my responsibilities would not have made such a request. The decision to bring you here was made by senior advisors on Myssar itself. My modest and admittedly negative input was disregarded."

For a long moment silence reigned among visitors and host. The reason for the director's coolness was now understood. Their presence on Daribb and the need to accommodate them and their search would take away from resources Twi'win plainly felt could be more usefully deployed elsewhere. Being Myssari, she was too polite to display her resentment openly. That did not mean she was prevented from displaying a patent lack of enthusiasm. This was evident in her tone as well as her posture.

"It is thought by some students of your culture that one of your own kind who might be fearful of us might in contrast respond positively to your appearance."

A simple explanation but one that made sense, he thought. Alone and wary of everything, a single surviving individual might well avoid contact with unknown aliens. Not every human had his gregarious personality.

"When can I go to this other city?"

"Whenever you wish. I am instructed to place all of the outpost's resources at your disposal." Her attitude toward the visitors and their objective stayed just the cordial side of frigid. "I would suggest, though, remaining here a day or so to acclimate yourself to your new surroundings as well as to familiarize yourselves with the layout of our outpost. While the gravity here is virtually the same as that on Treth and Seraboth, the atmosphere is denser and, self-evidently, far more moist. It can make for breathing difficulties, especially if one is called upon to exert themselves."

That might be true for Myssari, he thought. As for himself, he found the damp air refreshing. His third lung would not need to engage here. Despite that, the director's suggestion was a reasonable one.

"Your advice is welcome." He glanced at his companions. "Hopefully, my friends won't have any trouble. Despite your very understandable doubts I think they are still enthused about the report that's brought us here. I know I am."

"As I stated, I believe it remains nothing more than a slight possibility." Good scientist that she was, Twi'win did not outright deny the prospect lest she be proven wrong. "Despite repeating the scouts' flyover, we are still left with only the initial questionable sighting."

"I think you are being overly negative," Bac'cul told her. "If the Science Sectionary had not thought highly of the original report, they would not have gone to the trouble of sending us here."

Twi'win turned her head halfway to the right before letting it swing back. "It is my hope you may find something to justify their expectations," she replied dryly, "along with the loss of time, personnel, and material resources."

Ruslan hoped to find something more than that. The director's continued disparagement of her automatics' findings notwithstanding, he hoped to find a hammer with which to shatter his loneliness.

8

Not only was the outpost on Daribb smaller than the research base on Treth, it had been in operation less than half as long. Many of the creature comforts he and his companions had enjoyed on the world they had previously visited were greatly reduced or not available at all. Add to that the perpetual gloom that contrasted greatly with the bright sunshine of the previous station and it was easy to understand why the outpost's Myssari staff, dedicated as they were, went about their daily routines with considerably less bounce in their tripartite step.

Preparations were made to transport Ruslan and his companions to the ruined city where the scouts had made their dubious sighting. Though Twi'win's cold appraisal of the possibilities and barely concealed resentment at their presence had dimmed his early excitement, he was still eager to see for himself, as were Kel'les, Bac'cul, and Cor'rin.

While proper attire was available to outfit the visiting Myssari, no such gear existed that would accommodate his taller, narrower, bipedal human frame. Amid grumbling, several sets of the special glider boots that the Myssari used to skate atop the slick, muddy surface were cannibalized to provide him with secure footing.

"How does the creature stay upright on only two legs?" The outpost's chief engineer was watching as Ruslan experimented with ski-walking on the improvised gliders. Standing beside the intermet, Cor'rin was no less intent on the human's efforts.

"There is something within the species' hearing mechanism that aids them in staying upright. Although we have only the one live specimen available for study, examination of numerous ca- davers confirms that the internal physiology is common to all and to both sexes. I confess that the process never ceases to astonish me. It is not perfect, however. I have seen him fall."

"I don't wonder." The engineer simultaneously admired and sympathized with the human's struggles to master the use of the modified gliders. "The possibility appears not to bother him."

"It depends how he lands. The skeletal structure is sound but, as anyone can see, absurdly top-heavy." As if to confirm her anal- ysis, Ruslan promptly tumbled forward, overcorrected by flailing his arms and kicking outward with his feet, and landed on his backside with an appreciable splash. Fortunately, the surface on which he was practicing was inside the outpost. While approxi- mating the consistency of the ground outside, it was nowhere near as thick with dissolved soil and organic solids. When he rose, helped up by Kel'les, his pants were damp but not dirty.

"I wonder how long it will take him to master the gliders well enough to walk outside?" The engineer did not sound optimistic. Cor'rin was quick to step to Ruslan's defense.

"I think you will be surprised. From having studied him for a period of years, I can assure you that the human is very adapt- able."

The engineer made a high-pitched gargling sound. "Not adapt- able enough, or they wouldn't be one individual shy of extinction." His body pivoted while he continued to gaze at her. "I have work to do. We are perpetually shorthanded here."

His guest indicated that she understood. "A fact of which your director never ceases to remind us."

It was midmorning of the following day before everyone, including Ruslan, felt he was competent enough on the gliders to consider commencing their search. It could have begun earlier but everyone felt it was important that the human be able to fully participate. That meant being able to enter narrow passageways and travel down crumbling corridors on his own, without the aid of machinery. He felt as strongly about that as did his hosts.

From the air, the decaying city the outpost's xenologists had identified as Dinabu was dauntingly extensive. Ruslan regarded the sprawling, decaying metropolis with concern. Even if the outpost's automatics *had* seen something worthwhile, it could be anywhere within the crumbling depths below. Just because the pair of driftecs touched down at the exact coordinates that had been recorded by the scouts did not mean that whatever they had seen remained in the vicinity. Searching the city on foot could take years, even with advanced Myssari detection equipment. How many years Ruslan had remaining to him could only be estimated.

Sitting in the driftec, then, he was wasting time. As soon as the disembarkation portal opened, he was outside.

Whatever had prompted his kind to settle such a glum, soggy world remained a matter for speculation. If there were valuable minerals, the mines had yet to be found. Perhaps there were interesting indigenous food sources, he told himself as he stepped down off the battered metal landing platform. Possibly non-synthesizable organics. The answer would lie in the local records that Twi'win's limited staff of linguists was methodically deciphering.

Walking on instead of in the omnipresent muck involved sliding one's feet backward and forward, as if skiing on snow. Snow, however, did not gurgle beneath one's feet. As he followed Bac'cul and their outpost guide toward the nearest large buildings, he wondered how deep the thick brown mud was beneath their feet. Maybe deep enough to swallow a man before he could utter a sound and without leaving the slightest indication he had ever been. It was a sobering thought and he was careful to keep his balance.

There was nothing remarkable about the entrance to the structure where the scouts had seen . . . something. Save for adaptations to the local climate, the interior was not all that different from the dozens, the hundreds, of abandoned buildings he had explored on Seraboth. There were similar devices, similar layouts, similar furniture. The same forlorn assortment of forsaken personal items. The same vestiges of a vanished people. The same pain.

Nothing moving, though. With the collapse of the city's infrastructure following the obliterating sweep of the Aura Malignance, there was no possibility of utilizing local power or other facilities. While the necessary machinery was present, it was badly in need of repair and restoration, thanks to the depredations of local flora and fauna. In tandem with his companions he activated the illumination function of the modified Myssari exploration vest he now wore. This enabled him to better see his surroundings and his companions to see him. Looking like a swarm of oversized fireflies, they spread out to inspect each room in the building.

Ordinary Myssari would have been unsettled by the gloom and strange noises. Not the accompanying team of researchers from the outpost. They were familiar with Daribb's lugubrious moods. Ruslan's companions, however, were used to brighter, more cheerful surroundings. Even devastated Seraboth had boasted blue skies and sunshine.

Gazing at his present environs, he wasn't sure he wanted them to be better illuminated. Unclassified scum pooled in the corners of violated buildings, while white-tendriled quasi-fungi climbed the posts that supported aboveground walkways. Where the latter had collapsed, he and his friends had to traverse the mud.

Directional lights mounted on individual vests allowed them to search recesses and crannies within the interconnected buildings. Heat-seeking sensors told the lights where to aim. Ruslan's picked out a large mass of black fur that, when targeted, dissolved into a mad mob of multi-legged, pink-bellied creatures with top-mounted eyes and oversized teeth. He was not surprised. Similar creatures thrived on Seraboth and on Myssar itself. The frantic dark-furred beings followed a rule of evolution that was standard where higher lifeforms had developed. Breed often, have large litters, dwell in those places that are shunned by more dominant creatures, and your species will be a success. He grunted at the irony. Humans had bred infrequently, had small litters, and chose to live in the most amenable regions. Small furry things survived. Humanity had not.

The structural complex that had been singled out by the outpost's scouts was a warren of interconnected rooms and chambers. A hospital, he thought as he glided ever deeper into its unidentified recesses and examined his surroundings. Or perhaps some kind of food-processing facility. There were no signs to guide him, print having given way millennia ago to electronic identifiers that could easily be attached to or embedded in walls. Take away their respective power sources, though, and you took away the words. Thousands of years after the invention of printing, there was still something to be said in favor of ink and crushed graphite.

A touch of anticipation sparked through him as he found a cabinet, its transparent doors broken out, that was filled with actual printed books. Some higher-up's private collection, no doubt, or treasured symbols of the facility through which he strode. He was perusing one, delightedly flipping through the manually operated pages, when he heard the noise.

"Hello?" He placed the book he had been studying back into its home in the cabinet. "Who's there? Can you speak?"

Had he imagined it? No—the sound was repeated. Something was moving, rustling, deeper within the complex, teasing his hearing, teasing his imagination. A Myssari would have answered him; therefore it was not Myssari. Paralleling his rising excitement, a hundred possibilities flashed through his mind.

If the source of the noise was the subject of the scouts' disputed report, it might have forgotten how to talk. Or it might have suffered an injury that prevented it from speaking. Forced to subsist alone on a ruined world, a plague survivor might be naturally suspicious of any new sound, even one that was made up of familiar words.

That was it, he told himself. Having for many years now spoken nothing but Myssari, he had called out in that alien language. He immediately repeated his query, this time first in the formal interstellar tongue utilized by all human-settled worlds and then in the colloquial dialect of Seraboth. His lips and tongue remembered the words without effort.

The rustling noises ceased. Whatever was making them had heard him and was responding. With caution, but responding. Had their positions been reversed, he was sure he would have been no less prudent. As he continued to advance he could not keep images so long repressed from expanding in his mind. Would it be a man, perhaps his own age? Or one younger; strong and able to assist him as he grew older? Would it be a woman?

"It's all right." He kept repeating the mantra in both formal and colloquial. "I'm human. A survivor of the Malignance like yourself." Shuffling aside debris with his glider-clad feet, he entered a large, high-ceilinged chamber. The intricate, faceted skylight had long since fallen in. "My name is Ruslan. Ruslan . . ."

He couldn't remember his other name. It didn't matter. "I'm from Seraboth. I'm here with the nonhumans who operate a nearby scientific outpost. They're friends. They've been good to me. They've . . . helped me." He extended a hand in case the other was watching closely. "They'll help you, too, if you let them. I'll help you. They just want to—"

A dark shape exploded from the mound of debris off to his

right. It was bipedal and human-sized. The proportions were right. Even the hair was right: light brown and long. But it was not human. A second's glance, which was about all the time he had, was enough to show that. He felt sudden terror and crushing disappointment all at once. Out of the corner of an eye, he saw two more of the creatures emerging from behind the trash mountain, watching to see how the ambush went before they risked their own hides by joining in the attack.

Reeling, stumbling backward, Ruslan managed to throw himself to one side an instant before powerful four-fingered hands could wrap themselves around his neck. His reflexes were not what they had been as a young man, but they were good enough. As the creature landed and turned, Ruslan fumbled for the sidearm he had been issued. He had argued with Twi'win about the need for him to carry a weapon. If he made it back, he would make it a point to apologize to her in person.

The creature's wiry hair extended all the way to the backs of its legs. Like the Myssari, it was multi-jointed, though not so extensively as the Vrizan. Two bulging, round eyes were arranged in a pair facing forward, while two smaller orbs protruded from either side of the ovoid of a skull, giving the animal superb peripheral vision on a world noted for its murky atmosphere. With the exclusion of the exceptional mane, its brown, ochre-splotched body was utterly hairless. For all Ruslan could gather from his one hurried glance at its nakedness, it might just as well reproduce by budding or spores as sexually.

All of this impressed itself on his mind as he drew his weapon and took aim at the crouching alien. Before he could depress the trigger, something hard and muscular struck his right side. His impact-shocked fingers released the sidearm, which went tumbling to the damp, grimy floor. As he struggled with what felt like a massive bundle of live wires, the second creature turned to face him. Up close he could see that it had a protruding ridge of bone where a nose would be but no visible nostrils. No such ambiguity clouded the identity of the gaping mouth, whose parted jaws revealed sturdy incisors and molars arranged in double rows. A maw that could both rip and chew, it was presently inclining toward his face.

A part of him realized dimly that from a distance, and not a great one at that, such a being could easily be mistaken for human by even a well-programmed Myssari automatic. The matter of multiple joints aside, the native possessed the requisite number of limbs in approximately the same places, four manipulative digits instead of five, a head in the right location, and similar proportions. The flowing hair could easily conceal the left-skull and right-skull flanking eyes, while from anywhere but up close the central facial bony ridge looked very much like a human nose. Yes, the confusion was understandable. That his demise was imminent in no way affected the disappointment of his realization.

A bright light flashed in his eyes, blinding him. It was due not to the release of his body's protective endorphins but to a perfectly placed discharge of energy from a weapon wielded by one of his Myssari escorts. As he blinked in furious pain, Ruslan's vision cleared enough for him to see that where tooth and maw had loomed ever closer to his face, smoke now rose from a small crater where the alien's head had been. The decapitated body slowly fell to its left. Maintaining their grip even in death, the powerful four-fingered hands that held him now dragged him to the ground.

More shots were fired, driving the remaining pair of frustrated, screeching creatures from the chamber. As the outpost escorts pursued them, familiar figures rushed to Ruslan's aid. Kel'les arrived first, followed by Cor'rin and Bac'cul. Their largely inflexible faces prohibited expressions of concern, but he could see the apprehension in their eyes and hear clearly the strain in their voices.

"I'm fine," Ruslan assured them. Balancing on two legs, Bac'cul used his third to brace himself against the headless native corpse. Utilizing all three arms, he soon had the human free from the dead creature's death grasp. "It was a near thing, though," he added as he rose to his feet.

"We heard noises." Cor'rin was staring at him out of her small violet eyes. "Then the sound of a weapon being discharged and we came as fast as we could." She looked past him, in the direction taken by the fleeing natives and the pursuing Myssari. "Your survival is a tribute to the skill of our escorts. I would not have dared to take a shot while you were held so close in the native's embrace."

"Weapons schooling comprises only the most peripheral portion of our field training." Though Bac'cul had an irritating fetish for elucidating the obvious, an exhausted Ruslan could not find it in his heart to venture even the slightest dollop of his usual sarcasm.

He was exhausted, and crushed. Twi'win's pessimism had trumped his original zeal. Observed in passing from a distance and from the air, the ferocious native creatures he had encountered could easily pass muster as possible humans. While it was not conclusive that the ones who had attacked him were representative of the same species that had been spotted and recorded by the Daribb outpost's airborne automatics, neither was it an unreasonable assumption. Discouraged and depressed, he felt that he could hear Twi'win's acerbic comments already.

He did not have long to wait to hear the actual ones.

"You *must* allow us to continue searching." There was as much intensity in Bac'cul's voice as Ruslan had ever heard from the usually even-toned Myssari.

Strange the situation was. Though he was sitting with his back to the discussion, Ruslan did not miss a word. As he stared out the back of the outpost's three-sided observation tower, his gaze swept over the interminable sea of shallow mudflats. In the distance a wan sun was setting, its sickly hue unable to render the sunset anything other than ailing. From within the mud a few desultory bubbles rose and burst, signifying the presence of something unwholesome beneath the surface whose sole current activity consisted of breaking alien wind. Nothing that was not artificial rose above the murk; not a tree, not a bush, not a blade of grass. Daribb was a world ruled by suck and slime—sad, smelly, and sinking in upon itself.

Yet his kind had seen fit to settle here, to lift buildings and travelways above the murk, to raise children and expand civilization and find, as always, something to exploit. Now they were gone and all was ruin, falling in upon itself and left to the haunts of local bipeds who resembled their past masters only in the most rudimentary shape and size.

He was very tired. He had helped the Myssari on Seraboth. He had helped them on Myssar itself and most recently on Treth. Surely there was no more they could learn from him. He had explained and demonstrated and utilized and performed. He was done remembering. They could preserve his exhausted body however they wished, alongside the many others they had recovered from the unpremeditated catacombs of a dozen worlds. Dimensional recordings of him talking and moving would live after him to amaze each new generation of Myssari youth. He would not be present to hear their muted equivalent of laughter and endure their stares and gestures.

There was no question that they valued what he had done in helping to explain and preserve something of human culture. Having lived an ordinary life until the coming of the Aura Malignance, he was proud of the fact that he had contributed something special, if only to the knowledge base of another species. Who else could make such a claim? Certainly not any human inhabitant of Daribb: there were no human inhabitants of Daribb. He had already acknowledged as much to the outpost's director.

Bac'cul and Cor'rin, however, were not so willing to give up.

Having traveled a long way from Treth at considerable cost to their department, they were not ready to concede to reality, pack their belongings, turn around, and go home. Besides, Cor'rin was arguing as she confronted Director Twi'win, it would be several sixparts before a ship could be designated to pick them up and take them back to Myssar. Why not utilize the time remaining to continue the search? Smiling tautly to himself as he continued to stare out the window, Ruslan knew the answer. Twi'win's reply to Cor'rin confirmed it.

"You must think we have no other use for our limited resources here than to escort you around Dinabu. There are other human settlements and cities that cry out for exploration." She gestured with all three hands, executing a complex pattern in the air in front of her. "Should we return to Dinabu, I am sure there is an excellent chance that we would once again encounter the same welcoming 'humans' there that your party did yesterday."

"Just because our initial search was interrupted by hostile indigenes does not mean there are no surviving humans in the city." Cor'rin was emphatic. "Absence of proof is not proof of absence."

"You will need to come up with more than clever words to persuade me to allocate additional resources to what I have regarded from the beginning as a wasteful undertaking."

Though he paid close attention, Ruslan did not participate in the ongoing debate. It would have been useless to do so. His words would have carried no weight and he saw no point in opening himself to embarrassment. He was an artifact. A highly valued one to be sure, but one that retained precious little control over his own destiny. Where the Myssari were concerned, expediency always took precedence over compassion. Just because he wanted to continue the search, which despite his near-fatal encounter with local lifeforms he very much wished to do, did not mean that his desires would make one whit of difference to the outpost director. Or, for that matter, to Bac'cul and Cor'rin.

Kel'les, now—Kel'les had become friend enough to side with

Ruslan against the others. At least Ruslan thought so. He was unsure what the actual result would be if he ever put that friendship
to a serious test. He was uncertain he wanted to.

He urged on Bac'cul and Cor'rin's efforts silently, knowing that
to inject himself and his opinions aloud would only be likely to
stiffen Twi'win's opposition. If the outpost director would not
yield to the urging of two esteemed scientists of her own kind, she
surely would be immune to the entreaties of a single alien.

Having no standing in what was essentially a disagreement in-
volving science and economics, Kel'les sidled over to stand beside
the human. "Bac'cul and Cor'rin are making as good a case as
they can. I feel that their reasoning is sound."

Turning away from a panorama that featured endless muck
and sallow sunlight, Ruslan murmured softly to his trisymmetrical
friend. "I've lived among your kind long enough to know that one
thing both our species had in common was the inevitable triumph
of cost over reason." He nodded to where the three Myssari continued in passionate but characteristically soft-voiced debate.
"Though in this case Twi'win is such a disbeliever in the possibility of finding any human survivors that I think she would refuse
our requests even if she had access to ten times the needed supplies
and personnel."

As he finished, something fist-sized, dull red, and multi-legged
slammed into the observation tower's transparent wall. The resulting organic splatter was unpleasant to look upon and he turned
away even as the structure's automated maintenance gear swung
into action to remove the stain left behind by the unfortunate
leaper.

Kel'les's small, lipless mouth flexed. "The director is required
to accommodate us. The orders came directly from Myssar."

Ruslan nodded, a gesture his companion knew well. "She's required to do so only insofar as is practical with respect to local
conditions." He gestured in the direction of the dispute, which, by

Myssari standards, was growing positively heated. "Orders or not, it all comes down to a decision by Twi'win."

As he and Kel'les looked on, the debate came to a sudden end. Feeling that the abruptness of it did not bode well for their continued efforts, Ruslan was apprehensive when his companions ambled over to rejoin him. Twi'win did not join them, disappearing into the lift shaft that would carry her away from the topmost portion of the observation tower. He was not upset that she departed without speaking to him. There was no reason for her to deal directly with what was nothing more than a valuable specimen.

With Bac'cul's and Cor'rin's postures conveying a mix of excitement and resignation, he hardly knew what to think. They were quick to enlighten him.

"We have struck a compromise."

He nodded tersely. "As is always the Myssari way. Is the compromise in our favor or against it?"

The two researchers exchanged a look before Cor'rin turned back to the human. "Twi'win has agreed to authorize one more full-scale visit to Dinabu and to nowhere but that city. That is where the single disputed sighting by the outpost's automatics took place, and she is convinced there is no reason to look elsewhere. After that, if we wish to continue searching, we will have to request additional resources from Myssar."

"I understand. In that event, do you think your department will provide them?"

"Difficult to say." The pupils of Bac'cul's orange-red eyes narrowed. "Two expensive failures would be unlikely to inspire calls to underwrite any subsequent excursions."

Ruslan's mouth tightened. "Then we'd better make the best of this forthcoming outing."

Cor'rin gestured her agreement. "We have to make our own preparations. The day following tomorrow the weather is supposed to be amenable. We should go then, as soon as possible and before the director has additional time to reflect on options and change her mind."

She departed with Bac'cul, the two of them moving with commendable speed, their three-legged gait looking as unsteady to Ruslan's eyes as his bipedal stride undoubtedly did to them. He turned back to his minder.

"Tell me your opinion, Kel'les. Honestly—do you think the outpost's automatics saw a human?"

His friend demurred. "I am hardly in a position to comment, Ruslan. I am neither scientist nor engineer."

"But you saw the images. The same ones as everyone else. If I wanted a researcher's opinion, I'd ask Bac'cul or Cor'rin. I want yours." He eyed his companion intently.

Trapped by the human's words and stare, a clearly uncomfortable Kel'les could do nothing but answer. Honestly, as his friend had requested.

"I must confess I found them to be, at best, inconclusive."

Ruslan was silent for a moment, then nodded solemnly. "Thank you, Kel'les. But we're going to conduct the second search anyway."

"Of course we are. One must be certain, and the chance may not present itself again."

"I know that it won't," he replied.

Because by the time any kind of similar opportunity materialized, he told himself, he would in all likelihood be little but a valued memory in the annals of Myssari science.

9

———

Though the Myssari were by nature not an especially demonstrative species, there was even less visible enthusiasm than usual among the team from the outpost as the trio of driftecs skimmed across the slime toward Dinabu. The enervating dullness of the journey over the monotonous yellow-brown landscape was broken only by the occasional attack. Mounted by local predatory lifeforms that dwelled beneath the viscous surface of the endless mudflats, these attacks took the form of the desperate upward thrusting of arms, tentacles, and assorted alien gripping apparatuses for which Ruslan had no name. Preoccupied with thoughts of what they might find in the desolate city they were approaching, he spared these occasional fruitless assaults only the most cursory of glances. His Myssari hosts evinced an equal lack of concern. Too slow and too clumsy to present any real danger, the flailing limbs of local predators immersed in mud clutched only the empty air that was warmed by the wake of the speeding driftecs.

Limited in resources and modest in aim, the expedition touched down on the opposite side of Dinabu from the previous search site. Although this was also much farther from the location where the outpost's automatic scouts had made their sighting, Ruslan did not object. He was fully aware his presence and that of his not-so-esteemed Myssari colleagues was resented by many of the researchers assigned (some said condemned) to Daribb. The present outing had barely been approved. Voicing objection to any part of it at this early stage was liable to see it terminated prematurely.

If naught else, the visit was rich with nostalgia. Living as he had for decades on Myssar, he had fallen out of familiarity with many of the simpler accoutrements of human life. Seeing abandoned eating utensils, entertainment displays, food storage and preparation facilities, even the mechanisms necessary for performing basic hygiene, brought back memories of a happier youth on Seraboth before the arrival of the Aura Malignance. Both children's and adult toys were scattered throughout the corroding buildings. Noting them, he flashed an ironic smile at no one in particular. Now all the players were gone and only one functional toy remained: him.

That was not being fair to the Myssari, he knew. Specimen or not, they had treated him with respect, if not outright reverence. How he reacted to that was his problem, not one imposed on him from without.

"Do not wander off by yourself," the escort leader had warned him. "Remember what nearly happened last time."

Ruslan remembered. He also had never been one for taking orders. At least, not since his last human order-giver had expired in a hospital in Seraboth's capital city. Ruslan recalled the death day clearly. Lying on the bed, his aged supervisor had drawn a last, desperate breath, eyes bulging in desperation. The awful sight had quickly been blocked by the attending physician, who less than an hour later collapsed and died on top of his patient. There had been very few patients or health professionals left alive by the time the plague-resistant Ruslan left the building for the last time.

The structure through which he was presently walking was definitely no hospital, he reflected as he edged away from Bac'cul and the others. When he wanted to be by himself, not even the devoted Kel'les could keep up with him. From their very beginnings humans had always been good at hiding. The ancient survival trait now lent stealth to his curiosity as he turned sharply to his right and disappeared behind a small escarpment of oversized but lightweight storage containers.

He was not wholly reckless. Making his way across the platforms and walkways that rose above the murky surface, he took care to stay inland wherever possible, aware from the driftec flyovers of the greater dangers that lurked in deeper holes in the mud. The section of city through which he was walking bore some resemblance to the small fishing villages he remembered from visits to ocean shores on Seraboth, though there were no fish on Daribb and, for that matter, no oceans. But the mudflats teemed with hidden life; not all of it lethal, no doubt some of it edible.

One of the first things settlers of a new world strove to learn was which local organics were ingestible and which were toxic. Crumbling craft of local design, warehouses, cranes, and deactivated shocknets all pointed to a local industry that, if not designed to catch fish, was clearly intended to gather something. In the absence of sea or field, they suggested a once-thriving local commerce founded on gathering the bounty of the mudflats.

A gap loomed ahead in the walkway he was traversing. While his athletic days were largely behind him, the breach was not significant and he jumped it easily. Nothing rose from the muck below to snap at him, though the stink of organic decay was pronounced. He wrinkled his nose. Daribb was ripe with the stench of decomposition. A moon would have helped, nudging tides that would have washed the shores of the city. But Daribb had no moon. And not much else, he was coming to believe, save the ghosts of the long dead. Fatigue magnified his dejection.

He was ready to turn back, more than ready, when for the second time in as many visits dank and depressing Dinabu tantalized his hearing with unidentified sounds. One hand dropped to his sidearm as he listened intently. This time he would not be surprised, would not be caught off guard by whatever came gnashing out of the ruins. Shrieks and rumbles, rapid-fire coughs and chitterings, assailed his ears. He let his hand relax. Somewhere in the depths the local lifeforms were disputing among themselves and it was none of his business.

He didn't care how fascinating they might be, or if they comprised representatives of one or more new indigenous species. Let the exploration team's xenologists assemble themselves to record the goings-on. He wanted none of it. Rising from the twisted ceramic beam where he had paused to rest, he turned to rejoin his companions. Bac'cul and Cor'rin might not be ready to leave, but he was. He found that he was looking forward to the return to Myssar. There would be no retirement for him there, only comfort and a tending to his needs. Even his death would be valuable to the Myssari scientists who were fascinated by all things human. They would watch and study his passing with as much interest as they had his life, carefully recording his last wheezing breaths, solicitously noting the stoppage of his heart, the shrinking activity of his synapses, the final forceful exhalation of his collapsing lungs. . . .

He turned so sharply he nearly fell on the weather-warped walkway. That last sound—had he imagined it? Strikingly different in tone and timbre from the preponderance of guttural hooting and hollering, it had pierced him as cleanly as a surgical probe. While he was trying to analyze it, to decide if he had really heard it or if his hearing was playing tricks on him, it resounded again. Several times, increasing in pitch.

A scream. An undeniably human scream. Underscored by overtones he had not heard in decades except in recordings salvaged and offered up for his inspection and explanation by Myssari xenologists. Feminine overtones. The screamer was female.

He began to run, drawing his sidearm as he did so. As he raced in the direction of the screaming, he silently cursed every obstacle in his path, every shortened stride that kept him from reaching its source that much sooner. As he ran he spoke, haltingly and with difficulty, to the aural pickup that clung to his chest like an iridescent blue insect.

"Kel'les! Bac'cul, Cor'rin! I'm monitoring what sounds like local creatures fighting, but there's something else. It sounds hu—" Mindful of earlier disappointments and opprobrium, he leavened his call with caution. "I think it *might* be human. I don't have visual yet."

Initial exhilaration gave way to prudence. What if the screams were being made by the Daribbian equivalent of a Serabothian mocking climber? What if what he was hearing was nothing more than the mindless replication of shouts once made by now long-dead inhabitants of the city, perfect reproductions passed down through generations of masterfully imitative indigenous creatures?

As to the source of the wild howling and bleating, he had no illusions. This was confirmed as he rounded a corner and came upon a choice chunk of chaos.

The fight between two groups of the long-haired hunters, one of whom had nearly killed him in the course of his previous visit, was ongoing and fierce. Battling with clubs, spears, and crude axes, more than twenty of the creatures were flailing away madly at one another. In the absence of anything resembling a combat strategy, sheer unfocused energy prevailed. Skulls were bashed, limbs broken, bodies sliced and stabbed. Whether they had noticed his arrival or not he could not tell, but none of the combatants paid him the least attention. Formed into a semicircle, one group was attempting to defend a pile of still-intact building supplies while being assailed by their adversaries. Though slightly outnumbered, the first group was managing to hold their assailants at bay.

Then Ruslan saw that what the first group was so zealously defending was not building supplies.

Initially he was so stunned he did not react. More than half a century had passed since he had last set eyes on another living human being. Despite the scouting report that had brought him and his companions to Daribb, he had not really, in his heart, expected to encounter one. Now he found himself staring through the red flush of battle at a struggling, unkempt figure that even at a distance the cynical Twi'win herself not could mistake for a native.

He knew he ought to wait for the others. Intervening on his own might get the both of them killed. But at any moment a stray blade, a thrown spear, might destroy his last chance to feel the flesh of a fellow live human pressed against his own. Blurting his discovery into his pickup, he raised his sidearm and rushed heedlessly forward, yelling and firing as he went. His charge would have been more impressive had he been a few decades younger. His speed would have been better, and his reaction time. The avalanche of adrenaline that shot through him helped to compensate for the passage of years, however, and he did have on his side the significant benefit of complete surprise.

Neither of the two contesting groups of primitive bipeds had ever seen an advanced weapon before. While the flashes of light from the muzzle of his sidearm were little more than distractions, the devastating consequences of the energy bursts they unleashed manifested themselves in the form of obliterated heads, severed limbs, and flowering guts.

When one or two of the creatures showed signs of challenging him, they were quickly dissuaded by the hasty departure of their fellows. Deprived of backup, these braver members of the two tribes joined their colleagues in flight. Low on the intelligence scale they might be, but they possessed enough cognizance to recognize

superior firepower when it was shown to them. Smoke and the
smell of burning flesh rose from the corpses they left behind. They
made no effort to take the bodies of their dead with them. It was
likely that as soon as Ruslan left the scene the survivors would
return; to recover, to bury, perhaps to consume. He knew next to
nothing of the biology of the local aborigines, nor did he much
care. His attention was focused solely on the small figure that was
huddling at the back of the mountain of material. Dust coated the
surfaces of boxes and crates like brown sugar, indicating that they
had not been touched in a very long time.

Slowing down as he approached, he lowered his weapon and
extended his other hand, fingers splayed in open invitation.

"It's all right. It's okay. I'm human, like . . . like you are. My
name is Ruslan." In the absence of a response, he continued. "I
come from a world called Seraboth. Like this world, Daribb, it
was once part of the human expansion. Now I live with a race
called the Myssari. They're not very human, but they're quite nice.
They've taken good care of me."

He was starting to worry that after a probable lifetime of
scrambling and hiding to survive, this singular survivor might bolt
in fear. It struck him that he had no proof of her existence to show
his companions. As a non-researcher, he carried no recording device with him. His roughly modified clothing was not equipped
with the integrated scientific instrumentation that smoothly
adorned Bac'cul's and Cor'rin's attire. If this individual ran from
him, he would have to somehow convince the Myssari that he had
indeed encountered another live human, and that might not be so
easy. In the absence of any confirming facts or visual proof, even
Kel'les would be reluctant to accept such a claim.

He maintained his cautious approach to the survivor. Fearful of
doing something to spook her, he kept his voice low, the tone insistent but gently pleading.

"I can help you. My friends can help you. I've lived among the
Myssari for many years. They only want to ask questions of us.

They can get you away from here, off this world, to a safe place. I'll be with you every step of the way." He swallowed hard. "Can you speak? Please, won't you at least tell me your name? I haven't heard a nonrecorded human voice in decades and I'm . . . lonely. Aren't you lonely?"

Save for the peculiar songlike thrumming of small creatures moving within the pile of debris, it was completely silent around them. Then, from within the mass of containers, came something he never thought to hear again: the unrecorded voice of a human female. It shocked his ears.

"My name is Cherpa."

An enormous smile creased his face and he halted his advance. "It's very nice to meet you, Cherpa. Won't you come out so I can see you better? I'm sure you can see me, and so you can see that I won't do you any harm."

A human shape emerged from the shadows. It was short and slender and nearly cloaked in hair the color of weak chocolate. No wonder the brief, indistinct recording made by the outpost's automatics had been so inconclusive. With hair that reached to the backs of her knees, the survivor, from a distance, would look very much like a small example of the indigenous tribal bipeds. Cherpa had the barest nub of an upturned nose and wide, curious blue eyes. His heart fell even as his spirits rose. The clash of images and thoughts that had dominated his imagination ever since he had identified the survivor as female vanished in a puff of wishful thinking.

She looked to be about eleven.

His very wide smile subsided somewhat. With as deep a sigh as his more than middle-aged chest could muster, he extended a hand once more. "It's very, very good to meet another human, Cherpa." His gaze rose to scan the mountain of material behind her as he tried to frame the question he dreaded but which had to be asked. "Where are your parents?"

"Gone and dead, dead and gone, their bones gnawed and their

faces flawed." Her reply took the form of a girlish singsong leavened with melancholy. In front of him, she began to dance. "Mary,
Mary, relativistically contrary, how does your gravity flow? Depends on the size of your bottom, gottum, sottum." She ceased
twirling, staring up at him. "Do you have any food? I like mine
live, but I can eat dead things when I have to, when I have to. Too
much to do but got to eat to grew, to grew you. To grew you? Who
knew?"

The muscles around his eyes tensed but he held back. Not for
his sake but for hers. It was going to take time, he knew. Time to
mend, time to see if a change of surroundings would help. Until
then he could only guess at how crazy she was and how far from
reality she had slipped. He extended his arms, offering a hug, but
she skipped warily out of his reach. Her gaze narrowed as her tone
turned ferocious.

"No touch! Touching is bad. Touching is kills."

"I'm not one of them." He gestured in the direction taken by
the fleeing natives. "I'm human just like you."

She shook her head violently. "Different meant. You're big and
strong, like them." Turning her head, she spat in the direction of
the departed predators. "Gnaw Cherpa's bones while she moans."

"No." He made no further move to advance toward her, rely-
ing on reason and his voice. "I'm just . . ." It struck him then. He
had no way of knowing how old she had been when her parents
had died. It was possible she did not recall her father and, not remembering, saw this new mature male only as something different. He didn't want to be a father figure. He had wanted . . . he
had wanted . . .

It didn't matter what he had wanted. It didn't matter what he
had twirled and danced with in his mind's eye. She was eleven.
Or so.

"I'm a man, Cherpa. You're a girl. Yes, we're different, but
we're a lot more alike than we're different. I'm like your father.
We're the same species."

"Big," she repeated warily. He stayed where he was, being patient, giving her time to study, to evaluate him.

Finally she came forward, advancing hesitantly, the wide blue eyes glazed. Glazing over the haunting, he decided. He could not imagine what her life had been like, surviving alone and abandoned in a place like Dinabu. When she finally spoke again, it was decisively.

"I'll call you Bogo."

He could not quite swallow his quick responsive laugh. "That's not a very dignified name for the last man alive. My name is Ruslan."

"Bogo." She seemed pleased with herself. He gave a mental shrug. If it made her happy, if it led her to cooperate—Bogo it was.

"You can call me whatever you want, Cherpa." This time when he extended a welcoming arm, she did not retreat. But neither did she allow him to embrace her. Within her protective psychosis she remained guarded. He would have to deal with it as best he could and hope; hope that with time and care and tenderness the protective mask of madness would fall away. "Let's go and meet my friends. You'll like them. They're . . . funny."

His respected, highly educated companions probably would not have appreciated his description, but his sole concern of the moment was to get her away from an area where she surely knew every hiding place and back to the outpost before she could change her mind about him.

One childish hand reached out to touch his bare forearm. The small slender fingers should have been soft and smooth. Instead they were tough and wiry. The callused tips stroked his skin. He didn't move; just stood still, letting her explore him like a kitten with a new toy. Her hand withdrew.

"You feel like me." Her tone was as solemn as her expression. "I remember others like me." Turning her head, she nodded in the direction taken by the departed two-legged predators. "Others like me gone to food, every one."

"I'm sorry," he murmured. "But if you will come with me, I promise you won't go to food."

Her eyes widened still further as she turned back to him. "Promise? Cross your heart and hope to remove it?"

"Cross my heart and—hope to remove it." Putting his hands on his knees, he squatted so that his face was level with hers. "In fact, if you come with me and decide that I'm lying, I'll let you remove it yourself."

"Give me a knife and I can do that." He did not think she was boasting.

"Well then." For a third time he extended a hopeful hand. This time she took it.

"You have nice hands, Bogo. No claws."

"No claws," he agreed. "My friends the Myssari don't have claws, either. In fact, their hands are smoother than a human's. They don't even have fingerprints."

"What's a fingerprint? Is it like a scratch?"

"More like art. I'll show you, later." Addressing his pickup, he uttered a key word. Nothing. Puzzled, he looked down.

He had forgotten to activate the communications device. No wonder none of his companions had arrived in response to his frantic calling. Nudging the appropriate tab, he was pleasantly surprised when Kel'les answered instead of one of the scientists or escorts from the outpost. His minder's tone was anxious.

"Ruslan? We have not heard from you in some time. We were about to—"

"I'm fine and on my way back," he said, hurrying to allay his handler's concern. "And I have company. When you see her, you'll understand the confusion that arose from the automatics' report."

"You make funny sounds." Cherpa was looking up at him. He was careful to let her hold his hand instead of gripping hers. He did not want her to feel as if he was attempting to pull her along.

"That's Myssarian, the language of my friends," he explained. "It's very straightforward and not hard for a human to learn. I'll teach you myself. Until then you'll have to wear a translator. I did, too, when they first found me."

She pondered this as they made their way across pedestrian walkways that were strewn like disembodied tendons above the mudflats and throughout the empty city. "So you were alone, too? Like me, except that these Miserables found you?"

"Myssari," he corrected her. "They're very nice people. Don't let their appearance frighten you. They have three arms and three legs and more joints than we do."

Her reaction was not what he expected. She clapped her hands and looked delighted. "An extra arm and an extra leg! You're right, Bogo—they *are* funny. I don't think I'll be scared at all."

After the life you've likely had, he thought somberly, *I doubt there's much that could scare you.* Still, he didn't want to take any chances. It would be heartbreaking if, after having found another living human, something caused her to panic, flee, and lose herself back in the dark viscera of the city. Nor did he want to do anything that might result in having to restrain her against her will. Given her apparently precarious state of mental health, pushing her too hard might well result in sending her over a psychological cliff from which her remaining degree of sanity might never recover.

He knew what the Myssari reaction would be. Restraining their eagerness to study her was not going to be easy. Presented with a second living representative of the species, and one of the opposite gender at that, they were going to want to poke, probe, measure, and record the girl down to the smallest detail. He was going to have to impress on them that she was not only immature but mentally unsettled. Examine the crystal too closely and too often and you are liable to shatter it. An outcome like that would crush both him and his alien associates.

An ancient human expression come down through the centuries would have to define his position. What was it . . . "*Cave canum*"? No. "Back down"? No . . . "Back off." Yes, that was it.

Where Cherpa was concerned, the impatient Myssari were going to have to back off lest they damage the very subject they wished to appreciate.

That would extend to the removal of any viable eggs whenever the girl became sexually mature. Desperately as they wished to reestablish the human species, they were going to have to continue to focus on cloning his cells and those of the recently deceased rather than actual breeding. Theoretically, his own sperm ought to be serviceable for another twenty years or so, if not longer. While he did not wish to contemplate such activities, he knew that he must, if for no other reason than that it would be one of the first issues the Myssari would raise.

Was her psychosis inheritable? Had she been crazy from birth? He had a sudden vision of a successfully resurrected humankind— all mad. Would that, after all, be so very different from the species that had created and disseminated the Aura Malignance?

For now, he pushed the unsettling images from his mind. The girl had just been found. She was about to be introduced to aliens and an alien society. Unlike the mature individual he had been when a Myssari exploration team had found him wandering on Seraboth, she had no reference points for such an encounter. In contrast, he'd had access to more than a hundred years of studying and learning, albeit largely self-directed. In the absence of such experience, he would have to direct for her. He would have to explain, to teach, to assure. Whether she would let him or not remained to be seen.

In dreaming of finding another human alive, he had fantasized himself as a mate. Not a teacher. But he resolved to accept the destiny Fate had handed him with as much grace as possible.

The small, leather-tough hand that firmly gripped his made it easier for him to acquiesce to that inevitability.

She might have found his description of the Myssari amusing, but it turned out that his own estimation of her courageousness had been overdone. When she saw them approaching in their exploration gear, Bac'cul in the lead, she let out a cross between a scream and a squeak and tried to bolt. Gripping her hand tightly (he told himself it was for purposes of reassurance and not restraint), he knelt down and hurried to calm her.

"Hey, hey! . . . Relax, Cherpa. They're friends, I told you." He put on his best smile. "You said they sounded funny. Just look at them. They are funny-looking, aren't they?" The pull on his hand, the frantic desire to escape, grew less insistent. Her wide-eyed gaze flicked rapidly between him and the approaching Myssari. He kept talking—fast, but not so fast as to suggest panic. "See how they walk? Sometimes the middle leg first and then the other two, sometimes one-two-three, one-two-three." He leaned closer and she did not pull away. "You know what's *really* funny?" She shook her head uncertainly. "Watching a Myssari trip over all three of its own feet."

Her brows drew together, an indication that internal visualization was hard at work. Then she smiled. It was the second-most-beautiful thing he had seen that day, following his first full glimpse of the long-tressed girl.

"My friends will be your friends," he promised her. "They can be a lot of fun. You know what else is fun?" The Myssari team was almost upon them now and he made sure to keep his body between them and her. "A haircut. See?" Reaching up, he ran his palm across a pate that was covered with very short gray follicles. "But we won't cut yours this short. Unless you want it this short." He hoped she would not say yes. Though it was an utterly unscientific, culturally antique thought, he was inordinately pleased when she did not.

To their credit, the Myssari slowed their advance despite their unconcealed excitement.

"Another human!" Cor'rin was breathing hard as she stared. "And an immature female at that. I never thought to see such a thing. Wonderful, wonderful!" Forcing her gaze away from the wide-eyed newcomer, she regarded Ruslan. "Is she healthy?"

Not "What is her name?" or "How is she feeling?" Ruslan thought. As a Myssari scientist, Cor'rin's first concern was for the viability of the new specimen. He decided he could not blame her for being characteristic of her own species. Still, the researcher's query rankled slightly.

"No, she's not fine." He looked on intently as Bac'cul and several other members of the exploration team formed a curious, reverential semicircle behind Cherpa. Reassured by Ruslan, she studied them in turn, more curious now than afraid. She could not understand anything they were saying about her, of course. Language learning would take time. Meanwhile there would be mechanical translators, perfectly efficient thanks to Myssari technology and his assistance with corrections.

They were examining her as if she were a new genus of arthropod. It was a look he knew intimately, having himself been subject to it on more occasions than he could count. Cherpa appeared to be handling the attention very well. What was actually going through her mind as she withstood the intense alien scrutiny remained unknown. At least, he told himself, she wasn't running in circles and screaming or coiling into a fetal position. Thus far her madness seemed drawn from a source that, as such things went, was comparatively benign.

"Look at the extent of follicular growth." Informed that Cor'rin was also female, the bright-eyed Cherpa was allowing the Myssari researcher to handle her long hair. Nine limber, soft-tipped fingers trolled through the auburn tresses. "Contrast it with Ruslan's."

"I could have had the same," he pointed out. "Via simple genetic manipulation or chemical stimulation. I chose to let nature take its course." He nodded at the now surrounded girl. "That's what has happened with her. It will have to be trimmed back, if only for hygienic reasons. But not too much." Moving closer, he smiled down at the girl. Her initial fears now banished by the humorous appearance and gentle touch of the Myssari scientists, she grinned loopily back at him.

"Will you let your hair be cut, Cherpa? I'll do it myself if you don't want the Myssari to do it—though I think one of their medical personnel would do a better job than me."

"Funny Bogo; of course you can cut my hair! It's just hair. I used to hide behind it. I don't have to hide anymore, do I?" Looking around, she met many of the small-eyed stares that were openly marveling at her. "I embrace funny, run from nasty. No hasty-nasties here." Her voice fell slightly as her attitude grew more serious. "We are going away from here, aren't we?"

He nodded encouragingly. "No hasty-nasties where we're going, I promise you. Just lots of real food and new clothes."

"I'd like to have some new clothes." Her voice faded. "I remember that I had some once, a long time ago. My mo . . . my mo—"

A great gush of tears erupted from her. Alarmed by the unexpected outpouring, the Myssari hastily retreated. Bac'cul looked downright terrified. *Afraid of losing the new specimen,* Ruslan mused unfairly as he moved to hold the girl and let her wring out her sobs against him. Even while they were staring concernedly, at least two of the researchers were checking to make certain their automatic recorders were functioning properly. Cherpa's anguish constituted a unique display, one that outside of studied historical recordings of human children was entirely new to the Myssari. Dedicated researchers that they were, they were not about to miss preserving a moment of it.

Ruslan found himself thinking that the first one of them that mentioned possible reproductive possibilities was going to receive a punch to its facial foreridge. The girl was awakening in him all manner of instincts he thought long forgotten. Ancient genetic information was being roused. It was astounding. It was remarkable. For the first time in decades he felt . . . protective. Alien though the emotion might be, and unnecessary, he did not reject it.

Taking a small, individual specimen recovery tube from his

pack, Bac'cul contemplated obtaining a sample of the lubricating fluid that was spilling from the immature human's eyes. He was anxious to learn if its composition differed from that of the male mature specimen Ruslan. It was not the human who intervened to prevent him, however, but one of his own kind. Startled, he looked to his left. It was the intermet Kel'les who had interrupted the scientist's proposed course of action.

"I believe I perceive your intention. I recommend postponement. As was often the case with Ruslan, I am certain there will be ample future opportunity to acquire the sample you wish to take."

While Bac'cul technically outranked the human's personal handler, the researcher decided not to make an issue of the minor confrontation. Not without fully satisfying his curiosity, however.

"Why should I not proceed?"

Kel'les gestured toward the humans. "Observe the interaction. Note the intimacy of the respective stances. An elder male is comforting a distraught juvenile. One whose mental state is, according to Ruslan, perilous. From the extensive time I have spent in Ruslan's company, I deduce that interruption at such a moment could be interpreted as unnecessarily provocative."

Bac'cul indicated his uncertainty. "I am not sure that I follow your reasoning."

Kel'les obligingly abridged it. "There are times when Ruslan takes objection to being treated as a thing. Now that he is functioning in caring mode, I believe his reaction to what he might perceive as an insensitive intrusion would be detrimental to your ultimate purpose."

The researcher was taken aback. "You're not suggesting he might resist my attempt physically?"

"I am suggesting precisely that," a tense Kel'les replied.

Bac'cul didn't hesitate. He returned the collection cup to its holder. He was not fearful that the human might hurt him: he was afraid that the human might hurt himself. As he looked on he realized that there was wisdom in Kel'les's intervention that could be applied beyond the immediate situation. The history of Ruslan's presence among the Myssari had shown that it had taken some time to fully gain the human's trust. Similarly, gaining the girl's confidence was likely to take at least as long. As with Ruslan, it would be vital to have her full cooperation in order to best advance the field of human studies. As a specimen, she was plainly going to be around for longer than the older male. Bac'cul's withholding his immediate interest was therefore based entirely on a respect for good science and not at all on empathy for a distressed fellow sentient. It was just good sense, if not good sensitivity.

Having lived long among the Myssari, Ruslan would have understood this reasoning. But that did not mean he would have liked it.

10

————

It was as the team was packing to leave Dinabu for the last time that Ruslan felt a tug on his arm. That the touch was slightly but noticeably warmer than that of a Myssari immediately identified the owner of the insistent fingers.

"Can't go yet." An anxious Cherpa was gazing up at him. "Won't go yet. Won't. I'll suck in my breath until I turn inside out. I'll wriggle—"

"Easy, easy." By now the soothing tone he had adopted whenever he was in her presence came unbidden to him. "What's wrong? Why don't you want to leave yet?"

"Need something. Can't forget." Turning, she gestured in the direction of the city. "You need to come with me to get it. Three-legs need to come with me to get it." Her expression was deadly serious. "We'll need guns. Lots of guns."

"There's that kind of danger?" he inquired gently.

Her head turned slightly to one side and she eyed him as if he had suddenly morphed into one of the eel-like creatures that lived their whole lives in the slimier portions of the endless mudflats.

"No. I'm making it all up. I'm crazy, remember? Crazy and 'leven. I want lots of guns because there's *no* danger. What do you think?"

Where Cherpa was concerned, he hoped for intelligence. He wished for sanity. He had not expected scorn.

"Lots of guns it is." He started away. "I'll tell Bac'cul and Cor'rin and they'll inform the escort leader. When do you want to do this?"

"Right now. This minute. Yesterday." She was plainly troubled. "I shouldn't have come with you without it, but your appearance slapped my brain and it didn't stop shaking until today."

"We'll get ready as fast as possible," he assured her.

What could be so important? he wondered. A nicfile containing her personal records, perhaps with images of her parents? A visual life history of the kind people used to carry around with them on Seraboth, contained in a tiny device that recorded one's every action, every utterance? The Myssari would treat any such material as invaluable since the contents could be corroborated by her, by a living human being. All he had to do was suggest that was the case and the escort she was requesting should be immediately forthcoming.

More than a dozen armed Myssari from the outpost accompanied him and the girl as they retraced their steps back to the section of the city where he had initially encountered her. It being essentially a recovery operation with an as yet undefined target, a quick in and out allowing no time for field research, Bac'cul and Cor'rin remained behind with the driftecs. In the event a flash extraction was required, they would be in constant contact with the compact expeditionary group.

Having been attacked twice now by the local bipedal aborigines, Ruslan was more than a little wary of every dark alley and

overhang, every crumbling ledge. Back once more among the devastated reaches she had called home, the effervescent Cherpa had
gone silent. She had survived here alone through stealth and caution. The presence of armed Myssari around her did not result in
a sudden change in habit.

So she was the only one not taken by surprise when the parallel
walkways being utilized by her new friends erupted beneath them.

"Nalack!" she screamed as she bolted for the safety of a nearby
structure.

The name meant nothing to Ruslan. The creature's appearance
meant everything. "Nalack" might not even be a name, he told
himself as he threw himself to one side while simultaneously struggling to draw his sidearm. It might be a curse. Both seemed appli-
cable to the shape that was rising out of the muck.

It looked like the mother of all nematodes. Coated in a special
mucus that allowed it to slip rapidly through the mudflats in search
of food, the slick snakelike body terminated in a spray of two-
meter-long tentacles that themselves were coated with thousands
of tiny barbs. Unable to escape, trapped prey would be ingested as
the head-mouth folded in upon itself, pushing the incipient meal
backward down the long gullet. There were no visible eyes or
other sensory organs.

Twice as thick as his own torso, the upper portion of the muscular dark brown body emerged farther from the mud and struck
at the scattering of Myssari. Many shots were fired but none struck
home. Taking aim at the flailing *nalack* was like trying to draw a
bead on an uncontrolled hose. Metal, ceramic, and blended graphite flowered in fragments as the missed blasts struck the surrounding buildings.

A frantic Ruslan heard a sickening crunching sound as one of
the escorts was snapped up by the thrashing head-mouth. Impaled
on dozens of backward-facing barbs, the unfortunate Myssari's
bones snapped and crumpled as his body was forced down the
predator's throat. It was a sacrifice not in vain. In order to begin

the process of swallowing, the *nalack* had to slow its wild gyrations. This allowed the doomed escort's comrades to pause in their flight and take proper aim. Convulsed by repeated hits from their weapons, the *nalack* shuddered, thrust several times at its now well-concealed tormentors, and finally fell, a coil of extirpated muscularity that collapsed in upon itself. Its subsidence sent a shower of mud and dirty water cascading over anyone unfortunate enough to be sheltering nearby, including Ruslan. As the *nalack* spasmed through its final death throes in the muck, it regurgitated its most recent meal. Hardened from their tour of duty on Daribb, the companions of the dead and broken Myssari dealt with his remains far better than Ruslan, who turned away and threw up.

It was only when he had finished wiping his mouth with the back of his bare forearm that he remembered Cherpa.

Responding to the *nalack*'s attack faster than any of her companions, she had ducked into an open, protective doorway the instant the monster pseudo-worm had erupted from its hiding place within the harbor flats. Ruslan hurried toward the opening where she had disappeared, absently brushing at the filth that covered him as he ran, all manner of worrisome thoughts rushing through his mind. Given her still-uncertain state of mind, it was possible to imagine a raft of possible scenarios, few of them good. The appearance of the *nalack* might have driven her over the edge on which she had been teetering. Panic might have wiped memory of him and the Myssari from her mind. Revitalized fear could have sent her fleeing into the depths of the empty city. The inability of the Myssari to deal instantly with the threat posed by the predator, much less detect it before it attacked, could have led her to conclude that there was no safety in throwing in her lot with them.

His gaze swept the interior of the building into which she had fled. There was no sign of her, no indication she had ever been there. Behind him the sorrowful Myssari escorts were bundling up their dead comrade. There was no wailing, no heaving sobs. The

Myssari did not cry. Their anguish was private. Ruslan's throat constricted. Even had they been biologically able to produce tears, his friends would have found the act of weeping an unforgivable imposition on those around them.

They had better be prepared to deal with it, though. If they didn't find the girl, an increasingly distraught Ruslan was going to put on an exhibition of grief that would go down as unprecedented in the annals of Myssari xenological research.

He let the escorts deal with their deceased associate for as long as he dared before informing them of the situation.

"We should call in the others." The leader of the escorts was beyond upset, though one would never have guessed it from the intermet's controlled demeanor. "The lifeform detection gear on the driftecs far exceeds the capabilities of our hand-carried instrumentation."

Ruslan nodded ready agreement, not bothering to consider if the escorts would correctly interpret the meaning of the gesture. "Do it now." He gestured over a shoulder, toward the building where Cherpa had vanished. "But we can't wait for them to get here. We have to move now. The longer we wait, the deeper into the city she's liable to run. I only found her the first time because she was being threatened by the natives." He licked his lips. "She's likely to have a network of deep, protected hiding places where we won't be able to find her even with advanced search-and-locate equipment."

While the escort leader relayed the request together with a report on the *nalack* assault, Ruslan reentered the structure where the girl had taken refuge. He blamed himself. Though his reaction to the predator's assault had been instinctive, it was no excuse. His first thought should have been for Cherpa. The knowledge that she had reacted and bolted before he'd had a chance to respond did little to assuage the deep remorse he felt. If they didn't find her, the Myssari would be greatly disappointed. His reaction would be far worse than disappointment. He would be alone. Again. A lone human dwelling among billions of tripodal aliens. An isolated specimen. A miserable . . .

"Hi, Bogo!"

He gaped. There she was, walking in his direction as though nothing untoward had happened. Not only was she unhurt, she was smiling. A big, bold, self-satisfied smile the likes of which he had feared he might never seen again.

"You must have killed the *nalack* or you'd be dead by now." Peering past the stunned Ruslan, her gaze fell upon the curved, tightly wound corpse of the imposing predator. "Yep, you killed it, all right. Good for you. Better for you than being dead." There was pride in her voice. "Since you all were busy, I went and got what I needed."

He noticed that her left hand was holding something behind her. Though masked by shadow, it seemed too big to be a nicslip.

"You got what you needed," he repeated uncertainly.

She nodded vigorously. "We can go now. It's okay. The three of us can go."

She held up the doll.

It was made of some soft material, though whether natural or synthetic he could not tell. One eye was missing. The hair was a tangle and, interestingly, as long as Cherpa's. The formal bright green singlet it wore had been torn and crudely patched numerous times. He made a mental nod. Green would be a popular color on a dull-brown world like Daribb. Like most modern toys for children, it had once doubtless been capable of movement, speech, and a modicum of artificial intelligence. Power source long since drained, it hung limp and mute in the girl's hand. He swallowed hard.

"What's her name?"

"Oola. I think it was something else once but I can't remember. I don't know where 'Oola' comes from."

"Doesn't matter." He put a hand on her shoulder. "If Oola's happy with her name, we should be, too."

Cherpa nodded and spoke in a small voice. "I couldn't leave without her. She'd never forgive me. I'd never forgive me."

"Of course you couldn't leave without her. Now there are three humans to be friends with the Myssari, right?"

For a moment the girl looked confused. Then her voice strengthened. "That's right. I've talked to Oola and she said that the Myssari people can study her, too. I like you, Ruslan." Her other hand came up to take his. "You're not just funny. You're nice."

No, I'm not, he thought. But he didn't correct her.

If Ruslan's arrival at the outpost had caused a minor sensation, Cherpa's resulted in something close to a partial shutdown of activity. Everyone wanted a look at the first surviving human juvenile. As a prerequisite of their deployment to an archeological site like Daribb, support personnel as well as researchers were required to study and learn all they could about human history. This included details on biology. None missed the significance of a chance to observe a second live human who was not only an immature specimen but of the opposite gender from the only other known survivor.

Cherpa tolerated the stares with remarkable equanimity, Ruslan thought. Much better than he had when he had first been brought to Myssar. Perhaps her slightly skewed outlook on existence provided something of a shield, her inclination to mild madness interposing itself between reality and whatever she chose to believe. When fitted with a translator, she proved able to ignore the numerous comments she could now understand.

At a private meeting with Twi'win and Hoh'nun, the chief of the outpost's scientific contingent, she examined and touched everything within reach. Other researchers, including Bac'cul and Cor'rin, were also present. Watching the girl as she delightedly studied and fingered everything from furniture to electronic controls, Ruslan decided that she was going to have an easier time adapting to her new Myssari surroundings than he ever had. He had already spoken to his companions about finding a suitable Kel'les-equivalent to serve as her minder. The girl's rapid adjustment extended even to letting the Myssari handle her precious doll.

"Oola can take care of herself," she had explained when Ruslan had tentatively conveyed the request. "As long as I'm close by, she knows she'll be okay."

While Cherpa explored her new surroundings, he was left to contemplate the incongruous sight of the outpost's senior researcher and two subordinates studying the raggedy remnants of what once must have been a fairly advanced children's toy.

"Our offspring do not play with small artificial replicas of themselves." Hoh'nun was repeatedly turning the doll over and over in his three hands. "A Myssari child would find such a diminutive replicant unsettling."

Bac'cul spoke up. "You say the artifact was once capable of speech and movement?"

Ruslan nodded. "I never played with anything like it myself, but I remember other children on Seraboth being accompanied by similar homunculi. Most were equipped with rudimentary artificial intelligence as well as the ability to perambulate on their own. The human word for it is 'doll.' As you point out, there is no Myssari equivalent."

Cor'rin gestured her bemusement. "Why would any juvenile wish the companionship of something artificial when they could have the company of others?"

"Dolls and playmates aren't mutually exclusive among human children. Sometimes children would play with one another's toys, or even trade them."

She looked horrified. "You mean they would establish a relationship with the device and then voluntarily part with it?"

He smiled. "You should know from your studies, Cor'rin, that our bonds with objects aren't as powerful as they are among the Myssari."

Hoh'nun held the doll out at arm's length. Oola stared back in silence. "There is more to this than it appears. I believe further examination of such relationships may lead to greater insight into the human psyche, perhaps even to the cause of the ultimate species self-rejection embodied in the creation of the great plague."

Ruslan frowned slightly. "It's just a doll."

The chief researcher lowered the artifact. It hung limply from one three-fingered hand. "Everything that motivates a mature sentient species is latent in the childhood of its individuals. Sometimes such things are only perceptible to distanced outside observers."

Ruslan shrugged. "Observe away." There was no point in arguing with a Myssari researcher. They were going to derive their opinions about humankind irrespective of anything he might say.

Cor'rin sensed his irritation. "The request has been transmitted for the next ship in the vicinity to detour to pick us up. We have achieved everything here that we hoped would be possible. Prior to our departure you must take time to prepare the juvenile as best you can for her new life on Myssar."

Yes, the specimen has to be preconditioned for a healthy life in the zoo, he thought unenthusiastically. *It is incumbent on the senior ape to instruct the younger.* Despite Cherpa's slight mental unbalance he did not foresee any difficulty. He had spent enough time on blighted Daribb to know she would be far happier on civilized, sanitized Myssar. In fact, he couldn't wait to leave, either. He'd seen more than enough of Daribb and its aggressive native lifeforms and its grime-frosted landscape to last him a lifetime.

Unhappily, there were other aggressive lifeforms who were not native. They soon manifested themselves.

11

——

From the solitary nighttime scout Ruslan had encountered on his ill-conceived walking excursion to the individual members of the more insistent delegation that had responded to the scout's report, the Vrizan on Treth had been stiffly correct if not exactly convivial. No such pretensions afflicted the faction that descended on the outpost the following night.

As he helped Cherpa to dress he reflected angrily on the fact that no one had bothered to tell him that, just as on Treth, the Vrizan also had their research teams hard at work on Daribb. No doubt Twi'win and her colleagues had seen no reason to mention it, since he and his colleagues were unlikely to have any contact with representatives of that competing and competitive species. Well, the unlikely had happened.

It took the form of alarms and warnings that sounded both on private and general communications. This was followed by a broadcast cautioning that the outpost's security had been violated and that resistance was being organized. Distant sharp echoes suggested that small arms were being employed. While he was sorry for what Cherpa had been forced to endure while growing up and surviving on her own, at that moment he was grateful for her enforced maturity. He did not have to rustle her awake. The instant he touched her shoulder, she was wide-eyed and alert.

"We have to get dressed, Cherpa. There's a problem." She nodded, watching him intently, and did not try to contradict him or waste time with unnecessary questions. "There's another sentient species, the Vrizan, who are also studying this world. They—they and the Myssari don't really seem to like each other much. For one thing, they argue over who should own certain scientific discoveries." As he talked she was sliding into a singlet that fit like a second skin. "Right now I think they're arguing over who owns us."

Fully clad, she snatched up the doll and held it close. "Are they nice people, too, like the Myssari?"

He started to reply and found himself hesitating. What, after all, did he know about Vrizan society beyond what his three-legged friends had told him? His brief encounters with them had been nothing if not contradictory. For all he knew, the people of their homeworld might be as accommodating and supportive as those of Myssar.

The Myssari, however, were a known quantity. He recalled the confrontation on Treth. Regardless of the scout's blandishments and whatever other racial characteristics they possessed, the Vrizan there, at least, had shown themselves to be interested in him but notably less . . . polite than the Myssari.

Snatching up a water dispenser and a couple of sucrose-laden twists—Myssari snacks that were perfectly acceptable to the human digestive system—he took her hand.

"Where are we going, Bogo?" Taking two steps to his every stride, she kept pace easily.

"I don't know yet," he muttered. "I don't know." What he did know was that he did not want to be caught between two violently disputatious groups of aliens. "We have to hide, at least for a little while. And I haven't any idea where to hide. I don't know this outpost very well."

She smiled brightly. "I know where we can hide."

He eyed her in surprise. "You do? Where?" Higher up within the outpost the sound of fighting rose and fell, angry waves of noise crashing on an insufficiently distant shore.

"Outside."

He stared at her. "We can't 'hide' outside. There are dangerous animals outside and . . ."

He stopped. How could he presume to lecture someone who had grown up and survived all their life in this hostile environment on the dangers of native fauna? She knew more about what lurked in the mudflats than he could learn if he had years in which to study it. But there was also the matter of her mental imbalance. Did she know what she was talking about, or was she just being innocently agreeable?

Something loud and metallic went *smash* in the distance. Bending, he brought his face close to hers. "What does Oola say?"

Cherpa looked at her doll. "Oola says if there's danger we should get the hell out of here *right now*."

He straightened. "Come on then."

They encountered no one, Myssari or Vrizan, as he led the way down toward the only one of the outpost's surface-level exits he could recall having passed and identified. It was helpful that it lay on the opposite side of the installation from the driftec landing platform, which by now was possibly under the control of the encroaching Vrizan. Myssari resistance to their intrusion would likewise be concentrated in that area. Indeed, as he and Cherpa descended a stairwell designed to accommodate its three-legged builders, the sounds of fighting receded into the distance.

It occurred to him that they could remain where they were, hiding in the stairwell, in the hope that the Myssari would beat off the incursion. On the other hand, if he was wrong . . .

Beset by circumstances that were nothing if not confusing, he opted to keep moving. Moments later they were standing in the maintenance chamber he remembered from the one formal tour of the outpost to which he and his companions had been subjected. Then he had thought it a waste of time; now he was grateful for it.

All that was required to get the membrane lock that was integrated into the portal to yield was the touch of his warm hand. Holding on to the side of the opening, he leaned forward and looked out. In the absence of a moon, it was exceedingly dark. Swinging himself out and around so that he was facing the exterior of the structure, he took a couple of steps downward. Other than the fact that the wide individual rungs were spaced more closely together vertically than they would have been on a human ladder, primate hands and feet had no difficulty negotiating a descent intended for Myssari technicians. The close spacing, he decided, would make it easier for Cherpa.

Tilting back his head to face the portal, he held tight to a rung with one hand and extended the other upward. "Come on, Cherpa. It's okay. I'll help you—"

Scampering past him while still clinging to her doll, she sped down the entire length of the ladder and dropped silently into the mud before he had time to fully react. Her upturned face barely illuminated by starlight, she met his gaze.

"Hurry *up*, Bogo!"

Carefully making his way down the rest of the ladder, he resolved that from now on he would not offer help to the girl unless she specifically requested his assistance.

It was late enough for the mud to have shucked off most of the day's accumulated heat. Following her lead, he lay down in it and turned on his back so that only his face was exposed. The dark, clammy ooze immediately began to seep into his clothing, finding openings where he imagined none existed, working its way into the corners and crevices of his body. He tried not to think of the glut of alien microorganisms that were being carried along on the tide of organic sludge.

"This way," she urged him. "Like this."

Looking to his left, he saw that utilizing a modified back crab crawl, she had begun to work her way away from the outpost. By dint of pushing and shoving, he mimicked her as best he could, though she had to repeatedly stop and wait for him to catch up.

Traveling on his back had its advantages, he persuaded himself. With all but a portion of their faces concealed by the mud, they were much less likely to be spotted by eager-eyed Vrizan, even if the intruders thought to scan the outpost's surroundings. Also, he could look back at the buildings as they moved away from them. In the dim light it was possible to make out little more than the integrated structure's general outline and the lights that gleamed from numerous ports. The sounds of fighting faded as they moved farther and farther away from the complex.

These were replaced by the natural night sounds of the mud-flats. Peeping and hooting, soft squeals and insistent squeaks, chirps and grunts and bellows began to compete for his attention. Occasionally turning his head from side to side revealed intermittent shadows rising above the flat surface only to disappear quickly into the depths. One time, the firmer ground beneath him sank away and he found himself struggling to swim back to more solid footing. The Myssari had constructed their outpost where the mudflats were shallowest. Elsewhere, he knew, the mud was kilometers deep. In such places lived relatives of the *nalack:* eyeless monsters he preferred not to envision.

The outpost's silhouette had grown small when he began to notice the lights around him. Half were comparatively motionless. The rest swarmed at varying speeds around his suspended form. They flickered to life like so many thousands of tiny, individual illuminators. Present in every color of the rainbow and in shapes ranging from the animated to the purely geometric, they brightened his immediate surroundings to the point where he could see Cherpa clearly. With only her face visible above the surface, she looked like a ceramic effigy from an ancient time, when humans had worn masks and makeup to celebrate pagan rituals.

It was a beautiful thing to see the bioluminescent creatures responding to his and her presence. It was disconcerting to feel them sliding along the bare skin of his arms and neck and wriggling upward against his legs and down past his shoulders. Knowing only the basics of Daribbian ecology, he could only hope that none of the tiny luminescent creatures were parasitic, and that if they were, his alien biology would repel instead of welcome them. Taking a risk, he raised his head and upper body out of the mud.

The oceanic flats in which they lay were coming alive with lights. Not millions this time but uncountable trillions. Seeing the look on his face, Cherpa clarified.

"The moglow happens every night. Didn't you know, Bogo?"

"No. No, I didn't know. Every night that I've been here I've been sound alseep, deep inside the outpost. I never thought to get up after dark to look at mud. None of the personnel assigned to the outpost bothered to tell me there might be something worth looking at."

"It's probably real familiar to them so they didn't think of it," she replied thoughtfully. "It's pretty, isn't it?"

He stared in awe at the multicolored, brightly illuminated surface of the mudflats. "Yes, it's pretty, Cherpa. Very, very pretty."

"Lots of nights I'd sneak to the edge of the docks and try to count all the colors. I like the night." Barely visible above the mud, her upturned face was the placid nexus of a maelstrom of tiny living stars and nebulae. "Most of the time I like it, but not always. Sometimes it eats."

Alarmed, he lay back down, once more submerging his upper body fully beneath the surface. "You mean the lights?"

She laughed softly, at once childlike and adult. "No, silly. The night. The night eats."

He considered pressing her for details but decided against it. If anything more dangerous than the diminutive light-emitting mud dwellers was nearby, it was just as well he remained ignorant of its presence. With escape being foremost in his mind, they had been forced to flee the outpost without a weapon. All he had to defend himself and Cherpa against an attack were his hands and feet. Though hardly proficient with either, he determined to place himself between any hostile lifeform and the girl. If they were assaulted, it could eat him first. He smiled grimly to himself. Had Bac'cul, Cor'rin, and the other Myssari scientists been present, they would have heartily approved his decision.

Meanwhile they could only chat quietly, wait to see what the dawn would bring, and float in the warm, slick mud, suspended between stars above and stars below.

The *neosone* was not interested in lights, either of the distant thermonuclear or the proximate organic variety. It was interested in food, a potential source of which had manifested itself close by. Drawn by the unusual set of vibrations in the mud, it had homed in rapidly on the source. It skimmed along just above the surface, propelled and supported by the electrical field generated by specialized cells within its broad but paper-thin body. Upon locating its prey, it would stun it with a powerful electric shock before contracting around it and enveloping it like a blanket. Then digestion could begin.

As it neared the source of the disturbance, it slowed, hovering just above the greasy surface. A line of primitive eyes along its front end could discern shape and color but no detail. Of one thing it was immediately certain: the two organisms floating before it were like nothing it had encountered before. Large and dense, they emitted no light whatsoever. Protein they possessed in plenty, but it was of a composition unfamiliar to the *neosone*. It hesitated. The two organisms were lying virtually motionless. A successful attack would require little effort.

The predator was not concerned should their substance prove indigestible. That it might be dodgy, or even toxic, was of more immediate concern. The only way to find out would be to taste. It moved closer, virtually indistinguishable from the mudflat itself. Still the prey creatures did not stir.

Then it perceived that the lesser of the potential victims was clutching a third, still smaller shape. In outline it perfectly mimicked the larger pair. But instead of potentially edible proteins, the third figure gave back no indication that it was composed of organic materials. Unable to fathom this discrepancy, the *neosone* held back. It could not understand why of three otherwise identical shapes, two should be patently organic and the third not.

In light of such confusion it determined that caution outweighed any hunger pangs. Expressing a stronger repulsion field, it rose slightly higher, accelerated, and shot off in search of safer, more familiar prey.

Lying on his back in the mud, his face turned skyward, an increasingly relaxed Ruslan noted what appeared to be a wispy cirrus cloud as it passed rapidly over him, momentarily obscuring the stars.

The Vrizan were far too clever to employ lethal weapons. Killing even one of the Myssari would have ignited trouble that would have led to repercussions far beyond Daribb. Every sidearm they carried was designed to stun or otherwise incapacitate its target, not to kill. Equally aware of the larger issues at stake, the Myssari responded in kind. The result was a pain-filled but ultimately bloodless battle that ended with the Vrizan in control of the outpost.

A pack of them confronted Twi'win, her top advisors, and the two visiting researchers in the upper conference chamber. The curved wall on one side had darkened considerably in response to the rising sun. All of the Myssari had been disarmed. Deprived of weaponry, Twi'win took the initiative with words. Just in case there should be confusion over the use of any particular invective, automatic translators were present on both sides.

"This outrage will not go unreported! You have attacked a station whose mandate is solely for peaceful scientific purposes."

"You have been visited by the personnel of a Vrizan installation whose mandate is solely for peaceful scientific purposes." In echoing her accusation, the commander of the Vrizan force was plainly not in the least troubled by Twi'win's outrage. "However, when another species flaunts their illegal presence on a world whose exploration rights have long since been awarded to the Vrizan Integument, that species should not expect the owners of those rights to demonstrate eternal patience." A hand gestured at their surroundings. "By treaty, this outpost should have been dismantled and abandoned long ago. Instead, it bears every hallmark of having been strengthened and expanded."

Turning to one of her advisors, Twi'win conferred with the intermet before replying. "This outpost was established before the terms of the treaty to which you refer was agreed upon. Its continued presence is therefore validated by precedence."

"It is not." The Vrizan commander was struggling to keep a leash on his anger.

Twi'win cleared her throat, which resulted in a high-pitched whistle bouncing through the chamber. "If you will scan Section Four, Subsection Twenty-two, of the treaty in question, it quite specifically states that—"

In a visually arresting display of alien circulation, the Vrizan commander's horizontally elongated cranium flushed crimson at the center before the intensifying tint spread outward toward the opposite ends of his head. At the same time, the row of small fleshy appendages atop his skull rippled like brown seaweed in a strong current.

"We are not here to debate the fine points of a treaty that was agreed upon and sealed elsewhere! Your continued presence constitutes violation enough. That you seek to remove artifacts that, by that same treaty, are the property of the Integument represents an escalation of provocation that could no longer be ignored!"

To a watching Bac'cul and Cor'rin, Twi'win proceeded to demonstrate an unexpected talent for feigning ignorance.

"I am sure I have no notion whatsoever of what you are talking about." Unable to blink, she executed the Myssari equivalent, which consisted of temporarily passing one hand across her eyes.

Once more the Vrizan commander was not taken aback. "A fool can play innocent only with another fool." His tone grew sharper still. "Do not make the mistake of thinking you are engaging with a fool."

"I would not presume to do so," Twi'win replied with mock seriousness.

"The property to which I refer involves an example of local life located and recovered from the human city known as Dinabu. Specifically, a live human being." Bac'cul and Cor'rin tried not to show their unease. Truly this Vrizan was no fool. "The report prepared by our automatics and reviewed by my staff suggests but does not confirm that it is an immature specimen. Enhanced imagery clearly shows it visible in the company of a mature example of the same supposedly extinct species."

Unable to remain quiet any longer in the face of the Vrizan's facts, Cor'rin spoke up. "The mature specimen's name is Ruslan, he was found by one of our exploration teams on the human-settled world of Seraboth, and he has been the property of the Myssari Combine for many, many time-parts!"

The Vrizan looked at her out of the large, swiveling eyes located at opposite ends of his elongated skull. "Your claim to the mature example of humankind is not in dispute here. We assert ownership rights only to the specimen that was found living on Daribb, in the city known as Dinabu, as is our entitlement by treaty." A humming sound that might have been laughter emerged from the depths of the commander's throat. "While your disagreeable continued presence here *may* have some basis in pre-treaty argument, our right to all archeological discoveries of importance is clear. The immature specimen—a female, I am told—belongs to us."

Though caught off guard by the Vrizan's entirely reasonable rejoinder, Twi'win recovered as best she was able. "The female juvenile will not be parted from the adult. Insofar as any of us knows, they are the last two surviving examples of their kind. Would you, who claim to be so much more civilized than us, so callously tear them apart?"

"Naturally we would prefer another course of action. What do you take us for?" The strange throaty humming sound came again. "You state that the Myssari have had possession of the adult human for a considerable period of time. Ample time, then, for you to have learned all you can from it. For the good of the juvenile, you should therefore commit both of them to our care." He paused a moment. "Ponder this, and then instruct me again on who has the better right to be called civilized."

It was a clever trap. Bac'cul knew that Twi'win could claim, truthfully, that she did not have the power to make such a decision. The Vrizan commander's response would doubtless be that he and his colleagues could wait until she received it from the proper authorities. The researcher tensed. Surely Twi'win would not agree to such a proposal, not even to stall for time. She would know, as he and Cor'rin knew, that the need to preserve harmony between competing interstellar governments could easily result in far-off Myssari functionaries making very bad decisions.

Twi'win therefore opted to avoid the snare entirely. "The specimens to which you refer are no longer here."

While startled by this pronouncement, Bac'cul and Cor'rin managed to conceal their surprise. The Vrizan rolled his eyes, an extraordinary sight. When they had ceased rotating at the ends of his skull, he spoke slowly and carefully.

"What did I just say about not thinking you were playing with a fool? Our automatics saw your heavily armed 'researchers' escort both humans into a driftec, which then lifted off and headed in this direction. This is the only Myssari infection on Daribb. No starships have entered this system since our own most recent resupply vessel."

Twi'win was adamant. "I repeat: the specimens to which you refer are no longer at this outpost."

"Then where are they?" The Vrizan made no attempt to hide his exasperation—or his rapidly diminishing patience. Though as interested in the answer as the Vrizan, Bac'cul and Cor'rin kept silent and waited.

The outpost director executed a gesture of complete puzzlement, which involved some intricate crossing of all three of her arms while slightly bowing her head toward the resultant geometric creation. "I am ashamed to admit that I do not know. None of us does. It is a terrible development that will reflect badly on all of our professional records."

"Do you expect us to be—" The Vrizan caught himself. "Our respective peoples have known each other for a very long time. We are as familiar with Myssari physiology as you are with ours. Ways of ascertaining whether or not a Myssari is telling the truth are not unknown to us." He paused to give Twi'win and her companions time to absorb the veiled threat.

Twi'win did not hesitate. As she reached out with her central arm, she extended the others to the sides. "As long as they produce no lasting adverse effects, we welcome whatever method of inquiry and interrogation you would like to employ. I offer myself as the first subject. You are also welcome to conduct a physical search of our facilities, which are entirely scientific and supportive in nature. I will provide guides to ensure that you miss nothing. If you feel that you are in any way being misled, please do feel free to point out in what respect that may be the case and your concerns will be addressed."

If Bac'cul and Cor'rin had been surprised by Twi'win's response thus far, her latest pronouncement left them shocked. No longer able to deny the existence of the two humans, was she now attempting to bluff the Vrizan commander? He did not seem a type who would be vulnerable to such an approach. His prompt reply confirmed it.

"We accept your offer. I promise that my people will disturb nothing beyond what is necessary to satisfy our interest, and that compensation will be offered for any damage that inadvertently transpires." Turning, he murmured to one of his two aides. The officer departed, presumably to organize the search.

"Barring any interference on the part of your staff, this scrutiny should not take long. We have lifeforce proximity detectors that will reveal the presence of any large beings even if they should be temporarily sealed within a wall or beneath a floor. I assure you that wherever you have hidden the specimens, they will be found." The smooth, sweeping gesture he executed bordered on the elegant. "Be assured that when they are found, no opprobrium will accrue to you. Were our positions reversed, I would myself try as hard as possible to secure such valuable specimens for future study. But they will be found and the juvenile, at least, removed. As to the fate of the mature individual, that can be discussed further once he has been recovered."

Cor'rin could stand it no longer. "You speak of him as if he is something to be studied under a microscope, like a slime mold! These surviving humans are as intelligent as any of their species. They are independent beings who possess the right to determine their own fate and future!"

Eyes set far apart locked on the researcher. "A fair and honest appraisal. In that light I will be certain to remind the adult of his options. I have been informed that such were presented to him on Treth, but that the manner and circumstances in which said choices were offered might not have been the most agreeable. I will try to do better." The Vrizan's command of Myssari sarcasm was commendable. "As 'civilized' beings, naturally you will offer no objection if, when presented with an alternative to living the rest of his natural life among the Myssari, he opts to voluntarily come with us and the juvenile." His tone hardened again. "The juvenile is Vrizan property. Her future is not negotiable."

Leaving behind one aide and a subordinate, the commander and his adjutant exited the conference chamber. Outside, the sun had risen high enough to turn the perpetually beleaguered sky a sick, sad shade of yellow-orange. In the conference chamber the Myssari gathered near one high, curving transparent wall. While never taking their eyes from them, the two Vrizan guards relaxed slightly.

Switching to a dialect less likely to be understood by their watchers even if they had the capability to overhear conversation at such a distance, an anxious Bac'cul immediately confronted the outpost director.

"What do you mean, you do not know where the humans are? If they are not in Ruslan's quarters, then they must be somewhere else within the outpost."

"Perhaps they heard or saw the Vrizan's arrival and, correctly interpreting their intentions, hurried themselves to the best hiding place they could imagine," an equally apprehensive Cor'rin added.

It did not bolster their confidence to see that Twi'win, now freed from confrontation with the Vrizan commander, suddenly appeared as uneasy as the two researchers.

"It is much easier to defy a captor when one only has to speak the truth. Unfortunately, that is the situation. I truly do have no idea where the humans have taken themselves. When the Vrizan appeared and made their intentions clear, the first thing I did was send armed personnel to watch over the specimens. They found

them fled. As to their present location"—she gestured with all
three hands—"what I told the foul Vrizan was true. I do not know
where they are or where they might have gone."

"Somewhere deep within the station." Bac'cul felt no relief in
his conviction. "Attempting to conceal themselves among the hy-
drologics, perhaps, or even the by-products treatment facilities."

"It will not matter in the end." A distraught Cor'rin was slowly
resigning herself to the possible loss of at least one if not both of
the two irreplaceable specimens. "You heard the commander. His
intentions as well as his species may be distasteful, but the Vrizan
are undeniably competent. They will find the humans."

"Do you think the adult will opt to go with them?" Twi'win
wanted to know. "If so, it will be a bad thing. Very bad."

"A serious loss to Myssari science," Bac'cul concurred. "He
refused their blandishments on Treth." Despite this observation
the researcher did not sound confident. "This Vrizan strikes me as
more persuasive. I cannot say what Ruslan's decision might be. He
has become settled with his life among us. But if they insist on taking the juvenile, I cannot envision a scenario where he would
abandon the only other living human he has encountered since his
youth on Seraboth."

"Kel'les might know." Cor'rin eyed her companions thoughtfully. "Where is Ruslan's handler now?"

Under guard, they could not leave the conference chamber to
look for the intermet whose permanent assignment was to look
after the human. In any event they would not have had much time
to search, because the Vrizan commander rejoined them much
sooner than expected. The agitated rustling of his leaflike cranial
appendages as well as the darkened color of his elongated visage
reflected his frustration. At any moment his annoyance threatened
to spill over into anger. His second-in-command and two additional armed aides appeared no less irritated.

"Your honesty is most irksome." Though far from expert in the
interpretation of Vrizan expressions, which were nearly as diverse

as those of humans, Bac'cul felt that it was with great effort that the commander was withholding a desire to shoot one of the restrained Myssari. *Any* one of the restrained Myssari.

"We had no reason to lie to you," Twi'win told him, demonstrating admirable poise.

Wide-spaced eyes zeroed in on her. "You had every reason to lie to us. Yet it appears you have not done so. Both the equipment we have and the personnel trained in its use have found no sign of the two humans. Nothing larger than a maggot escaped their notice. I must therefore conclude that the specimens are indeed no longer present within this illegitimate facility. This leads inevitably to the question of where they are at present."

Risking spontaneous demise, Cor'rin chirped, "Not here."

Penetrating eyes shifted their attention from the outpost's commander to the outspoken researcher. "Restating the obvious does nothing to sate my curiosity while simultaneously shortening my patience." The Vrizan came toward her. While taller and slightly more massive, he did not loom over her quite as much as did the human. "Perhaps you could be persuaded to reveal their present location?"

Sensing that his commander was on the verge of stepping beyond the bounds of propriety, his adjutant moved forward to place a limber hand on his superior's arm. As whenever a Vrizan moved, the soft supple crackling of numerous joints was plainly audible. The aide murmured something in Vrizani that the Myssari did not hear clearly. Favoring Cor'rin with a bifurcated stare that could only be described as murderous, the commander stepped back.

"Perhaps," the adjutant said, "in the absence of a visiting starship, the specimens have been moved to an orbiting station to await its arrival."

The commander gestured impatiently. "You know that the Myssari maintain several such extra-atmospheric monitors. We tolerate them because we know of them. To my knowledge all are wholly automatic and devoid of the means to sustain visitors even on a temporary basis."

"To your knowledge, yes," the aide pointed out. "It is conceivable that our knowledge is imperfect, just as it proved to be inadequate regarding the presence of surviving human lifeforms in the city of Dinabu."

"Just because our—" The commander paused sharply. "Dinabu. Of course." Returning his attention to the quietly watching Myssari, his slit of a mouth grew wider. "Where better to hide the specimens than where the immature one was found? I should congratulate you on your obviousness." He coughed orders at his subordinates, one of whom immediately commenced to spew a stream of instructions into an aural pickup. As the Vrizan moved to leave the conference chamber, the commander turned back to Twi'win and the others.

"I regret that it will be necessary to temporarily disable your communications and transportation capabilities. The respective locks and blocks that will be emplaced will automatically disengage in a day or two. By then we will have concluded our visit to your small outpost at Dinabu and, I believe, recovered our property. As to the matter of the adult human, we will discuss his future possibilities with him in a manner befitting the representatives of two *civilized* species. I promise you that no coercion will be involved. You will be informed of the outcome promptly."

As soon as they were gone Bac'cul and Cor'rin confronted the outpost director.

"Were you telling the whole truth when the shameful Vrizan queried you?" Bac'cul was beside himself at the thought of losing not only the newfound girl but Ruslan himself. "Have you had them sent to Dinabu?"

"If so they must be warned, somehow, and moved elsewhere!" Cor'rin was as distressed as her colleague. "As quickly as possible!" Her tone was anguished. "But if our transportation is disabled, how can we—"

"Would that I knew their location," a glum Twi'win interrupted the researcher. "What I told the Vrizan *was* the truth entire. I have no idea as to the present location of the two humans. This I do know: they cannot be hiding within the outpost. Vrizan technology is as advanced as our own; in certain aspects, perhaps more so. If the specimens were here, they would have been found."

Bac'cul was baffled. "Then . . . where could they be?"

The outpost director turned away from the two scientists and toward the interminable mudflats that stretched away from the research facility in every direction. "Only one conclusion is possible. If they are not hiding within the outpost, then they must be hiding without."

Cor'rin came up to stand and stare beside her. "Is that possible? Our pre-arrival studies suggested that the general environment is . . ."

"Hostile." Swiveling her head more than halfway around, Twi'win regarded her dismayed visitors. "Generally, not unrelievedly, so. While my personnel never venture outside unless they are armed and properly attired, I suppose it is conceivable that one with an intimate knowledge of the Daribbian environment might be able to survive its threats without protection."

"The juvenile!" Cor'rin exclaimed.

One of the director's hands gestured in a broad sweep at the surging, sucking surroundings outside. "As nearly all of the human presence here was concentrated in their empty cities, we have expended very little of our limited resources on the study of the mudflats themselves. Aggressive lifeforms aside, they constitute anything but a hospitable environment. The great majority of our work has focused on the derelict urban centers."

"Whereas humans who lived and matured here must have been forced to learn everything they could about *all* of their surroundings." Bac'cul's voice was full of rising hope. "We must begin a search of the immediate area!"

"How?" Twi'win regarded the researcher with a mixture of

compassion and frustration. "With our transportation immobilized we cannot cover any significant ground. We will have to wait until the driftecs are operational once again."

Cor'rin's frustration was palpable. "We cannot just squat here waiting for the Vrizan to return! And they will return, once they have finished fruitlessly scouring Dinabu for signs of the two specimens."

"Let them." Twi'win sounded anything but accommodating. "If they come back we will be ready for them. Prepared, I am confident my staff can stand them off. Next time they will not have the element of surprise."

"But," Bac'cul protested, "what about the humans?"

Already ambling toward the lift that would take her back down into the body of the outpost, the director looked back at him. "We can only hope they are safe and that when our driftecs are once more operational, we can find them before the Vrizan do." With her assistants in tow she entered the waiting lift and was gone.

Left to themselves, Bac'cul and Cor'rin turned their attention back to the vast mudflats above which the outpost stood, a lonely sentinel of civilization in an environment as intimidating as it was unpleasant.

"We could take Kel'les and go look for the humans ourselves," he suggested hesitantly.

"How?" She indicated the flat, yellow-brown horizon. "There are no landmarks, nothing to suggest which way they might have gone. If they were close by and standing erect, or even crouching, do you not think the meticulous Vrizan would have spotted them? If they could not locate them with instruments, how could we possibly find them on our own? If Ruslan and the child were walking on gliders, the Vrizan would surely have taken notice."

Bac'cul's mind was racing. "Humans have fewer joints than us but thicker bones and heavier muscles. It is conceivable they could make more progress without gliders and on foot than Myssari or Vrizan."

"Except that one of them is a juvenile, short and undeveloped."

"Trueso." Once again Bac'cul returned his gaze to the bleak, utterly flat landscape that surrounded them. "Then we are left with our original uncertainty: where are they?"

"Not in the belly of some indigenous predator, one hopes. If that is the case, then all our defensive posturing and all the belligerence of the Vrizan hold no more meaning than what can be found in a specimen cup of this all-pervasive muck."

12

———

The Myssari technician who was running the checkout on the organic recycling system was as relieved as the rest of his colleagues at the departure of the belligerent Vrizan. Though the majority of personnel had suffered no contact with the intruders, everyone knew that they had temporarily taken control of the station. All staff had been instructed to stand aside and not interfere as the Vrizan had conducted an incredibly thorough inspection of the outpost's facilities, though to what end and for what purpose most of the workers had no idea.

It was not important, the tech told herself. The Vrizan were gone now. All that mattered to her and her associates was that the intruders had left without doing any damage. They had been in a foul mood when they had arrived and had apparently encountered nothing to ameliorate their emotions by the time they departed. Wishing them all infected fundaments, she and her colleagues had resumed their daily work schedule as soon as the Vrizan had taken their leave.

Since no alarm or alert had sounded to indicate that they had returned, the tech was more than mildly startled when the exterior portal just ahead and to the right of her normal inspection track began to open from the outside. She immediately found herself debating whether or not to sound a warning. Surely if the Vrizan had come back, their approach, not to mention their actual arrival, would have been broadcast throughout the outpost? That left few alternative explanations for what she was seeing. To the best of her knowledge, there were no maintenance crews working on the exterior of this side of the facility. Those that were operating outside were doing so on the opposite side of the station from where she was standing. There was no reason for one or more members of those maintenance crews to be on this side. Additionally, if someone was having a problem with reentry, she and everyone else would have been notified to look out for them and to be ready to render assistance as needed.

All her excellent reasoning notwithstanding, the doorway continued to slide sideways into its receptacle. Diluted hazy sunlight poured in through the opening that resulted. She held off sounding an alarm. It was probably nothing. Declaring a false emergency would open her to station-wide ridicule.

Just as she had decided that the door opening was purely accidental, two figures stepped through the gap and into the accessway. Beyond the fact that they stood upright, she could recognize nothing about them. Completely covered in muck from the mudflats, all details of their true shapes were masked. Whatever facial features they possessed were turned away from the tech.

Daribbian indigenes! she thought wildly. If these were anything like their fellow creatures, they were doubtless both dangerous and hostile. She immediately voiced an alarm to her aural pickup.

It turned out to be the wrong decision. The ridicule she had hoped to avoid soon followed, though it was all good-natured.

Though the relief expressed by Bac'cul, Cor'rin, and Kel'les, not to mention Director Twi'win, at the safe return of the two specimens was expressive, the humans themselves seemed to care for nothing save access to a mist rinse. Only when they had thoroughly cleansed themselves of the mud that had provided them refuge did Ruslan take the time to explain where they had been and how they had avoided detection by the swarming Vrizan.

"Cherpa deserves all the credit." Seated in the relaxation lounge with a cold drink at hand, he was happy to relate the circumstances of their survival. "I didn't want to go outside, unarmed, but it was obvious that if we were going to avoid the Vrizan we had no other choice. So I followed her lead." He nodded toward the far side of the mood-changing chamber, where the girl was playing with her doll while finger-painting three-dimensional patterns on the wall. That the ever-changing scenes being displayed were of Myssari and not human-settled worlds did not matter to her. She found each and every one new and fascinating.

"But you were outside, and at *night*." Bac'cul could not keep the astonishment from his voice.

"The best knowledge is always local knowledge, I suppose. Once we managed to make our way some distance from the outpost—farther than I would have liked, I have to admit—we spent the rest of the night buried in the mud on our backs and being very, very still. For all I know, a hundred predators could have taken our measure and decided that we weren't worth the trouble, or that we were too alien to be considered digestible prey." He turned to Cor'rin. "Having spent more hours than I care to remember immersed in alien muck, I suppose the three of us should be checked for possible contamination, although I would think a human body would be an unsuitable host for local parasitic organisms."

"Still, a reasonable precaution," she agreed.

Bac'cul gestured uncertainly. "Excuse me, Ruslan: the *three* of you?"

Once more the human nodded in the direction of the wholly preoccupied girl. "To contribute to the juven— to Cherpa's mental health, you should at every opportunity treat her doll, the small human effigy she is never without, as a 'real' individual. She sees it as such. It's a function of a lingering traumatic childhood. It's also the only family she's got."

Cor'rin gestured understanding. "The information will be posted forefront in her records."

They were interrupted by the arrival of the director. It was shocking, Ruslan mused, how fundamentally Twi'win's attitude toward the visitors had changed since their discovery of Cherpa. It would have boded well for the future development of human-Myssari relations on Daribb . . . had there been any other humans on Daribb for the Myssari to relate to. Or any humans anywhere else, for that matter. Rejoining them, she settled herself down against a narrow Myssari seat. Her eyes were bright, her speech rapid.

"Details of the Vrizan intrusion have been reported to the appropriate authorities. There will be repercussions, albeit on a modest scale since no one was harmed, no permanent damage was done to the facility here, and nothing—such as invaluable live specimens—was taken." She glanced in the direction of the happily playing girl before turning to the attentive Ruslan. "Arrangements are in motion to get you and the juvenile off Daribb and to a Myssari world as quickly as possible."

"And Oola," Cor'rin added. "Do not forget Oola. She is human family as well."

The director gave the researcher a hard look but decided to seek explication later. "Ruslan, will you make ready the juvenile? Daribb being the only world she has ever known, it may well be that some significant mental preparation may be required in order for her to acquiesce comfortably to the departure."

He looked past the sharp-featured alien to where a delighted Cherpa was busily rearranging landscapes on the far wall. "I think your apprehension may be misplaced, Twi'win. She strikes me as extremely adaptable. She'd have to be, to survive here alone for we don't know how many years. Don't worry, though. I'll make sure she isn't going to throw a fit moments before we board for orbit. She'll be ready. I know I'll be." The unwanted attention of the Vrizan aside, he couldn't wait to get off this inhospitable, empty planet. He rose.

"In fact, I'll get started right now."

Leaving the four Myssari to their consultations, he walked over to where Cherpa, with the use of one finger, was presently sliding mountains into place to serve as the backdrop for an alpine lake. He studied the resultant vista.

"That's very pretty, Cherpa. Where is it?"

"Planet Here." She grinned and tapped the side of her head. "I've had lots of time to imagine places I'd like to be. This is one of them."

Unexpectedly, he felt his throat tightening as he surveyed a scene reminiscent of the mountains of Seraboth, and hastened to change the subject. "We're going to have to leave this place. Leave Daribb and go somewhere where the Vrizan people who just came for you and me can't find us."

"Okay."

So much for the need to prepare acquiescence and ensure mental stability, he thought dryly.

"You're sure you're all right with leaving behind . . . everything?"

"There isn't everything." Her tone was somber. "There's nothing. Not here. There are only things that want to eat you. I'd be real happy to go someplace where nothing wants to eat me." She hesitated. "Only one thing's-a-thing elsewise to take along though, maybe, perhaps."

Another toy to bring, he decided. Or a favorite piece of clothing, or some physical reminder of her family. He waited for the details. They were not what he had been expecting.

"Maybe we should bring the other person, too."

Confusion swirled his thoughts. "Another? There's another person?" Realization made him smile. "Oh, you mean Oola. Of course we're taking her with us."

Cherpa tucked the doll tighter against her. "Not Oola. Pahksen."

Pahksen? This was the first mention of any "Pahksen." Bearing in mind the girl's fragile mental state, Ruslan found himself wondering if the other "person" she was referring to might be imaginary. It was almost to be expected that someone her age in her condition would have invented an imaginary friend for company. Given ample time, he would have slowly and gently confronted her with the likelihood. With them waiting to be called for departure at any moment, he had no leeway for patience. He asked her straight out.

She shook her head and made a face. "Pahksen's not imaginary. Though lots of times I wish he was."

For a second time since he had arrived on Daribb, the faint stirring of a long-held hope was swiftly whisked away. "He," she had said. Ruslan set about questioning her further.

"Let me make sure I understand, Cherpa. You're saying there's another live human here?" It was not impossible that she was referring to a dead body she had named. An isolated child, much less one forced to endure her circumstances, could conceivably make a "friend" of anything. But she nodded affirmatively and without hesitation.

"But," he continued, "neither I nor any of the Myssari ever saw this person. If there's just the two of you left, I would think you'd try to stay together and help each other."

"I guess that makes sense," she admitted. "Except I don't make sense and Pahksen doesn't make sense and if you put the two of us together you'd have double nonsense, wouldn't you?" The face she had made earlier returned. "I don't like him and he doesn't like me, so we didn't spend much time together. Only when we had no choice. The difference is that I like lots of things and Pahksen, he doesn't like *anything*. He's nasty." She hugged her doll. "He said for someone my age to keep Oola with me all the time was stupid. *Stupid!*" She stared up at him. "You don't think it's stupid, do you, Bogo?"

"No . . . of course not."

Nasty or not, he thought furiously, the existence of a second surviving human would only further confirm the previously underappreciated work of the outpost's automatic scouts. When informed, Bac'cul and Cor'rin would be delirious with joy. The costly journey to Daribb could be classed as doubly successful. As for this as yet unmet Pahksen's purported irritability, as someone who had been known to suffer from bouts of unpleasantness himself, Ruslan was confident he could deal with him. What was critical now was to find and recover the second survivor before the Vrizan could do so.

"I'm guessing you and this Pahksen crossed paths in Dinabu, right?"

"Din . . . ?" For a moment she looked puzzled. Then she brightened. "Oh, you mean hometown. Yes, of course. I showed you how to move through the mud. I can move faster than that, but not fast enough to make it safely to another hometown."

He hardly dared ask, but had to. "If we go back to Dinabu for a, um, last visit, do you think you would be able to find Pahksen?"

With each of the girl's positive nods, he saw another honor accruing to his researcher friends. For such alien honors, he himself cared nothing. In contrast, the chance to meet with another human being was everything. To see another face, hear another voice, make contact with another person—that was everything. This Pahksen could be as disagreeable as he wished. Ruslan was positive he could eventually effect a change in the other's personality.

———

If anything, he underestimated the response among the Myssari. Twi'win and her staff were as energized at the prospect of recovering another live human as Bac'cul and Cor'rin. As a freshly constituted and well-armed team set off once more for the city of Dinabu, their greatest fear was that the ever-attentive Vrizan might already have located and extricated the human Pahksen. Cherpa seemed far less concerned at the likelihood.

"Pahksen's different from me but also like me. One way we're a lot alike is that we both know how to hide."

Cor'rin glanced at the girl across the interior of the masked driftec as it skimmed along above the mudflats. "The Vrizan—the other people who will be looking for him—have very advanced ways of finding people."

Cherpa stared right back at the Myssari scientist. "Hide we know. You wouldn't have found me if Bogo hadn't heard the sounds of me being attacked. I wouldn't be surprised to learn that Pahksen had been watching the whole time."

Ruslan's expression darkened. "You mean he could have been watching the fight, seen the danger you were in, and still made no move to help you?"

She shrugged as if the imagined scenario was of no consequence. "I told you: Pahksen, he's nasty. He wouldn't risk his life for me. That's okay." In the context of what she said next, her bright smile was more than a little disconcerting. "I wouldn't risk mine to save his, either."

Two surviving human beings on the entire planet, Ruslan thought, *and they can't stand each other. A fitting metaphor for the entire species.* For all that, he was looking forward to meeting this reprehensible Pahksen. *If* they could find him.

Deliberative scans from the slowing driftecs revealed a heartening absence of Vrizan and Vrizan craft, either occupied or automatic. That did not mean, he told himself as he prepared to disembark, that the cunning competitors of the Myssari were not present. But it was better than having alarms go off in the presence of a dozen watching craft.

They set down not far from the port area where Ruslan had first encountered Cherpa. This time all personnel, including the two researchers from Myssar, disembarked with weapons in hand. Twi'win was taking no chances with either dangerous indigenous lifeforms or possible marauding Vrizan. Not with the irreplaceable Ruslan and Cherpa in their midst. With the girl and her doll leading the way, the generous deployment from the outpost pushed past the outskirts and into the depths of the long-silent city.

They spent the day rummaging through collapsing buildings, sites overgrown with crawling gunk, and long-abandoned vehicles. While Daribb's diminutive but voracious flora and fauna had devoured tens of thousands of bones, there were still numerous bodies scattered about. The sight did not unnerve either Cherpa or Ruslan. Each had grown up on a world littered with the skeletal detritus of their kind. Neither was a stranger to the apocalyptic aftermath of the Aura Malignance.

As night fell they were forced to return to the safety of the temporary shelters that had been set up alongside the driftecs. Though the Myssari outpost was a scientific and not a military installation, its technicians had managed to come up with some convincing camouflage, both physical and electronic, to screen the visitors from possible Vrizan scrutiny. Continued anonymity would be the only way of gauging the effectiveness of the improvised effort.

Despite Cherpa's best efforts at tracking, in three days of intensive searching they found no sign of another live human being. Ruslan was beginning to wonder anew if her male acquaintance was, as he had earlier suspected, only imaginary. Or if she really wanted them to find someone with whom she admittedly did not get along.

On the fourth day of searching, they still had not found him— but something found them.

It was very large, very active, and repulsively amorphous. Rising out of an expanding breach in a disintegrating city street, it looked at first as if a thick perceptive glob of the surrounding mudflats had somehow acquired sentience and decided to go on the rampage. Only after more of its columnar, elastic body emerged from the gap did Ruslan and the hastily scattering Myssari realize that it comprised a single entity. Multiple brown pseudopods flailed at the evasive, scuttling escorts. The Myssari were not fast, but they were quick, and their trisymmetrical forms made it difficult for a predator to predict which direction they were going to run.

"Mushwack!" Cherpa screamed as she ran. Despite his longer legs it was an effort for Ruslan to keep up with her.

Behind them the Myssari were firing repeatedly into the building-sized body of the creature. As bursts from their weapons struck the twisting, writhing form, gaseous bubbles rose and burst from its epidermis. The smell that arose from the vicinity of these strikes was beyond sickening. Survivors of dead worlds rife with decomposition, the two humans dealt with the miasma better than the Myssari, some of whom were forced to turn away and retch. It was left to their more resilient companions to finally drive the creature back down into the opening from which it had emerged.

There were no deaths, but several of the Myssari had suffered bad falls while avoiding the *mushwack*'s grasping limbs. Thankfully, none of the injuries were life-threatening. With their injured treated and bandaged, the remaining members of the expedition were soon ready, if not particularly eager, to resume the search.

They were preparing to head deeper still into the shell of the city when Ruslan felt Cherpa tugging on his left arm. Her left, of course, was reserved for cradling Oola.

"He's here," she said simply.

Quickly he looked around, scanning their immediate surroundings. He saw nothing but ruins. Taking note, Bac'cul and Cor'rin moved closer to the specimens.

"What is it, Ruslan?" Cor'rin's own narrower gaze strove to mimic the human's.

"Cherpa says he's here."

Tired from the brief but intense battle with the *mushwack*, both researchers were rejuvenated by his words. "Where? I see nothing," a rapidly pivoting Bac'cul declared.

"Nor do I." Ruslan bent toward the girl. "Where is he, Cherpa?"

Raising an arm, she pointed. "Up there. That open-sided building, second floor." She raised her voice. "Come out, Pahksen! I see you! These are my new friends. I'm going away with them, away from this place, forever. To a place where there are no bad things. Where nothing will try to eat you." Reaching over, she put her arm around Ruslan's waist, startling him. It was a very adult gesture. "Look—another one of us! A grown-up! Come down, if you want this to be the last *mushwack* you ever see."

Nothing moved. Ruslan, the researchers, their escorts, all were staring at the gaping second floor where Cherpa had pointed. Squint as he might, he could discern nothing but abandoned furniture and crumbling superstructure. Then part of the superstructure stood up. Without speaking, it jumped from the second floor onto a mound of debris. Emerging from the resultant cloud of dust, a figure came toward them. The nearer it came, the larger it grew, until it stood confronting Ruslan. Indisputably, there were now three live humans gathered on the debris-littered walkway. Bac'cul and Cor'rin were recording like mad, euphoric at the sight of a third live human. Crowding close to Ruslan, Cherpa was clearly less than overjoyed.

Far more than a boy, not yet quite a man, Pahksen was as tall as Ruslan. No more than seventeen or so, Ruslan decided. Youth and adult regarded each other: the latter with appreciation, the former with suspicion. Remembering how it was done, Ruslan extended a hand.

"Pleasure to meet another survivor. My name's Ruslan."

"Pahksen." No hand reached out to accept the older man's offering. Whether this constituted a deliberate snub, indicated general wariness, or was because both of the youth's hands were needed to support the very large rifle he was holding Ruslan could not say. He fully intended to find out later.

Pahksen's blond hair was long, nowhere near as long as Cherpa's had before it had been cut back at the outpost. He was lanky as a willow tree, all lean muscle and darting blue eyes. These danced methodically over Ruslan and Cherpa before pausing to consider the watching Myssari. Eventually they returned to Cherpa. She did not move toward her fellow survivor but neither did she retreat, comfortable as she was in Ruslan's presence.

"The man's a man, sure, but what are all these other ugly things?"

"They're called Myssari," she told him. "They're good people." Her gaze flicked upward to the face of the individual whose waist she held. "They helped Ruslan. He's from another world called Seraboth."

"Never heard of it." Pahksen continued to hold the power rifle as though he might opt to utilize it at any moment. While Ruslan would have preferred that the youth deactivate it, he did not begrudge him the ongoing tension. Introductions were still in progress, and something like the *mushwack* or the aggressive natives might put in an appearance at any time.

"He's been with these funny three-legs for a long time," Cherpa explained. "He says their homeworld is a nice place to live, they make sure he has anything he wants, and they appreciate all the help he's given them while they try to learn everything they can about our kind. He says they'll do the same for me, and I believe him. Anyway, it's nasty here. You know that. I don't suppose it could be nastier where they live."

"Unless he's lying." The youth's gaze, which was inordinately intense, focused sharply on Ruslan. "How about it, old man? You lying?"

Ruslan was not sure which bothered him more: the fact that the youth continued to grip the rifle as if at any moment he might choose to turn it on his rescuers or the fact that he had been referred to as an old man.

"You don't want to shake my hand, fine. You don't want to believe me or Cherpa, that's fine, too. Much as the Myssari want you to join us, no one's going to force you. You can stay here and deal with the local lifeforms on your own, if that's your wish. I'm offering you respect and comfort for the rest of your life, free of worry about where your next meal is coming from or about becoming something else's meal yourself. It's entirely your choice."

For the first time, the muzzle of the rifle dropped toward the ground. "And what do they want in return? Every lifeform-to-lifeform exchange is a trade-off."

"The Myssari desire only information. Like any civilized species, being of a curious nature they seek to learn about the unknown. Until we outsmarted ourselves, humankind was a respectable species. Daribb isn't an isolated world, you know."

"I know that." Pahksen fairly spat his reply. "D'you think I'm stupid?"

Naturally confrontational, Ruslan wondered, or a learned trait? He would hopefully have ample time to find out. Whichever, it was an attitude that could be corrected. Good food and safe surroundings would work to mollify the youth's hostility.

"We're all gone. Every last million of us. Except, apparently, for we three standing here, right now, this minute. The Myssari are very curious about us, about our civilization. They're at least as smart as we are. Or were. But there are aspects to human culture no study of records and artifacts, no matter how passionate, can properly parse. That's where I've come in. I've helped with explanations. You can, too, you and Cherpa. You'll outlive me and be even more valuable to them." He looked around. "You can join in helping the Myssari to understand us, or you can stay here and retain ownership of . . . all this."

A few small, unseen creatures continued their scampering

among the ruins. For a long moment their calls were all that was heard echoing among the crumbling walls and pavements. To Ruslan's relief the youth finally eased his aggressive grip on the rifle, setting the butt down on the ground.

"I'm not sure I believe in any of this," the younger man muttered. "But I believe in what I can see. You're real enough, and you look healthy enough. I don't know if that means that these things are treating you as well as you say or that they're fattening you for an eventual meal, but Cherpa's no dummy." He eyed the girl, who did everything but stick her tongue out at him. "If she's going with you and voluntarily, then there must be something to what you say." He shrugged. "Anyway, it'd be a change."

Cor'rin had edged forward until she was standing very close to Ruslan. Now she whispered to him. "Is the new human coming with us or not? We can sedate him if you think it would facilitate matters."

"Temporarily it would," he answered in Myssarian. "It might also mean the end of any eventual cooperation once he was revived. Let's proceed without such measures, at least for the moment. Yes, he has agreed to come with us, though he is exhibiting a remarkable lack of enthusiasm. I'm hoping time and good treatment will ease his concerns." Turning back to the frowning Pahksen, who had understood none of the conversation between man and Myssari, he provided an explanation.

"The individual to whom I've been speaking is Cor'rin. She's a scientist." Turning, he pointed. "That's Bac'cul, her colleague. The rest of the Myssari work at a scientific station not terribly far from here. We can leave to go there now, unless there are objects of a personal nature you'd like to take with you."

Pahksen pursed his lips, thinking. "Can I bring my gun?"

"Of course," Ruslan assured him expansively. "Bring anything you want. The Myssari are not fearful of you, and you have no reason to be afraid of them."

"I'm alive because I'm afraid," the youth shot back. "I'm even afraid when I'm asleep. If you had to live like I have, you'd be the same way."

Though I wouldn't be as surly toward my fellow humans, Ruslan thought. *Patience.* The youngster was understandably twitchy. Time and Myssari good treatment would smooth down the rough edges.

"Anything besides the weapon?" Ruslan asked him.

"A few small things. I'll be right back."

Moving with the grace of a longer-limbed predecessor primate, he disappeared back into the rubble only to return sooner than Ruslan had expected. A bag of some green synthetic material was slung over one shoulder. Time enough later to inquire about the contents, Ruslan knew. The important thing now was to get him and Cherpa back to the outpost, and both of them off Daribb before Vrizan belligerence had a reason to reassert itself. He smiled at the thought.

The multi-jointed bipeds would be more than upset to know that not one but two surviving humans had been living right under their collective if nearly nonexistent noses. Ruslan had no intention of thumbing his own at them.

As far as he was concerned, everything revolved around securing a comfortable future for three surviving humans. If this provoked a serious clash of science and diplomacy between two alien civilizations, so be it. If he had learned anything at all from the decades he had spent among the Myssari, it was that it was always best, where and when possible, to reduce matters of seemingly great import to the most basic equations.

13

———

To the best of Ruslan's knowledge, the Vrizan never learned how not one but two human survivors had been spirited off Daribb. There was a moment of tension when the ship that had been diverted to pick up the Myssari scientific team was queried by one of the Vrizanian automated satellites, but it passed swiftly enough when the orbiting station accepted the explanation that the arriving starship was simply engaging in a routine replenishment of supplies and exchange of personnel.

It was not until he was back on Myssar that Ruslan finally relaxed. Or rather, relaxed as much as Cherpa would permit. From the moment she stepped into the orbital lift, a stream of questions and exclamations spilled from her lips that no volume of responses was able to quench. Striving his best to satisfy her, he achieved only partial success. Between the girl's boundless curiosity and sometimes convoluted reasoning and Pahksen's unshakable paranoia, Ruslan had very little time left to himself.

So it was that when Kel'les informed him that Bac'cul and Cor'rin desired his solo presence in the antechamber of his continuously monitored home, he was actually thankful for a few moments away from the two youthful Daribbian survivors.

"We appreciate everything you are doing to please the female and placate the younger male," Bac'cul assured him. "Your participation in acclimatizing them to wholly Myssari surroundings has been invaluable."

Ruslan tried not to smirk. "If you mean that I managed to get Pahksen to finally surrender his gun, yeah, I'll take credit for that."

He had eventually succeeded in doing so by convincing the suspicious youth that he could retrieve his weapon whenever he wished, simply by making the request. That was not true, of course. Accommodating though they might be, the Myssari had no intention of allowing a member of another species, however irreplaceable, to go wandering about Myssar in possession of a killing weapon. If a citizen were to be injured by the alien apparatus, even accidentally, it could cause untold damage to the ongoing program of human studies. It was enough that Pahksen believed he could have his gun back at any time.

"They appear to be adapting quite well," Cor'rin added. "What is your current opinion?"

Ruslan considered. "Cherpa doesn't understand everything she's being shown or told, but I'm convinced full understanding will come with time. It may matter to you that she adapts to everything immediately, but it doesn't matter to her. One reason she was able to survive as a lone child on Daribb was that she invented her own private world. She was able to retreat into herself, into her own mind. She still does it on occasion but I can see her resorting to it less and less. The same is as true of human offspring as it is of Myssari: the younger they are, the easier they adapt to new circumstances. I believe she's doing extremely well and will prove a great help to your research programs for a long time to come."

"And the older youth, the male?" Cor'rin pressed him.

Ruslan hesitated. "He's still chary of everything. I can't go so far as to say that he's less mistrustful than he was on Daribb, but he's certainly no worse."

The three Myssari exchanged a glance.

"That is less than encouraging. I had hoped for better results to pass along to the Sectionary." Bac'cul was plainly unhappy.

"What else can we do to reassure him?" Kel'les asked. "He refuses a minder."

"I'll keep trying to put him at ease." Ruslan tried to sound optimistic. "The best thing you can do is the same thing you did with me: give him whatever he wants, within reason, and when you have to refuse a request be sure to provide an explanation. The more comfortable he becomes with his surroundings, the more he'll relax, and the more he relaxes, the more he'll come to accept his new life here."

Ruslan found the next exchange of glances bemusing. The Myssari were hesitating about something. He turned to Kel'les, who could not refuse a question from him.

"Am I missing something here? Is there something I'm not being told?"

The intermet started to reply but ended up deferring to Cor'rin. She explained with unusual care.

"We are under pressure from the General Science Sectionary to begin the resurrection of your species. As you will remember, the project was to proceed with or without your consent, via cloning if necessary." In the absence of an Adam's apple, it was difficult to tell if she was swallowing nervously. "The acquisition of two young humans of breeding age renders the need to clone not only superfluous but—"

"Just a goddamn minute—if you please," he added, remembering Myssari civil protocol. "First of all, while Pahksen may or may not be of breeding age, Cherpa certainly is not. Second of all, they don't happen to much like each other."

"You will fix that." Was Bac'cul's observation a statement of hope, Ruslan wondered, or an order? His tone turned emphatic.

"I can supply information. I can answer questions. I can't work miracles. Anyway, it's far too soon to contemplate the two of them engaging in . . ." He searched for the right words. ". . . natural reproduction. You don't even know if either one of them is fertile."

"The male is." Cor'rin did not hesitate. "An examination was carried out while he slept."

Now, that'll make him less distrustful, a pained Ruslan thought. "I'd keep that particular information from him just now." He realized he was almost afraid to ask the next question. No, not afraid, he corrected himself. Queasy. "Did you also 'examine' Cherpa?"

"We refrained," Bac'cul told him. Ruslan was unaccountably relieved. His stomach settled. "Bearing in mind not what you have told us so much as information about such matters that we have gleaned from our years of research into human biology."

Kel'les was no less curious than the more highly trained colleagues. "Are you saying, Ruslan, that mutual dislike makes it physically impossible for them to breed?"

"No," the human muttered, "I'm not saying that at all. I'm just saying that now is not the time. It's far too early to schedule the process." His gaze switched back and forth between the two scientists. "I know that when Cherpa comes of age, you can remove eggs from her and sperm from Pahksen whether they agree to the respective extractions or not. What I am trying to convey is that it will be of more interest to you and better for the future of human revivification if you allow the process to proceed naturally."

"And if it does not?" Bac'cul was staring at him evenly.

Ruslan shut his eyes. "Then I can't stop you from doing what your superiors order you to do. I can object, but I can't stop it. I know that." Opening his eyes, he regarded the both of them once more. "There's a proper way of letting such things eventuate and a wrong way. From a technical standpoint both can produce the end result you wish. I'm just saying it would be better, and more beneficial in the end, to do it the proper way."

The Myssari triumvirate was silent until Cor'rin spoke up. "We will relay everything you have said to the Sectionary. I believe Yah'thom, at least, will back you up. Whether that will be enough to sway the majority opinion I do not know." She eyed her co-workers. "There are those who are impatient to commence this."

"Where science is concerned, impatience can work for good or for bad." Bac'cul's comforting words notwithstanding, the male researcher was clearly more ambivalent than his partners. "Every suggestion you have made in the course of our research has proven itself worthwhile. We will hope that this latest of yours meets with the same approval when it is communicated to our superiors. Meanwhile you will of course continue your work with the two young humans in helping them to adapt to their new lives on Myssar."

As if he had any choice, he thought, despite all the fine words and gifts and promises. But he did not voice his reaction out loud.

14

———

There was no reason for them to visit Tespo. There were better beaches close to Pe'leoek than the one that fronted the extensive coastal scientific complex. Instead, for today's sojourn Ruslan opted to take his two charges to Velet. Though the group of small, sandy islands lay some sixty kilometers offshore from the capital city, they were as close as the nearest public teleport platform.

In the five years since they had been *rescued* (it sounded so much better than "abducted," the ever-cynical Ruslan thought) from Daribb, both young survivors had matured mentally as well as physically. Pahksen was now taller than Ruslan. With access to proper nutrition for the first time in his life, the once lanky adolescent had also filled out considerably. While still subscribing to a certain degree of the guardedness that had initially defined him, thanks to Ruslan's efforts and the unending kindness of the Myssari he had mellowed from his feral hunter-gatherer days on Daribb. As for his younger counterpart . . .

If Ruslan and Pahksen were minor celebrities within the Myssari Combine, Cherpa was all but venerated. Wherever they went, every local desired to be recorded in her company, or touch the famous auburn follicles that had grown out (though not to knee length this time), or listen to her distinctive human laugh. Something about the melodious sound, so different from the far more subdued Myssari vocalizations of amusement, struck the humans' hosts as irresistible. Ruslan quite understood. The girl's laughter had nearly the same effect on him.

As had Pahksen, she had also matured physically. Her physical transformation was a wonderment to the Myssari, who knew of such changes only from the recordings they had salvaged from now-uninhabited human worlds. While many of those historical records featured perfectly preserved three-dimensional reproductions, they could not in any way begin to match the reality.

Yet always lurking in the background was the insistence of the Sectionary for Human History and Culture that the resurrection of the species be initiated. Twice a year Ruslan had to go, with Kel'les and Bac'cul and Cor'rin by his side, to plead before Yah'thom's contemporaries that the time had not yet arrived for natural reproduction to commence and that instigating it via artificial insemination of surgically removed eggs and sperm would likely have deleterious effects on the pair of progenitors. Each time, he and his friends managed to persuade the senior scientists to postpone said proceedings for another half year.

Such efforts could not succeed forever, he knew. Through their extensive research into human affairs, the Sectionary knew as well as he did when young humans reached sexual maturity and became capable of reproduction. Only his insistence that rushing matters could result in permanent psychological damage managed to sustain an increasingly tenuous status quo.

It helped that while the relationship between Pahksen and Cherpa had improved since their removal from Daribb, it gave no indication of edging toward intimacy. Ruslan often thought that the two youths had little in common besides their humanity. That could still change with time, he knew. While Pahksen was now in his early twenties, Cherpa was only sixteen or so, their exact ages being unverifiable. Though the young man's interests had broadened upon his arrival on Myssar and his exposure to Myssari civilization, none appeared to include romance. This simultaneously puzzled and relieved Ruslan.

Of course, it could all change tomorrow, he told himself. A touch, a glance, a spark, would be all that would be necessary to light the fuse. Then—fireworks. The Sectionary would be pleased.

Today, however, was all about unvisited islands, warm water, and exotic flora and fauna. Velet was a popular getaway among the citizens of Pe'leoek, but at this time of the year it ought not to be crowded. He told himself the day trip was for Pahksen's and Cherpa's benefit, but in reality it was as much for him as for them. As ever, the oceans of Myssar continued to remind him of the slightly less salty seas of Seraboth.

They dispensed with clothing as soon as they arrived. Neither of the two youths had been inculcated with anything resembling a nudity phobia, and the few locals who saw them regarded the naked bodies no differently from when they were clad. To the enchanted Myssari, both genders of the famous human survivors appeared equally exotic.

Cherpa was first into the water, splashing and laughing, trying to catch the spongy, nearly transparent bubble-like forms of startled *basetch* as they rose from the disturbed surface and tried to drift out of her way. Pahksen entered the shallow turquoise sea more deliberately, projecting a dignity that was heartfelt if somewhat misplaced. Seated on the beach of bright pink and green olivine sand, a contented Ruslan leaned back on his elbows and looked on. Beside him, Kel'les had lowered his body down into the center of the tripod formed by his legs. Ruslan smiled at the sight. No matter how many years he lived among the Myssari, he would never be able to think of a squatting individual as anything other than a triangular head in a basket.

"They have adapted very well as they have grown."

Ruslan glanced at his friend. "The young always have an easier time of it." He indicated the only other pair of human shapes on Myssar. Both were taut of body and sleek with youth. "Pahksen knows more about your technology than I ever would, and Cherpa speaks better Myssari than—well, than most Myssari."

"She has a natural feel for linguistics," Kel'les confirmed. "Did you know that she now speaks the major Vrizan and Hahk'na dialects as well?"

Ruslan's eyebrows rose. "I knew she was working with Vrizani. I didn't know she had been studying Hahk'nan."

"Oh. I hope I have not spoiled a surprise."

"I don't think so." Ruslan turned his gaze back toward the water. The glare moderated accordingly. The aging lenses of his eyes had been replaced by Myssari technicians several years ago. He could override their programming by simply thinking about it. Experts at rejuvenating their own bodies, the Myssari considered the devising of replacement parts for humans an engineering challenge. His left hip was artificial as well, a perfect reproduction built up of calcium- and phosphorus-based organosynth compounds. The resulting construction fooled not only his brain but his circulatory and nervous systems as well. Young and healthy, Cherpa and Pahksen had not yet required any such surgical interventions.

Kel'les gestured toward an irregular object lying on the sand nearby. "Despite her increasing maturity the female still maintains possession of the effigy."

Ruslan regarded the doll. "It's all she has of her childhood. Probably a gift from one of her parents. I never asked."

"Nor will I," Kel'les admitted. "As you know, the Myssari hold personal privacy in high regard."

For other Myssari, Ruslan thought. *Not so much for valuable specimens.*

"Your love of immersing yourselves in water continues to astonish us," his minder continued. Given the Myssari body design, all angles and awkwardness, Ruslan understood their innate hydrophobia. Myssari physicality was admirably suited to numerous activities, but swimming was not among them. They were the antithesis of streamlined.

"I regret to say that the General Sectionary's impatience continues unabated."

"With regard to what?" Having heard the declaration many times before, Ruslan was sure he knew the answer, but wanted to hear it from Kel'les's mouth.

"I think you know," his minder continued, confirming all suspicions. "It concerns the matter of commencing human repopulation through natural means. With each half year that passes, the forces clamoring for intensive cloning are strengthened. This is especially so since the female has reached reproductive status."

It was too beautiful a day and setting to serve as a slave to the inexorable. "Surely we can put off the Sectionary for another year or so." Something small, green, and many-winged landed on his right big toe. He brushed at it idly and it flew off on a complaining whistle.

"I was told you would say that."

He chuckled. "So the Sectionary has become so expert in predicting human responses that they can now divine what I'm going to say?"

"They are studious, and the staff has not been idle." Once again Kel'les indicated the two young, strong humans relaxing in the water. "However, it was decided, once again, not to force the issue."

"Glad to hear it." Ruslan considered the matter settled. But it was not.

"In their desire to accelerate the course of natural events, the

Sectionary has decided that placing the youths in more familiar surroundings might induce—or even inspire—them to initiate the process of natural reproduction."

That got Ruslan's attention. "You don't mean the Sectionary intends to send them back to Daribb?"

Kel'les was alarmed. "Nothing so foolish! If nothing else, the Vrizan are still there. But it was noted that there are numerous empty worlds on which the old human infrastructure is far better preserved than on Daribb. Seraboth, for example."

"The Aura Malignance—" Ruslan began, only to have Kel'les atypically cut him off.

"Your homeworld has been thoroughly scrutinized. No sign of the great plague nor its virulent method of dispersal has ever been found on Seraboth. It died out when the last vulnerable hosts—the entire human population except yourself—expired. Seraboth is clean and has been so for some time. The surviving infrastructure there is far better preserved than on Daribb or comparable other worlds." The intermet gestured toward the young humans frolicking in the tepid sea. "It would be a suitable place to reestablish your kind." Small bright eyes met Ruslan's. "You, of course, could opt to remain on Myssar, where your honorary citizenship will never expire."

"It's not my choice to say," he finally replied. "Will it be their choice?"

"I am assured by Bac'cul that no coercion is being contemplated. The young humans will be offered the option. Whatever inducements the Sectionary can muster will of course be presented to them, though it is difficult for me to imagine what more can be offered. The same option will apply to you."

He did not need to think about it. Having spent much of his adult life never expecting to set eyes on another living human, he was not about to let his two fellow survivors depart to pursue a future in which he would not participate. There was still sage advice to be passed on from an adult to youngsters, and as the only adult, he was bound to deliver it. If Cherpa and Pahksen decided to move to Seraboth, he would certainly go with them.

Despite all the decades he had spent living on Myssar and among its civilized, courteous people, the thought of leaving it permanently behind did not give him pause. It was a gentle world, and an accepting one, but it was not a civilization that had been developed of and for humans. A return to Seraboth, the world of his birth, would not constitute a hardship. He did not point out to the honestly concerned intermet that he, Ruslan, had never been offered the option to go back and live where the Myssari had found him.

Thoughts of home led him to another topic. One that had been seemingly set aside when the two young survivors had been discovered.

"Old Earth. What of my request? What of the search? For years now I've heard nothing. Has it all been forgotten? I've kept my part of the agreement to help in restoring the species; first by allowing my cells to be cloned and stored and subsequently by assisting in the growth and mental maturation of the two younger survivors."

"It is not forgotten," Kel'les told him. "I am assured that the work goes on." His tone was apologetic and, insofar as Ruslan could tell, sincere. "Within the restrictions imposed by limited resources, true, but it goes on. You knew when you first made the bargain that the chances of locating the original human homeworld were limited."

He dug one foot into the multicolored sand. Though something unseen tickled a toe, he did not withdraw his foot. Civilization on Myssar was so old and deeply established that those dangerous indigenous lifeforms that remained, no matter how large or small, survived only in carefully managed refuges. Nothing that dwelled in the sand, especially on a beach frequented by visiting city-dwellers, could harm him.

"After five years I'd say they were more than limited. I'd say they were nonexistent."

"Ah." Kel'les's head rotated almost completely around before once more meeting the human's gaze. "You have no confidence in our scientists."

Ruslan shrugged. "I'm a realist. Always have been. It helps a lot."

"Exactly the attitude necessary to aid the two young adult humans in their development." The intermet rose, torso traveling in a straight line upward. "I will inform Cor'rin and the other members of the project of our conversation. They in turn will notify the Sectionary. May I also pass the word that should the youths opt to move to Seraboth you will go with them?"

Ruslan was no longer gazing at his minder or even at the two youngsters. His attention reached to the far horizon. What did it matter, after all, if he moved? Wasn't one horizon much like another? A line dividing sky and sea, or sky and land. He lived at this end of the line of sight, wherever it might happen to terminate.

"Sure," he replied. "There's nothing holding me here."

As incapable as the Myssari were of complex facial expression, he nonetheless suspected that he might have hurt the minder's feelings. He offered no apology.

After all, on the day he had been removed from Seraboth, none had been tendered to him.

As the Myssari hoped, the change of setting did indeed stimulate excitement in Pahksen and Cherpa. Excitement at the prospect of returning to a once human-dominated world, excitement at encountering artifacts and relics closely linked to their own kind, excitement at the discovery of surviving human foods in gardens and on farms whose genetic lineage could be traced back to seeds that had originated on old Earth itself. Excitement, yes—but no spark.

Personality-wise, the two young humans remained as they had been on Myssar. Cherpa was ebullient, outgoing, energized by everything she saw and encountered, even if on occasion her verbalizations could turn addled. Pahksen was straightforward, determined, and suspicious of everything new but willing to learn. When certain hoped-for interpersonal developments did not occur, the members of the General Science Sectionary found themselves frustrated anew on an entirely different world.

Once again Ruslan had to persuade the Myssari senior scientists to be patient. Once again they restrained themselves. They would continue to hold off on compulsory artificial reproduction in the hopes that as the two young humans became more and more comfortable on the old-new world, they would be drawn closer together and Nature would take its course. The Sectionary would not, Kel'les repeatedly informed him, remain patient forever. As it turned out, the matter that never failed to focus everyone's attention, Ruslan and Myssari alike, did indeed finally come to a head.

But not in the manner everyone expected.

No one could have failed to appreciate the natural beauty of the setting where Ruslan had chosen to live on Seraboth. Kel'les and the other Myssari were surprised when he informed them he did not want to return to the city where they had found him so very many years ago. Why should he go back there, he told them, when he had the best of the planet to choose from? No objection to his choice was raised by Pahksen or Cherpa, who after all knew nothing of his world. So it was that he'd had the Myssari restore a group of small but elaborate private homes located on a rocky peninsula that jutted out into one of Seraboth's smaller seas. The views were spectacular and the climate salubrious. Cherpa was delighted with the location, while Pahksen gruntingly assented.

"Always the sea. Always the openness," Bac'cul had commented when he had first been shown the site.

"Always whenever possible," Ruslan had told him. "At least when it's water and not liquid methane or something equally exotic. Besides, the homes were designed as vacation retreats and were in an unusually good state of preservation. There'll be one for each of us and they're close to one another. I can keep an eye on the youngsters while each of them adapts individually to their new habitat."

Indeed, both Cherpa and Pahksen took to their new residences with a zest that only served to confirm the Sectionary's foresight in instigating the move from Myssar. As time passed, everyone settled in. Even the resident Myssari, comprised of rotating teams from Myssar, took the time to customize the buildings that had been adapted by them for their research facilities. They had the benefit of assistance from fellow scientists who had been researching Serabothian civilization for decades.

Having come to know their initial specimen intimately over the years, the Myssari understood that Ruslan enjoyed having time to himself. Since there were no Myssari scheduled to visit him for study that morning and as none had contacted him to do so, he was startled to feel a hand on his shoulder. The swift spinning of his seat, suspended as it was an appropriate distance off the unforgiving ground, forced the individual who had accosted him to retreat a couple of steps. A surprised Ruslan found himself staring up at Pahksen.

In the two years since migrating from Myssar, the young man had stopped growing upward, but not outward. Recalling the lithe and hungry young Pahksen of Daribb, it was difficult for Ruslan to look at him now and realize he was seeing the same person. No longer needing to fight to survive and with everything he might desire provided by the helpful Myssari, the whiplike survivor had ballooned into a large and lazy young man. As evidenced by his occasional irritated outbursts, the old mental roughness was still there, but the body was on the cusp of surrendering to sloth.

This was, Ruslan mused as he waited to see what his visitor wanted, in sharp contrast to Cherpa, who seemingly by simply wishing it to be so had matured into a spectacular, healthy young woman. One who nonetheless rarely went anywhere without a certain repeatedly rejuvenated old toy in tow. Ruslan had to smile to himself every time he thought of the doll Oola. It might not qualify as a human survivor, but it certainly made the grade as a survivor of human culture.

It was a truly beautiful morning, he thought, and now Pahksen was showing him an expression designed to spoil it. He sighed inwardly.

"What is it this time? Another breakdown in communications? Cor'rin told you that the station techs are working on it."

"You're half right, I think." The much younger man unslung a pack from his back and set it on the hard ground. As he did so a cluster of purple and yellow thushpins hurriedly uprooted themselves and scampered away in all directions, seeking safety from the crushing weight of the descending pack. Ruslan regarded the minor floral genocide with displeasure. Pahksen was careless about such things. This was not Daribb. He no longer had to worry about defending himself from the local flora and fauna. Seraboth was and always had been a benign world. Old habits die slowly, Ruslan told himself, manufacturing an excuse for the youth's indifference.

Positioning the cushioned floating disc by subtly shifting his body mass, he spun his chair so that he was looking straight at his visitor. "Then I must also be half wrong."

"You're right about the communications but wrong about the source." Pahksen indicated a second nearby, empty chair. "May I sit down?"

Odd, Ruslan thought. There were and never had been any formalities between them. But he welcomed the unusual degree of civility. "You don't need my permission for that. You don't need my permission for anything, Pahksen. You know that."

"I always felt that I did. Part of it's the age difference, I suppose." He was looking down at his pack, toying with the shoulder straps. "I know that the Myssari want Cherpa and me to make a baby. Or babies, I guess I should say. They want to restart the species."

This was nothing new, Ruslan thought. So eager were the Myssari, they could not have hid their intentions had they tried. Which, being inhumanly straightforward, they did not.

"Doesn't sound like there's a communications problem there." He leaned forward, the disc tilting him toward the youth. "What's wrong?"

Pahksen raised his gaze. "I'm willing. More than willing. But when I put the matter to Cherpa, she always has an excuse. She's too young, she's too uncertain, she's too this, too that."

"She is still a bit young," a patient Ruslan pointed out.

"Not biologically. And with the best Myssari specialists in human physiology overseeing everything from conception to birth, it's highly unlikely there would be any dangerous complications. You know what I think the real problem is?"

Ruslan had played the elder advisor for years now. "Tell me."

"I don't think Cherpa likes me."

"Don't be ridiculous, Pahksen. You're the only other surviving human. How could she not like you?"

The younger man's nostrils flared ever so slightly. "*You* don't like me."

Ruslan was genuinely startled. "That's absurd! Of course I like you. I'd like any fellow survivor, automatically. How could I not? It's wonderful to have your company, to just sit like this and talk with another human being. You're developing into a fine individual. Everyone has growing pains, and yes, you're no different. If I criticize you occasionally, it's only because I want to do everything possible to assist in your maturation."

"You don't criticize Cherpa." Pahksen's tone was accusatory.

"Of course I do. Anyway, how would you know the details of how much I do or not? There are plenty of times she and I are together and you're not around, just like right now it's only you and me. How do you know what I say to her when you're not present?"

A peculiar undertone crept into the younger man's voice. "What *do* you say to her when I'm not around?"

It took a long moment for Ruslan to comprehend the full import of Pahksen's query. When he finally did so, it took him a longer moment to overcome his shock and gather his thoughts enough to compose an appropriate response. It was hard to accept, but the youngster's own words were the proof of it: his youthful, raging paranoia still retained its grasp.

"You're not . . ." He hesitated and started over again. "You're not implying, in any way, shape, or form, Pahksen, that you think there's anything *physical* between Cherpa and me?"

The younger man shrugged with mock indifference. "How would I know, with all the times you two are together and I'm 'not around'?"

A stunned Ruslan leaned back in his seat, which rocked slightly at the sudden weight shift. "I don't know what to say."

"You could start by denying it." Fingers continued to play with the backpack's straps.

"Fine, no problem. I deny it. Utterly and completely."

"I've seen the way you look at her sometimes."

"Pahksen, I'm older than both of you put together."

"No. You're just old." Satisfaction and frustration competed for dominance in the youth's rejoinder.

"Okay, sure: I'm old. Doesn't that satisfy you, then?"

"No, it doesn't. Because while you're old, you're not too old. I know—I checked the records. So I know you're not too old to

have sex, or even to reproduce. You're healthy enough. I've wondered for years now why Cherpa won't have anything to do with
me, why she doesn't like me. It's so obvious I feel like a complete
idiot for not seeing it before. She won't have anything to do with
me because she's waiting for an invitation from *you*." His tone
hardened. "If it hasn't been accepted already."

What could he say? Ruslan wondered. How could he respond?
He needed to convince Pahksen once and for all that his bizarre
fantasies were nothing more than that—the imaginings of a disturbed, unsettled mind that lacked self-confidence. A mind perhaps more disturbed and unsettled, he suddenly realized, than
anyone had suspected. The Myssari would not have noticed. Not
even the specialists among them were sufficiently attuned to human
psychology. With only three examples to choose from, they could
hardly be blamed for that.

But there was someone who *could* be held to account: Ruslan
himself. How had he missed the signals? How had he ignored the
signs? Judging from the intensity of Pahksen's stare and the crisp,
certain timbre of his voice, this had been building up in him for
some time.

It was good it was out in the open now, though, Ruslan told
himself. A symptom revealed was a symptom that could be treated.
The first step was to straightforwardly refute the youth's claims.
This had been done. The next was to deal with his baseless obses-
sion. In order to do so effectively, the patient would have to understand the need for, as well as participate willingly in, his own
therapy.

"I've denied your unfounded suspicions, Pahksen. I'll do whatever you think necessary to reassure you further. And I'd prefer
not to bring Cherpa into this."

The youth nodded. "We're in agreement on something, then. I
don't want her to know about this, either. As to its resolution, I've
already constructed what I think will be a believable scenario that
will resolve everything."

Feeling better now that the problem was out in the open and that Pahksen appeared to have worked out a way to deal with it, a relieved Ruslan nodded approvingly. "That's most encouraging. What did you have in mind?"

Leaning forward, Pahksen rummaged in his pack until he brought out the neural neutralizer. An uncomprehending Ruslan stared at the weapon as the younger man calmly explained.

"I'm going to kill you."

15

"One shot from this will cause all the electrical activity in your body to cease." Pahksen held the weapon firmly in both hands: a necessity since it was designed to be gripped by three sets of Myssari fingers. "Your brain will cease to function and your heart will stop. It will be quick and there should be very little pain." His mouth twisted slightly. "I'm a survivor, not a sadist. It's very Myssari in its way. They're real problem-solvers."

A stunned Ruslan chose his words carefully, aware that any one of them might be his last. "They're also exceedingly civilized. What you intend is not . . . polite."

Pahksen shrugged again. As he did so the muzzle of the neutralizer wavered slightly—but not enough for Ruslan to rush the younger man. The distance between them was too great, and despite his increased size and corresponding loss of conditioning, Pahksen's reflexes were still those of a young man who had been

forced to survive alone on a world emptied of humans and populated by dangerous creatures. His tone remained bitter.

"You want Cherpa for yourself. I can see that she's waiting for
you and that's why she won't have anything to do with me. The
solution is pretty straightforward."

Ruslan did not take his eyes off the muzzle of the gun. "How
do you think she'll look at you when it's made known that you're
responsible for my death?"

"Won't happen." The younger man was utterly self-assured.
"As I told you, I've put together a sequence of events that will
convince anyone you took your own life."

"Why would I do that?" *Stall,* Ruslan told himself, *stall, stall,*
in the hope that he could come up with something to change the
troubled young man's mind.

"You're old. You're tired. You're bored. There are plenty of
commonsense reasons. You want Cherpa and me to carry on the
species without your interference, even if it's unintentional. Don't
worry—I've worked everything out in great detail. I think you'd
be proud of me."

"I *am* proud of you, Pahksen. You've adapted very well both to
a new world and to Myssari supervision. Don't throw all that
away on behalf of a false conviction. There are only three of us
left. There's no reason to reduce that by a third."

"You mean by a turd. With you removed from the picture,
Cherpa will have no one else to talk to, no one else to confide in,
except me." Once again the tip of the neutralizer shifted as its
wielder waved it for emphasis. "The Myssari won't care. You
think they care about you? All they're interested in is their human
studies, and they want more humans to study. Well, Cherpa and I
will give them a handful to study. And if she's still unwilling after
you've been removed from the scene, then I'll just explain to the
Myssari that a certain amount of force is sometimes required in
order to ensure successful procreation. I'm willing to bet they'll
take my side of the argument. Anything to produce offspring to

commence repopulation of their favorite nearly extinct species. If she needs someone to confide in and she continues to shun me, she can always talk to that stupid doll of hers!" He spat to one side. "That's a piece of rag that needs to find its way over a cliff at the first opportunity."

On the word "opportunity" the beleaguered Ruslan saw his last chance. Having tensed his muscles while Pahksen ranted, he now threw himself forward. The suddenness of the gesture caused the hovering chair to heave him outward and away from its comforting curve.

He felt a brief sting in his left shoulder as he slammed into the seated Pahksen. Trying to balance the seating needs of two individuals, the disc on which Pahksen had been reposing began to rock and swerve wildly, threatening to dump both men to the ground. Desperately gripping Pahksen's wrist with both hands, Ruslan sought to wring the neutralizer free from the younger man's grasp. Untrained in matters such as personal combat, all he knew to do was hang on as tightly as he could while keeping the muzzle of the weapon pointed away from him.

A far more toughened survivor, Pahksen had a much better idea what to do. But he was in poor shape, his survival days from Daribb many years behind him. Additionally, the rocking, contorting, hovering seat constituted an awkward platform on which to try to execute any kind of close-combat maneuver. As they fought for possession of the gun on the violently gyrating disc, Ruslan knew that whoever finally wrested control of the weapon would be the only winner.

It was then that he had a small epiphany.

Letting his muscles go slack, he released his grip on the other man's wrist and lay back against the wide, circular seat. He had come to a decision with which he was unexpectedly comfortable. He had done enough for the species, he decided. More than enough. Having been given everything by the Myssari, he wanted for nothing, and had not for many decades now. Except the op-

portunity to see old Earth, and that plainly was not going to happen. Understanding this, he felt it was incumbent on him to allow
the resurrection of humankind to proceed to the next level. He
wasn't really worried about Cherpa. She could and would handle
Pahksen. Doubtless she would calm him down. With nothing left
to fear, with no one however imaginary competing for her attention, Pahksen would probably settle down quickly. If his, Ruslan's, removal from the scene was what was ultimately necessary
to advance the restoration of humanity, it was a sacrifice that he
was willing to make.

Tired. He was so tired. He recalled an ancient human tale he
had read long ago, during his growing up on Seraboth when he
believed himself to be the last living human in the galaxy. Whether
it came from an incident true or fictional he did not know, but it
had stayed with him.

It is a far, far better thing that I do than I have ever done, he
repeated to himself. *It is a far, far better rest that I go to than . . .*

Now seated above his erstwhile rival, a grimly triumphant
Pahksen started to raise and position the neutralizer. It looked as
if he had a few choice last words for the man he was about to
murder. And then he fell over. A baffled Ruslan watched the
younger man topple forward. In seeming slow motion, Pahksen
fell to his right, his eyes closing like tiny shades as he toppled.
Near the end of his preternaturally slow descent, the first droplets
of blood entered Ruslan's line of sight.

As the younger man tumbled to one side it was as if one human-
sized silhouette was being peeled away to reveal a second that had
been concealed behind the first. Having resigned himself to death,
a still very much alive but unmoving Ruslan saw that Cherpa had
come up unseen behind the pair of combatants. In both hands she
gripped a very large rock. As he gaped at her, trying to process
what had just happened, she dropped it and stumbled backward a
couple of steps.

Slowly he sat up in the rapidly stabilizing chair and looked to his left, over the side of the disc. Pahksen was lying on the ground, facedown and unmoving. Several yellow-orange thushpins that had fled his fall were now crowding cautiously back in search of their hastily abandoned holes in the soil. They would not be able to shift the considerable bulk of the motionless human, Ruslan knew. Swinging his legs over the side of the disc, he stood up. As he did so Cherpa came up beside him. Normally he would have been instantly alert to her proximity, to her warmth, to her smell. Not now. Together they stared at the motionless figure.

Ruslan bent down and lightly touched the prone body's chest, neck, and face. Spreading rapidly from the skull onto the ground was a dark pool that formed a halo around the skull like those found on ancient religious icons. He straightened.

"I think you've killed him." Ruslan spoke as calmly and quietly as a Myssari. He did not think that, at that moment, they would have been proud. On the contrary, he knew that the death of one of their three prize specimens would be enough to seriously upset even the normally understanding Cor'rin. Holding Oola tight against her chest, Cherpa stared at the dead body.

"I didn't mean to. I didn't want to. But he was going to kill you. I couldn't let him kill you, Bogo. You rescued me. I couldn't let him, net him, vet him." Her apology was bracketed not by remorse but with irritation. "He was *mean,* Pahksen was. Even on Daribb he was mean. I hoped when we got here that Seraboth and the Myssari would suck some of the mean out of him, but all the attention and fawning and caring just made him puff up with self-importance." Her regret was perfunctory. "I'm sorry, Bogo. I tried to be nice to him. I really did. I know"—she turned her face away—"I know what the Myssari wanted from the two of us. They didn't hide it."

He felt he should say something. "Committed scientists are rarely good at hiding that to which they are dedicated. It—didn't bother you?"

"What? The constant emphasis on reproduction? No. I understood. I just couldn't do it. I kept waiting for Pahksen to do something . . . nice. I studied the old records. I know what romance is. It's not like I expected flowers, or an invitation to a moonlit walk, or ancient courting rituals." She eyed the body anew. "I just wanted him to be nice, thrice. And he never could be, he never was. I guess all the bad memories of Daribb and Dinabu never left him, no matter how hard the Myssari tried to put him at ease."

Ruslan reached for the communicator tab at his ear, then hesitated. The Myssari were going to be very, very unhappy. Doubtless the Sectionary would immediately authorize the cloning program. Given what had happened, he could hardly raise more objections. Quite unintentionally, the events of the previous few minutes would only confirm what hard-line Myssari researchers had long claimed: that humankind could not be trusted with its own rejuvenation. He nodded at the rapidly cooling corpse.

"He was jealous, you know. That's what finally caused him to eschew reason and lose control."

"Jealous?" Her brow furrowed. "Of what?"

"Our relationship. You and I."

"Our 'relationship'?" She still didn't understand. Then, abruptly, she did. One hand went to her mouth and she stared, not at the body this time, but at him. "You mean he thought . . . ? That's crazy! That's insane!"

"I told him that. He wouldn't believe me."

He paused, then went on: "Many elements among the Myssari scientific community will be distraught. Some will believe their worst theories confirmed. All will wonder if this is yet another, probably the last, example of why our species died out. They'll say anew that it was because we couldn't control our baser instincts, everything from individual conflicts to intersystem wars. I always felt it was my duty to counter such arguments. Now . . ." He shrugged. "I don't have much of a logic leg left to stand on." He looked back at her.

"You may have saved my life, Cherpa, but you've only postponed my death. Myssari science will keep me alive for a long time yet, but all other things being equal, you're destined to outlive me. When that day comes—and barring accident or the unforeseen, come it will—you'll take over from me. You'll be the last human." He sighed heavily. "It's not a particularly enjoyable job."

"Maybe," she replied softly, "maybe the Myssari will find more of us. I know they're always looking. Cor'rin told me so."

He nodded tersely. "Sure. And maybe one day they'll find old Earth, too. The universe thrives on maybes." He went ahead and activated the communications tab. "No point in waiting any longer to inform our friends. They have to be told. Their shock won't prevent them from getting here as fast as possible with the equipment necessary to preserve the body. They'll want some of it for study and some of it to keep for possible replacement material." He met her gaze evenly. "They'll especially want to preserve his sperm."

She didn't flinch. There was nothing about the Myssari program to re-create humankind with which she was unfamiliar. "Bogo, do you think there's a gene in humans that's responsible for unwarranted aggression?"

"If there is, I sincerely hope it's highly recessive. We'll discuss that with Bac'cul and Cor'rin and the others. When the project moves to the next step, they won't want to make any mistakes." Once again he indicated the dead Pahksen. "They'll leave the doing of that to live humans."

By the standards of contemporary interstellar communication, reaction was swift.

Like much of the main research installation on Seraboth, the room was suspended over the Halafari River, which ran through the center of the long-uninhabited human city of Chalfar. Wishing to preserve the human city in as original a condition as possible, the Myssari had thrown their own imported facilities from one shore to the other in a succession of parallel arches over the river. Select study modules boasted transparent floors, both for research and aesthetic reasons. Such was the floor in the room in which he and Cherpa presently found themselves. Looking down between the furnishings, he could see the cataracts of the Halafari raging below. The boiling waters were only a little less angry than the Myssari who were presently glaring at him.

Though he felt he had prepared himself for the expected confrontation, Ruslan was still taken aback by the perceptible chill. Among the assembled, only Kel'les seemed his usual self, though pointedly subdued. Gathered in the chamber along with Bac'cul and Cor'rin were several senior members of the Seraboth research staff. While their faces were largely inflexible, Ruslan had learned over the decades that something of a Myssari's state of mind could be inferred by the rapidity and frequency of their eye blinks. At the moment, he felt he was the subject of numerous stares that were totally absolute in their unblinking. If there was any sympathy for him among the assembled besides that of his minder and old friend, Kel'les, he was not detecting it. He decided not to wait for formal introductions.

"Look, I'm sorry for what happened. It should have been avoided and I wish it had turned out differently. I know how hard you've tried to accommodate my individual interests and outlook, and the encounter probably could have been handled differently." He finished lamely. "It was a human thing."

Cherpa then proceeded to undo every iota of his careful diplomacy.

"I wish Pahksen hadn't died but I'm not sorry I hit him." She nodded toward Ruslan. "It was him be stopped or Bogo be died. So I acted. I'd act again if I had to." She paused thoughtfully. "Maybe next time I'd use a smaller rock, but I didn't have time to look around and choose. Growing up on Daribb, I learned to always go with what was readily available even if it wasn't my first choice."

As chief of the Seraboth study bloc, Gos'sil was the one who replied. His tone was not sympathetic. "One-third of the galaxy's surviving human population is now extinguished, and at the hands of one of its own kind. Although I serve more in the capacity of administrator than scientist, I begin to comprehend how a supposedly intelligent species was capable of utterly annihilating itself."

Lowering his gaze, Ruslan let his thoughts wander to the rush of white water beneath the transparent floor. "Do what you want with me but leave Cherpa out of it. She came to my defense. Instinctively, not with forethought. The unfortunate demise of Pahksen was an accident."

A confused Cor'rin responded. "Are you implying that some sort of punishment might be forthcoming, Ruslan? What would we gain by that? The resurrection program has suffered a serious blow. The last thing anyone connected with the process would wish to do is damage it further. We have no choice but to continue to deal with you as we have done previously."

He lifted his head. "Then what are you going to do?"

Gos'sil and his colleagues were focused on Ruslan. "The restoration process will commence as soon as you and Cherpa are returned to Myssar. Natural, viable reproductive components will be utilized. Fertilization will be induced and offspring nurtured."

It was as Ruslan had feared. He addressed the pronouncement quickly.

"You can't do that."

"Of course we can." Ruslan was surprised but not shocked to hear from Bac'cul. Friend or not, he was as much a Myssari scientist as Gos'sil or any other representative of the Sectionary. "I tell you that from many years of study our specialists in the matter are more familiar with the process than would be the average human. Certainly more so than yourself and a young, inexperienced, uneducated female."

"It's not right," he shot back.

"What obscure moral issues you may attempt to cite are sub-

sumed in the far greater need to resurrect your species." Cor'rin
was empathetic but unyielding. "You may choose to deny yourself
a future, but we will not allow you to deny it to your kind." She
leaned back on her two rearmost legs and crossed the third over
her left side.

"What if I refuse cooperation?"

"You have already agreed to cooperate in the process," Bac'cul
reminded him. "You agreed to do so when we made the bargain
to search for your original homeworld. Nothing was said about
the need to find it: only to commence a search. We have upheld
and continue to uphold our part of the agreement." Pausing, he
added in a less strident tone, "I am sorry that the seeking has
proved fruitless. None would have wished it to be successful more
than I."

Unpersuaded, Ruslan fought back. "The bargain referred to involved my agreeing to provide cells for cloning. Nothing was said
about mimicking natural human reproduction. As far as that goes,
I choose not to cooperate." He crossed his arms over his chest in
a gesture whose meaning only a few of those present would recognize.

It didn't matter. Bac'cul politely but coolly explained why. "I
repeat: the process will commence upon your return to Myssar. It
has been decided that your cooperation in the matter is not required."

Ruslan's jaw tightened. "I won't let you do it to her. You can't
force her to bear Pahksen's offspring!"

"We have no wish to risk damage to our sole female specimen,"
Gos'sil assured him. "Founded on human biology, the construction and maintenance of a number of artificial wombs is a simple
matter of organic engineering. As to the other . . ."

As Cherpa stepped forward she placed an open palm over her
lower abdomen. "You don't have to do anything by force. I'll vol-
unteer my eggs. Take what you want."

Startled and hurt, Ruslan turned to her. "Cherpa, you don't

have to agree to this! Even though we're not Myssari, there are
legal-ethical edicts available to us on Myssar that we can invoke.
You don't have to see your eggs fertilized with the sperm of the
man you killed, someone you didn't like and who tormented you
through—"

Cor'rin interrupted him. As usual, her highly restrictive expression was unreadable. "Who said we were going to use genetic
material from the deceased specimen?"

"I assumed that because—" He broke off as realization hit
home. "You're not referring to me, Cor'rin. Surely not to me."

"Unless there is another human male of whose existence we are
unaware—yes, we are referring to you, Ruslan."

He swallowed and started to say something, only to find the
words bunching up unintelligibly in his throat. Moving close,
Cherpa put a hand on his shoulder.

"It's okay, Bogo. It's not only okay, it's special okay."

They were all staring at him, waiting for a response. So many
Myssari eyes. So many inhuman eyes. He was being asked to consider a possibility that had barely, if ever, impinged on his consciousness.

"I don't—I think of Cherpa as a distant daughter, not as a
mate."

"No 'mating' will be involved, Ruslan." Bac'cul was once more
the phlegmatic scientist. "Not in the traditional sense. You have
only the most tenuous genetic connection to each other. You are
not even from the same world. You are both human. Where basal
matters of reproduction are concerned, the age difference is im-
material. All that matters is biological viability."

Looking down past his feet toward the surging river, Ruslan
wished he were in it. "What if my 'genetic material' isn't viable
any longer?"

"Then we will have no choice but to use the corresponding reproductive components salvaged from the body of the deceased
Pahksen." There was neither apology nor hesitation in Cor'rin's

voice. "If it eventuates that we follow that course of action, we will have to deal with the possibility of inherited psychological abnormalities when and if they manifest themselves in the course of the resultant offsprings' maturation."

The Myssari were plainly adamant. Given no choice, a reluctant Ruslan decided it was better to concede than to flail fruitlessly against something that had already been decided.

"Since Cherpa's willing to contribute, I suppose I might as well also," he sighed. Thick with satisfaction, a group susurration filled the room. A compliant specimen, the assembled researchers knew, always produced better results than one that was study-averse. "But it will be via a strictly controlled and deliberate laboratory methodology, as you say."

Among the Myssari only Cor'rin and one or two other of the scientists were noticeably disappointed. To the rest the method of reproduction was a sideshow. A potentially interesting one from a scientific and cultural-historical standpoint, to be sure, but unimportant compared to the far greater desire to see humankind brought back as a viable species.

With the matter settled, the gathering dispersed; the researchers to their work, Gos'sil and his assistants to their administrative duties, Cherpa to resume her ongoing perusal of surviving human entertainment sounds and visuals. Only Ruslan was left aimless, unsure what to do next.

Wandering out of the research complex, he made his way down to the riverside. Much of the original vitreous but rough-surfaced promenade had survived, allowing him to walk safely beside the foaming, roaring waterway. Cleverly diverted streamlets threaded their way like aqueous tentacles through the material of the walkway itself, lending a dynamic, almost organic feel to his stroll as streams of rushing water danced beneath his feet.

He had put off the business of human reproduction as long as he could. Then Cherpa and Pahksen had come into the picture, reinforcing the determination of the Myssari to commence restoration of his species. Pahksen was likely out of it now, but the manner of his passing had pushed the Myssari beyond politeness. Ruslan knew there was nothing more he could do. His hosts were going to begin bringing back humankind no matter what he said or did.

He hoped they knew what they were doing.

16

———

In addition to being accounted the last man alive, once back on Myssar Ruslan found himself embarking on the strangest fatherhood in human history.

Focusing on twenty of Cherpa's carefully extracted eggs, Myssari scientists who had spent a good portion of their professional lives analyzing records relating to human reproduction succeeded in successfully fertilizing sixteen of them utilizing Ruslan's sperm. Implanted into artificial wombs designed and built with as much care as any equivalent Myssari device, they rapidly developed into viable embryos. After endless years of collapse thanks to the now extinct Aura Malignance, the human race was once more on the road to regeneration.

Ruslan had mixed feelings. Not about restoring humankind: having been interminably exposed to Myssari determination, he had long since come to accept the project's inevitability. No, his concern revolved around being an actual father. While other dedicated and highly trained Myssari would of necessity take on the responsibility of raising the hoped-for sixteen infants, there would come a time when his physical presence, not to mention his actual direction, would assume an unavoidable and important role in their development as humans. Cherpa would naturally assist as well, but considering that her upbringing had deviated far more from the norm than had Ruslan's, it would fall largely upon him to help ensure that the children developed normally.

Healthy, active, and as intrigued by the world around them as any human infants had ever been, the sixteen had reached the uniform age of three when news arrived that jolted his world. Fittingly, it was not a scientist or administrator who delivered it but his old friend and minder, Kel'les. They had remained in contact even though Ruslan was so familiar with and integrated into Myssari culture that he no longer required an interlocutor. Instead of needing one himself, he had taken on the same duties with regard to Cherpa.

The two humans were leaving the crèche for the day when the intermet confronted them near the exit. So obviously excited was Kel'les that s'he was swaying on all three feet. Unlike a human who rocks from side to side or front to back, when a Myssari sways they make small circles around the axis of their central spine. A concerned Ruslan reached out a hand to steady his former mentor.

"Something's wrong, Kel'les. Tell us." He nodded back the way they had come. "Hopefully it doesn't involve the children." Knowing that a change of heart or direction within the Myssari General Sectionary could shut down the entire project was a fear he had carried with him since the birth of his multiple unexpected offspring.

"Nothing is wrong," Kel'les told him. "On the contrary, everything is right."

Taking a cue from her mentor, Cherpa relaxed. "Then what is it?"

Gazing intently at Ruslan, Kel'les blurted his response. "Your Earth. They have found your Earth. The human homeworld."

So completely immersed had he become in the new experience of fatherhood that Ruslan had all but forgotten about the presumably failed search upon which he had originally made his full cooperation with the project contingent. To hear from Kel'les that it had not only not been forgotten but was now apparently successful served to upend his cosmos yet again. Every time he thought it stabilized, the universe smacked him in the face with some new and unexpected revelation. This time, for once, it was not unwelcome. He also found it hard to believe.

"This is a joke." Yes, that had to be it. Though more restrained than humankind had been, the Myssari were not without humor of their own. Kel'les, perhaps with Cor'rin's or Bac'cul's connivance, was playing a joke on Cherpa and him.

The intermet's reaction belied Ruslan's suspicions. "The announcement is not made to provoke laughter, friend Ruslan. It is the truth, delivered direct from the Exploration Sectionary."

Ruslan lapsed into a daze. Having no emotional involvement invested in the revelation, a curious Cherpa could only stand and observe the byplay between the two old friends.

"How—how can they be sure?" Was that his voice doing the questioning? Ruslan wondered. It was such an old voice, such a cynical voice. Although the children did not think so. Poking at sensitive spots, pulling on his nose and ears and hair while laughing at his discomfort, they were never less than delighted to be near to their papa Ruslan.

"You forget," Kel'les told him. "There are records. From Seraboth, from Daribb, from a hundred other now empty human-settled worlds. In the absence of coordinates, we have thousands of detailed descriptions of the human homeworld. Thousands of descriptions and thousands of images. I am told there can be no mistake. Too many of those thousands are excellent matches."

S'he was joyous. "It is some considerable distance away, but nothing that cannot be negotiated."

Ruslan had to sit down. He was joined by a concerned Cherpa. Though tending at times to the complicated, their relationship since the death of Pahksen had been wholly platonic, more father and daughter than father and mother. Theirs was surely a partnership passing strange, though no more so than the unique set of circumstances in which they found themselves.

"Earth." When properly enunciated, the one word itself carried more significance than a hundred complete sentences. His gaze wandered before once again finding the intermet's face. "What—what is it like?"

"Quite pleasant, according to the initial reports. Perfectly habitable, with no sign of any Malignance-related organisms. Deprived of hosts in which to live, that genetically engineered virulence died out more than a hundred years ago on Seraboth and far earlier than that on your homeworld. It is once more a safe place for humans to live. Is that what you would like to do now that it has been rediscovered, Ruslan? Live on your Earth?"

Never having expected to be offered such an option, he had nothing prepared in the way of a clear-cut response. "I . . . don't know. I suppose the first thing is to go and have a look at the place. You said it was distant. Do you think a visit can be arranged?"

"Arranged?" Kel'les's tone grew even more expansive. "They are all but straining to hold back the follow-up expedition in hopes that you would consent to participate."

Ruslan nodded once and looked to his left. "Cherpa?"

"Of course Oola and I will come."

His gaze narrowed slightly in surprise. "What about the children? You're not worried about them?" If they both went, who would look after the crèche? He found himself hesitating, torn between old desire and new responsibility.

The Myssari, he told himself, had taken good care of him. Their specialists knew more about human children than either he or Cherpa. He persuaded himself that all would be well enough until the two adult humans returned.

She promptly confirmed his conclusions. "Why should they concern me? Each one can call on a dozen affectionate and respectful minders. To them I am only a bigger child. And I like it that way."

"All right then." He looked back at Kel'les. "Inform the Sectionary that their two adult specimens would be pleased to join the next mission to visit Earth. While there we'll be happy to impart our observations." He paused. "Though I can't predict what my reaction, at least, is likely to be."

"Your excitement," Kel'les replied, "may arise from a different place, but rest assured it is shared. I will be coming as well, of course." Peering past Ruslan, the intermet addressed the other human in the room. "It has been remarked upon that ever since arriving here from Daribb years ago, you have never requested a minder of your own. Considering where we are about to go, it was suggested that you might wish to have one assigned to you now. It need not be an intermet. You may request any gender."

"I never asked for one," she responded, "because I always had one." She put an arm around Ruslan's shoulders and smiled. "Even if he's short a couple of limbs."

Feeling the weight of her arm on him, Ruslan reflected that his life had finally come full circle: from refugee to relic to occupying the place in another human's life of a Myssari technician. It was a strange feeling—one of many he had experienced over the last several decades.

He wondered how it would compare to his first sight of Earth.

Cherpa, of course, had nothing with which to compare the reality of the discovery, so Ruslan was relieved to see that the actual third planet from the modest star looked exactly like the images he had dreamed over while wandering in the wilderness that had over-taken Seraboth.

Just like in all the old recordings, there were the blue oceans, extensive and gemstone bright. The white clouds, highlighted by a massive storm rotating over the largest body of water. The fabled continents with their splotches of lowland brown and forest green and desert beige. The mountain ranges whose names he had mem-orized from the ancient records, and the winding rivers, and the unpretentious ice fields that streaked the highly developed south-ern continent. All achingly familiar. As the ship slowed toward orbit he resolved that he would not cry.

He had no trouble keeping the resolution. Earth was beautiful, yes, but it was just another human-suitable world. Seraboth was beautiful, too, and there were many others. His kind had settled few that looked like Daribb. Rearrange the land masses and the seas below and he might be looking at any of a hundred habitable worlds, all of which had at least one thing in common.

None presently supported human life.

The landing party touched down in a mild temperate zone to the south of a massive upraised plateau bordered by the highest range of mountains. Despite their sky-scraping height only the topmost peaks flashed ragged caps of snow. On the ground the disintegrating detritus of a lost civilization was everywhere, and not just in the nearby deserted cities.

"As well to set down here as in open country." Disembarking from the lander, a cautious Bac'cul sniffed the breathable but thick alien atmosphere. His air intake clenched at the strange odors but his lungs did not reject them. "This is as intensively developed a region as any that was observed from orbit. Were there to be any survivors, calculations suggest this would be as good a place to seek them as any."

Having walked a short distance away from the landing craft, Ruslan crouched and dug his right hand into soil moist from a recent rain. Holding it up to his nose, he inhaled deeply. Earth of Earth. It smelled . . . right. Rising, he wiped the dark crumbles from his palm. Smelling the homeworld was sufficient. He was not about to taste it. Nearby, Myssari technicians were already at work erecting the inflatable and pourable components that were to be the foundations of the new scientific station. Life-support facilities would go up first so that the landing team would not have to go back and forth to the supply starship in orbit. The site had been selected following distillation of thousands of factors. There was permanent water, interesting topography, flora and fauna in plenty, and a vast spray of ruins easily accessible for study.

"What would you like to do now?" Cor'rin had joined Kel'les and the two humans. "The technical and construction teams have their work to do, and the other researchers are already unpacking their field gear. I have arranged for a small driftec to be put at our disposal."

" 'Do'?" Just as on Myssar when Kel'les had first told him that the human homeworld had been found, Ruslan once more found himself at a loss for a ready response. "I don't know. Believe it or not, I hadn't thought about it." He gestured at the surrounding greenery. "I always thought that just coming here would be enough."

"It can be, if you think it so." Cherpa danced away from them, spinning and leaping and flinging her hands in the air, her long hair flying in imitation of the fast-moving cirrus clouds overhead. "You can join me, Bogo, or just sit and stare there at the air and glare." Coming to a halt, she pointed toward the sharp outline of distant mountains. "We should go there, too!" She resumed her joyous pirouetting.

Watching her, he mused that there was a time when he might have joined in her carefree prancing. That time had passed. Thanks to the ongoing efforts of the best Myssari biotechs, his body was still in excellent condition. But while they might have been geniuses, they were not wizards. They could repair the exigencies of time but they could not reverse it. He felt like exploring, but leaping and frolicking for the pure pleasure of it was now beyond him. Of the human-studies specialists on the starship, there were at least one or two who would join the camp, but this was not Myssar and this was no place to break an aging ankle.

The extensive skeletal remains of the city beckoned, as did nearby temples and castles that were far older still. The Myssari who had decided on the landing site had chosen well. While Cherpa twirled happily through the landscape, he stayed where he was and contemplated that which he had dreamed of: the earth, the sky, the vegetation, the mountains, a nearby stream flamboyant with a skirt of overhanging verdure. He stood quietly and soaked it all up: sights, sounds, smells. He was content.

By nightfall he found, to his considerable shock, that he missed Myssar.

This Earth, this third planet from its warm yellow sun, was the human homeworld for true—but it was not his home. It fulfilled that purpose only in memory. Seraboth was his homeworld and Myssar his home. The realization shocked him; his acceptance of it stunned him. Much as he felt privileged to stand where he stood, he longed for his comfortable, familiar abode in Pe'leoek, with its on-demand entertainment and food and instant access to beaches and the entire breadth of knowledge of the Myssari. If the ruined city spread out before the landing party had been intact and swarming with members of his species, he might have felt differently. But neither was so. It was a beautiful place but an empty one: void of company, conversation, and convenience. They would study it and make recordings and then he and Cherpa and the Myssari who had brought them all this way would go . . . home. He would finish out his existence on Myssar among the aliens with whom, socially at least, he had become one.

But what of Cherpa? What did she want? And what would be best for their meticulously nurtured offspring? If the restoration program continued to prove successful, there would be more of them, with adequate genetic variation assured through expert Myssari scientific tinkering. At what point would the resurrection of humanity need to be relocated to a human world in order to fully validate the effort? Given his own feelings, would it not be better to transplant the program now to a world once populated by humans? Before the children, like himself, so habituated to Myssar that moving them offworld might prove culturally counterproductive? If so, why move them and the program to someplace like Seraboth when Earth itself awaited? Would it not make the most sense to first reestablish his species on the world that gave it birth?

Cherpa and the children were not yet wedded to Myssar. For him it was too late. Much as he might wish for it philosophically, he knew he could become an Earthman only under duress. He had been away from human company long enough for a crucial part of him to have faded away, to have become lost. Wishing that it were otherwise would not make it so.

The madness that had once afflicted and protected Cherpa on Daribb had given way to an unbridled joy in life. She would be a fine Earth mother for the children, someone they could look up to and admire. For whatever good the Myssari sociologists thought it would do, he would be content to make fatherly visits and declaim what pearls of wisdom he could conjure. But he would not, he could not, live here permanently.

Rising from where he had been sitting, he ascended the remainder of the low hill and turned to look back toward the main part of the enormous, empty city. The jagged spires of abandoned towers loomed over a sprawl of smaller buildings that reached to the horizon. It must have been a grand place once, he told himself, spilling over with energy and life. All gone now. Like the rest of humanity, as dead as the Aura Malignance that had wiped out the species. Or nearly wiped it out. It was too late for him to reclaim humankind's birthplace. That was a task that would be left to the children and to the irrepressible Cherpa.

Closer, seemingly at his feet and reinforced by a steady stream of personnel and equipment arriving from the ship in orbit, the diligent Myssari were erecting the framework of what would become their preliminary outpost on Earth. Xenoarcheologists were hard at work gathering the first of thousands of artifacts that had been abandoned in the course of the great dying. Once these had been properly catalogued and classified, they would find their way into repositories scattered across the Combine. So it would be done, he told himself as he started back down the hill.

Overhead a flock of noisy unnamed birds was winging its way toward the high mountains. The surrounding underbrush was full of similarly vocal feathered songsters. It struck him that in none of the other places where he had spent time, from Seraboth to Myssar to Daribb, had he encountered so much airborne song. If humans had been the chorus of Earth, then its birds had been its trumpets.

Have to acquire some recordings from the Myssari xenologists, he told himself as he continued to pick his way down the slight slope. He might not be able to live full-time on Earth, but he could take its music with him.

The Myssari expedition had been on Earth for several sublime terrestrial weeks before the first discordant note declared itself.

While no restrictions were placed on Ruslan's or Cherpa's movements, the leader of the expedition insisted that they carry sidearms with them on the walks the two humans took frequently. Ruslan scheduled his forays for times when he was not aiding the archeologists in identifying the purpose or providing the names of recovered relics. Sometimes Cherpa went with him. On other occasions they hiked separately, since he preferred the morning hours, while she favored the evening.

Sidearms were necessary because in the absence of humans Earth's fauna had recovered in numbers not seen on the planet since before the rise of humankind. Not all of these revived species were benign. In particular the expedition's xenologists singled out in the vicinity of the landing area three examples of large carnivorous felines, any one of which could easily make a meal of an unarmed human or Myssari. Neither was the big cats' normal prey. They knew nothing of Myssari, while humans had not been available for the taking for hundreds of years. Still, the way any large carnivore determines if something strange and new is good to eat is to taste it, and both the Myssari and the two humans preferred to avoid that possibility.

Between the weapon slung at his hip and the always-on locator/communicator that floated near his lips, Ruslan felt no compunction about wandering through the ruins and the forest that had taken over streets and buildings. Doing so made him feel as if he were a youth again back home on Seraboth, wandering aimlessly in search of sustenance and company, finding ample supplies of the former and none of the latter. Sometimes he went into the ruins with Cherpa, sometimes with a Myssari scientific team.

This morning he was alone. Packs of lesser primates scattered before him, chattering but not complaining at the way history had turned out. This world was theirs once again. Clearly they were happy it was so, despite the disappearance centuries ago of the last handouts. Enormous trees sent powerful aboveground roots searching and curling through the collapsing structures, co-conspirators with the wind and rain in the eternal process of decomposition. Ruslan clambered over and around them, through empty buildings with collapsed roofs, seeking revelation and finding only destruction.

Movement in front of him caused him to pause and put one

hand on his weapon. Mindful of the warning about the surviving large native carnivores, he let his forefinger slip down to activate the gun. He did not want to kill anything on a world from which so much life had been taken, but if attacked he would have no hesitation in defending himself.

The predatory nature of the creature that rose before him might have been debatable. Its origin was not.

Gripping a sidearm of its own, the Vrizan approached deliberately. Several more appeared off to Ruslan's right and left. Drawing his own weapon with his right hand, he murmured to his aural pickup.

"Ruslan speaking. There are Vrizan here. They are armed and closing in on me. I doubt I could outrun them, so I'm not going to try. I'll attempt to stall them while waiting for pickup."

"You are wasting your words, human." The lead Vrizan lowered her (recent study allowed Ruslan to distinguish gender among the Myssari's rivals) weapon. "Your communications device has been smothered since first we detected you."

He held his ground. "I have only your word for that. And I still have my weapon." He gestured with the sidearm.

"You are welcome to retain it." She continued to advance. "Are you going to shoot me?" She indicated her companions, who now numbered more than a dozen. "What then if we shoot you in return?"

"You won't shoot me." He was outrageously confident. "I'm too valuable."

That halted her. "To kill, yes, but we also have devices that will incapacitate without causing damage. Why make yourself uncomfortable? Killing me would only ensure that. As you surmise, the last thing we wish to do is harm you."

"Then what do you wish to do?" The longer he could keep the conversation going, he knew, the more time it would give for the Myssari to reach him. Unless, of course, the Vrizan was telling the truth and his locator signal was being masked.

"Treat you as the unique individual you are. Provide for you for the remainder of your life. Show you things to which no Myssari has access. You refused our offer on Treth."

His thoughts churned furiously. "So, you know about that?"

"Such unique information spreads rapidly and widely. The arrival here of your transporting vessel was noted immediately. It was decided that no action was to be taken and that any investigations its personnel wished to carry out would be allowed to proceed without interference. Then your presence and that of your fellow human was detected. Swift correlation was made with your earlier presence on Daribb. Records of that encounter were reviewed. As a consequence, two decisions were rendered. The first was that if an amenable situation presented itself, we were to try once again to convince you to come with us and aid the Integument in its studies and research into human history and culture."

"Forget it." Ruslan gripped his sidearm more tightly. "What's the second decision?"

The Vrizan officer was staring at him intently. "To use force to compel you to comply if the first decision failed to produce the desired result." At a gesture from one slender many-jointed arm, the other Vrizan resumed closing in around the specimen.

Ruslan realized he could delay them no longer. Nor could he run fast enough to escape. All he could do was fire. He had no doubt that would produce the kind of reaction the Vrizan had described, probably leaving him provisionally paralyzed. No matter how valuable they considered him, if he killed someone they would be less likely to treat him with the kind of deference they were showing now. But if he surrendered to the Vrizan, before long the Myssari would find his lack of verbal communication puzzling, then alarming. Even if his smothered locator still showed him wandering safely, a lack of response on his part would rouse them to come looking for him. He would have to rely on that.

Forming up into an escort, the Vrizan led him out through the back of the ruined building. He was a bit startled to discover that their leader had been telling the truth about allowing him to keep his sidearm. No one tried to take it from him. Then it occurred to him that if they could smother his locator and communicator, they might well have the technology to do the same to his weapon. He hoped he would not be forced to find out.

In contrast to a Myssari driftec, the flyer they placed him in was larger and more powerful, plainly designed to cover longer distances at higher speeds. Rising much higher into the atmosphere than a driftec could manage, it then accelerated westward. Given the rate of speed at which they were traveling, it was not long before he started worrying how the Myssari, when they did start searching, were ever going to find him.

Left alone, he took the first mental steps toward resigning himself to a new life, in a new captivity. In the decades he had lived among them, the Myssari had been pleasant, even deferential. What would life among the Vrizan be like? Having now encountered them several times, he knew them to be more brusque, more contentious than his current longtime hosts. Except where he was concerned. The alien society into which he would be placed would be different, but his treatment might well be similar. How he would respond remained to be seen.

He would miss Kel'les, and Bac'cul and Cor'rin, and even Yah'thol. Then he thought of Cherpa and the sixteen children and started to weep. The Vrizan leader, having positioned herself near her prize, regarded the display with unconcealed curiosity.

"You expel salt water from your eyes. This is a voluntary physical reaction to your situation?"

"Yes and no." Using the back of his bare right arm, Ruslan wiped at his face. "It is an involuntary human expression of sorrow that I'm making no attempt to repress."

"You have no reason to grieve," the Vrizan assured him. "You will be treated with the utmost care and respect and will be given whatever you wish."

"I 'wish' to return to my friends."

"They are not your friends. They are your keepers. You mistake cold scientific calculation for sincere friendship."

He stared back at her, having a hard time trying to decide on which of the widely spaced eyes to focus. "As opposed to the Vrizan?"

She surprised him again. "No. We are also operating under the aegis of cold scientific calculation. The difference is that I am admitting it to you."

17

When the atmospheric transit vehicle finally descended low enough for him to once more distinguish individual surface features, Ruslan found himself shocked at the size and extent of the Vrizan outpost. He quickly decided that "outpost" was inadequate to describe what he was seeing. It was at least a station and possibly large enough to qualify as a full-fledged base. The fact that the majority of it threaded its way along the bottom of a narrow, high-walled desert canyon could explain why it had not been detected by the initial, necessarily perfunctory Myssari survey.

He became aware that in addition to the team leader, another nearby Vrizan was watching him closely. Speaking Myssari, the alien responded to the human's stare with an explanation.

"I am Abinahhs Uit Oln. You may call me by any of my three identifiers."

Presuming the Vrizan was expecting a reaction, Ruslan complied. "I am Ruslan. You may call me by any one of three identifiers: angry, outraged, and uncooperative."

"Sarcasm. The plentiful records left by your kind are rife with it. Fascinating to encounter it in life instead of merely in endless folios of dead speech. I am thinking it is even more effective in the original language than when transshipped via the feeble Myssari tongue."

"In that case I am sorry you don't speak my original language," a glum Ruslan retorted, "so that I could provide you with multiple, more extreme examples."

"In goodening time." The Vrizan seemed remarkably even-tempered. "I look forward to it."

"What about my unrelieved hostility?" Ruslan challenged him as their craft leveled off to land. "You have that to look forward to as well."

The alien's temperament was unshakable. "That will wither. Time and superior treatment are remarkably effective emollients."

"I don't believe I'll have a chance to experience them." The transport touched down with the slightest of bumps. "My friends are looking for me even as we speak."

"I know that they are." The Vrizan was no less certain than the specimen. "It is possible that they will locate this settlement before we can get you offworld. You will be interested to know that an appropriate Myssari vessel has already been dispatched in our general direction, though it is traveling at a slower speed, is still a considerable distance from here, and can have no idea of exactly where you have been taken."

Ruslan replied with confidence. "You can be certain they'll find me. And when they do, you'll wish you . . ." He halted, frowning. Unsure of what he had just heard, he sought clarification. "Did you say 'settlement'?"

"I am pleased that my command of a debased language is sufficiently competent for comprehension by a third party. 'Settlement' is the correct term, yes." Rising from his seat, he gestured toward the back of the passenger compartment, his multi-jointed right arm flowing like a wave. "Please, Ruslan the angry, outraged, and uncooperative. Set aside your three harsh modifiers long enough to exit this craft of your own volition. It would displease me ethically and you physically were it to prove necessary to carry you off."

Ruslan hesitated. Understanding that there was nothing to be gained by engaging in futile obtuseness (at least at this moment in time), he rose and followed the Vrizan. Two especially large examples of their kind fell in wordlessly behind him. He smiled with grim satisfaction. Though he had nowhere to run to, he was pleased by the notion that they feared such a possibility.

In contrast to the smooth architectural arcs preferred by the Myssari, Vrizan structural design favored conjoined shapes that could be sharply angled as well as curved. Startlingly, some of it was strongly reminiscent of buildings on Seraboth. That the structures boasted a more familiar appearance in no way made them inviting. He knew what the Vrizan wanted with him: the leader of the abduction team had told him as much. As a surviving human he was a living fount of information about his long-vanished kind. In return for details, explication, and explanation, they would doubtless treat him as well as Abinahhs claimed. There was no reason to do otherwise.

As had often been the case on Myssar, he would very much have liked to have been less popular.

They entered a building whose interior had been cleverly tailored to match the tinted sandstone in which it was set. An assortment of automatons whisked around them, some gliding along the smooth, patterned floor, others airborne. Every Vrizan they passed paused to stare at the marvelous acquisition that was Ruslan. He ignored them even to the extent of forgoing obscene gestures. They would have been meaningless in any case and he was too tired to engage in a futile exercise in primitive personal satisfaction. He found himself unable to restrain his own curiosity.

"What kind of 'settlement' are you talking about?"

"Why, a permanent one, of course." Stepping aside, Abinahhs allowed the human to enter the room first.

Ruslan inhaled softly. Of all the things he had expected to encounter within the Vrizan outpost, calculated beauty was not among them.

The room duplicated, down to the smallest detail, a waterfall-dominated slot canyon. The original probably was to be found nearby, he decided as he entered. At the base of the musical spill of cool water was a small rock-lined pool. That the permanent rainbow that angled across the artful cascade was artificially generated made it no less beautiful. Native terrestrial plants fringed the pond. Benches that appeared to be hewn from solid sandstone proved to be composed of much softer and more accommodating synthetics. He sat without having to be told.

The dragonfly that appeared before his eyes paused in chromatic contemplation before flitting away. Brief as the encounter was, he could not tell if it was an actual insect or an artificial construct.

Abinahhs had taken a seat opposite—on a cushion much more like a human seat than a Myssari rest bar. The faux sandstone sank beneath his weight. His widely spaced eyes regarded the human. Ruslan did not doubt for a second that his every word, movement, and eye blink was being recorded by unseen pickups for study later. Never having had a live human to examine, Vrizan xenologists would doubtless be salivating over each individual image. Assuming their digestive processes produced saliva. He knew less about their kind than they did about his.

"You can't have a permanent settlement here," he said sharply.

"Why not?" Abinahhs was nothing if not straightforward. The formality Ruslan had come to associate with the Myssari seemed absent among the Vrizan. They were almost . . . affable. Brusque, but affable.

No, he corrected himself. Friendly overtures did not involve abduction. He remained wary.

"You can't because this is Earth, homeworld to my kind, the place where my species evolved, built a civilization through trial and error, and eventually leaped out to the stars."

"A commendable progression, to be sure. No one is arguing with that. Let me know when you require food or drink and it will be provided." One long, nearly flexible arm swept wide to take in the surroundings outside the windowless chamber. "Which brings forward the question: where are your kind?"

Ruslan tensed but tried not to show it. Not that the Vrizan was likely to pick up on any physical clues anyway. "You know the answer to that question. As a human it's not something of which I'm proud even though I, personally, am not responsible for what happened to my species. I'm a victim of the hereditary forces of rampant hubris." This last was awkward to translate into Myssari. He managed, though he was not sure his translation carried with it the full weight of intended sarcasm.

Rising from his seat, Abinahhs began to pace back and forth in front of the specimen—anxious pacing being another trait Ruslan apparently shared with his captors.

"This world is, by the definition of any civilization, habitable but uninhabited. Respect for previous dominant species does not preclude replacing them. Your Earth is a beautiful world. Why should it not once again resound to the actions and words and deeds of an advanced civilization? That it would not be a human civilization is regrettable but irrelevant. Others of your kind would of course be welcome to settle here among us, with all rights and privileges. Indeed, they would be greeted with excitement and pleasure—were there any left to greet."

Realization struck Ruslan hard. "You've made a formal claim. The Vrizan are claiming Earth."

Abinahhs did not bother to deny it. "Of course we have. With a world as welcoming as this, we would have put forth a claim whether a previous civilization existed here or not." *Was that empathy in his voice?* Ruslan wondered. "Your kind built a civilization, vast and advanced. And then destroyed it. I am afraid the claim of a single survivor does not outweigh that of a vital, developing species such as my own. What would you do with this world if you contested our claim? Preserve an entire habitable planet for one individual and his memories? Humankind was unimaginably destructive. Your comment suggests that in addition to unchecked aggression, unbridled greed was also encoded in its genes."

Ruslan found the string of accusations disorienting. The Vrizan was trying to make him feel guilty about wanting to keep Earth from becoming home to another species. No wonder Abinahhs had been chosen to confront him. The alien's forensic talents extended beyond linguistics.

"There is one thing that might persuade my government to abandon its claim, though you would have to deal separately with the Myssari and all other claimants. And were the Vrizan to withdraw, I assure you there would be others. One thing that we would regard as more valuable than this world."

At first angry, then frustrated, Ruslan was now bewildered. "I don't have anything to trade. Everything I have are gifts from the Myssari."

"Then you affirm you are not a scientist, and avow you know nothing of the science of the great plague that exterminated your kind, or its origins?"

Shock replaced bewilderment. "Why on . . . Earth"—he had to smile at the irony inherent in his words—"would you want to know anything about the Aura Malignance? Even if I knew something about it, the details would be of no use to you. While I personally don't know much beyond the fact that it destroyed my civilization and my species, I do know that the active vector affected only human beings. Not other mammals, not even close relatives like lesser primates. Only *Homo sapiens*. It would be useless to you."

The elongated head turned directly toward the specimen. "You underestimate the capabilities of Vrizan science. Our biologists are very competent. A variant that could be held in reserve for use only as a final defensive weapon would be a potent deterrent against any threat to my species. Since we are a more mature race than humankind, such a development would be engineered so that it could pose no threat to us."

Which meant, Ruslan realized, that any genetic manipulation of the Aura Malignance would be targeted against possible adversaries of the Vrizan. The Myssari, for example.

"I'm sure you have highly skilled experts in the field of biological warfare." On arrival at the settlement the peaceful surroundings had lulled him into relaxing. That was gone now, the first stirrings of tranquility purged by Abinahhs's alarming words. "Whatever you may think of us, it can't be any worse than what we thought of ourselves. Arrogance was the end of humanity, not the plague."

"Then we will be safe and all will be well." Abinahhs was quietly reassuring. "The Vrizan are not arrogant." Though the small tooth-lined mouth twisted slightly, Ruslan was not confident enough to call it a smile. "Loud at times, perhaps. Dynamic certainly. But not arrogant. Particularly dangerous research is carried out on quarantined artificial stations or otherwise uninhabited moons. In weapons research, isolation is the key to safety. Your kind forgot that."

It was an observation with which Ruslan did not feel qualified to quarrel.

"It doesn't matter. I can't help you reconstruct the Aura Malignance. Before society collapsed on my homeworld of Seraboth, I was a mid-level administrator. I'm only special genetically." He touched the fingers of his left hand to the side of his head. "Up here I'm unremittingly ordinary." Once again he had to decide on which of the Vrizan's widely spaced eyes to focus. "You can imprison me, torture me, it doesn't matter: I can't give up information I don't possess."

Both of the Vrizan's eyes rolled upward in their highly flexible sockets as Abinahhs's tone wavered. "You think us so much less civilized than the Myssari that we would resort to such methods? I do not know whether to feel hurt or sadness."

"The Myssari didn't abduct me from Seraboth."

The alien eyes returned to him. "It would have been preferred that you change your living arrangements voluntarily. I can assure you that this forced repositioning was not done lightly. In the end the desperate need of the Integument for a human's insight into the history of your kind overrode all other considerations. Any possible knowledge of the workings of the great plague you might have possessed aside."

Ruslan nodded sagely. "And if I refuse to cooperate in your researches into the history of my kind, what then? Will my refusal override all other considerations and 'such methods' of persuasion then come into play?"

Abinahhs was on the verge of replying when the ground shook. The decorative waterfall ceased flowing into the ornamental pool. Dust fell in slow motion from the ceiling as a shadow momentarily dimmed the illumination in the room. As light was restored the Vrizan replied to a comment in his own language that briefly sounded from an unseen source. Initially shaken, Ruslan now relaxed and allowed himself a slight smile.

"I don't know who you're talking to but I can guess. My friends have arrived."

Speaking anew in Myssarian, a plainly disturbed Abinahhs stared at him. A second concussion rattled the chamber. "It is not possible for them to have found you so soon. All electronic emissions from the gear you carry are systematically blocked."

Leaning back in the sandstone-hued but responsive seat, Ruslan shrugged. "I don't know how they've done it either, and damn quick, too." His smile widened. "The Vrizan aren't the only ones who can boast of advanced technologies."

With neither the Vrizan settlers and scientists nor the recent Myssari arrivals prepared for a military encounter, both sides were limited to deploying small arms intended only to repel dangerous terrestrial lifeforms. Escorted out of the research complex and onto the surface, Ruslan found himself wishing for a club, or better yet a spear. The nexus of a potential conflict, he was the only one who was defenseless.

In the center of the settlement's scientific station, an artesian well tapped by the settlers supplied a rotating series of free-floating tubes. Water leaped from one suspended, brightly colored tube to another, arcs of liquid soaring through the air like wingless flying fish. He blinked at the brightness of sunlight that was harsher here than at the landing site chosen by the Myssari. How *had* they located him if, as an abashed Abinahhs claimed, the broadcast from his locator unit had been smothered?

The composure he had successfully maintained ever since his capture was shaken by the sight of Cherpa among the grim-faced Myssari who had come for him.

"Bogo!" She had to raise her voice to make herself heard above the harmonious rush of flying water. "Have they hurt you?"

"I'm fine." Brightly tinted, irregularly shaped hydrothermic tiles beneath his feet helped to cool the air around him. He looked to his left. Abinahhs was not armed, but the several dozen Vrizan who accompanied him were.

He wondered why they had brought him out of the underground reception room when they could have rushed him to some hidden cell. Then he realized that if the Myssari had managed to track him down so far from their landing site, they would likely have no trouble locating him within this single settlement. By bringing him out and showing that he was safe and unharmed, the Vrizan were being preemptive in defense of their actions. Justifying them, however, would require circumlocutions of logic he doubted would satisfy the Myssari. His friends would want him back. He smiled to himself. Even if they were for some reason amenable to a loan of some kind, a furious Cherpa was not going to permit it. One of the Myssari—through the intense sunlight it looked like Cor'rin—had to keep putting all three hands on the enraged young woman's right forearm to keep her from drawing her sidearm.

"How did you find me?" he called out. The Myssari expedition's second-in-command, an unusually tall and slender intermet named Jih'hune, stepped forward.

"It is a matter of some sensitivity and therefore questionable as to whether or not I am authorized to provide an explanation."

Ruslan stared back. "Are you afraid of exposing something to the Vrizan?" Beside him, Abinahhs rippled an arm.

Jih'hune hesitated, then came to a decision on his own. "The sensitivity to which I refer involves you personally. It is not a question of technological exclusion. I was not instructed that you *not* be told. Merely that the information not be volunteered."

"You're not volunteering," Ruslan snapped. "I'm asking."

The intermet's discomfort was increasing proportionate to the number of armed Vrizan who continued to arrive, but the group of tightly packed Myssari held their ground.

"When you were found on Seraboth, it was instantly recognized that Myssari science had acquired an invaluable asset. One my people would be distressed to lose."

An impatient Ruslan waved the words away. "I'm reminded of my value daily. What has that got to do with how you found me?"

"Measures were taken during the initial medical examinations to ensure that what was found could not be lost." When a still-bemused Ruslan did not comment, Jih'hune continued. His tone was not quite apologetic. "Your circulatory system was infused with a harmless but permanent biological marker. To the right equipment the unique signature is detectable even from high orbit. In any ecology you stand out, Ruslan. When you did not return from your last walk and we were unable to contact you, a call went out to our supply ship in orbit. With the landing site as locus, scans were performed in widening concentric circles until your personal identifier was finally located. It took some time; otherwise we would have arrived here sooner." Looking past the human, the intermet glanced at Abinahhs.

"In the course of searching for our friend, we encountered the inadequately masked electronic signatures of your base here. That in turn rendered locating him much easier."

From specimen to friend in a few sentences, Ruslan mused. The Myssari second-in-command was not untrained in the art of negotiation. Cherpa, on the other hand . . .

"Let him go or I'll permanently divide the space between your eyes!" She continued to wrestle with Cor'rin as the Myssari researcher struggled to keep the human's weapon holstered.

"We desired nothing more than a few moments of private conversation." Once again Abinahhs's strange mouth contorted. "Surely as Myssari you can appreciate that."

Bac'cul stepped forward. Ruslan had not noticed him among the arrivals until now. "You have had more than enough time alone with our property, whose return we would now appreciate."

So much for his brief sojourn as a "friend," Ruslan thought. He was back to being a specimen again.

"As civilized beings," Abinahhs replied smoothly, "you will appreciate that the 'property' may have an opinion of its own in this matter." The elongated skull turned to face Ruslan. "I apologize for the method employed to bring you here. That need not affect your choice of destinies." With one arm gesturing as sinuously as a snake swimming on the surface of a lake, he indicated the anxious Myssari. "Ruslan, you may return to whatever life they have provided for you. Or you can remain here, with us, and we will deed you a continent."

He blinked. "Excuse me? A continent?"

"Whichever one you choose. It will be defined as your personal property. No Vrizan will set foot on it without your permission." One limber hand waved at Cherpa. "This is the first we know of the existence of a mature human female. From my own personal studies of your kind, she would appear to be of breeding age. You could reseed your homeworld. We would be happy to assist."

The growing tension on the Myssari side was palpable. Ruslan ignored it. He also volunteered nothing about the children already maturing on Myssar. "And what would you want in return?"

"To watch. To observe. To study how a species as bewildering as yours regenerates itself. To teach you and to learn from you."

Ruslan considered. "What if I lay claim to the whole planet?"

Abinahhs was equally firm in denial. "You have no claim to it. Though it is the homeworld of your species, it has been devoid of sentient life for a considerable time and is therefore a legitimate site for colonization. You cannot even claim it as your personal home, as you come from another world entirely. The Integument is in a position to make good use of it. Without an immense and likely unavailable amount of direct assistance, you are unable to do so."

"The Myssari could provide assistance as extensive as anything you can promise."

Abinahhs made no attempt to deny it. "That is true. But they have no claim to this world. Not even an automatic survey drone has preceded this first visit of theirs. In any formal dispute between governments, they would be forced to contend with our conflicting and already well-established position." Looking past Ruslan, he raised his voice. His Myssarian was perfectly intelligible.

"What of this matter, triploids? Will you dispute the Vrizan claim to this world? Will you fight for it?"

Jih'hune replied far more quickly than Ruslan would have liked.

"At this point in time we exert claim only to our friend, the human Ruslan. The Vrizan presence here has been noted. It will be discussed, but not here, now, or by us. As you are surely aware, as an expeditionary study force we hold no diplomatic portfolio."

A stunned Cherpa turned to the Myssari who continued to exert a restraining grip on the young woman's right arm. "What's he saying? You're giving the Vrizan the Earth?"

"We are giving them nothing." The researcher looked as uncomfortable as she felt. "As Jih'hune declared, the matter will be discussed. By higher authorities than ourselves." Turning her head ninety degrees, she indicated the now substantial crowd of armed Vrizan that had gathered to watch the confrontation. "It cannot be denied that they have a valid claim. This settlement is far more than a study outpost. As we slowed to land here I could see evidence of the beginnings of both agriculture and mining. Such developments declare their intentions far more unarguably than recorded words. And there may well be other such bases as this. It will be difficult to dislodge them."

Blue eyes widened. "So you're not going to fight for my homeworld?"

Cor'rin stiffened. "As you say, Earth is your homeworld. We would not fight for Daribb; we might do so for Seraboth. Colonization claims are much about precedence and the establishment of community. We can assert that for Ruslan's homeworld but not for Daribb. And most assuredly not for Earth. It may be your ancient homeworld, but to the Combine as well as to the Vrizan it is only one more habitable world among hundreds. Valuable, yes. Worth fighting over, most likely not." Removing one hand from Cherpa's arm, she gestured at the Vrizan with the other two.

"As concerns Ruslan himself, I am not worried about their weapons. I am worried about their offer. By any standards it is generous."

Setting aside for the moment any notions of interceding with violence, a suddenly concerned Cherpa joined the researcher in staring across the colorful pavement at the man who had been her mentor and who was, however indirectly, the father of her offspring.

"You don't seriously—you don't think Bogo will accept? Do you?"

"As I said: a generous offer. As we learned on Daribb, the Vrizan badly want access to the knowledge only a live human can give them. They need not have offered to do anything but match what we have provided. Instead, they have gone beyond that. What they have proposed is considerably more beguiling. A vast locale on the human homeworld itself where your kind might regenerate entirely free from all but requested and permitted outside help."

"It doesn't matter. He won't accept." Cherpa straightened. "I know Bogo. He's going to turn them down."

Small bright eyes regarded her from beneath inflexible bony brows. "How can you be so certain?"

"Because while Bogo may be human, he's also become part Myssari."

"I and my kind are flattered." Cor'rin made a gesture rich with gratitude. But she did not take her third hand off Cherpa's gun arm. "For discussion's sake, though, if he should prove your assessment wrong, what will you do? Will you return with us to the outpost or will you go with him?"

Cherpa did not reply. It was a possibility she had not considered. It was one she did not want to consider.

The Myssari were silent, waiting. It was left to the gathering Vrizan to murmur and mutter among themselves. Only those who were members of the scientific community, led by Abinahhs, understood what was at stake. Having waited through an increasingly tense silence on the part of the human specimen, the Vrizan researcher was visibly relieved when Ruslan's eyes finally turned back to him.

"You know," Ruslan said calmly, "if you had never brought up the subject of learning the secrets of the Aura Malignance, I might seriously have considered accepting your offer." He shook his head. "In contrast, no request of the sort was ever broached to me by the Myssari, not ever. It makes my choice easy." So saying, he turned away and started across the open plaza that haloed the wonderful fountain. No Vrizan moved to stop him. Any one of them could have raised a weapon and easily brought him down, he knew. Shot or paralyzed him right in the back. He knew nothing of the sort would happen. However covetous of another species' property, one did not risk damage to it if it happened to be an irreplaceable scientific specimen.

Pulling away from Cor'rin and separating herself from the band of armed Myssari, Cherpa slammed into him so hard and wrapped her arms around him so tightly that he nearly lost his footing.

"Bogo! I told Cor'rin you wouldn't stay with the Vrizan. I told her!"

She was right, he knew, but perhaps not for the reasons she thought.

"So, I'm back." Turning, he gently freed himself from her embrace. "Abinahhs! I want you and your kind off my homeworld. I want you to know that I'll be working toward that end."

The Vrizan gestured complacently. "And what of the Myssari? Do you wish them to leave this world as well? Or are you— exhibiting what I believe from my studies of the ancient human language is called 'hypocrisy'—content to have them swarm here in numbers you wish to deny us?"

"That's a matter to decide in the future," he shot back.

Abinahhs was disappointed but not defeated. "By not you, or me, or any of the stone-faced triploids who now surround you with a perceptible air of greedy possessiveness. Until that decision is made, we will remain and continue with our proposed expansion here." His gaze switched to the carefully watching Jih'hune. "Meanwhile the sexless one and the rest of his kind can stay, so long as their distant outpost makes no attempt to interfere with our progress and confines itself to work of a scientific nature. Whenever you find it unutterably boring, Ruslan, you and the female are welcome to visit us. With assurances you will be returned."

Unable to stay silent any longer, one of the armed Myssari started to speak. "The assurances of the Vrizan are *not*—" Set upon by those next to him, he was quickly silenced by wiser, more experienced comrades. Much as they might have shared his suppressed sentiments, they could not permit the speaker's independent action. Scientists did not start wars with settlers.

While his invaluable human charges were once more at ease in each other's company, Jih'hune did not allow himself to relax until the transport once again set down safely within the perimeter that had been established by the Myssari around their expanding outpost. Kel'les was the first to greet his old human friend. Though the recovery sortie had been completely successful, it was a somber group who reported to the head of the expeditionary team.

As a senior explorer who had commanded more than a dozen primary expeditions to other worlds, Sat'shan was in every sense of the term world-weary. Nothing in her long career had prepared her for the situation in which she now found herself. Seated at a recently activated command station within the second of the landing team's completed buildings, she contemplated the mix of human and Myssari assembled before her. Her first question was not directed at the salvaged specimen, nor intended for his equally irreplaceable female companion, nor even the accompanying researchers who specialized in human studies.

"Do you think they will try to mount a full-scale assault?" she asked her second-in-command directly.

"They have weapons," Jih'hune informed her, "but from what I observed they are modest and intended for defense against the indigenous dangerous lifeforms. I saw nothing of a military nature."

"From what you observed." Sat'shan's mind was working furiously: deliberating possibilities, making plans, considering and discarding options. "What about what you could not see?"

"There is no reason for them to have a significant military presence here," her adjutant insisted. "There is nothing to defend save vast expanses of empty land and numerous archeological sites. The latter are surely of interest, but hardly worth the outlay of a military commitment."

Unless one of your aims is to discover the workings of the most devastating biological weapon ever utilized in this arm of the galaxy. For now Ruslan chose to keep that information to himself. He did not wish to spark undue panic among the Myssari, much less do anything that might ignite an actual conflict.

"You speak sense." The outpost commander was in agreement. "If they wished to forcibly contest possession of the specimen Ruslan, they would have done so within the familiar confines of their settlement. Indeed, they likely would have tried to prevent your transport from landing. Your preliminary report describes their settlement as extensive."

Three arms gestured as one. "Even cursory scans suggest it is intended to provide permanent support for colonists numbering in the thousands. It is likely there are similar projects under way elsewhere on the planetary surface." The intermet indicated the silent male human. "Ruslan says that the Vrizan plan to lodge a formal claim to possession of the planet and to develop it as a full-fledged colony."

"That is distressing. The Sectionary will be displeased." Sharp yellow-orange eyes regarded both humans. "It would be natural for you to be distraught at this development. I can understand if not feel your pain. This is your ancestral homeworld."

Ruslan stepped forward. "I know it doesn't make sense, logically. Our connection"—he nodded toward Cherpa—"to this world is only through history and sentiment. We were both born on other worlds. But the connection, however tenuous, exists. It is there, in our minds and in our hearts. Is there anything short of war the Combine can do to stop the Vrizan from turning Earth into a colony of theirs?"

"Their claim can of course be contested. Jih'hune says that the Vrizan offered the pair of you an entire continent to develop as your own. Doubtless they feel by the time you could reproduce sufficiently to populate even a small community, they will have expanded across the rest of the planetary surface to a degree that would render any future claims by a resurgent humankind pointless. It is plain they do not know about the reproductive program for your kind that has begun on Myssar. Human reproduction by natural methods is slow, it is true. The Sectionary's program will produce offspring far faster."

She almost added, "than you two," but caught herself. It was widely known that while they demonstrated varying degrees of affection toward one another, the two human specimens before her had declined to engage in actual reproductive activity. Myssari cultural sensitivity demanded that the subject be avoided unless mention of it otherwise proved necessary.

"The program, under your supervision, will grow the human population of Earth far faster than the Vrizan realize. Whether it will grow fast enough to deter them from their own plans only future developments can answer."

Cherpa had been silent long enough. "It would improve the prospect if you'd kill the lot of them."

Taking the junior specimen's comparative youth into consideration, Sat'shan leavened her reply with characteristic politeness.

"You are impulsive. A deeply rooted human trait that has not always stood your species in good stead. The Combine would never agree to go to war with the Vrizan over a world to which their adversaries have a prior and better claim. In the name of science, not affairs of state, the Sectionary will do all it can to support the regeneration and repatriation of your species here. But there will be no fighting. Too many worlds full of life clamor for support to risk skirmishing over one that reeks of death. You will have to fight the plans of the Vrizan with ethics and argument."

Cherpa muttered under her breath, "I'd rather have a lot of guns."

Sat'shan was not moved. "We will go through the steps of contesting the Vrizan claim via diplomatic channels. It may slow but likely will not halt their work here. Perhaps they may find it unworthy of extensive investment. History is spotted with instances of one species laying claim to a world not in order to develop it for themselves but simply to deny it to others. We will see if that is how they feel about your Earth." She turned away from Cherpa and looked at Ruslan.

"I am glad you are safely returned to us, Ruslan. Kel'les will, as always, see to your needs and those of your companion. I request only that you engage in no additional unescorted jaunts, no matter how tempting the surroundings. If you wish to explore further, a driftec and driver will be put at your disposal. I am sure Bac'cul, Cor'rin, and the rest of the scientific detachment will be more than pleased to accompany you on any excursions you care to propose. Now, if you will all excuse me, I have an outpost to organize and complex communications to prepare for transmission."

Outside, Cherpa walked alongside Ruslan as they made their way toward the portion of the residential quarters that had been allotted to them. "What do you think, Bogo? Can anything stop the settlers from making Earth a colony of Vriza? Can we?" She looked outward, toward the silent abandoned city. "Can our offspring?"

Lost in thought, Ruslan didn't reply immediately. Pondering her queries, he realized he did not know the answers. But one thing he did know. For some time now he had grown bored with existence. His mind was tired, his body was worn, his spirit was exhausted. Now, here on Earth, he felt rejuvenated. For that he had the Vrizan to thank. They had offered him a continent but they had given him something far more vital.

A cause.

18

———

Notwithstanding the Vrizan's promise not to intervene in any efforts Ruslan made to establish a revived human presence on Earth, he and Cherpa as well as the administering Myssari were convinced that the long-headed claimants to humankind's home-world continued to monitor their every move at the growing out-post. While far smaller than the Vrizan settlement Ruslan had been "encouraged" to visit, the new Myssari base grew steadily as the Combine government contributed increasing resources to its expansion.

Whether Vrizan monitoring instrumentation was sensitive enough to detect the presence of human children at the outpost was the subject of some debate among Myssari scientists. If so, no comment was forthcoming. While every effort was made to keep the youthful human arrivals from Myssar under cover, Cherpa was unwilling to restrict them to what would have amounted to a closed environment. Earth was their homeworld, too, and they deserved to be allowed to experience its surface, sights, and sounds.

The presence of a dozen or so humans of any size was unlikely to cause the Vrizan much concern. Not when balanced against the presence of several thousand of their own already established colonists. Once placed in orbit, high-resolution Myssari scanners had soon confirmed the presence of half a dozen other Vrizan settlement sites in various stages of construction. By the time the Myssari human reproduction program succeeded in producing a hundred adult humans, the Vrizan and their claim to Earth would be far too deeply established to contest. They would own the place by right of development. Half a world away, an agricultural footprint had already been established in a second northern continent. Low-level industrial development was sure to follow. Though a vanished humankind had done its best, it still had only managed to make use of the most accessible of the planet's resources. Much remained for a high-tech civilization like the Vrizan to exploit.

Ruslan knew they had to contest the Vrizan claim. If it was too late for him and Cherpa, there had to be a way for their engineered offspring to reclaim ownership of the homeworld. He never missed an opportunity to push the Myssari to take a firmer stand against the wide-headed interlopers. But while the scientists and researchers who came and went at the outpost were of similar mind, the government of the Combine was forced to consider issues of far greater import. Certainly Earth was a pleasant world and the reestablishment of its dominant sentient species a matter of great scientific interest. Determining its ownership, however, was not something for which the Myssari were willing to go to war.

The situation was made more difficult because the General Science Sectionary absolutely refused to send every young human to join the outpost. Having invested so much in starting to resurrect the human species, its members were not about to risk everything they had worked for by exposing all the offspring to potential hostile action on the part of the Vrizan. So some were sent to Earth while others remained on Myssar. Occasionally the children were allowed to exchange places. But the spatial dichotomy remained.

While not as large as some settled oxygen-atmosphere planets, Earth was more than expansive enough to allow both Vrizan and Myssari scientific teams to explore at their leisure without ever encountering each other. At once frustrated and energized by the course events were taking, Ruslan tried to divert his thoughts by joining the Myssari researchers whenever they chose to explore another new corner of the globe.

Such excursions were inevitably satisfactory without being re-velatory. The empty, decaying cities were always interesting to explore, especially those that predated the era of stellar expansions. Orbital surveys revealed the most interesting sites. Of course, the Vrizan had access to equivalent search technology. Though he'd had no personal contact with humankind's lost civilizations other than what he had acquired since his arrival, the thought of the Vrizan picking through the vestiges of human society and carrying off whatever they liked for study elsewhere created a permanent discomfort he was unable to shake off. That their Myssari counterparts were equally avaricious when it came to the possessive study of human relics was no consolation.

When accompanying these expeditions, he took the opportunity to examine any newly unearthed artifacts himself. Cherpa was less interested. She often chose to remain behind with the children, devoting more and more of her time to them. It was gratifying to see that her new domestic avocation had in no way muted her individuality, though working with the children did succeed in filing off the sharp edges of her personality that had once been defined as madness.

When Jih'hune caught up with Ruslan near the outpost perimeter, there was no reason to think that the assistant outpost commander brought with him anything other than ordinary news. Watching rainbow-hued fish describing lazy arcs within the crystal-clear stream that marked the outpost's northern boundary while soaking up the warmth of the original Sol, Ruslan was not really in the mood to go out on yet another expedition to help excited Myssari researchers plow through the fascinating but frequently repetitive detritus of human civilization.

What Jih'hune told him soon changed his mind.

"We have come across an interesting anomaly."

With a sigh of resignation Ruslan turned away from the dancing fish. A small component of humankind had made a terrible mistake in concocting and releasing the Aura Malignance. Their only saving grace was that it affected only humans. *We all swim in our own little universe,* he thought. He wrenched his attention back to reality.

"I suppose I'm as interested as anyone in anomalies. What does this particular one involve?"

"As is normal when exploring a new world—or in the case of your Earth, a new old world—as many scanning instruments as possible are put into orbit subsequent to the initial landing. These have been sending back data ever since our first days on the surface. Enough are in place so that our researchers can begin to pick out the most interesting sites for investigation. One such location appears to exist far to the northwest of here, on the edge of the main continental mass. In itself it is unexceptional. However, it appears to be the locus of a series of weak, intermittent electronic emissions."

"Emissions?" The last dreams of chromatic swimmers faded from Ruslan's thoughts. "What kind of emissions? Automated, certainly."

"Of course. That much is immediately apparent. The high variability of their intermittency suggests the broadcast source is running out of power, or perhaps is failing due to lack of maintenance. That they emanate from this one otherwise undistinguished location is intriguing. Enough so that Bac'cul will be given charge of the on-site scouting party himself. There is no evidence that the

Vrizan, who have tended to focus their development and exploration efforts on prime agricultural land or major urban sites, have been active in the indicated area. As near as our orbiters can tell, it is so far unvisited. Of course, there may be a good reason for that. There may simply be nothing of interest there to see." Small intense eyes met those of the human.

"On the assumption that there just may be an unusual artifact or two at the locale, I am requested by Sat'shan to ask that both you and the female specimen join the expedition. Once a preliminary survey of the site has been compiled, it is likely that your presence will not be requested on future visits, assuming any are forthcoming."

This was normal procedure, Ruslan knew. Have one or both of the adult humans along on a first visit to any particularly interesting new archeological location. Set them free to identify and explain any relics new to Myssari science. Then return them to their principal task of supervising the progress of the younger specimens. The routine was familiar. But this business of a flickering electronic emission was something different.

"Of course I'll go. I'm sure Cherpa will, too." As Jih'hune pivoted to leave, Ruslan put out a hand to forestall him. "One more thing. If this is a new development, maybe the last remnant of an old broadcasting system or some such, I'd still expect that the Vrizan would have been all over and through it by now."

"One would, considering how much longer they have been here." Jih'hune did not dispute the human's observation. "However, they are so intent on developing and expanding their settlements that it is likely they have diverted resources which otherwise would have been employed in the service of pure science. If orbiters are occupied hunting for ore deposits or exceptional agricultural sites or the ruins of the most impressive ancient cities, something like a few intermittent electronic indications might well be overlooked, or filed away for future examination, or relegated to the realm of the not immediately cost-effective. That is not to say they are unaware of the frail transmission: only that if so, our scan from orbit shows no sign of there having been a Vrizan visitation." He pondered. "There is probably nothing to it. A relay point of some kind, perhaps, or a portion of an early meteorological prediction system. You have no notion of what such an emission might signify?"

Ruslan shook his head, a human gesture with which any Myssari researcher was by now fully familiar. "Not a clue. But I suppose it might be worth a quick visit."

"If nothing else," Jih'hune continued, "the locus lies in an area we have not yet explored. The ruins of many major human conurbations lie comparatively close by, which further suggests that this may have something to do with an early human form of communication. No human city of size lies farther north than this site. The climatological zone from which the emission arises is not one favored by your kind."

"Makes it all the more interesting, then," Ruslan agreed by way of parting. "I'll tell Cherpa. She's ready for another break from dealing with the children, I think. When is this outing scheduled?"

"Not for several days next." Ambling easily on all three legs, Jih'hune headed back toward the recently finished administration building. "There is nothing in the finding to suggest that haste is indicated."

Their destination lay a considerable distance from the outpost, but not so far that suborbital transport was required. A boosted driftec was sufficient. Staying within atmosphere also allowed Ruslan and Cherpa to drink in the planetary panorama that unfolded beneath them. Seas and mountains, once fertile plain now completely overgrown by native vegetation, and the shredded geometric patterns of empty cities blended into a sumptuous visual whole that was as much a feast for the eyes as it was sorrow for the soul. All lost, all wasted, all slowly sinking back into the folds of the planet from whence humankind had drawn the original sculptures, he thought, with only himself and Cherpa left to try to uphold the memories of a once great civilization. And the children, he reminded himself. Not to forget the children.

The terrain where they finally descended was beautiful but not welcoming. Cold and tectonically warped, it had been diced by glaciers whose retreating footprints took the form of permanent slaps of ice and snow. Temperature-wise it was a radical departure from where the outpost was located. That they were properly dressed and prepared was thanks to the information that had been sent back by the Myssari probes in orbit.

Appropriate attire notwithstanding, the humans found themselves shivering slightly as they emerged from the driftec. Myssari did not shiver, but with their especially sensitive extremities overbundled, they were awkward and graceless. With the representatives of neither species willing to risk frostbite, it was evident from the start than any in-depth work would have to be done by weather-immune machines.

Hard country, Ruslan thought as he and Cherpa followed the pair of techs toward the nexus of the orbiters' discovery. Not the place one would expect to find something of survivable significance. The terrain was striking, but it was not nearly as convivial as the outpost. Certainly Pe'leoek on Myssar was more amenably sited. He hoped the Myssari researchers would not want to stay too long.

There was nothing encouraging to see. No crumbling city towers, no expansive urban development, no suggestions of vast, mysterious industrial enterprises. Only rock and snow and a sky that was, admittedly, bluer than any he had yet viewed from the planetary surface. Blueness wasn't enough to keep him interested. At least Cherpa had flowers to fawn over. Petite and brightly colored, they poked their colorful heads up everywhere a roothold could be found in the rocky soil.

"There." Having come up behind his friend, Kel'les was pointing with two hands. Ruslan noted that the flesh of his mentor's face and neck was tightening like drying leather, a sure sign of aging among the Myssari. With a start he realized that he had never seriously contemplated what his life would be like without Kel'les around to counsel him at every turn. He had just assumed the Myssari would outlive him. That was clearly not necessarily the case and he would have to find a way to deal with it. For now he preferred to think that the epidermal contractions he was seeing on his friend were due to the midday cold and not the vagaries of advancing age.

The techs had stopped. Or rather, their forward progress had been halted. Beneath a lip of overhanging granite and sunk within a cliff face was a single door. Perhaps three times Ruslan's height and equally wide, it was a simple square slab of remarkably unweathered metal. Perhaps early terrestrial steel, he thought, though it was imbued with a faint golden hue he had never seen before. Leaving Cherpa to her flower gathering, he joined the techs, Bac'cul, and Kel'les in examining the barrier. Having grown adept over the decades at anticipating researchers' questions, he answered the first before it had to be asked.

"No, I don't know what it is or what it's made of. I can't imagine what lies behind it or why such a doorway happens to be located here, in such an inhospitable and inaccessible place."

Having temporarily removed his gloves, one tech was intent on the flat pane of instrumentation he was manipulating with all three hands as he made slow passes over the door with the device. "I am having trouble obtaining a compositional analysis. Certainly there is iron present in quantity."

"That is not surprising." The tech's companion resolutely kept her hands and sensitive fingers bundled in protective material. "As we were on approach, scans recorded the presence nearby of an iron mine of exceptional dimensions." She indicated the mute bar-

rier before them. "Perhaps this is a storage facility for pure, re-
fined product from that mine."

"Except that we detected no evidence of such a refinery." Her
colleague continued to study his readouts. "Which is not proof
one did not exist here in earlier times. The machinery may have
been removed for use elsewhere."

"I would say it is a repository." Everyone turned to look at
Bac'cul. "Similar in design and purpose to others we have found
scattered around human-settled worlds. A place intended to safe-
guard and conserve important relics and materials. The Vrizan
boast of having found one far to the northwest of here that was
filled with preserved seeds and animal parts." He indicated the
barrier. "I suspect we may find something similar when we enter
here."

"Enter how?" The still fully clothed tech used one thickly
gloved hand to gesture at the barrier. "Other repositories that we
have found and inventoried had physical handles built into the
doors, or electronic sensors awaiting input."

Bac'cul indicated his understanding. "The smaller ones, yes. All
human entrances of this size were originally controlled by electronic recognition devices. I admit I see no such inviting panels or
optics here. They would of course no longer be functional in any
case. So we will have to force an entrance. It will hardly be the first
time." He glanced at Ruslan.

"No objection," the human advisor told him. Why should he
care if the scientists blew the door? He was not especially interested to see what lay on the other side. Compared to what was
easily accessible on a planetary surface, the contents of similar
repositories on Seraboth had been of only marginal interest. He
doubted it would be much different here. And the sooner they
learned what was within, the sooner they could return to the
warmth and comfort of the outpost.

An optical cutter was brought from the driftec. Not wishing to damage the portal any more than was necessary to gain entrance, its operators activated it on low power and turned its beam on the lower right-hand corner of the entryway. The coherent beam lanced out and struck the barrier, layering irresistible energy onto the featureless material.

Nothing happened.

The metal, if that's what it was, did not even grow warm. Conferring, the device's operators gradually increased the strength of the cutting beam until it was at maximum. A small circular glow appeared as a halo where the beam was contacting the barrier. But no hole was cut and no material melted. The frustrated operators continued to pour power into the attempt until Bac'cul called a halt. He walked up to the unharmed doorway and ran a gloved hand carefully over the spot where the beam had been aimed.

"We have something new here." Though his tone was unchanged, there was an undeniable touch of excitement in his voice. "This is the first time we have encountered an obstruction our field gear could not penetrate." He looked back at the small group gathered behind him. "We will have to go back to base and return here with more powerful equipment. Ruslan? Any suggestions?"

The human shook his head. "I don't have any idea what it's made of, and I agree we should return to the outpost. I'm cold."

"We are all suffering from the climate." No less ready than Ruslan to leave the place, Kel'les was already starting back to where the driftec had set down. "Though I am no scientist, as far as I see, for all the promise this location holds we might as well wait for the seasons to change before we return."

"It is true there are easier sites to study," the female researcher said. "Though I am always curious to see that which is hidden from me."

"We need not return with a full scientific complement," her companion said. "It might be better to let one of the materials scientists study the obstruction before a second attempt is made at penetration."

They continued to discuss the discovery and how best to proceed as they walked back toward the driftec. Carrying their equipment between them, the operators of the cutter led the way. No one thought to call to Cherpa to cease her flower gathering and hurry up to join them.

Preoccupied with her botanical collecting, she had not joined the others in studying the barrier. Now she lingered behind in order to conduct her own brief examination. Curious, she removed the protective warming glove from her right hand and let it slide down the face of the remarkably unpitted, uneroded barrier. Ruslan had already performed the same gesture. But his hand had remained gloved.

"Cold," she murmured.

Something like a rising wind whispered in her ears. It was not the wind. It was far away and deep down, a sigh from the past.

Startled, she stepped back as the barrier rose almost silently in front of her.

Hearing the surprised exclamations in Myssarian, Ruslan turned in time to see the last of the barrier disappear into the roof of the overhang like a claw being retracted into a cat's paw. Setting down the cutter, the two operators joined the human and the researchers in rushing to the unexpected opening. Clustering together just outside the now revealed entrance, humans and Myssari alike found themselves staring down a perfectly cylindrical tunnel. The walls were of bare rock that had been polished to a decorative shine, though whether as a consequence of a deliberately decorative touch or the process of digging none of them could say. The entrance was not vast, but it was impressive.

Ruslan stared at her. "What did you do?"

She spread her hands. "Nothing. I just ran my palm down it. My bare hand." She mimed the motion. "And up it went."

"What now?" Bac'cul asked, staring at him. So were the other researchers. As if merely by being a human confronted with an enigmatic human relic, he would instinctively know what to do

next. He smiled ruefully. In such a situation his ignorance probably exceeded theirs.

Less vexed by informational deficiencies, Cherpa started down
the tunnel. As she did so successive segments of the walls, ceiling,
and floors flared to light. Ruslan turned to Bac'cul and shrugged.
"Old human game. Follow the leader."

"She is not a leader," Bac'cul insisted as he joined Ruslan in
entering. "She has no idea how she is doing what she is doing."

"Are you interested in explanations or results?" Ruslan challenged him. The researcher said no more.

They walked for quite a while, until even the beauty of the polished granite that surrounded them grew tiresome. Bac'cul was
about to call for a return to the driftec so they could unload pow-
ered ground transportation, when the tunnel took a sudden bend
to the left. Confronting them were half a dozen identical mechanical complexities. Here at least Ruslan could supply some useful
information drawn from his early years on Seraboth.

"Those are lifts. The design is a little different from what I'm
familiar with, but I don't think there's any mistaking the purpose."

The lead male researcher considered. "Do you think they are
functional?"

"No," Ruslan replied, "but I didn't think the outer door was
functional, and there was no reason to expect internal illumination in this place to be functional, either. The door responded to
Cherpa's touch. So has the interior lighting." As he spoke he was
removing the glove from his right hand. "Let's try a gender variant."

Eying her colleague, the second researcher hesitated. "Do we
really want to do this now, here? Should we not return to the
driftec and first seek wider concord?"

"From whom?" Her companion gazed back at her. "Sat'shan?
Jih'hune? Sectionary advisors on Myssar? We are here; all others
are elsewhere." He looked to Bac'cul. "Any worthwhile discovery

embodies an element of risk. But as superior, the decision is yours to make."

Bac'cul hesitated. Then he turned to Ruslan and Cherpa. "No. This is *their* heritage. The decision on whether or not to proceed is theirs."

While the Myssari waited, Ruslan looked over at Cherpa. Her collection pack was overflowing with wildflowers. "What do you think? I'd prefer that you go back to the driftec and wait. You can always come in later and have a look at whatever we might find."

She smiled back at him. "I've never been the one to come in later, Bogo. You know that."

"That's what I thought you'd say." He turned back to Bac'cul and the other Myssari. "I think the first sentient sentiment voiced by my species may have been, 'Let's see where this goes.' "

Bac'cul gestured appreciatively. "A little boldness frequently yields worthwhile rewards. But I would try one small experiment first."

Removing one of his three gloves, he stepped past Ruslan and entered the nearest of the multiple lifts. Three Myssari fingers trailed down the interior wall, over what looked like a bare panel, and across several metallic extrusions. When nothing happened, he replaced the glove and stepped aside. Kel'les, the two cutter operators, and the pair of researchers joined him. With Cherpa looking on, Ruslan repeated Bac'cul's stroking. Touching the interior wall produced no reaction, but sliding his palm over the naked panel produced a humming noise. Without further sound and as smoothly as if it were a piece of wood settling onto still water, the lift began to descend. As it did so, lights came on to illuminate the shaft around them. Smooth and gleaming, it was a perfect vertical facsimile of the tunnel through which they had entered.

And seemingly just as interminable . . .

19

_____

There were no intermediate floors or levels: only surface and abyss. Individual instruments capable of measuring depth all agreed the descent was considerable.

Despite having no idea what to expect when the lift finally slowed, stopped, and allowed them to disembark, it is fair to say both humans and Myssari were initially disappointed. The chamber that illuminated as they entered was exceptional only for its state of preservation. Little but dust marred the vitreous surfaces of walls and floors. Of visible instrumentation there was none. But, Ruslan reminded himself, the impressive surface portal that had barred the way inward had similarly been devoid of recognizable tactilities but had proven to have hidden functionality. Might not the same be true of here . . . whatever "here" was?

Other than being a deeply buried and not especially large open space, it was impossible to tell. The apparently empty chamber was hardly awe-inspiring. Maintaining a brisk but not stressful pace, they soon reached the far end. This consisted of a wall of solid black glass, though whether of synthetic composition or something akin to natural obsidian Ruslan could not tell. Aware that from a scientific standpoint he was completely out of his depth, he prudently offered no opinion. There was one thing he did feel reasonably certain of: whatever still-functioning system had turned on the illumination was also providing fresh air. A perceptible breeze caressed his face, and it had been pre-warmed.

In contrast to his hesitation the Myssari were bursting with speculation. That was all they could do in the absence of written or engraved material that they might have interpreted. In the entire amorphous space there was not a single sign, warning, or instruction. Other than the bumps and protrusions that marred its otherwise smooth walls and ceiling, the chamber was a blank slate. Both humans confessed ignorance of their surroundings.

"I've never seen anything like it." Ruslan's eyes roved the roof and its integrated lighting system. "It has to be a place of some importance. The depth at which it's located and the impenetrable doorway speak to that." Lowering his gaze, he indicated the places where instruments ought to be but where only shimmering blank curves of flowing metallic glass gleamed in the subdued light. "My first guess would be that it's a place to store data of some kind. My people often used deep places to keep valuable information."

Bac'cul was running the three fingers of his middle hand over one of the nearby wall's featureless protuberances. "If that is the case, then there should be a way to access whatever is stored here . . . if indeed anything is. I see nothing resembling a control or even an aural pickup."

"The outer door." Excited to be able to contribute an idea, Kel'les sidled up next to Cherpa and put a hand on her shoulder. "It responded to her touch." S'he gestured meaningfully at the nearest wall protrusion. "Perhaps . . . ?"

The young woman glanced at Ruslan, who nodded encouragement. Kel'les and Bac'cul made way for her as she stepped forward. Reaching out with her right hand, she boldly stroked the lustrous material. Applying varying amounts of pressure, she repeated the gesture several times . . . all to no effect. Bac'cul consoled the intermet.

"It was a worthy thought and a worthwhile attempt." His gaze swept the silent chamber. "If anything here besides the facility of illumination is still functional, there must be another way to stimulate activity. Now that we know the location, we can return with specialists who are better equipped to conduct an analysis." When the intermet did not respond, the researcher added, "Kel'les? Has all the time you have spent in human company rendered you incapable of responding politely to a compliment?"

Ruslan's minder was not being discourteous. Staring past the researcher, s'he was reduced to pointing.

One of the larger wall outcroppings behind Bac'cul had quietly begun to emit a soft yellow glow. Pivoting, the startled researcher could only stare at it in silence. The same was true of the two wide-eyed humans close by him.

Something was emerging from the base of the outcropping. Shocking in their simplicity and ordinariness, the pair of neatly booted human feet descended slowly into a lower portion of the protrusion. As they did so the outcropping began to emerge from the wall. Turning parallel to the floor, it slowly turned transparent. A tube, Ruslan thought, or capsule of some kind. The shod feet were followed by the rest of the body. It was male, less than two meters in height, and clothed in some understated, velour-like, dark blue material. Its eyes were closed, its hair close-cropped, its features unremarkable save for a somewhat prominent nose. It was undeniably human. Or at the very least, Ruslan told himself through his rising excitement, humanoid.

One by one, ten similar capsules began to emerge outward from the seemingly solid wall. Inspection begat disappointment when it was discovered that the other nine were empty and devoid of internal illumination.

Putting his face so close to the single occupied transparency that his breath fogged the curving exterior, Ruslan peered hard at the body within. It lay utterly still. The clothed chest did not rise and fall, the nostrils did not flex. Insofar as he could tell, respiration was nonexistent.

In the hushed air of the chamber, the bold female voice that addressed them without warning but clearly and with great precision made the two humans jump and the tripodal Myssari quiver slightly.

"Template established. Install pattern number one?" A single word pregnant with portent caught Ruslan's attention.

Swallowing, he replied as evenly as he could to the voice whose source remained unseen. "What template? What kind of 'pattern'?"

The synthvoice stayed silent. Insistent it was not, he decided, unlike thousands of other exchanges he had engaged in so long ago while working with artificial intelligences at his old profession on Seraboth. Irrespective of purpose, the build behind artificial intelligences on the world of his birth had been similar across all platforms no matter what their intended purpose. The lack of response to his query suggested design paradigms might be different here.

That supposition remained valid for less than ten seconds.

The hint of impatience in the AI's voice was unmistakable and possibly deliberate. *"Install pattern number one?"*

Before Ruslan could reply, Bac'cul stepped forward to place his hands on the human's right shoulder, elbow, and forearm.

"We are moving too fast here and now. Haste is the parent of mistakes."

"I know, but—"

Quickly the researcher cut him off. "It is likely that this place has remained in a state of stasis for hundreds of years. Another few days of delay before observing it in full operation is unlikely to detrimentally compromise its functions, whatever those may ultimately be. Our group is only charged with exploration and discovery, not with explication." He indicated the faceless imago lying within the capsule. "To ensure that everything that can be learned is learned and that no mistakes are made, we must inform Base of what we have found. Experts there can determine better than we how best to proceed."

Ruslan wanted to argue that he knew how to proceed, except that he realized he did not. The operative AI was being cooperative, if curt. He felt it would continue to be so. But he could not support what he felt with any assurance. So he hesitated, aware that as well as the Myssari, Cherpa was watching him closely.

It was typical of the Myssari to be cautious. And Bac'cul was probably correct in noting that there were specialists at the outpost who would have a better idea of how to move forward with the investigation of whatever kind of facility it was that they had found and reactivated.

What did the AI mean by "template"? Was it indicative of the clothed human form that now lay within the transparent capsule? When it spoke of installing "pattern number one," was it referring to some generalized appearance, or to a ware component, or something else? His ignorance throbbed like a headache. Although the present surroundings were very different—the body was fully attired, and it was not floating in a liquid suspension—he could not escape memories of the ineffective resurrection center on Treth. Was the purpose of this deeply buried underground center similar to that of the revivification center on that colony world? Instead of row upon row of waiting people, there was only the single human shape. If the intention was resurrection, why were nine of the ten capsules empty?

Bac'cul's communicator abruptly hummed for attention. As the researcher listened his body seemed to sink downward on all three legs. This well-recognized Myssari posture immediately put Ruslan and Cherpa on alert. Their concern was thoroughly justified.

As he closed the communication a disconsolate Bac'cul eyed them both. His tone was flat.

"The Vrizan are here."

Cherpa's expression reflected her shock. "How?"

"I do not know. No one does. Perhaps one of their orbiters has been tracking our progress all along, and the length of our stay in this seemingly empty region has drawn their attention. I am informed that a large atmospheric transport of theirs has set down beside our vehicle. They are insistent to know what is going on and what we are doing here."

"Just tell them that we—" Ruslan began.

The researcher cut him off. "They have seen the open entrance. I suspect it is unlikely they can detect lifeforms at this depth. Also, they have not yet alluded to such a possibility to my subordinates. They must be dealt with before they proceed any farther." He locked eyes with first Ruslan, then Cherpa. "I must return to the surface and try to satisfy their curiosity while conceding as little specific information as possible." At a gesture from their superior, the rest of the Myssari party started moving toward the open lift. Framed by the other five inactivated lift portals, they looked small and alone.

"Someone should remain here in the event that the resident AI continues with its enigmatic questioning or offers alternative communication," Bac'cul told the humans. "This is a place of your kind. None of us is better able to interpret its communications or tease out possible hidden meanings than yourselves. I will return as soon as the Vrizan have been persuaded to leave." He turned to follow his colleagues.

The Myssari did not depart as fast as Bac'cul wished, however. It took a swipe of Cherpa's hand to activate the lift and send it accelerating upward. As it ascended, Ruslan considered the uncomfortable possibility that in the absence of an active lift at the bottom of the delivery shaft, the lights in the underground chamber might go out. That they did not, that they dimmed slightly but remained sufficient, likely attested to the presence in the room of the two humans.

Neither he nor Cherpa had to activate their own communicators. Always on, these would keep them in touch with the surface. With the departure of the Myssari, they found themselves alone deep in the Earth, with only each other for company in the cool, featureless, glassy surroundings.

Not quite alone, Ruslan reminded himself as he turned toward the single isolated source of warmer, yellower light. There remained the smartly clad slab of human within the capsule. Unlike the warm glow it continued to emit, the lack of motion within was not comforting.

As researcher and historian, Bac'cul liked nothing better than to spend multiple three-days at a time in the field, studying the artifacts and remnants of the wondrous but ultimately self-extinguishing human culture. Today, in the company of the only two mature surviving specimens of that singular species, a discovery had been made that was potentially of great significance. All he wished for was to return to the outpost, lay out the preliminary findings before his colleagues, and make preparations to return with some of them to commence an in-depth investigation of the fascinating newly discovered site.

That blissful strategy had been interrupted by the arrival of a Vrizan aircraft much larger than the driftec in which he and his team had traveled. The visitors were correspondingly greater in number. Furthermore, they were plainly equipped to do more than defend themselves against wandering terrestrial carnivores. In contrast, Bac'cul and his team carried only a few small sidearms. While well trained, in a serious fight they would be no match for a coterie of Vrizan soldiers. He would have to do battle with different weapons. Subterfuge, misdirection, and that old Myssari standby, unremitting civility.

Very tall, very determined, and very straightforward, the lead Vrizan would have none of it. Untutored in Myssarian, she utilized an electronic translator to address Bac'cul and the members of the scientific team who had gathered around him. The Vrizan's immediate attention, however, was not on the tripeds but on the internally lit circular opening in the mountainside behind them. Their multi-jointed arms folded almost tentacle-like around large weapons, two soldiers flanked her.

"I am called Zizanden Ait Orl."

"Bac'cul." A three-fingered hand fluttered, respectively and accusingly, at each of the soldiers. "We are researchers. There is no need for heavy weapons here."

Surprisingly, the Vrizan responded with a conciliatory gesture. The soldiers stepped back, to be replaced by a pair of unarmed males. If they were research specialists, Bac'cul mused worriedly, he might have been better off not objecting to the presence of the guns.

In typical forthright Vrizan fashion, Zizanden indicated the illuminated tunnel opening. "You have found something of significance."

"We have found something," Bac'cul admitted. There was no point in denying what the Vrizan could see with their own eyes. "Thus far it has not proven to be of any especial consequence. It may be a human depository. That has yet to be determined. It may well be empty. We arrived here only this morning." Striving to assume a defiant pose, he added, "Our agreement with Vriza allows us to study anything we discover."

Inherently imperious, Zizanden looked down at him. "You do not need to lecture me on the details of the agreement. Though I do not personally subscribe to its tenets, I am bound by the details." Once more her gaze rose to the circular opening, trying to penetrate its depths. "I do not accept your claim to have found nothing. I do accept that you have not had time to study or evaluate it, because the same orbital locator that detected your presence here recorded it, as you truthfully declare, only this morning." Her tone grew less martial. "Might I suggest that it would be of scientific benefit to all, not to mention conducive to the amelioration of relations, if examination of this site were to proceed on a joint basis?"

Bac'cul tried to sound accommodating without actually committing to anything. "The ramifications of your suggestion extend beyond the limits of my individual professional mandate. It is something for my superiors to determine. Meanwhile, since we have found nothing worth examining, might I counter-suggest that matters remain as they are until those occupying more senior levels of responsibility than you or I decide how to proceed?"

That put the Vrizan in the position of possibly making decisions that would later be overridden. Recognizing the ploy, Zizanden opted to change the thrust of the conversation.

"Even at this distance I can see that the cave, or tunnel, is beautifully machined and internally lit. The ancient humans were not known for expending such effort to protect or conceal 'nothing.' "

Unable to deny this without admitting an ignorance he did not possess, Bac'cul countered, "I agree. As further study, quite possibly by the kind of conjoined research group you propose, may well prove."

"Come now, three-legs." Zizanden stared hard at her Myssari counterpart. "You have found more than a hole in the ground. What does it hold? Plant material, like the celebrated island depository to the north of here? Preserved fauna? Miscellaneous relics, artwork . . . what?"

"I have told you," Bac'cul insisted, "we have been here only a very short while and have not had time to probe the interior and its possible contents in any depth. But out of common interest and amity, I will agree to call a halt to further exploration until the question of possible joint exploration is settled by our respective superiors."

The Vrizan commander hesitated. Then, sufficiently pleased by what she determined to be her counterpart's willing acquiescence, she turned and snapped an order in her own language. To Bac'cul's relief the regular soldiers turned and headed back toward their waiting vessel. Even at a distance, their weapons had been discomfiting. With one more constructive gesture he felt he could convince the Vrizan to depart, if only for the remainder of the day. Such a gesture would be by far the best means of demonstrating to them that he and his team had nothing to hide.

"As a further indication of goodwill on the part of my people, I can tell you that the two well-known humans who advise the Science Sectionary are also here. They are present to aid in analyzing and identifying any artifacts of significance that may be found, though thus far none such have been located."

The Vrizan said something that was unrepeatable in polite company. Her translator struggled to convey it accurately. "There is no need to brag. We are aware of and envy the assistance they provide your researchers. By formal agreement between our governments, we are no longer permitted to try to persuade them to provide such services for us."

Meaning they are now safe from your egregious efforts at abduction, Bac'cul thought with satisfaction. Having more or less successfully befriended, discouraged, and finally misled the Vrizan, there was but one thing left to do to conclude the matter. He addressed his communicator, making sure the Vrizan could overhear him clearly.

"Ruslan, Cherpa—everything out here has been settled satisfactorily. Please come out so that you can confirm to our Vrizan friends that the tunnel holds nothing worthy of immediate examination, and so that you may bid them a mutually agreeable farewell."

———

Isolated from the confrontation, Ruslan and Cherpa listened to the research team leader's words—and worried, and wondered.

"I'm sure Bac'cul wants us to close down the place. He just couldn't say so in front of the Vrizan." Ruslan's words lingered in the still air. "As we leave, you or I will stroke the relevant section of wall and the outside barrier will come down. Then the Vrizan won't be able to get inside no matter what they decide to do next. This place will be sealed tight again."

Bright blue eyes met his. "You think that will be the end of it, Bogo? I don't trust the Vrizan no matter how much they quote the compact between their government and the Combine. You know me." Her expression tightened. "I'd rather be talking from behind a gun."

He smiled. "Me, I'm used to fighting with pages and pages of detail. That's what I'm really afraid of: that exploration of this place will get bogged down in bureaucratic infighting between both governments. And worse, that the Myssari will accommodate the Vrizan's wishes and allow for co-investigation of this place. I don't know that I like the idea of the broadheads wandering around in here."

Her words fell to a whisper. "Bogo, I don't know that I like the idea of the Myssari doing so, either."

He frowned. "I'm not sure I follow you, Cherpa."

Spreading her arms wide, she indicated their subterranean surrounds. "This installation is special, Bogo. We don't know special for what, but it's special for something. If not revivification, then something else. I know it. I *feel* it. This place is not for the Vrizan. It's not for the Myssari, either." Her eyes met his once again. "It's for us. For humans. Whatever it does. Whatever it means."

It was silent in the chamber for some minutes. Eventually he looked back at her. "All right. I'll stay behind. You bring down the barrier on your way out. Say that I'm waiting until everyone else decides what to do."

"There's no food down here," she pointed out quietly. "No water."

He shrugged. "I'll come out when everybody else leaves. There's water outside. Maybe you can leave me some rations where I can find them at the landing site. I won't be here forever."

"You don't know if the barrier will respond to you. So far I'm the one who has done all the touch-activating with it."

"I'll take that chance."

She stepped back and shook her head. "If you're staying, I'm staying, too."

"Cherpa . . ." he began, "what about the children at the outpost?"

"Their Myssari handlers will watch over them. They do most of that work now anyway. Kel'les will be there to help them." She smiled and began to laugh, her glee bouncing around the room like loose neutrons. Her laughter sent him back, all the way back to the first time he had heard it, wild and free, in the ruins of Daribb. It had not changed much. But she had.

"If at least one of us doesn't come out, the Vrizan are liable to get suspicious and decide to come looking for us."

A twinkle in her eye, she turned and started away from him. "I'll fix that. I'll fix *them*."

He started to call her back from where she had headed toward the lift, but relented. When she was younger, she would always listen to him, always take his advice. That had changed as she grew older and matured. She still listened to him . . . but she did not always take his suggestions. Nowadays Cherpa was going to do what Cherpa felt needed to be done. Contrary to his thinking, things usually turned out well enough. So he did what he always did in such situations.

Sat back, relaxed, and waited.

No one noticed her right away as she made her way down the last stretch of tunnel up top and approached the exit. But by the time she could feel the colder air from outside on her face, both Myssari and Vrizan had taken notice of her appearance. Walking briskly toward the outside, she smiled and offered a cheerful wave. Idly she observed that the Vrizan standing beside Bac'cul was female and quite tall. At the end of one wave, her left hand descended. As it did so it slid down the interior wall of the tunnel near the exit. In the absence of visible indicators, she hoped she had made contact with the appropriate place. Or perhaps it didn't matter, she thought. Perhaps the entire length of tunnel was one immense instrument sensitive to the presence and touch of a human being.

She did not have long to ponder the matter, because as soon as her bare hand made contact with the wall, the thick, heavy barrier began to descend. It came down fast, though not so fast that she failed to observe Bac'cul's startled reaction and the Vrizan's angry response. Led by the tall female, several of the visitors rushed toward the tunnel. They failed to reach it only seconds before the base of the dark barrier slid into its matching groove in the ground.

Myssari and Vrizan alike might have been yelling loudly at her from the other side. They might have been firing weapons at the doorway. She had no way of knowing because she could hear nothing. Pleased and relieved, she spun and retraced her steps at a fast walk, heading for the waiting rank of lifts. To find out if another of the six was functional, she would try a different one this time. She and Bogo were committed now. Even if they weren't sure to what.

"We're secure." Lying flat on the smooth floor, she put her hands behind her head and gazed at the softly radiant ceiling. The inexplicable contentment that had enveloped her ever since she had been freed from the hell that was her childhood on Daribb had bequeathed her the aspect of a tarnished angel. "For how long I don't know. But the Myssari couldn't break through the door. I imagine the Vrizan can't do any better." Rolling her head to one side, she met his gaze. "I imagine that after a while they'll both agree to listen to whatever we decide and we can ensure that whatever happens here is done to our satisfaction, not theirs. The Myssari are always willing to accommodate us. The Vrizan are belligerent, but they're not stupid. I'm willing to bet they'll fall in line with whatever arrangement we make with the Myssari."

Ruslan was less sanguine. "Unless they brought heavy weapons with them. If they did, they're liable to try forcing an entrance before agreeing to anything. The Vrizan I've met turn reasonable only when all their other methods of achieving what they want have failed."

From where she lay sprawled on her back on the floor, Cherpa mustered a shrug. "We'll just have to wait and see. I really think that door will keep them out."

"I wonder . . ." Ruslan's thoughts were drifting. "Important institutions on Seraboth were protected by mechanized safeguards. Even after most of the population had succumbed to the Aura Malignance, you had to be careful trying to enter certain buildings because their defensive automatics still functioned." Slowly he scrutinized their silent surroundings, from the slightly arched ceiling to the unmoving figure lying within the single transparent cylinder. "Though we're still not certain of its purpose, it's not inconceivable that a place like this is similarly protected."

Sitting up, Cherpa wrapped her forearms around her knees and hugged them to her chest. "If it's not, then maybe it's not as important as we think."

"Maybe there are defenses but they're not automatic and have to be activated." He studied the rippling walls and their inscrutable projections. "It would help if we could find something like a switch or haptic contact or other control."

She pursed her lips. "Maybe all you have to do is ask." For no particular reason she gestured upward. "Whatever kind of AI is implanted here is capable of speech. We know it listens because it has already asked for one reply."

He remained doubtful. "It asked a short question to which we could supply no answer. That may be all it's programmed to do."

"Only one way to find out." Rising to her feet, she cupped her hands to her mouth, and before he could restrain her or offer a counterargument, she was yelling at the top of her lungs.

"HEY! BE CAREFUL! NONHUMAN BIPEDS MAY TRY TO FORCE THEIR WAY IN HERE! DON'T LET THEM IN!" Lowering her hands, she grinned at the look on his face. "That should do it, if there's anything that can be done."

He swallowed before replying. "Admittedly, most of my contact on Seraboth was with administrative instrumentation, but in my experience AI's tend not to be deaf."

Extending her arms out to her sides, she performed a perfect pirouette before bowing in his direction. The woman before him was all grown up, Ruslan knew, but parts of the wild girl with whom he had bathed in the muck of Daribb were still present. They were also liable to rise to the surface at unexpected and sometimes awkward moments.

"I wanted to make sure that there was no equivocation in any response." Disarmingly, she giggled.

"What response?" he countered. "Nothing's happening."

"What about that?" She pointed. Upward again.

The overhead illumination was changing. The warm yellow glow was taking on overtones of pale orange and carmine. Lowering his gaze, he saw that the walls were coming alive. Swimming through the vitreous material like bioluminescent ocean dwellers, blobs of brighter colors began to congregate at various high points while darker hues concentrated themselves in dips and crevices. While most of the new lights shone steadily, a few surged with recurring pulsations. Looking down, a mesmerized Ruslan saw that the floor beneath him was now likewise alive with dancing luminosities. A subtle vibration filtered upward through his feet. The heartbeat of distant machinery coming alive after a long dormancy was perceptible in the depths. He looked over at an equally enthralled Cherpa.

"Something's happening. I wish we knew what." Remembering his communicator, he attempted to call Bac'cul. His efforts met with silence. He contemplated the information displayed on the readout before glancing up. His voice was grim.

"We're being blocked."

"You cannot do this. We had an agreement."

The Vrizan Zizanden did not look down at the Myssari researcher. Her attention was on the tech team that was positioning the shock cannon they had unloaded from their transport.

"Our agreement was to share information about this archeological site. This will be done. But in order to share information, we must first acquire it. Whether in response to an action by the female human or something else, the entrance to the site is now shut. Since it cannot be opened by pacific means, we will open it by those means that are available to us."

"But the doorway itself is an artifact!" A protesting Bac'cul waved all three arms in the direction of the heavy weapon. " 'Opening' it in this fashion will render it useless for study."

"It is a door," Zizanden observed curtly. "It is not unique."

Seeing that he was making no progress with the headstrong Vrizan commander, Bac'cul backed away and moved to rejoin his equally aghast colleagues. He did not need the situation explained to him. By forcing an entrance to the site while simultaneously insisting they would "share" any discoveries, the Vrizan hoped to conduct a preliminary survey and exploration of their own before the Myssari could conceal or mask anything of special significance. Had their positions been switched, Bac'cul might have felt similarly. Except no Myssari would resort to so crude a means of

gaining entrance to a blocked site. Outnumbered and heavily outgunned, his team could do little except retreat to the vicinity of
their driftec. From there they could wait, watch, and wonder if the
Vrizan weapon would succeed in penetrating the barrier when
their own less powerful devices had failed.

Knowing that the two humans inside deserved to know what
was going on, he turned away from the Vrizan so that his communicator was shielded by his body. He stared at the device. The
signal that had earlier reached to and from the depths without any
difficulty was now failing to make contact. Were the Vrizan blocking it? There was no obvious reason why they should be doing so.

He was trying to decide what to try next when the peculiar
half-ring, half-thump of a Vrizan shock cannon letting loose commanded his attention and he put aside his concern over the inability to make contact with the two humans.

When the blast ring struck the barrier, the resulting concussion
stunned the aural organs of everyone present. Bac'cul found himself flinching as he turned his head sharply away from the physically painful reverberation. When he rotated it back, he saw that
the barrier had not been so much as dented. It was as if the Vrizan
weapon had not fired at all. In the distance the commander was
railing at her crew as they prepared to fire again. This time Bac'cul
and his team members would be prepared for the consequences.
Hearing organs were shielded. A number of the more painfully affected had opted to retreat into the driftec in search of additional
protection.

As he waited for the next burst to be unleashed, Bac'cul was
accosted by one of his techs. Silently the intermet held up one of
several small field monitors. Though the instrument was highly
compact, its floating readouts were bright and easy to see. Besides
monitoring such mundanities as temperature, moisture levels,
solar radiation, and more, one glowing graphic indicated the
strength of any nearby ambient energy. On a developed world like
Myssar, it would be displaying a rainbow of colors. On Earth, one

or two minimal indications might appear when the instrument was in the presence of not-quite-dead automatics or other machinery. Bac'cul understood the readout he was seeing even though he could not comprehend it.

The information being displayed indicated that the levels being detected exceeded the device's measuring capacity. This impossibility was the last thing the researcher remembered seeing before he lost consciousness.

When he regained his senses and was able to finally stand on three shaky legs, he saw that he had been blown off his feet several body lengths from where he had been standing. Whistling in pain, the technician with the monitor was struggling to rise nearby. Similar high-pitched whines of distress came from other mission personnel as they slowly recovered from the shock wave. They were being helped and treated for their mostly minor injuries by colleagues who had taken early refuge on the driftec and had thus been shielded. The driftec itself had been shoved several lengths backward, leaving a shallow trough in the soil and snow.

Still unsteady on his feet, though far more stable than a human would have been if subjected to similar circumstances, he turned back toward the mountainside. The dark doorway that blocked access to the tunnel and the mysteries beyond was intact and undamaged. The Vrizan weapon was . . . gone. So was the team responsible for its operation, along with their commander, Zizanden. So was the Vrizan air transport craft. A handful of Vrizan lay scattered about, struggling to recover from the concussion. Some of those who had been standing closer to the shock cannon were missing important body parts. Myssari from the driftec rushed to help them.

Where the heavy weapon had been emplaced there was now a bowl-like depression in the earth, as smooth as if it had been scooped out and then polished to a high shine. A similar indentation in the ground occupied the place where the Vrizan transport had been parked. There was no dust in the air, no smoke, no evidence of an explosion. Stumbling over to the nearer of the two depressions, Bac'cul sank down and cautiously ran the three fingers of one hand over the edge. The smooth curve was warm to the touch. As he recalled his own team's initial attempt to blast through the tunnel door, a chill ran down his spine.

He hurriedly readjusted his communicator's settings. It was with considerable frustration that he finally set it aside. Communication with the two humans was still interdicted. As he stood surveying the destruction, he could only wonder if the blockage was involuntary or not. Pivoting, he moved to check on the condition of his injured colleagues and the surviving Vrizan. His body was still stunned but his mind was working furiously.

As a scientist engaged in cutting-edge research, he favored the predictable. It was therefore disconcerting to have to consider the possibility that the subjects of his research might now be in control of it.

20

The overriding sensation was as if they were now standing in an amorphous container filled with colored fire. Except the temperature was unchanged and the brilliant lights remained constrained within the surrounding walls, floor, and ceiling. It was a cold conflagration. Feeling his age as well as his ignorance, Ruslan turned to the ever-ebullient young woman nearby.

"What do we do now?" He indicated his communicator. "We don't know what, if anything, is happening up top. I can't get in touch with Bac'cul or any other member of the expedition."

Cherpa was grinning anew. Broadly, he reassured himself . . . not maniacally. "We warned the AI about possible danger," she said. "I don't hear any footsteps or voices. Until we do, I imagine we're still secure down here. If it responded to a warning, maybe it will respond to a question."

He frowned. "What kind of question? We don't want to do anything hasty, Cherpa."

"Of course we do. She who hesitates stays immobile. As to what kind of question," she added teasingly, "you just formulated it." Once again she raised her voice, though this time not as piercingly as before.

"Hey, whatever-wherever you are! What do we do now?"

That a response was forthcoming was gratifying. That it was no more than a repetition of what had gone before was more than disappointing.

"Install pattern number one?"

They had no idea what that meant nor to what the unseen AI might be referring, but by now there was no stopping the irrepressible Cherpa. Before Ruslan could caution her further, she had already replied, energetically and authoritatively.

"Yes!"

No verbal response was forthcoming—but the pulsating aurora that surrounded them underwent an immediate and perceptible shift in hue. New colors appeared, while old ones faded away. Configurations changed, roiled, darted through the walls. Cherpa did not have to point at their focus: Ruslan saw it, too.

The capsule containing the static human form had become enveloped in a refulgence so intense they had to squint in order to be able to look directly at it. Searching for change, Ruslan thought he could see the clothed chest within starting to rise and fall, but he couldn't be certain. Nor was he sure he saw the closed eyelids fluttering.

Further speculation was rendered moot when the top half of the capsule abruptly opened to one side and the figure within sat up. As soon as it stepped out and away from the transparency, the lid reclosed and a new shape slid into the vacated space. The replacement was female, as were four of the nine figures that now occupied the remaining and heretofore empty cylinders. They reposed face up, fully clothed and unmoving.

The intense illumination in which the first capsule had been

bathed rapidly subsided to its previous state. As an awestruck
Ruslan and Cherpa looked on, the individual who had emerged
slowly turned a complete circle. Apparently satisfied with his surroundings, he finally focused his attention on the other occupants
of the chamber. The unaltered voice of the AI echoed softly through
the underground.

"Install patterns numbers two through eleven?"

Ruslan was having a difficult time dividing his attention between the revived man and the female shape that now occupied
the nearest of the ten capsules. She looked to be about his age,
perhaps slightly younger. Long-buried yearnings began to flicker
within him. Would she, could she, be revived as rapidly and apparently as successfully as her male predecessor? If so, how might she
respond to him? How might he respond to her? Save for Cherpa,
his whole life had been bereft of female companionship. For an
entirely selfish moment the future of his species seemed incidental
to long-suppressed personal considerations.

The resurrected man spoke. His accent was thick and difficult
but ultimately comprehensible. It unsettled Ruslan, but not in a
bad way. It was as if his insides had momentarily turned to jelly.
The man was speaking in the tones, in the highs and lows, of old
Earth. Like him, the speech he was employing was an artifact . . .
an artifact brought back to life.

Something bumped Ruslan's left side. Wide-eyed, Cherpa had
moved to stand next to him. Together they listened raptly to the
upright relic.

"My name is Nashrudden Megas Chin." Prolongation of the
ensuing silence jolted Ruslan into realizing he was expected to respond to this introduction.

"I'm called Ruslan. I've forgotten my other names. When you're
the last of your kind, you tend to shed extraneous information
pretty quickly." He nodded to his left. "This is Cherpa."

"Mated?" the revivee asked politely.

Ruslan wondered if he was blushing. Somehow, when another human voiced it, the query came out sounding entirely different than when it was propounded by a Myssari.

"No, no. A friend."

"A very good friend." Reaching up, Cherpa put a hand on Ruslan's shoulder. "He saved me. Saved my life and my mind."

"Others?" the man asked. It struck Ruslan that Nashrudden was no more voluble than the AI that had revived him.

"Some children," Ruslan told him. "Our offspring, produced through artificial insemination. Our Myssari friends are looking after them."

"Myssari?"

"A nonhuman species." Ruslan did his best to explain. "One of the alien intelligences humankind always believed were out there. They exist, and there are many of them. They arrived in our area of the galaxy just as the Aura Malignance was killing off the last of us." Curiosity was turning to empathy. "I'm guessing you have been contained in this place for at least a couple of hundred years."

"But not you." The more the man talked, Ruslan reflected, the easier he became to understand.

"No." Once again Ruslan nodded toward Cherpa. "There may be others, but as far as I know I'm the only one on my homeworld, Seraboth, who was born with a natural immunity to the plague. Likewise Cherpa and—one other—on her world, Daribb."

The newly resurrected man nodded understandingly. "You also cannot be carriers. If that were the case or if any vestige of the Aura Malignance remained on Earth, the Preservation Project system would not have allowed me to be revived. I know: I helped to design it and oversaw much of the final construction and installation. It is because of my knowledge of the system that I am first to be revived. It means that this world, at least, is clean. It may be hoped that the same is true of all others. Without humans in which to propagate, the Malignance should have long since died out. As we again move off-world we will be cautious, just in case. A repeat of the cataclysm cannot be allowed to happen."

"The Myssari will help," Ruslan said encouragingly. "They have an entire scientific branch devoted to the study of our species and its culture. So do the Vrizan, and probably some of the other intelligences as well."

"Other intelligences." Nashrudden shook his head in disbelief. "A difficult concept for one of my time to grasp. I wonder if their scientists could have found a way to halt the plague. Something else we will never know." His expression brightened. "But my re-vivification proves the Earth is free of the Malignance. We will not repeat the mistakes of the past. This world and the others our spe-cies settled will once again resound to a multiplicity of human voices and the full range of human activity!"

Ruslan and Cherpa exchanged a glance before he replied. "Concerning that, there are good things to say. But there are also some . . . complications."

With her help he proceeded as best he could to fill in the scien-tist on two hundred years of missing history—and the current so-ciopolitical reality in this human-blighted corner of the cosmos.

No one knew how much time had passed since their disquisition had begun. No one much cared. Nashrudden Megas Chin was both fascinated and much pleased.

"Instruments were set in place to unobtrusively record every-thing that might transpire since the Project was initiated. The re-sults of that effort will eventually be scrutinized. But they cannot, they could not, record for posterity the events of elsewhere. I am indebted for your input on the state, however sad, of the colonized worlds."

"I'm sorry I can't remember more, or in greater detail." Ruslan was apologetic. "I'm—I was—a mid-level administrator, not a historian." He glanced at the young woman next to him and smiled. "Cherpa was too young and put-upon to be anything except a survivor." He turned back to the scientist. "What happens now?"

"Continuance." Raising his voice conspicuously, he addressed the unseen but omnipresent AI. "Install patterns two through eleven." With a smile that was almost shy, he added, to his new companions, "My coworkers. Once they are revived, the Project can resume in earnest."

Frowning, Ruslan indicated their surroundings. "We haven't explored every corner of this chamber, but it doesn't seem big enough to hold or support very many people. And what about food and water?"

"Did you think this single room was the extent of the space accorded to the Project?" Nashrudden gestured at the floor. "This is only the uppermost, supervisory level. Many others lie beneath us. All were stocked with carefully prepared long-term supplies. The same is true of similar installations hidden elsewhere on the other continents. But this one, this place, was designed to be reawakened first. My colleagues and I are the scientists, the designers, the engineers, the technicians. First we are revived, then we can more speedily awaken the others. The Project's reach is wide." Turning, he started toward the ten now fully occupied cylinders. "Some of my friends may find resurrection disconcerting. I need to make myself available to reassure them."

Ruslan gestured toward the cylinders. "This is all very different from a similar arrangement I saw on Treth. There the bodies were held in a liquid suspension."

"I imagine that when the Aura Malignance struck, the science here was more advanced than anything that was achieved on any of the colonies." Standing at the foot of the nearest cylinder, Nashrudden watched as the light enveloping it began to intensify— a now familiar development to the two onlookers. "It's easier to preserve individualities and memories when they're separated from the physical corpus. Restoration involves reintegration of non-corporeal memories with the original biological form."

Shielding his eyes from the intensifying glow, Ruslan struggled to understand. "You mean you removed the memories and thoughts of everyone who was stored for later revival?"

"Not removed. Copied out. Restoration involves writing over the original. The result is the same." He smiled anew, though Ruslan could hardly see him now through the intense auroras that enveloped all ten of the cylinders. "*I* certainly feel the same."

A question had been bothering Cherpa. "Why would a system designed to preserve humans when everyone else was dying off need a live human to reactivate it?" She gestured upward. "Would the supervising AI periodically sweep the surface for evidence of the Malignance and, after a reasonable time, awaken you if no plague was detected?"

Nashrudden looked back at her. "Surface sweeps would only indicate when the Earth itself was free of plague. Had that been the programming, we all could have been revived only to have the Malignance return, carried by an infected human from one of the colony worlds. Then all would truly have been lost." He smiled. "The presence of uninfected humans was the signal for which the instrumentation was designed to wait."

Unable to comprehend a science capable of shuttling human individualities around like so many collections of numbers, Ruslan did as he had done with every piece of incomprehensibility he had encountered since his years alone on Seraboth.

He simply accepted it.

The food and drink whose location was revealed by the AI in response to their query was old but impeccably preserved. Even so, Ruslan was reluctant to try it. Cherpa felt no such restraint, digging into the contents of the self-heating rehydrating containers

with as much gusto as if they had been prepared yesterday. A
ravenously hungry Nashrudden joined her, as did the first ten of
his revived colleagues. Not wishing to be left out of the Earth's
first revivification conclave, a hesitant Ruslan eventually joined in.
Compared to decades of Myssari fare, the revived provisions were
a riot in his mouth. In a sense he was eating history. His apprecia-
tive digestive system made no unnecessary distinctions.

When he thought Nashrudden could spare a moment from
helping his colleagues with the process of revivification, Ruslan
asked him how they now expected to care for themselves. That the
Myssari would help, gladly and freely, he had no doubt. But if
there were many . . .

"Appropriate resources were stored in many safe locations
across the planet," the resurrected scientist told him. "Food, additional clothing, instrumentation, machinery, even a few personal
items each individual was allowed to sequester. Enough so that the
species could rebuild and begin anew . . . hopefully this time with
more care, common sense, and ethics. It has been a costly lesson."

"Repositories." Cherpa had come up behind them. "Only this
time for people and not objects."

"They could be called such, yes." Nashrudden smiled at her.
"You're very pretty. I haven't been out of body so long that I've
forgotten what those parameters are like."

She did not blush, blushing being a behavior that is not innate
and must be learned. She simply accepted the compliment.

"And you are very brave—allowing yourself to be the first to be
revived without having any idea what kind of world you might be
entering."

"I was also, as far as I know, the last to have his individuality
extracted and body preserved." The scientist shook his head. "But
I'm not brave. The brave were those who were still healthy, still
untouched by the Aura Malignance, but who did not have their
selves extracted and their bodies placed in stasis. The ones who
remained outside and aboveground to ensure that each facility

was functioning as planned before being sealed. The brave ones died. The rest of us"—he gestured at the increasing crowd of the revived—"are the fortunate placeholders." Wiping at his eyes, he took a deep breath before once more turning a soulful gaze on Ruslan.

"How many others are there on the colonies? How many other survivors off-Earth?"

Ruslan and Cherpa exchanged a glance before he replied. "You're looking at them."

A stunned Nashrudden stared at him uncomprehendingly. "Two? Just . . . two?"

"There were three," Ruslan told him apologetically, "but there was an unfortunate incident."

"Two. Out of millions upon millions of colonists." He fought to speak. "I wish I could believe in a hell, if only as a just final resting place for those who developed and propagated the Aura Malignance." There was more he wanted to say but it was interrupted by the onset of weeping.

Ruslan and Cherpa looked on, embarrassed, not knowing how to respond. There wasn't anything they could do, really. Sufficient and appropriate words did not exist to describe a near-extinction to someone who had not experienced it.

More three-days than Bac'cul cared to remember had passed since the two human specimens had sealed themselves within the mountain. Spread out around him were all the scientific and engineering resources the Myssari outpost could bring to bear. These were augmented by the presence of an equal quantity of Vrizan material and equipment. Having agreed to work together to try to enter the mountain by means that would not see those making the attempt violently deconstructed, the teams put in place by the two reluctantly cooperating species had thus far managed to achieve a share in nothing except failure. Two attempts to bypass the doorway—

one to the left of it and the other working downward from the top of the mountain—had ceased when material of the same composition as the doorway had been encountered beneath the overlying rock.

It had just been decided to bore a hole and then excavate horizontally in an effort to interdict the lift shaft from one side when Cor'rin came running to alert him. That she had chosen to do so in person instead of employing her communicator said much. He had never seen her move so fast, rocking from side to side as she entered the field office located near the back of the portable building.

"Something I think you should see." Beneath her heavy brows her eyes were glittering. "Something I think everyone should see. Recording will ensure that they will, though they will have neither the joy nor the astonishment that comes with actual physical proximity." Without further explanation she all but pulled him away from his resting bench. In her mind urgency overrode the incivility.

Once outside and again confronted with the source of so much recent anxiety and confusion, he understood her insistence without having to have it explained to him.

The impervious door blocking entry into the mountain had risen to expose the tunnel beyond. The smooth, illuminated passageway looked exactly as Bac'cul remembered it save for one difference.

It was crowded.

The specimens Ruslan and Cherpa led the way. They were joined by a human male of indeterminate age whose mat of facial hair reminded Bac'cul of Ruslan's appearance the first time the researcher had encountered Seraboth's sole survivor. These three were followed by others. Hundreds of others. Having spent much of his professional life studying human history in the hopes of one day being fortunate enough to encounter a single live human,

Bac'cul was overwhelmed by the sight that now swelled before him.

How extraordinarily different they are from one another! he reflected. In height and girth, in epidermal tinting and hirsuteness, in facial features and physical structure. Such diversity within a single species and even within the same gender was unknown among the Myssari and all other civilized races. It was as if the fine details of the species' genetic code ran rampant over reason. Why should one be so much taller than another, or darker, or wider? It made no sense, but to a specialist like himself the bewildering parade offered an abundance of delights.

Having spent fruitful decades among the Myssari, Ruslan was able to hazard a guess at the thoughts that must be going through the researcher's mind. Grinning, he gestured toward his and Cherpa's unanticipated companion.

"Bac'cul, may I present Nashrudden Megas Chin. A scientist of his time, recently revived. Together with a few of his closest friends and colleagues." He translated for the newly resurrected scientist. "I think you two would work well together."

Having been properly introduced, the dazed Bac'cul responded automatically with the traditional Myssari embrace. Nashrudden flinched but otherwise accepted the three-armed clinch manfully. Having arrived in haste to join the group, Cor'rin followed with a greeting of her own, as did Kel'les. Formalities concluded, Ruslan and Cherpa proceeded to fill in the astonished Myssari on everything they had learned.

They had almost finished when the attention of human and Myssari alike was diverted by the hum of an arriving air transport. It was larger than the one that had preceded it. The anxious troops who emerged to be greeted by their few still-stunned surviving comrades were more heavily armed than their predecessors. They had been prepared to confront a Myssari scientific team and perhaps a pair of humans. Met by the sight of more than a thousand of the latter, all apparently as healthy as they were diverse, their commander and his suborns were taken aback as to how to proceed.

Taking pity on them and fully sympathizing with their shock, Bac'cul took it upon himself to make the next set of introductions. The Vrizan officer struggled to make sense of what he was seeing. In contrast, the human Nashrudden appeared utterly at ease with the arrival of a new set of aliens.

"So these are the Vrizan?" he asked Cherpa. "The species you said is desirous of laying claim to and settling Earth?" When she nodded confirmation, the scientist walked directly up to the Vrizan commander. They were of equal height, Ruslan noted, and, craniums aside, truly more alike than human and Myssari.

"Tell him, if it is a him, that the people of Earth are returning from a long sleep to reclaim their homeworld."

She translated into Myssari, and then back again when the Vrizan replied via his translator. "Commander Kanathel Uri Eln extends his greetings and wants to know how many people of Earth are going to return."

"We are but the first of many. All returns start small. Tell him."

She proceeded to do so. Physically capable of far more facial expression than a Myssari though less than a human, the Vrizan honored himself with as extreme a variety of facial tics and contortions as Ruslan had yet observed in one of his kind. When the commander finally found his voice again, it was to put another question to the human via Cherpa.

"Assuming your claim was to be upheld by the relevant authorities, he wishes to know what you would plan to do with the existing settlements the Vrizan have worked hard to establish here."

Nashrudden met the alien's gaze as evenly as he could. "Tell him that while I must consult with others of my kind, I see no reason why they should not remain. There are many . . . empty

spaces . . . that could do with the ameliorating touch of civilization. Any civilization. Devastating as it is, a mass die-off of one's
own kind is a powerful argument for future cooperation." When
Bac'cul started to object, the scientist added that the Myssari were
welcome to establish similar projects of their own. "All assistance
will be gratefully welcomed. It may be hoped that we have knowledge we can share with you as much as you can share with us. The
knowledge of the living," he concluded, "to complement that of
the dead."

While not entirely happy with the human's assertions, the Vrizan saw no civilized means of contesting it. It was not for a minor
functionary like Kanathel to decide anyway. The rendering of such
momentous decisions was the province of his superiors. He was
glad it was so. It was not a decision he would have wished to make
on his own. When all communication with the field team that had
preceded him failed, he had been ordered to assemble a rescue
team and proceed to the site at speed. It is safe to say that whatever he was expecting to find, the presence of hundreds of live
humans, with more continuing to file out of the tunnel every minute, had not figured into his planning.

Was the human who spoke no Myssari telling the truth when
he claimed there would soon be many more of his resurrected kind
spreading out across this world? Though rather more aggressive
than the Myssari, the Vrizan were no less ethical than their tripodal rivals. The commander knew there could be no valid excuse to
mount a war for a world that was being reclaimed by its original
inhabitants. Additionally, the collective wisdom of a race that had
successfully settled dozens of worlds was surely worth far more
than any single habitable planet. If the human scientist was to be
taken at his word, his kind were willing to freely share much of
that knowledge. It behooved the Vrizan to begin the relationship
on good terms with them. Lastly, his people were far more firmly
established on the human homeworld than the awkward Myssari.

Trusting the human female to continue translating honestly, he raised one hand and turned it upside down in presentation to the revived scientist.

"You are most generous. I personally look forward to assisting your people in fully reclaiming this world."

"As do the Myssari," put in Bac'cul hastily. Though no diplomat, he could evaluate a critical situation when he saw one. "The Combine will provide you with any and all the help that you need."

"As will the Vrizan." Commander and research team leader glared at each other.

Leaving the two alien representatives to engage in an ongoing confrontation that was chilly but polite, the three humans edged away to greet and explain the current situation to as many of the revived as they could.

Eventually a driftec arrived to carry the original exploration team back to the Myssari outpost. Nashrudden and several of his colleagues went along. Looking back as he prepared to board the transport, Ruslan could see the resurrected humans organizing themselves into groups. As they began their work, repositories would be unearthed, automatics activated, and supplies distributed. Reconstruction would begin soon enough. Aid already promised by the Vrizan and the Myssari would help to speed recovery. Earth, humankind's Earth, would live again. This time there would be no mistakes.

He entered the driftec and took a seat across from Cherpa, who was engaged in animated conversation with Nashrudden. The two were about the same age, Ruslan reflected. She had never seen a man her own age. Something sharp and painful lanced through him, faded like a burn, and was gone. *This was right,* he told himself as he watched them. Heavy as it lay within him, he could not find it in himself to object to rightness.

The woman who sat down beside him was one of the first ten following Nashrudden to be revived. She appeared older than the scientist but not by much. Her eyes, Ruslan noted, were very violet.

"You're Ruslan, aren't you?" She gestured across the way. "Nashrudden told me about you. You're a natural immune from, I think he said, Seraboth. I'm Elehna. Elehna Anchez, one of the last to be extracted and have her body put in stasis. Like Nashrudden." When he said nothing, she smiled. "You know what used to be said: the last shall be first?"

He finally remembered to nod, trying not to stare. "Yes, I'm Ruslan. Ruslan . . . I don't remember the rest."

"Well, Ruslan-I-don't-remember-the-rest, Nashrudden says that you have lived and survived among these trisymmetrical aliens ever since they plucked you off your homeworld, and I really would like to hear everything you can tell me about your experiences. In detail."

He found himself, automatically, smiling back. It was a smile that just kept getting wider and wider.

"And me? I've waited most of my life for the chance to tell you."

"There will be others," she told him. "They'll want to know what you know, too."

"I'm happy to start with you." He truly was. "How many others have to be revived? How much work remains to be done to bring them all back into the light? How many thousands will walk the surface of the homeworld again?"

"Thousands?" She looked at him strangely. "The Project head didn't tell you?"

He shook his head. "I just assumed thousands."

Her expression shifted from warm to serious. "Ruslan, there are *three billion* of us."

ABOUT THE AUTHOR

ALAN DEAN FOSTER has written in a variety of genres, including hard science fiction, fantasy, horror, detective, western, historical, and contemporary fiction. He is the author of several *New York Times* bestsellers and the popular Pip & Flinx novels, as well as novelizations of several films, including *Transformers, Star Wars,* the first three *Alien* films, and the most recent one, *Alien: Covenant*. Foster and his wife, JoAnn Oxley, live in Prescott, Arizona, in a house built of brick that was salvaged from an early-twentieth-century miners' brothel. He is currently at work on several new novels and media projects.

alandeanfoster.com
Facebook.com/AlanDeanFoster

ABOUT THE TYPE

This book was set in Sabon, a typeface designed by the well-known German typographer Jan Tschichold (1902–74). Sabon's design is based upon the original letter forms of sixteenth-century French type designer Claude Garamond and was created specifically to be used for three sources: foundry type for hand composition, Linotype, and Monotype. Tschichold named his typeface for the famous Frankfurt typefounder Jacques Sabon (c. 1520–80).